Fool's Gold

FOOL'S GOLD

WILLIAM W. JOHNSTONE

and J.A. JOHNSTONE

PINNACLE BOOKS
Kensington Publishing Corp.
kensingtonbooks.com

PINNACLE BOOKS are published by

Kensington Publishing Corp.
900 Third Avenue
New York, NY 10022

PUBLISHER'S NOTE: Following the death of William W. Johnstone, the Johnstone family is working with a carefully selected writer to organize and complete Mr. Johnstone's outlines and many unfinished manuscripts to create additional novels in all of his series, like The Last Gunfighter, Mountain Man, and Eagles, among others. This novel was inspired by Mr. Johnstone's superb storytelling.

First Pinnacle Trade Paperback Printing: July 2026

ISBN: 978-0-7860-5075-8

ISBN: 978-0-7860-5076-5 (ebook)

10 9 8 7 6 5 4 3 2 1

Printed in the United States of America

The authorized representative in the EU for product safety and compliance
is eucomply OU, Parnu mnt 139b-14, Apt 123
Tallinn, Berlin 11317, hello@eucompliancepartner.com.

Fool's Gold

BOOK I

Chapter 1

A full yellow moon hung low in the darkening sky as the man in black rode into town.

Although covered by a light coating of dust, his jacket and trousers were still dark, as his shirt front was still distinctively white and cut by the severe black string tie of the saddlebag preacher. A worn black homburg sat level on the man's head, and his face held a watchful expression—so watchful that it seemed almost fierce, although the wrinkles around the mouth and eyes suggested a capacity for warmth.

The man in black was strong as the Rock upon which he based his faith, but his own rock was worn smooth by a lifetime of service and suffering. He had learned how to be both firm and gentle. It was with just such firmness and gentleness that he drew on the horse's reins and paused on the hilltop to survey the town below.

Although shrouded by dusk, the town's features were still discernible. Rio Oro bore all the hallmarks of a gold mining boomtown. Buildings in various states of completion lined both sides of a wide, dirt main street. The man in black reckoned that street would be busy during daylight hours and, in wetter weather, likely a river of mud.

He spied several large buildings, most darkened at this hour, but the two spilling out light and music he figured for saloons or hotels, perhaps both. The building he sought was not visible from this height, but no matter. Deciding it was likely still under construction, he resolved to search for it once he arrived in town. For now, he tapped the horse's sides with booted heels and guided it down the narrow path of the draw to the valley floor.

A figure detached itself from the shadows of the outlying buildings as the preacher approached the outskirts of town. It took a few steps down the road toward the stranger before pausing to hook both arms around the wooden beam supporting a sign:

RIO ORO CITY LIMITS
JUDGE HORACE DAVENPORT, JUSTICE OF THE PEACE
CORD BENNETT, TOWN MARSHAL

"H-h-h-hi!" called the man holding on to the signpost. "W-w-welcome! My n-name's Hap!"

The man in black drew the reins on his mount and brought it to a stop. He cocked his head, studying the fellow who had introduced himself as Hap. His severe expression softened into a light smile.

"Well, hello, Mr. Hap," he said in a gravelly rumble. "It's nice to meet you. My name is Reverend Garrison Lomax."

"A r-r-reverend?" The slender man with the stutter snatched off his hat and held it before his chest. "W-w-well, gadzooks! You m-must be coming to fill the v-v-vacancy at our church!"

"Indeed I am, Hap. You wouldn't perchance happen to know where my church is, would you?"

"Yonder." Hap pointed. "I'll show you!"

"Much obliged."

Hap trotted ahead of Lomax down the dirt track that widened into Rio Oro's main street. The shops and dwellings on the outskirts were dark and the wooden sidewalks deserted. But there was light and activity a little farther up the way. Lomax followed Hap past the lit façades of two saloons, one on either side of the street. The sign on the one to his left was indistinct, but he could make out the word *Nugget* on the one to his right. Raucous voices rose from within, underlined by the jangle of an upright piano, badly played.

"L-lord, they're having a hoot in th-there!" cried Hap.

"Hmph. I can tell, from the painted women and bad music, it's a real den of iniquity." Lomax frowned. "I shall therefore be obliged to pay it a visit at the earliest opportunity."

"Planning to g-give 'em fire and brimstone, Preacher?"

"Perhaps." He scratched his cheek. "But more likely I'll just have a beer."

"Ha!"

Hap trotted another hundred yards ahead to pause at the intersection of the main street and its sole cross-street. The town was growing now, expanding cautiously outward on its new axis. A few ramshackle buildings clung to this new street's edges, and a cluster of shacks with Chinese lettering on them hugged the outskirts of the fledgling avenue. In a vacant lot across the way, the façade of a partially built church loomed in the shadows.

"There it is!" Hap cried proudly, flinging an arm at the building frame. "Volunteers been putting 'er up!"

"Hmph. Have you been helping, Hap?"

"Gadzooks, no! Th-they say I'm too s-stupid to be trusted with a hammer!"

"Is that right?" Lomax grimaced. "We'll have to do something about that."

Lomax studied the partially built structure, pleased with its dimensions and present condition. Yes, it would make a fine church for a town the size of Rio Oro. And if Lomax had his way, the congregation would expand, and additions would soon be necessary.

He knew from experience that towns and settlements grew up best with a godly presence in their midst. In a rough mining town such as this one, his work would very surely be cut out for him. Lomax clamped his eyes shut, breathing a short prayer to the Lord for the humility and fortitude necessary to do God's will in this new parish. When he was done, he opened his eyes and nodded at Hap.

"You've been mighty helpful, Hap," he said softly. "I'm obliged to you. What say we head back to that Nugget place, and I'll buy you a beer?"

"Why, s-sure!" Hap seemed surprised. "That's m-mighty kind of you!"

"Least I can do." Lomax nodded and turned his mount back toward the noise and music. "What's that building over yonder?" he asked, pointing at a tall shadow in the west.

"Ponder's lumber mill," replied Hap. "He's been d-doing good business lately!"

"I'm sure he has," said the preacher. With the gold rush in full swing, he reckoned places like Rio Oro, situated near large claims, were expanding by leaps and bounds. Growth meant building, and building meant lumber. Men like this fellow Ponder were getting fat on the expansion west.

Hap led them back to the town core. Turning onto the main street, they approached the lights and commotion from the two saloons.

"Do many folks live down in this part of town?" Lomax asked.

"G-gosh no, Reverend." Hap shook his head firmly. "Most people bunk f-further up thataway." He gestured vaguely over one shoulder. "Some f-folks do, though. I guess. Mr. Casterline has a loft above his office. Marshal does, too. And I reckon some of the s-soiled doves live in the rooms above the Nugget."

"Soiled doves, eh?" Lomax frowned. He did not disapprove of prostitution per se. Jesus himself had forgiven and uplifted such women, rescuing many from a life of sin. The preacher did not judge the women but knew they were often the victims of unscrupulous and controlling men—men for whom he nursed a righteous and bitter rage.

There was a hitching rail just outside the saloon whose full name was the Golden Nugget. Lomax dismounted and tied up his horse alongside a tired-looking paint and a long-suffering mule. Both stood despondent, so Lomax gave each a few gentle strokes on the way past. Soiled doves weren't the only creatures on God's earth in need of love and forgiveness. He followed Hap through the batwing doors into the barroom.

A scattering of tables occupied the main floor, which was ringed by a balcony above. Grouped around the tables were perhaps a half-dozen different clusters of men, some chatting, others engaged in card games. A long bar lined the left-hand wall. The piano stood against the right-hand wall, its player absent just now. A few women loitered in the shadows, their tattered clothes and hungry eyes telegraphing their profession even at a distance. As Lomax shook the dust from his hat, one drifted over and spoke to Hap.

"Hello, Hap," she said kindly. "It's nice to see you, but I figured you should know the Griffith brothers are here tonight."

"Oh?" Hap's eyes widened in sudden alarm, his attention turning toward three burly men clustered around a far table. "Well, I'm th-thinking I'd b-best be on my way then—"

"What are you talking about?" Lomax set his hat back on his head and laid a hand on Hap's shoulder. "C'mon, son. Let me buy you a beer."

But Hap shrank from the preacher's touch. "You d-don't understand, Preacher," he whispered. "Them Griffith b-boys h-hate m-me! Gadzooks, they're a terror! I d-don't want no t-trouble!"

"And you won't have any, I promise." Lomax wrapped an arm around Hap's shoulders, guiding him to the bar. "Come on with me."

The barkeep, a balding, mousy fellow, peered nervously at them from behind wire-rimmed spectacles as they approached. Leaning forward to buff the bar with a rag, he whispered urgently to Hap.

"Hiya, Hap," he said quietly. "Listen. The Griffith boys are—"

"Barkeep!" interrupted Lomax, slamming a palm down on the bar. "Two beers, if you please. One for me and one for my good friend, Hap, here."

Finishing this statement, he tossed a coin onto the bar before turning to lean his back against it, pushing his fingers into the front pockets of the vest under his black coat.

At the mention of Hap's name, the three burly men at the far table looked up. One, a snaggletoothed redhead, poked his nearest brother with an elbow and snickered. Then he rose and made his way toward the bar.

"Uh-oh," breathed Hap as the barkeep set two schooners of beer down before them.

"Relax, Hap," said Lomax, raising his beer and taking a sip. He studied the broad-shouldered redhead as he sauntered closer. He was a big man, a full head taller than Hap. He had an inch or two on the preacher as well. The redhead's clothes were worn but clean, his freckled face clean-shaven, and the smile on his lips puckish and charming.

But the slant of the eyes and the gleam in them spoke of a mean streak, one that became obvious as he posted himself before Hap and planted his hands on his hips.

"Well, well. If it ain't my old friend *Hap.*" This last word coincided with a slap on the back that caused Hap to stumble and spill some beer from his schooner. "I'm surprised to see you in here, Hap! Especially since we told you not to bother us. And yet here you come—"

"He's not bothering anybody."

Lomax's words, uttered in a voice that was low and guttural, sounded more like a growl than human speech. The redhead stopped speaking, affecting surprise as he did so. After a shocked second or two, he turned to Lomax.

"And who might you be?" he asked. "I don't believe we've been introduced."

"We haven't been introduced." Lomax set his beer on the bar and stepped up to the redhead. "Not formally, at any rate. But I'd say you've already made a first impression. And, son, I tell you: It ain't a good one."

At this, the redhead's eyes narrowed. Hap shifted nervously as the man balled his left hand into a fist and firmed his jaw. He knew the signs.

"I ain't your son," the redhead snarled.

"Damn right you're not. My son would have some manners." Lomax reached for his beer glass. "Tell you what. Why don't you run along back to your brothers over there? Leave me and my pal Hap in peace. We'll talk another day."

With that, Lomax turned his back on the man and leaned on the bar.

The stillness that fell over the barroom was glacial and complete. Every eye in the place was on the Griffith brother, waiting to see how he would react to such a calculated display of disrespect.

As it turned out, they didn't have to wait long. He reached out and grabbed Lomax's shoulder, intent on whipping him around. But he hadn't reckoned on a brimming schooner of beer crashing into the side of his head at full force. When it did, he went down like a bag of rocks.

CHAPTER 2

"Marshal!"

Cord Bennett surged awake and sat upright in the narrow bed upstairs from his office. He had been dreaming of his fiancée, Glory. In the dream she had been standing on the shore of a pond as he sank beneath the waves, one hand reaching out to her, his voice muffled by the rising water—a rushing noise that rose until it became . . .

"Marshal! Open up! It's Hap!"

He swung his stockinged feet to the floor. Cord slept in his work clothes when bunking here in town. He far preferred sleeping in the cabin he was building for himself and Glory up Ghost Canyon, a short piece from Rio Oro and within riding distance of the claim he owned. But a few nights of trouble in the saloons had convinced him to come down and spell his deputy, who had been doing night shift for a week.

He rose, stretched, and moved to the door, which he unlocked and opened a crack. Hap was alone on the outside steps leading up to the loft, breathing heavily from his run up from the street.

"Sheriff, you g-gotta come quick! The Griffith b-boys have g-got into a s-scrap with the new preacher over at the G-Golden Nugget!"

"The new preacher? He's here?" Dazedly, Cord groped for his gun belt and boots. "And he's gotten into a fight? *In the saloon?*"

"Truth be told, Marshal, he was defending me from Billy Griffith." Hap looked ashamed, although there was no reason for him to be. "Him and his two brothers are in town."

"Right." Cord clapped the hat down on his head and followed Hap downstairs at the double quick. It was for occasions such as this that he had chosen to sleep in town. Reaching the street, he pivoted and sprinted up Main Street.

The Golden Nugget was just a short distance away. The road's surface remained uneven from its mangling during the muddy season. Cord had to hop, dodge, and occasionally balance along the back of little dirt ridges to make headway. Before long, he reached the Nugget. His arrival coincided with a stampede of customers out the front door.

"Marshal, he's crazy!" hooted one old miner.

"Never seen a man fight like that before, Marshal!" echoed another.

Once the rush had passed, Cord approached the saloon. He heard a crash, a crunch of tinkling glass, and a scream, before it all went silent inside. Squaring up, he pushed through the batwing doors and beheld the spectacle inside.

Well, I'll be damned, he thought.

Sprawled out on the floor were the unconscious forms of Billy, Bobby, and Beau Griffith, the meanest bunch of ruffians in Rio Oro. They and their father, Ulysses, had arrived in town less than twelve weeks before but had already earned a reputation as the town's most hellacious hell-raisers. Cord and his deputy, Bart Blackstone, had been called to deal with them on more than one occasion. Each time had proved a donnybrook. But none of that prepared him for what he saw now.

Billy Griffith, lying curled up as if asleep, bled from a deep gash on the side of his head. Bobby and Beau both lay straight, stiff as boards, as though slammed by identical blows to exactly the right nerve to knock them out cold. The Griffith brothers, each more than two hundred pounds, were in deep hibernation.

And it all seemed to do with the man standing at the bar.

He was a big fellow—a looming, broad-shouldered bear of a man, with outsize hands, a barrel chest, and a pair of eagle-sharp eyes that found and fixed Cord Bennett the moment he entered the room. Cord knew at once this man had been responsible for the Griffith brothers' state and that, regardless of circumstances, he would never go against this man unarmed and alone.

"Well," said Cord, affecting a friendly tone. "Seems somebody decided to take a nap."

"Indeed they did. You would be the town marshal." The big man nodded. "Garrison Lomax. I had hoped our first meeting would be under more pleasant circumstances. I find myself posted to Rio Oro as pastor of the nascent church."

"I see." Cord flicked a glance down at the Griffiths to ensure they were still out before continuing. "Mind if I ask you, padre, are you armed? And, if so, would you be so kind as to surrender your weapon?"

"Certainly." With a deft flick of his right arm, the preacher reached around and plucked out a revolver from the belt at the small of his back. He handed it across to Cord deferentially, who recognized it as a modified Colt Walker. The preacher carried a version with a curtailed barrel. Cord had never seen one like it before.

"Much obliged, Reverend Lomax." His eyes scanned the room. One by one, the bar staff and soiled doves were emerging from hiding. "Truth be told, since I'm up, I might as well have a drink."

He kicked the toe of Billy Griffith's boot. "Care to help me haul these Sleeping Beauties to cells? Then we can reconvene here and you can give me a statement."

"Sounds very fine." The preacher drained his beer and placed his glass on the counter. He bent and hooked his hands under Billy's arms, lifting him from the sawdust-littered floor with seemingly effortless ease as Cord took Billy's legs.

It took three trips for the Griffith brothers to be piled neatly into the cell in Cord's office. They were still snoring soundly as he shut the door and led the way back to the Golden Nugget. Once there, he signaled to the barman for two beers.

"So, Reverend," he said. "Tell me your story."

Unlike Cord and his family, who had had a farm in the Ozark Mountains of Arkansas before heading west, Lomax was a city dweller. Born in Boston and abandoned at an orphanage, he had been raised in the care of the state. At sixteen, he fled the workhouse and fell in with a traveling carnival. Beginning as a roustabout, his bulk and temperament made him a natural for the boxing ring. He became the troupe's challenge pugilist, traversing several states by caravan and collecting coin from the men dumb enough to bet a dime they could knock him down. Most nights, Lomax could make two or three dollars in admission fees and tips. There were also plenty of men willing to buy him drinks and plenty of women eager to bed the beefy brawler. Life was good.

"Everything changed one evening in Richmond," he said. "I attended a service. Took place in a tent out under the stars. An evangelist was inviting folks forward to testify and be saved. I scoffed . . . at first. But I watched something amazing happen to those who chose to become converted. It was something I had to learn about. Something I had to follow."

Despite his lack of much formal education beyond the bare minimum, Lomax managed to gain acceptance to a Bible college.

It was to be the beginning of a lifelong adventure—and the closest Lomax would ever come to having a family of his own.

"Upon graduation, I was ordained to the ministry. I was assigned to the western circuit." Lomax took a healthy slug of beer and narrowed his eyes at Cord. "You mentioned having had brothers. Past tense. I hope they're not . . ."

"They are." Cord toasted the preacher with his mug. "Passed to glory. They helped establish this town. And they were among the first buried here. There was a great deal of violence and lawlessness when we arrived."

"Is that what drew you to become town marshal?"

"This?" Cord smiled self-consciously, fingertips straying up to stroke the star pinned to his vest. "It began as a provisional appointment. I wasn't expecting or intending to make this my work, but over time, it stuck. My family came here to stake a claim, so I understand these people. Understanding their hopes and frustrations makes it easier for me to reach them. Knock on wood, the worst of Rio Oro's growing pains are over, and now we can just focus on making the town grow."

"I'll raise a glass to that," said Lomax. He took a swallow of beer before saying, "Any chance you'll give me my gun back, Marshal?"

"Sure thing." Cord pulled the short-barreled pistol from his belt and handed it across. "Do most preachers carry guns these days?"

"The ones who ride out this way do, certain sure." Lomax received his weapon and vanished it back beneath his coat. "Being a saddlebag preacher in frontier territory is dangerous work even at the best of times. Having a piece and knowing how to use it is no violation of a man's vow to serve the Lord. Not how I see it, leastways."

As Lomax spoke, he reached up to scratch at his neck. As his shirt collar slipped down, Cord saw a band of bright red scar tissue circling the flesh of his throat.

"Ah." Lomax smiled and sat back. "My scars."

"That's a nasty one," Cord said. "How'd that happen?"

"It was a gift." Lomax offered a proud and bitter smile. "I was a guest, you see. Of the Apache."

"The *Apache*?" Cord breathed out slowly. "Lord, I've heard they're, well, I don't know what the word would be, but—"

"Diabolical." Lomax said it flatly, without rancor. "I was traveling by stage through the Arizona territory when they fell upon us. My God, it was terrifying. I was one of only two men left alive once their attack was finished. I think the fact that I fought them and had to be knocked cold bought me their respect. I was kept tied in the lodge of a large man who would come in and torture me from time to time. He used clubs. And a whip." Lomax touched his neck. "It went on for weeks until one night when he was out, I managed to untie myself and escape. I had lost a great deal of blood but would prefer to die on the run rather than as a miserable captive. By the grace of God, I made it."

Cord's respect for Lomax only grew. To escape captivity and live to tell the tale showed him to be a man of real fortitude. Such men were rare.

"Do you miss your family?" Lomax was watching Cord now, holding his beer just below his chin, waiting for Cord's answer to drink.

"Sure." He nodded. "It's not easy outliving your entire family. But I'm blessed to have my fiancée, and hers."

"Fiancée, eh?" Lomax flashed a grin. "You planning a church wedding?"

"Yes, Preacher, we sure are." Cord spread his hands. "We were just waiting for you to arrive. Glory—she's my girl—is going to be over the moon that you're finally here and we can be about the business of getting hitched."

"It will be my pleasure, Marshal." Lomax nodded gravely at this. "A town's leading citizens should be stable, family-oriented men.

When those in power lead ordered lives, it tends to flow downward to inform society and its institutions."

"Law and order are what this town needs," Cord affirmed.

"And children." Lomax's eyes twinkled. "You and Glory will have a special responsibility in that regard, you know."

"How do you figure?"

"Well, you're going to be married!" Lomax laughed. "Making children is a part of that!"

"I, uh, yeah." Cord smiled. "Yeah, I guess you're right."

"You don't sound too confident!"

"Oh, no." Cord grinned. "I'm just having a hard time getting over my good luck!"

Chapter 3

Cord managed to bed down and grab another few hours' sleep before full daylight. He woke with the sun streaming through the curtained window of his little loft and rose to peer down through the glass at the street below.

Already, Rio Oro pulsed with the morning rhythms of shop workers and saloonkeepers streaming to work, delivery wagons rolling from doorway to doorway, and the timbermen of Ponder's lumber mill lining up at the front gate to get into the yard.

A few lone horsemen threaded their way through traffic, one of whom was Clyde Casterline, heading out on an errand from the surveyor's office. Cord made a mental note to stop in and see him later. Then, with a tired sigh, he turned to the mirror, finger-combed his hair into place, dragged on his boots, and thumped downstairs to the marshal's office.

His was a simple work area—two desks and some chairs, a small potbellied wood stove for heat and coffee. A full quarter of the room was taken up by a cell large enough to accommodate a dozen men.

This morning, it held only three: the Griffith brothers. They were being watched from behind one of the desks by a large, bearded man who studied them as if planning to inflict violence upon their sleeping forms.

"Good day to you, sir," said the bearded man crisply. He spoke with a thick British accent. Cord moved to the stove and poured himself a cup of fresh coffee from the pot sitting on it.

"Good morning, Bart." Cord blew on the coffee before taking a cautious sip. He let the liquid rest in his mouth for a long moment before swallowing. His eyes teared up at the taste. "Boy, that's . . . great. Thanks, Bart."

The man behind the desk flashed a proud smile. Bartholomew "Boom Boom" Blackstone took immense pride in his ability to make perfectly awful coffee. His logic went something like this: Coffee is bad for you but useful in staying awake, so why not accentuate the effect by adding eye-wateringly bad flavor?

Having come from England with a pickax and a canvas bag full of mining tools, Blackstone had gone bust on his claim but made a place for himself in town as Cord's deputy. His nickname of Boom Boom was the result of his fondness for using blasting powder to work his claim.

"Yonder scoundrels remain unconscious, Marshal," Blackstone grumbled. "Shall I set up a hearing with Judge Davenport for when they wake?"

"No. Just cut them loose with a warning. Tell them I don't want to see them in town for a week." Cord took another hard swallow before setting down the cup.

"Who punched them up? He did a fine job, whoever he is," said Blackstone approvingly.

"Our new preacher. Reverend Lomax." Cord clapped his hat on his head. "Came into town last night."

"Is that a fact?" Blackstone grinned. "So, you and that pretty fiancée of yours will get that church wedding you always wanted!"

"Reckon so. I'm headed out to let her know about it right now."

Astride his horse and headed north along Main Street, Cord surveyed the storefronts and gaggle of pedestrians scurrying for the day's occupations. The morning rush usually lasted until about ten o'clock, when the day's temperature started to climb and sensible creatures sought refuge in the shade. They would emerge again around noon, headed home for lunch or down to one of the two saloons for lunch and a bracer. Cord paused as he drew level with a young woman emerging through the doorway of one.

The Bear Flag Saloon, virtually across the street from the Golden Nugget, was now owned and operated by Kat Olmsted, the woman who would soon be his sister-in-law. In the months since Cord had proposed to her sister Glory, Kat had developed a friendly, teasing relationship with the man who had done so much for her and her family since meeting up with him on the trail west. Kat, Glory, and their father, Abraham, had come to be almost substitutes for the family Cord had lost along the way.

"Hello, Marshal!" she called with a wave. "I hope you're not stopping by because I'm in some sort of trouble."

"No more than usual, Kat," he answered with a grin. "Heading up to see Glory and your pa. Any messages?"

"No, not that I can think right now. But thanks for asking." Kat flung a bucket of gray wash water into the street before pausing to push away a lock of stray hair with one sweaty wrist. "I heard tell there was a spot of trouble last night at the Nugget."

"There was. Griffith brothers came into town and went after Hap."

"Bullies!" she spat. "Why can't they just leave that poor boy alone?"

"After last night, I believe they will. Seems we have a new preacher in town."

"Oh?"

"Yep. Pretty good with his fists too. Laid out all three of them for spooking Hap. They're sleeping it off in jail right now."

"Is that so?" Kat giggled. "Shades of David and Goliath with this new padre, it sounds like!"

"Something like that, I reckon. Although he'd be Goliath. His name's Garrison Lomax. Big fellow. All dressed in black. You'll see him around."

"If he comes in here, he gets free drinks," Kat promised, hoisting her bucket and turning to go back inside. "I'd say beating the devil out of the Griffith brothers qualifies as the Lord's work. And God bless him for it!"

Cord was still chuckling at this as he rode out of town.

When Cord and his family first arrived in Rio Oro, they were every bit as green as the newcomers arriving today. Claims had been comparatively few back then, and they had had no problem finding one a short distance up the canyon outside of town. And, with God's grace and a little good luck, that claim had paid out beautifully.

But it had not all been sunshine and gold dust. Cord had come out here with his brothers Flint and Steve, and their father, Verne, who hadn't made it all the way to California. He had been killed during a battle with outlaws along the way.

After that, the brothers had stuck together through all the heartbreaks and disappointments greenhorns encounter in the gold mining business. Lies, betrayals, and misunderstandings a-plenty had led to the violent deaths of both Flint and Steve, leaving Cord alone in the world.

But he wasn't alone, he reminded himself.

Along the trail to California from the Ozarks, the Bennett family had fallen in with the Olmsteds. The widower Abraham and his two daughters, Katherine and Gloriana, had struck out to seek their fortune as well. When the Bennett claim yielded a lucky strike, Cord had hired Abraham to manage the claim on his behalf while he undertook the duties of town marshal. Abraham's honesty and uprightness made him a natural choice; Cord's growing love for Glory made him the inevitable one.

What had begun as a tiny camp on the river had burgeoned in the past year into a real settlement. The Bennett Claim, as it was now known, was demarcated by railroad ties laid end to end to form a kind of perimeter around the property. Set back from the river, two cabins loomed in the trees, one of which sent up a plume of smoke from its tin chimney.

A large sluice works occupied the major portion of the riverfront near which a healthy pile of tailings grew. Abraham stepped from around the back of the sluice as Cord approached, a bucket in hand and his battered hat fixed in its customary position on his tall forehead.

"Howdy, Cord!" Abraham's thin, bearded face lit up, and he changed course to intercept Cord. "How're things in town?"

"Big doings," Cord replied, reining to a halt. "The Griffith brothers are in jail."

"Oh?" Abraham chuckled. "What did those knuckleheads do this time?"

"They made the mistake of picking on poor Hap in the presence of our new town preacher. He laid all three of them out in the Nugget using nothing more than his bare fists, if you can believe it."

Abraham's bushy eyebrows jumped. "Is that right?" he asked, then hooted with laughter.

"It is." Cord chuckled, dismounting and shaking his head. "Busted them up pretty good. They were out cold on the barroom floor when I arrived. And there was Reverend Lomax, sipping a beer just as easy as you please."

"Well, I'll be darned!" Abraham's voice swelled with wonder. "God works in mysterious ways!"

"He does, at that." Cord glanced around. "Is Glory here?"

"She's up at the cabin, making dinner. You should stay and eat with us."

"Don't mind if I do."

Cord turned his steps to the cabin. As it did whenever he visited Glory, his heart began to beat more quickly. Excitement churned in his stomach, and he felt a surge of lightheadedness. Glory was the most wonderful woman—most wonderful *person*—Cord had ever met. And soon they would be united for life. He couldn't wait.

She had her back to the door when he stepped through, adding something to the cookpot bubbling on the stove. He just paused on the threshold and admired her for a minute before clearing his throat. She looked up, eyes brightening in recognition before she dropped the knife and flew into his arms.

"Cord!" She wrapped her arms around his back and pressed against him. "How are you?"

"I'm okay!" He laughed and squeezed back, holding her as he breathed in the rich scent of her red hair, of her womanly presence. "Lord, it's good to see you, honey."

They stood holding each other for a full minute until Abraham Olmsted cleared his throat in the doorway behind them.

"I hate to interrupt an intimate moment," he said. "But our chef requires this bucket of water."

"Sure thing, Pa!" Glory laughed and detached herself from Cord. "Just put it over there by the basin, would you, please?"

Abraham harumphed and trundled over to the basin, where he deposited the bucket before leaning over to take a deep draught of the cookpot's contents. "Now that smells wonderful," he enthused. "Are those them possums I hunted up yesterday?"

"They sure are, Pa." Glory stepped over and stirred the pot's contents with a ladle. "Got us some good stew here. Cord, why don't you set the table while Pa washes up?"

Cord did, and soon after, the three of them were saying grace over plates heaped with biscuits and stew.

"Cord's got some news." Abraham smirked and waggled his eyebrows at Glory as he spooned himself a helping of green beans.

"What's that, Cord?" Glory leaned toward him, chin in hand as her leg bumped his below the table.

"We've got ourselves a town preacher," Cord said. "Rode in last night. The Reverend Garrison Lomax. He aims to take over the building of the church, finish it up, and then fill the pews as quick as he can."

"So, we can have our church wedding?" Glory's excitement was plain in her voice.

"We can," Cord affirmed. "And we will. I already mentioned it to him and he's mighty excited at the prospect."

Glory launched herself from her chair to wrap her arms around him, overjoyed. He hugged her back, grateful for her happiness. Cord prayed for the strength to always put her happiness before all other things, including himself.

"He sounds like a helluva fella," said Abraham as Glory returned to her seat. "Cord says he laid out all three of the Griffith brothers all by hisself!"

"Cord, is that true?"

"Yep." Cord chuckled. "I left the three of them sleeping in a heap in the cell. Reckon they've probably woken up by now, splitting headaches and all."

Glory was impressed. "A man of God who's good with his fists." She shook her head. "Sounds exactly like the sort of preacher Rio Oro could use."

"Can't say I disagree," said Cord, helping himself to some beans.

Chapter 4

"I don't know how you can drink that stuff," Cord said the next morning as he watched Blackstone dunk a tea ball into a cup of freshly brewed hot water. "Why don't you just have some coffee like normal people?"

"Ah." Blackstone, his immense form hunched over his tiny cup, eyes narrowed in concentration as he carefully submerged and raised the ball, did not look up as he answered. "Tea is an acquired taste, Marshal. One is born to it, I suppose. In fact, I wouldn't be surprised to learn that native Brits like myself are born with a quantity of tea in our bloodstreams."

Cord smiled and shook his head as he watched Blackstone carefully sweeten his tea before leaning forward to take the most delicate sip. The big, burly Brit was about as fine a deputy as a marshal could want, even if he did retain his strange habits and expressions. Tea breaks, a fondness for bawdy music hall songs, and a reverence for England's Queen Victoria were among his eccentricities.

"Well, tea or coffee, it's all the same to me." Cord toasted him with his mug. "Here's to law and order."

"Chin-chin." Blackstone returned the salute and sipped noisily.

Cord heard feet hurtling along the wooden sidewalk, growing louder as they approached the marshal's office and stopped. Then came a pummeling on the doorframe.

"Someone's all in a twist!" exclaimed Blackstone, rising and pulling open the door to reveal Hap standing there, trembling.

"M-Marshal! Mr. B-Blackstone! You b-better come quick!"

Cord and Blackstone traded a look before setting down their respective cups and buckling on their gun belts.

"What's going on, Hap?" asked Cord, reaching for his hat.

"It's d-down at M-Mr. Ponder's lumberyard," Hap explained, leading them into the street. At this time of day, only a scattering of people were about. "Big t-t-trouble!"

"Is it the miners again?" Blackstone asked.

"I th-think so, deputy."

"Oh, Lord," groaned Cord. "Not this again."

Jeremiah Ponder was one of Rio Oro's big success stories. Something of a city slicker, the man had appeared in town with little more than his spectacles and a carpetbag. But within months, he had built up sufficient capital among the town officials and wealthier citizens to receive their support in establishing his lumber mill. Ponder had responded to their largesse by providing special orders—too-good deals on lumber with quick turnaround times. It was because of Ponder that the town had grown so fast.

Unfortunately, the man's professionalism did not extend to treating clients equally. While he lavished time and attention on the saloon and shopowners and the more well-to-do homesteaders who had come to start a life here, he had a tendency to bilk smaller clients. Ponder was known to overcharge on small jobs, cut corners, and deliver substandard lumber to the more hardscrabble among his customers. This included many of the miners.

"I wonder who he's upset this time," grumbled Blackstone as they hurried up the street.

A sinking feeling seized hold of Cord's gut as he caught sight of the fenced entrance to Ponder's mill. A group of maybe half a dozen men were clustered there. He could tell from their battered hats and boots and the cheap cut of their clothes that they were claim stakers—forty-niners like himself. New arrivals, they had each come determined to build a little cabin to pursue their piece of the gold rush dream.

And those dreams apparently had wrecked on the shore of Ponder's lumberyard. The scowls and fixed glares of the men, the clenched fists and muttered expressions of rage told Cord everything he needed to know. Ponder had found the wrong side of yet another group of customers, and they were not pleased about it.

As Cord and Blackstone drew level with the group, Cord could see one of the men arguing with Hansen, Ponder's yard foreman.

"—and provided what you asked for, no questions asked!" Hansen was saying. "You got no cause to complain!"

"That lumber you sold me was rotten!" The miner nearest Hansen, a man in a battered bowler hat, was red-faced with anger. "I was framing up my place when the whole shootin' match came down! Beams snapped like damned twigs!"

"Maybe you didn't calculate the weight balance correctly," Hansen countered.

"Weight balance?" The miner in the bowler hat thrust out a chunk of wood. "Look at it!"

Cord peered at the wood. Sure enough, the outside of the chunk looked just fine. But when the man tilted it, Cord could see the telltale signs of rot inside. The piece of timber had come from a rotten batch. That much was obvious.

"What do you have there?" demanded Hansen, squinting. "Oh. See? That's water rot. You probably left the planks out in the moisture and they—"

That was as far as he got before the miners broke out in a chorus of derision. They all apparently shared Bowler Hat's grievances to some extent or other. As their voices rose in complaint, a trio of miners joined them, swelling the crowd to ten. Cord stepped forward to take control of the situation.

"Why don't you fetch Mr. Ponder?" he asked Hansen pleasantly. "Seems this gentleman has a fair grievance."

"Mr. Ponder is busy," Hansen announced. "He's not taking visitors this morning."

"I'm not a visitor," Cord pointed out politely. "I'm the town marshal. You tell him I'd like a word with him, please."

The yard foreman seemed on the point of arguing when a guttural growl escaped Blackstone's chest. Hansen's face whitened, and he held up his hands in a gesture of surrender.

"I'll go get him!" he protested. "But he won't be happy about it!"

"Fine," said Cord. "I'll take my chances."

Hansen whirled and scuttled off into the yard, leaving Cord facing the group of agitated gold miners.

"Marshal, it's gotten bad," complained Bowler Hat. "A lot of us have been bilked by Ponder and we've had enough!"

"Maybe so," retorted Cord. "But that ain't an excuse to come here in a mob, all liver and lightning."

"He needs to answer for what he's done!" cried a voice in the crowd.

"This is a civilized town," snapped Cord, glaring in the direction of the voice. "And we aim to keep it that way!"

Hansen reappeared as he finished speaking. He came hurrying through the doorway of the lumber mill office ahead of Jeremiah Ponder. The mill boss stomped along behind him, plainly annoyed at being pulled from his desk. Cord could read his displeasure even at a distance.

"Here's Mr. Ponder," Hansen announced needlessly.

Cord studied Ponder. He was a rotund little man. Almost as big around as he was tall, he was a balding, red-faced little cuss. Wearing a canvas work apron, his spectacles pushed up onto his domed forehead, he was sweating, flushed, and obviously peeved as he planted his hands on his hips and glared at Cord.

"What's this all about, Marshal?" he demanded in a high, reedy voice. "I'm a busy man!"

"We appreciate you coming out to talk to us." Cord offered a nod. It paid to be courteous when speaking to town worthies. "Deputy Blackstone and I were called here in response to this crowd. I guess there are some folks here with a grievance about your product."

"I see." Ponder slid his spectacles back down to the bridge of his nose with a finger. Turning to the miners, he transformed himself into the figure of the concerned merchant, yet Cord could sense his annoyance as he addressed the group. "If there's a problem, fine. I'm glad to see to it. But don't be coming here to my shop and threatening my employees! Mr. Hansen is a trusted member of the Ponder Lumber family and I won't have him bullied, d'you hear?"

Bold words, thought Cord, doubting the man would have shown such bravado were it not for the presence of armed law enforcement.

"Here!" Bowler Hat stepped forward, thrusting the sample of rotted lumber under Ponder's nose. "I bought this from you and was using it to frame up a little shack on my claim! Got two walls framed up before the whole shebang came down! And this is what the lumber looked like when it snapped!"

Ponder flicked a suspicious glance at the man before deigning to study the wood. After a moment, he reached out and took the sample in hand and examined it through his spectacles, turning it this way and that and humming softly. Then he lowered his hands.

"I can see your point," he said quietly. "Looks like there was some inner rot. I'll work with you to come up with a compromise on what to do about it. But I won't have you blaming Mr. Hansen or any of the rest of my work crew!"

Before anyone could object, Ponder had raised his arms and was speaking to the crowd.

"We go and we cut the damn trees and haul the raw logs back here for processing. We choose the best we can and cut clean. We err on the side of generosity whenever possible! But we're not responsible for wood from a tree that's diseased or otherwise sick. How *can* we be?" He spread his hands in appeal. "We're not experts in biology! We just find the best trees we can and cut 'em up as neat as can be! Now, I'm sorry about this, I truly am. But let's be reasonable. Let's be gentlemen about this. Rio Oro is a civilized town."

At this echo of Cord's words, the marshal and Blackstone exchanged a glance. Blackstone rolled his eyes.

"Civilized?" exclaimed Bowler Hat. "What the hell does *civilized* mean to you, Ponder? Is it the civilized of decent folk doing honest business with one another? Or is it the *civilized* world where men of means seal a deal with a handshake while their fingers are crossed behind their backs?"

A murmur of shuffling and discontent arose at this. The crowd was definitely with Bowler Hat. To Cord, they resembled a corral full of steers jostling and nudging at the fence. The smallest event could spook and send them stampeding.

"All right, listen." Cord stepped forward. "Mr. Ponder here has offered to compensate this gentleman for his inconvenience. That's mighty generous of him. Now, if any of the rest of you have concerns, you bring them here individually. I'm not having any mob justice in this town. No, sir. This issue has been addressed and I am declaring this an unlawful assembly. You disperse and go back to your claims, now."

Bowler Hat turned as if to object. But the cold light in Cord's eyes, and the way his hand strayed to the butt of his pistol, discouraged him. The crowd remained in place for another moment or two before beginning to shuffle off in separate directions. Cord and

Blackstone watched them go before turning back to Ponder and Hansen.

"Well, that's handled." Cord sighed.

"How could you allow something like this to happen?" Ponder demanded. "You're the town marshal. Your job is to keep order here!"

"How could you sell rotten lumber?" Cord shot back. "You run the town mill. Your job is to provide sound building materials for the community. If I was you, I'd check my inventory and be careful of what I sell in the future."

Ponder seemed on the point of objecting but apparently thought better of it. He merely squared his jaw and firmed his lips before spinning and stalking back into his office. The door closed behind him with a slam.

"Now you've gone and upset him," Hansen muttered. "And we'll have to bear the brunt of it."

"Sounds like Ponder's the kind of man who likes to pick on his employees," Blackstone noted as Hansen scurried away.

"Sounds like a complete jackass to me," Cord said quietly.

CHAPTER 5

It didn't take long for Bowler Hat to cross Cord's trail again. His name, coincidentally enough, echoed that of his chosen headgear. Sy Bowles was a relatively new arrival in town, said to be from Delaware and known for having a quick temper.

Garrison Lomax had brought up Bowles's name once in conversation, saying the man was given to ridiculing the Scripture and the Church. While both Cord and Lomax agreed he was within his rights to do so, it revealed a tendency toward the argumentative, the outrageous, as well as a fondness for controversy.

"Some men are just built that way," Blackstone offered by way of comment on the subject. This was the afternoon after they had processed and released the Griffith brothers. They had remained out of town for a spell after that. But it was from them that Cord heard tell of the doings up-canyon.

It was Billy Griffith who came riding along the main street astride a sturdy mule, bundles of firewood wrapped in canvas and secured either side of the saddle for sale in the town. He stopped level with the door to the marshal's office. Cord stepped out onto the wooden sidewalk to greet him.

"Trouble out past our claim," Billy Griffith said simply. "Up-canyon about a mile. Two newcomers. Reckon one's pushed his boundary into the other's claim. It'll need seeing to."

Cord nodded. Billy looked down and gently tapped the sides of the donkey with his heels. As he rode off, Cord turned back into the office. Blackstone was dipping a tea ball into a cup of fresh hot water.

"Tea party's canceled," Cord announced. "We're going for a ride."

The Griffiths' claim was upstream of the grid staked out by Rio Oro's original prospectors. Cord had his claim down there, as did Olmsted and the others who had first registered at Casterline's assayer office. As more arrivals had come to swell the town's population, the claims had progressed upriver, venturing off sometimes into the tributary canyons with the water sources that fed the mainstream. It was in one of these that the trouble was brewing.

"That's the Bowles claim," Blackstone reported. "He's next to a fella named Antiglione, an Italian. I met him. Very jolly, very sweet man. I'm willing to bet it's Bowles that is the source of the problem."

"I'll take that into account," Cord said. "Thanks."

He set about giving it a good ponder as he and Blackstone rode from town, up the river trails past the original claims and further into the wilderness. Up here, the trees were thicker. And, to its credit, the river more than satisfied the needs of the surrounding fauna. It was cooler here, the branches shading the forest floor often shaken by a cool, off-river breeze. Dimly, somewhere upstream, rapids rushed. A lone jackrabbit skittered past as Cord picked out a path across the pine- and acorn-strewn forest floor.

After a while, he heard voices. At first, these mixed in with the blurry sound of the distant falls but gradually grew distinct as Cord and Blackstone advanced to the top of a pine-covered rise and gazed down the gentle slope to the riverside. A stone beach hugged the bend in the river at one end of which stood Bowles. He was not wearing his distinctive headgear. Stripped to his trousers, vest, and undershirt, he was sweaty and dirt-blackened, his bald pate glimmering with a touch of sunburn. The pickax he cradled in his hands was evidence he had been hard at work.

At the other end of the beach stood a stout, bald man. Shirtless and barefoot, he wore only a pair of dark knee pants. Although his stomach and chest were large, his arms bulged with muscle. Like Bowles, he was sweaty and soil-blackened, and the shovel he held gave proof of his labor. And he was engaged in a shouting match with Bowles.

"—got no call talkin' to me that way!" screamed Bowles.

"*Santa Diavolo!* You no come here, Bowles!" retorted Antiglione.

"I'll go wherever I damn want!"

"Is my claim!"

"Well. Aren't they a charming couple?" Blackstone quipped, pulling up his horse alongside Cord's.

Cord shook his head. "In a country as vast as ours, these two knuckleheads had to choose claims right next to each other?"

At some point during this exchange, the shouting between Bowles and Antiglione grew more shrill. Cord snapped his gaze back to the beach in time to see the Italian let fly with a rock.

The man's aim was impressive. It hurtled across the space between him and Bowles with lightning speed, and the sound of its impact on Bowles's head was a sharp *conk*!

Bowles staggered, stunned for a moment, before shaking his head, righting his stance, and glaring at Antiglione. Then he raised the pickax, loosed a horrifying shriek, and charged across the beach toward the other man.

"There they go!" cried Blackstone.

Cord spurred his horse toward the beach, his deputy right behind. The thunder of hooves rose just as Bowles reached Antiglione and swung down his pickax. It was intercepted in midflight by the old Italian's shovel. The two clanged off each other before all noise was eclipsed by the sound of a gunshot.

Bowles and Antiglione froze. Blinked. And turned toward Cord.

The marshal sat bolt upright in the saddle, his Colt Dragoon pointed skyward, still smoking from its last discharge.

"Cease and desist! Or I will shoot you both! Now, drop those tools! Go on, now!"

Antiglione complied immediately. Bowles affected a surly reluctance but finally consented to toss his pickax to the beach. Blackstone swung down to collect them and separate the two men. Cord remained mounted, glaring at them with frosty anger.

"This isn't how civilized men work out their differences," he said softly. "How's about you tell me and Deputy Blackstone what's going on here?"

As he said these words, Blackstone shouldered his way between the two men, dwarfing both. The fight seemed to leave them as Blackstone casually bent and scooped up shovel and pickax in one hand and threw them over a shoulder as easily as if they were balsa wood. Antiglione stepped back, put up his hands, and addressed Cord.

"I admit, Marshal Bennett, I was, how you say? In the wrong. I did wrong to throw rock. Mea culpa. I am sorry."

"That's right!" screeched Bowles, pointing and glaring. "You heard him, Marshal! He admits what he did! Arrest him!"

"Hold up just a second." Cord holstered the Dragoon before resting a forearm on the pommel of his saddle. "What about you, Mr. Bowles? What brings you here?"

"Why, I'm prospecting!"

"On Mr. Antiglione's claim?"

"This ain't his claim!"

"It is according to Clyde Casterline's records." Cord turned to Blackstone. "Isn't that right?"

"Sure is, Marshal." Blackstone dropped the shovel and pickax out of reach of the men and stood over them as he continued. "According to the documents filed and countersigned by both of you, the Bowles claim stops at the edge of that little headland back there." He pointed a hundred yards upriver. "Mr. Antiglione's claim begins here at this little stone beach."

"That's incorrect!" Bowles protested. "I'm sure it is!"

"And I'm sure you're wrong," said Cord. "We didn't come up here without first doing our homework, Mr. Bowles. Your conflict with Mr. Antiglione, here, is catching the notice of your fellow prospectors."

"Well, so what?" spat Bowles, angrily wheeling his arms. "It don't matter! He's not even *from* here!"

"I am an American citizen!" Antiglione raged indignantly. "I came onboard ship. I rode in the bottom decks, in the dark and stink, for weeks to get here! I work—two years digging holes, driving spikes on railroad. I save my money and come here! *This*!" He stomped the ground with one bare foot. "*This* my home, you *figlio di puttana*! I got every right to be here!"

Cord kept his face expressionless but could not help but be moved by the Italian man's story. More and more he was hearing such stories of the world's poor crossing oceans to get to America, working their fingers to the bone for the chance to make a new life. Although native-born himself, Cord could not help but feel admiration and respect for those who would risk so much for a chance to have what he took for granted: American citizenship. Cord privately felt that such immigrants had more of the adventurous American spirit in them than some of his fellow citizens, especially men like Bowles.

"As the marshal of these parts, I'm making a determination here." He pointed to the headland upriver that marked the boundary of Bowles's claim. "Mr. Bowles, I am ordering you in the name of the law to remain on your side of that headland. Failure to comply will lead to your arrest and incarceration. And Mr. Antiglione? Your boundary is the end of this beach. Don't cross it."

"On my honor, Marshal! It shall be as you say!"

"You got no right to do that!" Bowles exclaimed.

Cord's head snapped around, eyes narrowing. He urged his horse forward until he loomed over Bowles. Glaring down from this great height, his broad shoulders tensed and his voice icy, he gave the man a piece of his mind.

"Now you listen to me, you rambunctious troublemaker! I am the damn *law* in Rio Oro and the surrounding region. I am a peace officer sworn to uphold the law and the U.S. Constitution. And you will *not* tell me what I have the right to do and not to do! Do you understand me, Bowles? You do not dictate my duty to me. Nor do you disrespect my authority here, because to do so is to undermine the rule of law! Do I make myself clear?"

Bowles glared at Cord, his lips white from being pressed together so hard and angrily. At length, he drew a ragged breath, opened his mouth, and said, "Yes, sir, Marshal. You do. You make yourself plenty clear."

"Good." Cord backed up his mount a few feet and sighed. "You two stay the hell away from each other. If I have to come up here again, somebody is going to leave in irons. Understand?"

"Is-a very, *very* clear, Signore Marshal! Very clear to Antiglione! Very much clear!"

"Good." Cord smiled thinly. "Now gather up your tools and head home. You're both done working for the day."

Without another word, the two men gathered up the shovel and pickax and went their separate ways. Cord and Blackstone sat there mounted for another quarter hour to make sure neither of the combatants doubled back before turning and heading for town.

* * *

Cord was just packing up his desk at the end of the workday when the door to the marshal's office opened and Clyde Casterline poked his head in from the street. It was dusk, and the assayer's form was little more than an indistinct silhouette, although Cord could see he was still in his shirtsleeves, his spectacles pushed up onto his forehead. He had evidently just hurried straight over from work.

"Begging your pardon, Cord," he said quietly. "But I've got Sy Bowles in my office, and he's mad as a damned hatter. For good reason too. Seems the assayer's note of promise he received on his claim doesn't square with our records at the office. He says he's been cheated out of what he paid to demarcate as his property."

"Is that right?" This was unexpected. Casterline's office was known for its scrupulous recordkeeping.

"I remember Bowles and Antiglone both came during the busy season. I was using a clerk as an assistant at the time." Casterline shrugged. "The mistake's explained easily enough, but the responsibility is mine. I have both Bowles and Antiglione in my office now. Can you come?"

"Sure thing," said Cord. "Let's go."

Chapter 6

Bowles was hopping mad by the time Cord stepped through the door into Casterline's office. The evening shadows had already begun to streak the rear wall, darkening the clock where it sat above the mantel.

Antiglione, now clad in a jacket and boots, looked on sourly as his *neighbor* paced back and forth before the assayer and claims office counter. Normally closed at this hour, business was resumed as Casterline lifted the end portion of the counter and slipped behind it.

"Okay," said Cord, spreading his feet and crossing his arms. "What's going on here?"

Bowles whipped around, brandishing a folded paper he held in his left fist. "See this right here?" he demanded. "This is my notice of claim! Includes a section of map on it." He whirled on Casterline. "And this idiot marked it up wrong!"

"Take it easy," said Cord. "If there's been an error, Mr. Casterline will see to it. But there's no cause to be calling names."

Casterline lit a kerosene lamp, unrolled his claims map, and bent over it with a magnifying glass, comparing it to the notations on Bowles's claim sheet. After several moments, he sighed, straightened, and pushed the map across to Cord.

"There it is," he said simply. "There's the error."

Cord bent to the magnifying glass, comparing the dimensions of Bowles's claim as listed on his note to the section demarcated on the map. Sure enough, there was a discrepancy—a small one. It appeared his claim extended marginally beyond the headland Cord had seen at the riverside. This reduced the distance between Bowles's and Antiglione's claims.

"Yep," he said at length. "Seems there's been an error."

"It happens," admitted Casterline. "Not often, but it happens. I've written up a new notice for you, Mr. Bowles. And you—"

Bowles snatched the new notice from the assayer's fingers, pored over it, and then began shaking his head.

"Nope. This won't do." He slapped down the paper on the counter. "I want compensation for my inconvenience! I want my claim extended to the edge of that beach."

"Santa diavolo!" exclaimed Antiglione. "This is outrageous!"

"To the edge of that beach, I say! It's only fair!"

"Well, Mr. Bowles . . ." Casterline smiled softly. "You've got to understand, that's almost enough square footage to be its own claim entirely. And frankly, I'd prefer to offer that claim to a third party whom I could place between you and Mr. Antiglione, given how much—"

"I want it! And I demand legal satisfaction!"

Cord sighed. Glancing through the front window of Casterline's office, he noted the lights still on in the office of Judge Davenport, Rio Oro's justice of the peace. It seemed matters would have to be resolved with his assistance.

Horace Davenport had received his appointment as a territorial justice of the peace just a few months previously, but his presence was already keenly felt in town. A by-the-book judge, his edge was tempered by a kindly streak that could reveal itself on the most surprising occasions. Cord had seen him extend clemency to some nasty characters while coming down hard on what seemed to be law-abiding citizens. But on balance, Davenport seemed to have the pulse of the community under his thumb. The cumulative effect of his judgments had made itself manifest in a calmer, more peaceful, and law-abiding town.

And so it was with his customary quiet attentiveness that the fat, bearded justice listened first to Bowles, then to Casterline and Cord. Their testimony on the matter finished, he turned to Antiglione.

"Mr. Antiglione, sir. You've been rather quiet," grumbled the judge. "Do you have anything you wish to say?"

"Ah . . . your honor." Antiglione, hat in hand, shuffled his feet and looked down at the toes of his boots. "I just want to work my claim. My map is fine. I have no complaints. I just ask that Mr. Bowles stay away from my property, my claim. That is all, your honor."

"Quite reasonable and sensible." Davenport turned to Bowles. "Seems clear to me that you've been denied the rightful dimensions of your claim. Unintentionally, I believe. Mr. Casterline's reputation for fairness is legendary in these parts. He has the confidence of every miner on the river. To say nothing of law enforcement and this justice. But you apparently believe you are owed compensation?"

"Yes, your honor," said Bowles crisply. "I've been deprived of my rightful claim and believe I should be compensated."

"And so you shall be. But not in the way you want." Davenport turned to Casterline. "Clyde, you've done a good job, but you made a mistake on this claim. I'm sorry, but I have to fine you. Five dollars."

"Yes, your honor." Casterline nodded, taking the fine in the teeth and keeping his composure.

"You will pay that five dollars to Mr. Bowles. And the matter will be considered settled. Very well?"

Cord and Casterline nodded. Bowles fumed. This was not the outcome for which he had been hoping.

"And Mr. Antiglione? I wish you all the best on your claim, sir," said Davenport. "Do let us know if any further boundary disputes arise."

"I will, your honor! *Molte grazie!"*

One by one, they filed out of the judge's office. Cord remained behind, closing the door behind the last of them.

"Thank you, your honor," he said quietly.

"My pleasure, Cord." Davenport pushed out a chair with the toe of his boot. "Good timing. Something I needed to talk to you about anyhow. Go ahead and have a seat and I'll pour us a little bourbon."

"I won't say no to a free drink," Cord replied, taking a seat. He accepted the cool glass Davenport pressed into his hand.

"To your upcoming nuptials," the judge said, settling into his chair with a heavy sigh and raising his glass. "You and Miss Glory set a date yet?"

"Now that the preacher's come to town, it will be soon," Cord replied. "Soon as he gets that church of his finished."

"Yes. The church." The judge turned and gazed out the window toward the unfinished structure now obscured by darkness. "When I saw them put the foundation in, I knew the town was changing for the better. Things like a church, a library, a museum . . . They civilize a town. Along with folks like yourself, who wear badges and enforce the law. And men like myself, who interpret and rule upon it."

"Yes, Judge. Rio Oro *is* becoming civilized."

"Same thing's happening all over the territory," mused Davenport. "I've ridden extensively in my career. Been a circuit judge in a number of towns. Things usually follow the same course. Rough-hewn men come and put down stakes. They're followed by the merchants and the builders. Then the businessmen. Then the lawyers and the teachers and the preachers. Before you know it, there are skirts bustling in the streets and the womenfolk out organizing their bake sales and church picnics."

"I don't know that we're there yet, Judge."

"Maybe not." Davenport smiled. "But we will be soon. Along with everything that follows. If you catch my drift."

Cord assumed the judge was talking about children. He and Glory planned to make a few.

"Sadly, there's another side to civilization." Davenport sat forward and rummaged through a drawer. Producing an envelope, he sat back and drew out a sheet of paper marked by a clerk's careful script. "I expect you remember a fella named Patrick Elam?"

"I do." Cord's lips tightened. "I couldn't hardly forget a varmint like that. He used to own the Bear Flag Saloon. He and his posse of whip-wielding thugs got on the wrong side of the law. Had to put him down myself."

"And the saloon?" Davenport asked. "It's now owned by . . . ?"

"Kat Olmsted," Cord said. "Glory's sister. She was working for Elam when all the trouble happened. When the dust cleared, she took over." He shrugged. "Just seemed like a natural fit. She was helping Elam generate trade and run the place. Now she's the boss."

"Turns out Patrick Elam had a sister," said Davenport, waving the paper. "She has retained counsel and written to me, petitioning the court to return to her what is rightfully family property."

"Did Elam have a will?"

"Not that we've been able to find." Davenport shrugged helplessly. "But inheritance by next of kin is pretty much standard practice where such situations are concerned. She has indicated her intention to come to Rio Oro and claim what's hers. I've got to tell you, Cord, under the circumstances, things aren't looking too good for Kat's continued proprietorship."

Cord nodded. It was a bitter pill to swallow. But if Elam had a sister, then the Bear Flag should rightfully be hers.

"What is her name?" he asked.

"Dolores Whittaker," said Davenport. "I gather she goes by Dollie." He produced another piece of paper. "Received this letter too. She's making her way here from back East. This was sent from Chicago, so she's already on her way. Should be here any time."

Cord tensed. This was all happening a great deal faster than he would have liked. Someone would have to speak to Kat. It would not be a pleasant conversation.

"I reckon she'll probably come and see me when she arrives." Davenport folded and replaced the pages inside the envelope. "It's damned unfortunate for Kat. And it will be disruptive to the town. But, like we were just saying, civilization has its price."

"That it does." Cord set down the empty glass on a corner of the judge's desk. "Somebody will have to break the news to Kat, and I figure that should be me. I can take care of that tomorrow."

"Would you? That would be most helpful." Davenport drained the last of the bourbon from his own glass. "Tell her to feel free to drop in and speak to me. I plan to enforce the law, but I'm not heartless. A young woman finding herself at sixes and sevens in a situation like this is tragic. I'll help out where I can."

"We appreciate it, Judge."

"It's the least I can do." Davenport shrugged again. "Since I won't be performing your marriage ceremony, I still hope you'll invite me to the reception."

Cord smiled. "Count on it, your honor."

Cord returned to the marshal's office. Blackstone sat behind the desk and looked up when Cord entered.

"Everything all right?" he asked.

"More or less." Cord sighed and perched on the edge of his desk. "Turns out Patrick Elam, the man who used to run the Bear Flag, has a sister. She's been made aware of her brother's passing and is laying claim to the saloon as her rightful property."

"Is that right?" Blackstone was surprised. "That will come as something of a surprise to Miss Kat. She's put a great deal of effort into the place and built a solid clientele. The Bear Flag is basically her life's work."

"I know it." Cord shook his head. "It's a shame. But I suppose I can understand Elam's sister and her point of view. She's on her way to Rio Oro now. Should be here any day."

"Good thing that judge showed up," Blackstone replied. "I'd much rather the matter be settled in a court of law as opposed to guns in the main street."

Cord chuckled, despite being unsettled at the notion of two women facing off in a gunfight.

"We'll probably be a part of whatever happens." Cord yawned and stretched. "I'm going to bed. You got everything under control?"

"The night shift is on duty," said Blackstone.

Cord nodded and headed upstairs to bed.

CHAPTER 7

Cord wasn't looking forward to his conversation with Kat about Dolores Whittaker. He had developed a close bond with his fiancée's sister over the past year. Kat was a woman with a gift for making others feel welcome.

She also had a keen eye for business. Under her guidance, the Bear Flag had flourished despite the presence of the Golden Nugget. That two saloons situated right across the street from each other could both succeed in a town this size was surprising. Much of this came down to Kat's relentless hard work.

Cord waited until midafternoon before leaving the marshal's office to cross the street to the Bear Flag. This was the doldrums hour for both saloons. While busy during lunch and for an hour or so afterward, business slowed to a trickle between then and quitting time, when the crowd descended.

Kat used this lull to attend to the Bear Flag's practical details—cleaning, restocking, talking to employees, and making sure nothing was going on that she needed to know about. Cord wasn't surprised to see her standing on the wooden sidewalk by the batwing doors, broom in hand, as she joked with two of the waitresses. Kat was the sort who led her staff not by fear or reward but by a solid work ethic. The saloon girls and bartenders worshipped her, and she reciprocated by taking good care of them. The Bear Flag was a happy place to work, thanks to her.

"Miss Kat?" One of the bartenders stepped through the batwing doors as Cord approached. "I'm going down to the mercantile to pick up a few things for the bar. Do you need anything?"

"Oh, bless you, Burt. Yes." Kat shook the broom she was holding. "Fetch up a fresh broom for me, would you please? This one's damn near shot."

"Will do, Miss Kat." The bartender flipped her a salute and walked off down the street, accompanied by the two serving girls. Kat watched them go.

"Hello, there," said Cord, stepping up beside her. "How goes it today?"

"Hello, Cord." Kat leaned in and gave him a one-armed hug. "How's my future brother-in-law?"

"Doing all right, I suppose." He grinned. "Can't complain. Not that anyone would listen! Do you have a few minutes?"

"Certainly." She appeared startled. "Is everything okay?"

"Oh, yes." He shrugged. "Generally so, anyway. But there are just a few things I should let you know about. Confidentially, if possible."

"We can talk in my office." Kat leaned the broom up against the wall beside the doors. "Come on in. Would you care for some lemonade? One of the girls just whipped up a batch."

"Glass of lemonade sounds like just the thing right about now," Cord said. He followed her back through the mostly empty barroom with its scattering of tables. A woman knelt on the floor at the end of the bar by a wash bucket, cleaning the floorboards with a scrub brush and rag. Kat went behind the counter and poured two tall glasses of lemonade from a pitcher before leading Cord down a short hallway to a closed door.

Kat's office was a narrow room—a former closet that she had had widened and furnished. Now wide enough to accommodate a desk, a kerosene lamp, and two chairs, Kat's private sanctuary had a homey feel to it. A rug on the floor, a vase of flowers on a side table, and a few scrimshaw hangings made the place feel like a schoolroom or somebody's parlor.

Kat settled herself behind the desk and lit a kerosene lamp to augment the thin light from a narrow window. Cord settled into the surprisingly comfortable guest chair and looked around.

"Haven't been in here before," he admitted. "It's a cozy little nook."

"It is." Kat toasted him with her lemonade. "I had the door reinforced so almost no sound comes through it. I can disappear in here when things get crazy out in the saloon. My refuge from the madness. It's saved my life a few times."

"I bet." Cord sipped his lemonade, delighting in the fresh rush of moisture and flavor down his dry throat. It felt like a river invading a dry wash. "How's the business doing these days?"

"We cleared our debt last month. Finally!" She laughed. "In between what we owed Ponder for the lumber we used to finish the building and the charges Patrick had run up at the wholesale store, it took us a while to pay down both notes. But we managed. Now we're putting away some savings and making plans for the future."

"It's the future that I wanted to talk about," he said.

"The future of my business? Or our future as members of the same family?" She smiled teasingly. "You'll be the man of the family once you marry Glory."

"Nonsense! That's Abraham's job."

"My father is getting old, Cord. He'll be glad for the help. And we'll be glad to have you standing up for us and protecting us, me and Glory both."

"That's something I aim to do," he promised. "But no, I wanted to talk to you about something else. What legal arrangements, if any, did you have with Patrick Elam?"

"None." Kat shook her head. "I started out as an employee—kind of a hostess, helping people get seated, making folks feel welcome. Moved up from there to helping him run the place. When he died, I took over. Just seemed the natural thing under the circumstances."

"It sure did," Cord agreed. "And you've done a fine job, Kat. Kept these people employed and rendered the town a service. But something's come to my attention that you should know about. Turns out Patrick Elam had a next of kin."

Kat's eyes widened, but she said nothing, waiting for Cord to elaborate.

"Horace Davenport has received correspondence from a woman named Dolores Whittaker. She writes claiming to be Patrick Elam's sister. She's gotten wind of the existence of this place. Kat, she's claiming it should be hers by right of inheritance."

"I see." Given the news, her voice was remarkably calm.

"Did Patrick leave a will?"

Kat swallowed and looked at the floor, placing her hands on the desk in front of her, palms down, fingers spread. She was trying to collect herself, Cord recognized, fighting to maintain her equilibrium. What he had just unloaded on her was a shock—a big one. But she surprised him with her grit. Taking a deep, heavy breath, she looked up. Although watery, her gaze was steady. Her tone was firm.

"The only thing Patrick Elam left behind was a mess," she said. "After he died and his men scattered, I got hold of what documents he had related to the business. The account ledgers were chaotic. He was paying out almost exactly what this place took in on a nightly basis, and he had lines of credit with several merchants. A number had sent past due notices. Aside from the account books, a property deed for the land, and a few contracts, there was nothing else."

"So, no will."

"I never found one, no."

"That may not be a bad thing," Cord mused. "If he had a will that specifically mentioned next of kin, you would be out of luck. As it now stands, you have a fighting chance of hanging on to this place."

At this, Kat laughed—a harsh melody of climbing notes that ended on a dry exhale. "A fighting chance." She chuckled. "My word, Cord, you might just as well have given this place a second name. Up until a few weeks ago, just keeping the doors open and the staff paid was a touch-and-go prospect. In between paying off creditors and keeping the bar stocked, it's all we could do to make it from day to day. Last month was the first time since I took over that the budget has shown any improvement."

"Can't you cut costs?"

"Already have." She shrugged. "As close to the bone as I can."

"How about staff?"

"For most who work here, this job is all that stands between them and dire poverty. No." She rapped her knuckles on the desk. "The staff stays. Every one of them. Until they leave by their own choice."

"Right." Cord had to admire her sense of fairness. Like Glory, she was a good woman who wouldn't kick the needy into the dirt. "So, we're left with our current situation."

"Seems so."

"Look, it's all well and good for Dolores Whittaker to come here and present her case." He sat back and spread his hands. "But possession is nine points of the law. You're in the buckboard, reins in hand. She'll have to prove her claim in court before anything happens to disrupt life here at the Bear Flag."

"Yes and no." Kat sighed. "Cord, if she really is Patrick's sister, then I can't argue that she has a fair claim on the place. Now, don't get me wrong. I plan to fight for it. After all the work I put in, I'd be a fool not to. But I respect family, same as you." She leaned back and stared up at the ceiling. "Who knows what her life has been like? What she's been through? Could be she's a good woman who has nothing, and her brother's inheritance is the first stroke of good luck she's had in her lifetime. Lord, I think about you and Glory finding each other. It would be wrong to stand in the way of that. It's wrong to stand in the way of anyone else's destiny."

Cord was moved by her charity and sense of fairness. And he had to admire her ability to set her own interests aside in the service of a greater good. He himself had not always shown such righteous behavior.

"That's mighty understanding of you," he said quietly. "But one thing at a time. Let's see what happens when the woman arrives in town. Let her come and speak her piece. Meet with you and take a look over the place. Could be she'll see the state of things and change her mind."

"Could be," Kat agreed hopefully. "Could be she likes the way I run the place and decides to go partners. We have to see what she says once she gets here."

"Agreed." Cord could not help but feel a swell of admiration for the woman. Here she was, faced with the possibility of losing something she had rescued and built up with her own hands, and her first impulse was to be charitable. Cord breathed a prayer of thanks for the good fortune of finding Glory and her family. After the loss of his own, it was about as huge a blessing as any man could hope for.

"Well, Kat," he said. "You're taking it all very well. All right, then." He hauled himself out of the chair and stood upright. "Let's just keep an eye on the situation and see what happens."

"Agreed." She stood. "Thank you, Cord."

They walked out to the barroom. Cord stepped through the batwing doors into the quiet afternoon.

The streets of Rio Oro basked under warm sunlight. Soon, the heat of the day would pass, and the town would pick up speed as it moved toward nightfall. Cord had a bit of a ride ahead of him and decided to leave early. He would meander up the valley toward his claim and stop by the river to wash up on the way. He looked forward to a warm meal and familiar company.

He was halfway to his horse when the gunfire began.

CHAPTER 8

The bullet ricocheted, blasting up dirt a foot to Cord's left. He dove to his right, tucking and rolling as a second shot chased the first. He came to rest on his stomach, right hand clawing at his holster. A third shot—this one uncomfortably close. But where in damnation—?

There! A man in black partially concealed behind a porch pillar of the dry goods store. He was just leaning out from behind the pillar to take another shot when Cord's bullet chewed splinters from the wood near his head. The man ducked back behind the pillar. Cord rose to his knees.

A shot from another angle whined past his ear. Cord spun and blasted off a round. It was an instinctive move—an act of self-preservation. It should not have landed, but his time as a marshal had made him good with a gun.

The second assailant was kneeling behind a horse trough. Cord's bullet took out a corner of the trough, prompting a quantity of water to spill onto the street. Cord rolled again, rose, and ducked down an alley between two buildings to orient himself.

Two assailants, both in black hats and black dusters, had their features partially obscured, only their eyes visible above the bandannas wrapped around the lower half of each one's face. Cord was about to make a move when he realized there was a *third* gunman. Armed with a rifle, he had just stepped out onto the second-floor balcony of a rooming house across the street.

Cord was just lining up to take another shot when the creak of a door opening nearby alerted him to Blackstone's presence. The big Englishman, alerted by the sound of gunfire, had pulled on his belt with its two holsters and grabbed up a coach gun. Blackstone gripped the short, double-barreled weapon in both hands as he came stomping across the boardwalk to the street.

The man on the balcony spotted Blackstone first. His move to the railing alerted the Englishman. Despite his large size, Blackstone moved fast, whirling, bringing up the gun, and blasting both barrels at once. Part of the wooden railing blew apart, driving the gunman back into the building.

Cord took that opportunity to break out of the alley, pistol up and firing in the direction of the two assailants on the street. The gunman behind the water trough was kneeling, one hand on the trough's edge as his gun swept the street for targets. The man behind the porch pillar, meanwhile, nervously studied the shredded balcony railing as Blackstone reloaded.

Cord's bullet tearing through the fabric of his duster pulled him from his reverie. Cord fired again and the man jerked, his gun hand rising to stem the blood flow from his wounded left arm.

Blackstone, freshly reloaded, began moving slowly up the street in the direction of the building into which the balcony bushwhacker had ducked.

The gunman behind the water trough found Blackstone and dropped his sights on him. He must have been nervous because, despite having such a big target, his shot went wide, screaming past Blackstone to shatter the window of a store.

Rather than spooking the Englishman, the man's efforts seemed to enrage Blackstone, who immediately switched course and began blasting at the water trough with the coach gun. Two big booms and the trough disintegrated, the water that was still in it cascading out and creating a thick pool in the muddy street. The gunman yelped and dashed for cover.

The gunman from the balcony appeared in the doorway of the rooming house. Cord snapped off two shots, the second narrowly missing the man's head, forcing him back into the shadows. The wounded man across the street limped from porch pillar to porch pillar, heading in the same direction as his friend.

Cord skidded to a stop while Blackstone reloaded.

"You all right?" he asked.

"Oh, I'm just grand, thanks!" A slash of a smile appeared in the Englishman's bushy black beard. "Nothing to stir the blood like a good gunfight, yes?"

"If you say so." Blackstone's coolness under the circumstances was impressive. Cord gestured toward the rooming house. "We've got one of the varmints cornered in there. What say we head in?"

"Sounds like a fine idea!" Blackstone boomed, snapping shut the coach gun.

While the other two gunmen disappeared around the corner of the distant hostelry, Cord and Blackstone advanced on the rooming-house door. Reaching the sidewalk, they stepped up onto the wooden surface and flattened themselves against the walls to either side of the door. Crouching there, they heard voices approaching down the hallway from within. The footsteps accompanying those voices paused, then hurried in response to a loud noise from the second floor. A moment later, three women spilled through the door, one of whom was the rooming-house proprietor.

"Marshal, he went back upstairs!" she panted. "Most of the roomers fled through the back door, but some are still upstairs! Please hurry!"

"We will! Now get clear! Go into the saloon!"

The women did as they were told, running down the boardwalk to the Golden Nugget and flinging themselves through the batwing doors. After sharing a nod, Cord and Blackstone went in single file, Cord in the lead.

The rooming-house door led into a dark, narrow corridor with doors on either side. Most stood open, evidence of the lodgers' hasty flight. The corridor ended at a door with a glass window that was blocked by a table holding a vase of flowers. The hallway turned left there. Cord paused at the corner, crouched, and peered around. No gunshot chased him off, so he gave Blackstone a nod. Then, they went creeping down the hallway.

The corridor widened into a sort of entry hall. Cord saw more open doors flanking a staircase. He had just taken a single step toward the stairs when the man upstairs fired. The bullet punched a hole in the wooden floorboards, tearing a jagged oval in the floor. Cord ducked back into a doorway, his Dragoon up, waiting for more gunfire. But instead, he heard the thump of boots fleeing along an upstairs hallway. He turned to Blackstone.

"I'm going up. Cover me."

"Right." The big Englishman positioned the coach gun to fire without taking his eyes from the upstairs balcony railing. "Ready when you are, Marshal."

"All right, then."

Cord eased out of the doorway and across the entry hall toward the base of the stairs, eyes and pistol raised and ready. He could see flashes of the second-floor landing flickering between the balusters as he moved, but no sign of motion from above. He gained the bottom of the stairs and placed a booted foot upon the bottom step.

Nothing.

Adjusting his grip on the Dragoon, he began easing his way up the steps. Blessedly, each one took his weight and did not creak.

After a brief eternity, he reached the midpoint to the landing above. And still no response. He paused, breathed, and took another step.

The sudden blast of a gun was deafening in the close quarters. The gunman's bullet took another bite of wood. Cord crouched down as bits of the step above him shredded. He whipped up his gun and snapped back two shots. Then Blackstone's coach gun roared, and a portion of the landing railing disintegrated. Cord saw a flash of black duster fleeing along a hallway.

He sprinted up the steps two at a time into a haze of gun smoke. He could hear pounding bootsteps, see a vague shape in a black duster down the hall. As he watched, the shape turned, and he dove to the floor in time for another shot to whip over his head.

Whoever he was, the man was playing for keeps.

Cord scooted across the floor to plaster himself against the wall at the end of the hallway. Blackstone could be heard making his way ponderously up the steps behind him. Cord held up the Dragoon, ready to fire down the corridor in case the gunman went on the attack again.

He snuck a peek around a corner just as the man in the black duster threw open a door and disappeared inside one of the rooms along the hallway.

"He's inside a room. Six doors down," he told Blackstone, jerking his head to the right. "This side of the hallway."

"Flimsy doors." Blackstone shrugged. "Should go down with a good kick."

"You have to get there first."

"True enough."

Cord thought hard. Sending Blackstone first made little sense. His bulk would be heard coming down the hall, and the very size of the man made him an easy target in the narrow corridor.

No, he thought. He would have to go first, as low and fast as he could.

He turned to Blackstone. "You ready to cover me?"

"Ready, Marshal."

"Right. Here we go."

He edged into the hallway, keeping low. That would have been necessary anyway, given the thick pall of gun smoke hanging down from the ceiling. It filled most of the air in the corridor, ending just three feet above the carpet. Cord used the edge of the carpet as a guide, his ears alert.

So, when he heard the click of a door, he dove for the floor. A blast of gunfire exploded, bullets causing the smoke in the corridor to swish and eddy in their passage. More gunfire; the haze in the hall made it impossible for either the gunman or Cord to aim effectively.

Then Blackstone's coach gun sounded. Its blast, too, billowed the smoke, scattering it like storm clouds. The second barrel thickened the cloud. The reverberation jangled Cord's hearing, but he heard the door closing. The gunman had sought cover again. Now it was time to move. Hard.

"Bart?"

"Here, Marshal!"

"Let's go!"

They sprinted down the hallway, weapons raised. Cord skidded to a stop beside the room where the gunman had taken refuge. Blackstone was right behind him. He no sooner gained the doorway than he reared back and threw a shoulder against it.

Across the room, silk curtains billowed in the wind from an open window.

"There!"

They sprinted across the room. Reaching the window, Cord could see the man in black throw a leg over the balcony railing before disappearing.

"He's jumped!"

Cord and Blackstone rushed to the balcony's edge as a thunder of hooves erupted. They arrived in time to see the trio of gunmen gallop away on horseback, the wounded one favoring his arm. The horses raised a cloud of dust as they reached the end of the street and vanished out of town.

"Who the hell were *they*?" Blackstone exclaimed.

"I have absolutely no idea," replied Cord. "If I didn't know better, I'd say they were men we picked up and put in jail sometime back, but I didn't recognize a single one of them."

"Violent bloody lot," mused Blackstone. "In between the three of them, they probably blasted off a hundred rounds or more."

Cord's eyes narrowed as he peered into the dust left by the horsemen. "Bart, I need you to do some sleuthing for me. Ask around. See what you can find out about those three. Ride to the next town over, if you have to. But snoop around and find out what you can about them. Surely a trio that distinct would be remembered."

"I'd think so, Marshal," Blackstone agreed. "I'll pack up and light out at once."

"Good. Ride out. Find what you can. Come back quickly. I reckon we're likely due another visit from that crew, and when they come, I aim to be ready."

"We'll roll out the red carpet then, Marshal?"

"We'll roll it out. Or let them stain one for us."

Chapter 9

Cord's heart continued to beat heavily during his ride out of town. Although his path led him out along the opposite end of the street from the direction taken by the fleeing gunmen, he remained on high alert for ambush. There was a short, stony distance of uneven ground he had to cross before reaching the river with its patchwork of claims. Crossing this flatiron of rock and scrub, he kept his gun hand free and his eyes moving back and forth, scanning the path ahead as his ears remained alert for noises from either side and behind. After a few minutes, the hissing rush of the river filled his ears, and he began to relax.

Cord guided his horse down the shallow embankment to the stony beach on this side of the wide river. Two prospectors working a claim on the other side looked up and waved as he approached. Cord paused long enough to call across the water and ask them if they knew anything about the men he was after and, getting a negative answer, he pressed on upriver.

Another miner, this one on the same side of the river as Cord, paused in his work on a sluice to answer Cord's questions, again with no results. But like most of the miners, he was happy to see evidence of law enforcement out and about. Cord, charged with protecting these folks, was glad for their presence under the circumstances.

The narrow beach widened as he approached his own claim. A mile or so upriver from the older claims near the bottom, the Bennett Claim had begun to pay out handsomely in the past months. It was Cord's brothers who made the first strike, and the volume of gold had fallen and risen periodically since then. But a steady output was being taken right out of the ground and from the shallows of the river.

The profits had become sufficiently reliable for Cord to hire someone to work the claim. Abraham Olmsted had proven the perfect choice. He and his two daughters had tried their luck at finding gold without success. Bringing Abraham down to his claim and allowing him to set up house nearby had worked out beautifully for all concerned. Abraham had meaningful work, Kat and Glory had a place to stay, and Cord had a second home.

Abraham was just packing up his mining tools for the day when Cord rode onto the small spread, dismounting by the rushing river. The old man looked up, shading his eyes against the setting sun. Recognizing Cord, he threw a cheerful wave.

"We had a good day today!" he cried. Reaching into a pocket of his work apron, he withdrew a handful of tiny nuggets that he held out for Cord's inspection. "Take a look at these!"

Cord squinted down into Abraham's leathery palm. Just under a dozen golden pebbles formed a mound. Reaching down, Cord took one between thumb and forefinger. He brought the ridge of his thumbnail against its side and pressed. Sure enough, a tiny impression appeared in the rock's side.

"Soft," he said. "That's gold all right."

"I know it." Abraham took the pebble back from Cord and dropped it back into his apron pocket along with the rest. "It's a good day's work. Probably somewhere around a hundred dollars or more."

"If this strike keeps paying out as well as it has," Cord mused, "I may just retire as marshal."

"Don't do that! Lord, Cord!" Abraham laughed and grasped at his chest melodramatically. "Who'd keep order in this crazy town? I can't imagine anyone else doing that."

Cord chuckled. "I'm sure they'd eventually find somebody," he said. "C'mon, let's go inside. What's for dinner?"

"Glory's been working on it all afternoon," replied Abraham, throwing a shovel over one shoulder and leading the way to the cabin. "Got a big pot of rabbit and dumplings she was just putting the finishing touches on the last time I checked."

Abraham was right. Cord found himself enveloped in the warm scents of the kitchen as he crossed the threshold. Visible in the dim light of the cabin, Glory's slender form swayed slightly as she stirred the pot bubbling on the cast-iron stove.

"Not sure which is better," he said. "The way you look or the way that food smells."

Glory turned and favored him with a smile. "Now, Marshal Bennett," she said teasingly. "If a girl didn't know better, she might imagine you were trying to flirt with her."

Cord laughed. Glory laughed. And then the two of them were entwined in a deep, hard embrace.

"Hey, hey, you two!" chided Abraham with a grin on his weathered face. "You're not married yet."

With a laugh, Cord and Glory released each other and stepped back.

"You're a sight for sore eyes," he told her.

"So are you."

"Need help chopping or stirring?"

"Not a bit." She nodded toward the washbasin. "You go ahead

and wash up. I'll get you and Pa some coffee while we wait for the stew to finish simmering."

Cord did as he was told, figuring it was good practice for when they were married. He and Abraham liked to joke about how wives rule the roost, and how men become the ruled at the end of each workday. Although, truth be told, Cord felt more like a king than a servant as he sat down at the table and accepted a warm mug of fresh coffee from Glory.

"Will Kat be joining us?" he asked.

"She said she'd come by," Abraham answered. He blew on his coffee and took a tentative sip. "Things are keeping her busy at the Bear Flag these days. How about you? How was your day?"

"Oh . . . fine." He narrowed his eyes and considered mentioning the shoot-out at the rooming house. But that would keep until Kat arrived. For now, he preferred to luxuriate in the atmosphere of a normal home and family—one where violence and gunfire did not intrude. Cord decided to savor that luxury for as long as possible.

"I heard there was some trouble down at Ponder's mill," Abraham said. "What happened?"

"Seems he's started cutting corners with his product. Sy Bowles and a few friends showed up to register their dissatisfaction. Things got out of hand."

"Huh." Abraham grunted. "Some of the wood I used to finish out this place I bought from Ponder not long after he arrived. It was good lumber and he cut me a fair deal. In fact, *fair deal* was pretty much synonymous with *Ponder* for a time."

"I guess that's changed. He's looking to maximize profit."

"Like everyone else."

Glory returned to the table with a serving bowl filled to the brim with the savory mix of rabbit and dumplings. She set this down to exclamations of appreciation from both men before joining them at the table. The food laid out before them, its delicious odors wafting out to fill the cabin, they bowed their heads as Abraham said grace. When he finished, another voice chimed in with "Amen." Cord turned to see Kat standing in the doorway.

"Cord," she said. "Are you all right? I heard that you—"

"What?" Glory asked as her sister abruptly stopped what she was saying. Glory looked from Kat to Cord and back again. "Kat, what's going on?"

Kat entered the cabin and took a seat at the table. It was obvious to everyone that she was shaken. Cord couldn't blame her. It had been a rough afternoon at the Bear Flag.

"There was a shoot-out in town." Kat bit her lip as she glanced at Cord. "Three men were trying to kill Cord."

"Why didn't you say something?" Abraham asked his future son-in-law, his forehead creasing in a frown.

"Cord?" Glory reached out and grasped his hand.

Cord gave Glory what he hoped was a reassuring smile and squeezed her fingers before releasing them. Turning to Abraham, he said, "I wanted to wait until Kat got here to tell it. Also, there's been other news . . ." He paused, studying Kat. She didn't seem disinclined to his elaborating, so he did. "News that affects Kat and her work at the Bear Flag. But we can come back to that in a minute. Regarding the gunfight . . ."

Cord filled them in on the details of the event, describing the black-clad trio, the clash in the rooming house, and the final getaway on horseback. He related that he had tasked Blackstone with tracking down whatever information he could about the gang.

"Are you going to call for reinforcements?" Abraham asked, worried.

"I've sent Blackstone into the next town over to poke around, and he'll see about maybe getting some additional help in the form of deputies. But for now, forewarned is forearmed. And never worry." He patted Glory's hand. "We'll be ready for them if they come back."

"Let's hope they don't," she said with a shiver, spooning herself some greens. "You be careful, Cord Bennett. I won't have the man I aim to marry shot up by outlaws."

At this, Cord and Abraham shared a smile. Glory, for all her sweetness, was a strong and hardheaded woman. Cord wouldn't put it past her to mount up and personally go gunning for revenge against any who harmed him.

Abraham nudged Kat. "Cord mentioned something about news of you and the Bear Flag."

"Yes." Kat sat back, weary and deflated. "It turns out that Patrick Elam has a sister. And she wants the saloon."

"She *what*?" Glory was livid. "How dare she!"

"It's okay, Glory." Kat smiled wearily.

"But after all the *work* you've put in!"

"I know. I know." Kat waved a hand. "But I've been thinking about it. And talking it over with Cord here." She flashed a smile his way. "Look, there are things we can control and things we can't. Patrick Elam having a sister is one of them. I took over the Bear Flag after he passed and have built it into a good business. For all we know, his sister Dolores may be in poverty. Perhaps she's a widow. Could be this is the break she needs in her life and I'm able to provide it."

A long silence prevailed after this as Cord and Kat's family absorbed her words. At length, it was Abraham who broke the silence.

"That's mighty Christian of you," he allowed. "In fact, it's downright saintly. I don't know if I could do the same."

"Or me," said Glory. "Kat, you've got to fight for what's yours!"

"But Glory, it *isn't* mine." Kat's voice rose in frustration. "If you or Pa died, God forbid, what was yours should rightly come to the surviving kin. And Patrick Elam is no different. No. It's just common decency. It's just what's right. I'm not going to play games with another woman's inheritance. I'm willing to sit down and speak to her in a reasonable fashion and come to some sort of accommodation. Who knows? Maybe she'll keep me on as manager, like her brother did. But it's out of our hands. We have to leave it in God's and hope for the best."

Later, Cord and Glory stood together on the porch, looking up into the vast night sky.

"All those stars," she said dreamily, brushing up against him. "If you wished upon every single one . . ."

"You'd end up right where you started," he teased. "Wishing never got anyone anything."

"I wished for you," she replied, laying a hand on his arm. "And look what I got."

"You landed a big fish," he joked.

"I landed my dream." She wrapped her arms around him and squeezed. "Take care, Cord. Be careful and take good care."

Chapter 10

After supper with the Olmsteds, Cord rode upriver and slept the night in the partially finished cabin he was building for himself and Glory in Ghost Canyon. Up toward the north end of the river, where the water rushed down from the hills, Ghost Canyon had a few isolated claims that had mostly failed to pay out. The area seemed unlikely to see further claims, and so he had chosen it as the perfect place to build a home. He woke to clean, fresh air and the sound of rushing water. Deciding to take breakfast in town, he saddled up and headed back to Rio Oro.

He rode onto Main Street to the sound of sawing and hammering. Such activity was unusual at this early hour. Its source became clearer as he made his way toward the marshal's office. It was the undertaker, Forbes. Stripped to his shirtsleeves, he was fastening together the panels for two coffins he was busy building. Cord slowed as he passed, touching the brim of his hat as he did so.

"Morning," he said. "We have some fatalities?"

"The widow Stoddard passed last night, in the rooming house," said Forbes. "And the shoot-out yesterday. That gang took off on their horses without paying. Instead of coin, the stable hand got a bullet in the belly. Doc says he's not likely to make it."

"Okay." Cord's jaw tightened. "Thanks."

Blackstone was back already, much to Cord's surprise. The big Englishman was seated in a chair before the stove, legs stretched out, a weary look on his face as he sipped a cup of coffee and stared out the window.

"I had an interesting night," he said. "Rode east to Wakefield, figuring I would ask around in the saloon about those three duster-clad scoundrels. Only made it about halfway. Came across a wagon train that had stopped for the night and so visited with them for a while."

"Oh?" Cord helped himself to a tin cup and a serving of coffee. He took a seat in the chair beside Blackstone. Although the day was likely to be warm, the early morning still held a chill. He leaned closer to the stove.

"They were a religious community," Blackstone elaborated. "Interesting bunch. Got to speaking with one man. Fascinating fellow. A telegraph operator by trade back East, before he came out here. Accustomed to keeping his ear to the ground. I told him about our little run-in with those gunmen."

"Had he seen them?"

"He had not." Blackstone took a swallow of coffee. "But he had heard some rumors. They'd passed through Wakefield and points beyond. Says he heard tell of a group of professional gunfighters working in the area. Top dollar men. Hired killers." Blackstone paused. "A trio, working together."

"Hmm." Cord rose and moved to his desk, taking up a folder he used to keep old wanted posters. "A trio of gunfighters, eh?" He flipped through the posters. "Nothing in here."

"My friend seemed to think they came from somewhere back East, as did he." Blackstone nodded at the folder. "Doubt they'd be in there."

"Do me a favor and keep digging," Cord said. "Send a letter to the U.S. Marshal's office in Sacramento. They may have something."

"Already written," Blackstone said. "Just waiting for the post office to open so I can mail it."

"All right, then." Cord nodded. "Those men have a lot to answer for."

"Forbes told me about the stable hand," Blackstone said.

"Yeah." Cord drank more coffee and forced himself not to think about it.

Slowly, the town grew busier around them. Wagons and horse traffic began moving past the office window and pedestrian traffic clattered on the boardwalk outside. The early morning crowd, a mixture of miners and timberjacks from Ponder's mill, began hitting the saloon for a morning beer and breakfast.

Cord was making ready to join them when a knock sounded at the office door. He opened it and was surprised to be looking into the face of Hap. He seemed unusually agitated.

"Marshal." He shifted from foot to foot as he spoke. "M-Marshal, you b-better come q-quick. We got another p-problem."

"Is it the mill again?" Cord put down the coffee mug and reached for his hat.

"Gadzooks, n-no." Hap swallowed. "It's R-Reverend L-Lomax."

Lomax? Cord put some speed into his steps as he followed Hap. Timberjacks were already streaming through the gates of Ponder's mill as they turned the corner onto the unnamed side street where Lomax was building his church.

At first glance, everything seemed to be fine. The small street had its share of traffic. The few buildings there showed evidence of movement. The cluster of shacks clinging to the town's edge, populated by the small community of Chinese people in the region, was bustling with activity. One of the Chinese residents was leading a mule up the street. Cord spoke to him as he passed.

"Excuse me." Cord smiled. "Do you speak English?"

"Yes, I do." The Chinese man stopped and nodded a greeting to Hap. He spoke flawless English.

"Do you live down that way?" Cord gestured toward the Chinese section. "Hap, here, says there's been some problems with the church."

"Oh?" The Chinese man looked confused. "Really? I sure hope not. Reverend Lomax is already well-liked among our community."

"He's a good man," Cord agreed. "Seen or heard anything unusual in the past day or so?"

"Around here? No, I don't think so." The man peered left and right. "I smelled smoke last night. That was a little strange. I sleep with the window open, and my wife woke me up. Said she smelled smoke. I did too. But we checked around and it wasn't in our house, so we went back to sleep."

"That's helpful. Thanks for your time."

"Glad to help." The Chinese fellow tipped his hat. "I will keep my eyes open for you. My name is Li-Sen." He extended a hand.

"Cord Bennett." Cord shook. "Nice to meet you, Li-Sen. And thanks again."

"You're welcome." He turned to Hap. "Nice to see you, Hap."

"You t-too, Li-Sen!"

Cord watched Li-Sen walk off toward the main part of town. Then he bent his steps toward the half-finished church. He heard voices as he approached—the rumbling basso of Lomax and a reedy, nasal voice he recognized as belonging to Seb Grady.

Grady had moved to Rio Oro only six months ago but had already distinguished himself as the best carpenter in town. Half a dozen or more of the newer buildings were the result of his handiwork—fine, sturdy structures that were worth every penny spent on labor.

It was Grady who was speaking as Cord and Hap drew near.

"—came by just as I was lighting out," he said. "He arrived at the site early to take stock of things before we got to work. He's the one who found it. Oh, hello, Marshal."

"Marshal." Lomax nodded to Cord. "Glad to see you. We've got something of a problem."

"What's going on?" Cord asked.

"Come this way," said Grady. "We'll show you."

The carpenter led them around the edge of the church to the little yard in back where he had set up two worktables. It looked to be a busy area. Rows of tools were laid out on the tables, and someone had leaned a two-man saw against the back wall of the church. A few hatchets sat nearby. Grady led them through the work area toward something concealed beneath a canvas tarpaulin. Drawing level with one corner of the covering, Grady bent and hauled it back.

"Well," said Cord. "Isn't that interesting?"

A pile of finished lumber lay beneath the canvas. Stacked three feet high, it consisted mostly of long, narrow planks suitable for sealing the structure. The pile represented a healthy expenditure on building materials because it was good lumber.

But the far end of the stack was charred wreckage. Someone had set fire to the wood in an attempt to destroy the lumber, but the fire had smoldered out before finishing the job, leaving the stack of planks having the appearance of a set of oversize matches that had been lit, discarded, and arranged into a neat stack.

"It's not a dead loss per se," Grady was saying. "We can compensate for the loss by cutting off the burned ends and extending the cut planks with unburned bits from other planks. But it'll slow us down. Tedious, exacting work that we didn't count on having to do."

"It's all right, Mr. Grady," Lomax said. "You couldn't have prevented this. And neither could you, Marshal. A cowardly act of sabotage done under cover of darkness. An attempt to attack God's work in this town."

Cord studied the stack of fire-damaged timber in silence, flummoxed. It seemed like such a pointless crime. It was more in the line of vindictive pettiness than an out-and-out attack, as Lomax characterized it.

"I can't figure it out," he admitted at length. "Reverend, you made any enemies in town recently?"

"Aside from those Griffith brothers, I can't think of any." Lomax shrugged. "No, my work has been about spreading goodwill as far and as fast as I can."

"It can't be the Griffith brothers," said Grady. "I sometimes use Beau to help with hauling and fetching and the like. Tried to get him for this job, but they're out of town. Away somewhere." He flapped a hand to signify some far-off destination. "No idea where."

Cord nodded, then turned to Lomax. "Any thoughts?"

Lomax sighed, considering the situation before speaking to it. "I'm not sure," he said. "But Grady, you said something the other day. Something about miners and mill workers?"

"Right!" Grady snapped his fingers. "Marshal, now that the good reverend has mentioned it, I remember. There's been some problems lately between Mr. Ponder's workers and some of the miners—particularly the recent arrivals. I guess there've been issues with the quality of the wood they've been getting."

"I'm aware of that much," Cord allowed.

"Well, seems to be a persistent issue," Grady said. "I've gone to the lumberyard and back a few times. Seen more than a few yelling matches break out between timbermen and locals. And a fistfight the other day! It was quick and nasty and over fast, Marshal, so I doubt anyone called for you. But there is tension in the air. You can feel it."

Lomax spoke. "Mayhap one of the miners caught sight of this pile and decided to set it on fire out of . . . I don't know. Revenge? As a way of sullying Ponder's name? I don't know. Either that or . . ." He trailed off.

"Or what, Reverend?" Cord said.

Lomax appeared to hesitate before answering. When he did, he spoke in a slow and measured rhythm, as if wanting very much not to be misunderstood.

"Marshal, let's just say that not everyone is happy to see a minister take up residency in Rio Oro. And not everyone is happy about this church being built." He tapped the building frame. "There are some folks who consider religion to be old-fashioned. Outdated. Replaced by science. I've had some jeers thrown at me by locals—mostly miners. Could be one of them has decided to take a swing at the church."

"That's good to know too." Cord shuffled all these details together in his mind for evaluation. "This will take time to figure out. Meanwhile, Mr. Grady, you say you can make do for the moment?"

"Can do, Marshal."

"All right, then." Cord squinted into the distance. "We'll get to the bottom of this. Sooner or later."

CHAPTER 11

The stagecoach rattled into town, its team lathered and weary. The driver, stripped to his shirtsleeves, urged the animals onto Main Street with hoarse cries and a shaking of the reins while the armed man assigned to provide protection for passengers and cargo sat beside him on the driver's box.

In the dissipating heat of the late afternoon, the wheels kicked up billowing clouds of dust before slowing to a stop in front of the general store, which also served as the stagecoach station. The driver climbed down from the box and held open the door, offering his hand to steady the female passenger who disembarked first.

"Here we are, Mrs. Whittaker," he said. "Welcome to Rio Oro."

The woman planted herself on the ground, releasing the driver's hand and looking around. She was a handsome, well-proportioned woman in her early forties. The eyes above her prominent cheekbones were large, lending her an almost innocent air. But her conservative dress, crisp manner, and decisive movements bespoke a maturity and competence far beyond her lovely appearance.

"Thank you, Mr. Davis," she said. "Is that the hotel?"

"Yes, ma'am," said the driver. "Shall I carry your trunk over for you?"

"If you would be so kind." She smiled thinly and withdrew a calling card from her trim handbag. "Please offer them this and tell them that I will be along shortly to check in."

"I will, ma'am." The driver slipped the card into a vest pocket and set about unfastening the woman's trunk from the back luggage platform as she turned to walk down Main Street, her feminine form drawing the attention of passersby. She strolled confidently, moving with the slow assurance of a predator seeking prey.

Dolores Whittaker was no man's fool. She privately considered most men her inferior—blustering buffoons who postured to avoid actual conflict. Women she knew to be much more ruthless and deadly. Because with women there was always more at stake. They moved in close and always tried to do as much damage as quickly as possible. Dolores—or Dollie, as she preferred to be known—was an expert at that sort of infighting.

She spotted the Bear Flag Saloon quickly and crossed to the opposite side of the street to observe it unobtrusively. Stepping up onto the wooden boardwalk, she sauntered to a support pillar and leaned against it, her posture and position conveniently hiding her from view. She watched the Bear Flag from the corner of her eye for five minutes, paying attention to the comings and goings of patrons and picking out a few girls whom she suspected were employees. Making note of their faces, she moved down the sidewalk to the doorway of the saloon directly across from the Bear Flag. Pausing a short distance from the door, she noted the name Golden Nugget and the clean, quiet barroom within. She watched the interior for a few minutes before turning and heading back in the direction of the hotel.

She picked up her room key at the desk and headed straight to her accommodations. Her trunk had been sent up for her, and she doffed hat and gloves, pausing before the mirror to unpin her hair and watch it cascade down. With a smirk, she reached up and tugged down the sleeves of her blouse past her shoulders, accenting her cleavage and appreciating her own beauty.

She was honing a weapon—sharpening a blade. Like the serpent moving with slow assurance, she sorted through the images she had collected in her mind during her reconnaissance of the past few minutes. Assessing the lay of the land. Weighing the strengths and weaknesses of her target. Biding her time.

Finding her prey.

Dollie Whittaker had entered town adorned in the sensible traveling clothes of a modest city woman. In her flat-brimmed hat, tweed overcoat, and high-laced boots, she had looked every bit the prudish schoolmarm. But as dusk settled over the town and the day's heat dissipated and the night came, she emerged from the hotel, a woman transformed.

Her hair, a lustrous brown that tended toward red, was loose and full about her shoulders. For her modest blouse, she had substituted a low-cut, wine-red bodice fringed by short lace sleeves. Her arms were smooth and tanned and wrapped by a surprising cord of muscle that twisted her biceps. Those and her rough hands were the only indications of the significant physical strength she commanded behind her remarkable beauty.

She wore a wide skirt, a less expensive version of the plantation belle style. Its material was dowdy, but she had brightened it up with some embroidery of her own. She wore a pair of leather sandals after the fashion of Mexican women. Common enough for them, but daring for white society. Sultry and eye-catching, Dollie Whittaker was new in town, and she wanted everyone to know it.

She entered the barroom of the Golden Nugget, silencing the patrons by crossing the floor to the bar with a self-possessed assurance so strong that it bordered on the supernatural. As she reached the bar, the piano player returned from a break and began a slow waltz. The drama of the melody gave her the spotlight, her fluid gestures assuming a magical sense of timing as the song rolled out like a fanfare, announcing her arrival. She was here.

Center stage.

The she-wolf of Rio Oro.

It did not take long for the more confident men to size up the situation and muster up enough courage to make a play for her, after a short waiting game to see who would go first, who would assume that most precarious of roles and the one least likely to succeed. A monstrous self-assurance was called for. Either that or a monstrous recklessness.

As it happened, it was a monstrous stupidity that prompted the first man to step up.

Beau Griffith, arguably strongest of the Griffith brothers, approached Dollie, as if eager to demonstrate how he lacked in brains what he had in brawn.

"Would you care to—I mean, like to—dance?" the big man asked breathlessly, his eyes sliding down the visible portion of her legs to her daringly exposed calves, ankles, and feet. The piano player had struck up a lazy tune. But rather than dance, the women and interested men lingered around the edges of the dance floor and watched Beau Griffith take his shot.

Dollie Whittaker looked up with a sly smile, sliding her eye to the bartender as he drew up across from her. "I'll take a whiskey," she said coolly. Turning back to Beau, she placed her hands on her hips. "Well, aren't you a solid chunk of man! Lord, I imagine you can work all day and probably come home and dance all night, isn't that right, boy?"

Beau grinned and shrugged. "You bet!" he said in response.

"Then why haven't you managed to land yourself a wife?" She didn't break eye contact with him as her hand flashed out to capture the full whiskey glass the bartender placed before her.

"I . . ." Her question flummoxed him. "I live at home. With my brothers."

"I see. So that's how it is." Dollie Whittaker tipped back her head and stared coldly down her nose at him. "No. No, I don't think I want to dance with a boy who lives at home with his brothers. That sounds childish. A man who deserves my time and attention brings value to the world by producing wealth. He comes to the table with something to offer. Not with his, ah, hat in his hand. Like you're doing."

These words hung in the air, stinging. The dance hall girls eyed one another uneasily, for they all knew the Griffith brothers and were aware of the family's penchant for violence. The Griffith boys had wrecked many a barroom in their drunken rampages. Even women had occasionally tasted the lightning cruelty of their fists. And the dance hall girls knew from experience that not one man would dare step in when such a beating began.

But something in Dollie Whittaker's posture—in her straight-backed stance, iron gaze, and haughty manner—suggested that she was not a woman to be trifled with. She was in command of herself—and everyone in her presence. And she would tolerate no opposition to her will.

Beau Griffith slunk off, hat in hand.

It was one of the dance hall girls who approached next, but her intentions were not seductive. She merely slipped up beside Dollie, signaled for a glass of beer, and spoke softly while she had the newcomer's ear.

"You got some backbone, lady," she said. "Not that it's unwelcome at all. Lord, no. But Rio Oro can be a rough town. You'd best be ready to take care of business if things go wrong. If you catch my meaning."

The dance hall girl held Dollie's gaze as her beer came. She sipped it, giving Dollie her full attention. Dollie dropped her cold mask and favored the girl with a friendly smile.

"I'll remember that," she said. "And I appreciate you taking the trouble to warn me, I really do." Her smile widened as she lifted her left arm. "But as you can see, I take steps to secure my own safety."

The dance hall girl glanced down and saw the handle of a straight razor tucked discreetly into the leather belt of the skirt Dollie wore. The wear on the handle spoke of frequent use.

"I'm Clara." The dance hall girl held out her hand.

"Dollie." They shook. "Tell me, Clara. Who runs this establishment?"

A new voice spoke. "I do."

Dollie turned to the man who had spoken. He was an impressive figure, burly, barrel-chested, and wide-shouldered. His rough-hewn face, although not handsome, had a compelling quality to it.

His brown tweed suit was expensive. A glittering gold watch chain looped across his belly from one vest pocket to the other. Under the vest was a snowy white shirt with a ruffled front. A bright red cravat was at his throat.

And somewhere in the rugged landscape around Rio Oro, he had found a bright yellow flower that was pinned to his lapel.

"Teddy Harville," he introduced himself, extending a thick-fingered hand. "And I'd like to offer you your next drink on the house, Miss . . . ?"

"Dolores Whittaker." She smiled as she clasped his hand. His grip was gentle, although she could sense the strength he was capable of. "Call me Dollie."

"Dollie?" A grin spread across his face. "Dollie it is. Barkeep!" Harville thumped twice on the bar with the ornate silver handle of the walking stick he held in his other hand. "Give us a bottle and two glasses!" Turning to the dance hall girl, he added, "Get back to work, Clara."

"Sure." Clara rolled her eyes and wandered off.

With gestures of extravagant politeness designed to both honor the gorgeous newcomer as well as demonstrate a proprietary claim upon her, Harville conducted Dollie Whittaker to a table and held a chair. Once they were both settled and drinks poured, he raised a toast.

"To newcomers," he said. "And fond welcomes."

"I'll drink to that," she answered. "As well as to partnerships. Opportunities. And profit."

This was enough to turn Harville's attention from his appreciation of her beauty to another, far more elementary instinct. "Now you're speaking the kind of language dear to a businessman's heart, Miss Dollie." He carefully set down his glass, drink untouched. "Do please elaborate."

"I shall." She set down her own drink and leaned forward. "Mr. Harville, I will not dissemble with you. I can see you are a no-nonsense man of means. People such as us recognize each other. And by people like us, I mean those with sufficient capital to maximize opportunities to our advantage. I come to Rio Oro equipped with such means and a keen desire to acquire property and assets. I think we can work together to each other's mutual advantage."

"That sounds most attractive," he said. "Romantic possibilities aside, at the end of the day, what else is there besides money?"

"Oh, there will be plenty of time for both," she assured him. "At the end of the day."

With a smile, she tipped her glass to her lips and drank.

Chapter 12

Dollie Whittaker's presence didn't just turn heads for one memorable night at the Golden Nugget Saloon. Her presence in town was quickly noted by the womenfolk, a distinct minority in town, and known for being close-knit for mutual protection.

Clara received many questions as the first to have held an actual conversation with the newcomer. She dispensed her impressions sparingly, not wanting to cause harm to Dollie's reputation. Clara was kindhearted and given to discretion, but she was also smart enough to let her close friends—young women of her own class and occupation—know the important details.

"She's canny and sharp and carries a razor in her belt," she told the other dance hall gals.

"She's a buccaneer," remarked April, her best friend. "I know the type. You watch. She'll slice through Teddy Harville and half the men in this town like a mountain lion. Just wait and see if I'm not right!"

It was on the street that Glory first noticed Dollie Whittaker. She happened to be in town early, making a trip to the general store, when a figure emerged from the hotel entrance and began making her way up the boardwalk toward her. For some reason, Glory reacted with instinctive caution.

Something about the woman was unsettling. Her eyes were large in her narrow face. They trapped Glory immediately in their gaze—an expression of disquieting watchfulness. She wore a sensible tweed suit, a flat dark hat, and carried a satchel in her right hand. Glory thought she resembled an artist's model done up to look like a schoolmarm. She suppressed an involuntary shudder.

"Good morning," Glory said courteously as they made to pass each other.

"Good morning to you," the woman said, slowing. "Pardon me, but you wouldn't happen to know what time the land claims office opens, do you?"

"Why, that's Mr. Clyde Casterline's office," Glory said, pointing. "Mr. Casterline is an early riser and a conscientious public servant. He is also our assayer. Are you a prospector, Miss . . . ?"

But rather than speak her name, Dollie laughed. "A prospector? Dear me, no. Do I appear so athletic?"

Glory was still laughing politely when the woman brushed past with a curt thanks. It was only when she was some distance off that Glory realized she hadn't caught the stranger's name. She brought it up the next afternoon when she crossed paths with Cord at the house.

"I'd heard tell there's a new woman in town," he admitted. There were few enough females in Rio Oro that the addition of one was newsworthy. "Might even have caught a glimpse of her the other day. But I have yet to exchange words with her."

"Something about her . . ." Glory frowned. "I can't quite put my finger on it. But she's unsettling, Cord. Feels . . ."

"Feels how?"

"Dangerous," Glory said firmly. "Downright dangerous."

* * *

Those words haunted Cord the rest of that day and into the next, which was a day off for him as Bart Blackstone covered the marshal's office. He spent the morning in Ghost Canyon, working on the cabin.

Later, his work done, he ate a late lunch on the grass and recalled his discussion with Horace Davenport about Dollie Whittaker. He was fairly certain that was who Glory must have spotted. He decided to do some asking around.

Returning to town late in the afternoon, he tied up his horse outside the marshal's office and went for a walk. Blackstone, sitting on a bench in front of the hotel and keeping an eye on Main Street, nodded to Cord as he walked past.

Cord made his way up the main street, through a crowd that was more jovial than usual as folks relaxed and unwound as Saturday night approached. He smiled at young families out with their children, groups of youths strolling with their sweethearts, and the odd miner, scrubbed and cleaned up, ready to visit the saloon for some hard-earned fun. Cord did the rounds of the hotels and bars, finally pausing outside the door to the Golden Nugget.

There. Seated at a rear table by herself, jacket off, hat on the chair beside her, the woman leaned over a pair of leather-bound books, squinting at the details on the pages through spectacles. Cord recognized her at once as a new arrival.

As he approached, he took inventory of her features and understood at once why she made Glory uneasy. His time as a marshal had taught him to sniff out people who were comfortable with violence. And this woman, despite her spectacles and tweed, bore all the hallmarks of a hellcat once trouble broke loose.

"Excuse me."

Dollie Whittaker's gaze snapped up, eyes watchful and sharp before her expression softened into a welcoming smile. "Why, hello, Sheriff," she said, offering her hand. "It *is* sheriff, isn't it?

Or is it marshal? I have the most devilish time telling one from the other."

"Cord Bennett," he said, squeezing her fingers briefly before letting go. "And it's marshal, in this case." He gestured toward the empty chair. "May I sit?"

"I'm not under arrest, am I?"

"No. Why? Have you done something for which you should be arrested? Or ashamed?"

"Ashamed?" She gave a calculatedly girlish giggle. "Plenty of things. But I'm not sure I could be arrested for any of them."

"That's a fair point." Cord folded his arms. He noted that she still hadn't given him permission to sit. "You haven't told me your name."

"It's Dolores, Marshal."

Dolores Whittaker, I'll bet, he thought, but held his peace for now. He had figured out already it was best not to put all his cards on the table with this one.

"Very nice to meet you, Dolores," he said. "Welcome to Rio Oro."

"Thank you!"

"Mind if I take a seat?" Cord asked again. And without waiting for an answer this time, he drew the unoccupied chair toward himself and sat. Dolores seemed about to object, so he said, "I make it a point to introduce myself to visitors and passers-through. See, we don't get much news out this way. So it's helpful to talk to folks and hear the latest."

Dolores still seemed inclined to protest Cord's sitting down without an invitation but then thought the better of it. Like a boxer taking a few blows early in a match, then retreating to study the opponent's moves, she settled back in her chair and watched Cord, the ghost of a smile playing about her lips.

"You're a man who doesn't take no for an answer," she said.

"But you didn't *say* no," he pointed out. "In fact, you never answered the question."

"So you took what you wanted." She said this teasingly, but he sensed an undercurrent of sincerity. "Some women find that admirable."

"I reckon." He didn't rise to the bait. "But I also don't reckon I care so much about what this person or that finds admirable. You see, I'm only interested in the law."

"Have I broken any?"

"No." He settled his eyes on her. "But keeping the peace in this town requires that I know what's going on, and with whom. I like to know who's coming and going, and why. What brings you to Rio Oro?"

It was a direct question, and he sensed it landed badly. Dolores was not a woman who liked dealing in straightforward facts. She preferred lingering in gray areas, loitering in uncertainties. *Keeping people off-balance,* he thought. It was knowledge he filed away.

"Mr. Harville has been extremely kind," she began by way of response. "One would be hard-pressed to find a more generous or supportive business partner. But of course, the business environment in this town is still in its infancy. Why, you don't even have a proper chamber of commerce to speak of."

"So, you're a businesswoman." Cord gestured to one of the passing waitresses to bring him a coffee.

"Yes, I am." Dolores smiled brightly. "I come from a family of means. Or, more accurately, *married* into a family of means. My husband is deceased, and he died without issue. The proceeds from his business enterprise devolved to me upon his death."

"Mmm." Cord accepted the mug the waitress brought and took a careful sip. "Well, it's good of you to bring your generosity to our town. Lord knows, we could use some investment."

That last word seemed to calm her arch suspicions. "Investment is my chief concern," she admitted. "I have been protecting my family's interests for quite some time now. And the best way to protect what one has is to acquire more."

"I see." Cord kept his smile in place, even as he digested the ominous double meaning of her last statement. "And you're Mr. Harville's business partner?"

"Let's just say that I am making an investment," she clarified. "Something of a silent partner."

"You're, ah, interested in the saloon business?"

"I am. Why do you ask?"

"It's just not the sort of thing a woman typically gets herself involved in, if you catch my meaning."

"I'm not sure I do." She gestured through the window to the Bear Flag across the street. "Why, I have been given to understand that yonder establishment is run by a woman."

"It is." Cord's jaw tightened. She had let drop the detail that revealed her interest. He was now certain he was dealing with Dollie Whittaker. He would warn Kat the next time he saw her. Meanwhile, he looked around the Golden Nugget's interior. "What about this place?" he asked. "You planning on making some improvements here?"

"Oh, I do intend to suggest some. Certainly." She chuckled. "Mr. Harville has done a commendable job bringing the Golden Nugget along this far. But it could do with a woman's touch. Don't you agree?"

"I, uh, suppose so." The question took him aback so he retreated into a humorous response. "Most things men do are improved by a woman's touch."

"Most men in general," she corrected him. And her facial expression was that of a lioness lining up to pounce.

Sensing that he wasn't going to get anything more out of Dolores Whittaker, Cord beat a dignified and discreet retreat to his office. He decided to spend an hour getting some paperwork done.

He sat in the office, filing reports and completing the ever-growing list of dispatches he was required to send by mail to the marshal's office in Sacramento. When Blackstone came back in, Cord chatted for a few minutes before heading for the Bear Flag to speak to Kat.

"She's just left," said Reverend Lomax, who was alone at the bar. It was a quiet night in the Flag, with only a half dozen or so folks scattered at the tables. "She said she was heading up to check on her pa and sister."

"I'll be doing the same sooner or later myself," Cord said, and gestured for a beer. He leaned against the bar beside Lomax. "I was across the street earlier this morning. I met the new lady in town."

"That would be Dolores." Lomax's eyes narrowed as he said this, taking a sip of beer. "Yes, I met her yesterday."

"What do you think?"

Lomax remained silent for a long moment. When he spoke, it was with a seriousness Cord recognized the clergyman reserved for matters spiritual.

"There is a story in the Old Testament of what happened when Sisera brought his armies into the land of the Israelites," Lomax said quietly. "His chariots got bogged down in the mud and they were forced to walk. Eventually, he came to the tent of Yael, a Hebrew woman. She welcomed him in, covered him with a blanket, and gave him milk to drink."

"Sounds mighty neighborly."

"She was." Lomax raised his schooner of beer. "Until Sisera fell asleep. Then she drove a tent peg through his skull with a mallet."

CHAPTER 13

For the next few days following Cord's encounter with Dolores Whittaker in the Golden Nugget, Rio Oro seemed to settle into its new rhythms.

Garrison Lomax rolled up his sleeves and took on the foreman's duties for finishing his church. And he worked with a will. Many was the time Cord looked up from his desk to see the clergyman passing in the street driving a cart full of lumber or hauling a box of tools to the building site, his face and hands streaked with sweat and his black clothes covered in sawdust.

Under his supervision, the church climbed ever skyward, its walls now fully enclosed, its windows installed and reinforced. Cord marveled at the speed with which the building went up, wondering at the sudden burst in progress until the day he bumped into Li-Sen again.

"Reverend Lomax has hired three of us to work on the church," the Chinese man said with a weary grin. "He works us hard but pays fairly. He has been a good friend to our community."

"And you've been good friends to ours," said Cord, clapping a hand on the man's shoulder. "Thank you."

Ponder seemed pleased with all this progress too. Twice weekly loads of lumber left the mill gate, bound for Lomax's building site. According to the preacher, the wood seemed to be of fine quality. And its safety on the building site became guaranteed when Lomax set one of his Chinese laborers the task of guarding it overnight.

Despite this, tensions between Ponder's mill crew and the local miners continued to rise, albeit subtly. Blackstone reported being called to the Bear Flag a few times to stop fights between individuals and, increasingly, small groups of working men representing the two interests.

When those conflicts broke out in open use of chairs and lengths of chain as weapons, Cord spoke to Judge Davenport and the law put its foot down. By order of the justice of the peace, it was decreed that employees of Ponder's mill would refrain from entering the Golden Nugget and miners would refrain from entering the Bear Flag.

This temporary measure was implemented in the interest of public order and received no argument from either Kat or Teddy Harville. Far from lamenting the loss of customers, both seemed pleased at the notion of some peace and quiet returning to their establishments.

As for Dolores, she kept a low profile. In the hustle and bustle of busy schedules, Kat and Cord had yet to speak about her. But Cord kept his eyes peeled. She seemed increasingly involved in running the Golden Nugget and could often be seen bent over her ledger books or issuing instructions to staff.

Cord remained puzzled by her sudden authority until the day he happened upon her and Harville locked in a deep embrace out behind the Nugget. He watched them kissing and pressing against each other, their passion escaping in soft moans as Cord managed to slip away, unseen.

Bowles was another one keeping a low profile. After the claim-jumping incident with Antiglione, he had kept out of town and out of sight.

But gradually, he began making a reappearance. Cord noted his comings and goings—swift, furtive trips into stores for supplies. These soon became longer visits. He was often to be found drinking among the prospectors at the Golden Nugget and holding court among a group of gold miners that would gather across the street from Ponder's mill.

It was a rough group: Bowles, the Griffith brothers, and other assorted ruffians and ne'er-do-wells known around town. Cord wasn't sure what Bowles was up to, but given what he knew of the man, it couldn't be good whatever it was. He brought this up to Blackstone as they sat together in the marshal's office.

"Bowles is a coward, and all the more dangerous for it," Blackstone opined. "He's the kind of man unlikely to win a stand-up fight. So he'll talk and whisper and spread rumors. Create a base of support among those weak enough to be swayed by his nonsense. My guess is that he's planning some sort of revenge against Ponder and his men."

"I think you're probably right," Cord said. "But I doubt it's going to amount to much beyond name-calling. Maybe a scrap or two will break out in one of the saloons. But I don't see them arming up and going great guns at one another."

"I agree," said Blackstone. "They're not the type."

"Do you have to fiddle with that?" Cord asked, nodding to the small keg of blasting powder Blackstone held in his hands, turning it over and over.

"This? Oh. Sorry." The big Englishman slid the explosive under his desk. "Bad habits, you know."

Cord wondered how much blasting powder Boom Boom Blackstone kept in their office but decided not to ask.

"I *did* come across something of interest related to our gunmen," he said, closing the drawer and taking up a piece of paper on the desktop. "Received this letter from the U.S. Marshal's office."

"In Sacramento?"

"No, actually." Blackstone took out his reading spectacles. "In Washington, D.C. If you can believe that."

"Interesting." Blackstone had Cord's attention now. "What have we learned?"

Blackstone scanned the message briefly before answering.

"Something about how this was a trio operating in tandem suggested they might be part of a gang. To me, at any rate." He peered over the top of the letter. "Outlaws teaming up as pairs or rustlers in large groups are normal. But trios are unstable. Fractious. Yet this group acted effectively. So, I asked about known criminal trios, and one name came back. Gordon Anderson."

"Gordon Anderson," Cord repeated. "That's a name I've heard."

"Professional gunman. Operates principally in the Ozarks. Apparently, he and two associates have been working together, making a name for themselves in the region. Word is they recently left for points West."

Cord swallowed heavily.

"The Ozarks," said Blackstone. "Isn't that where you're from, Cord?"

The Ozarks . . .

The thought haunted Cord throughout the remainder of that morning and into the afternoon. It was a light day, duty-wise. This gave him time to walk around and do his usual checking on the various businesses. Showing a presence in town, he had discovered, headed off most problems before they could even begin. It also gave him time to think.

After a while, he stopped in at the livery stable for some feed before saddling his mount and lighting out from Rio Oro. The town fell away behind him as he followed the road that turned into a wagon trail a few hundred yards beyond city limits.

He took a turn-off onto an even smaller path that wound up into the hills above Rio Oro, pushing hard until he crested a rise that looked down over Main Street. Then he reined to a halt and stared into the distance.

It seemed like an eternity ago that Cord had been living on a farm in the Boston Mountain region of the Ozarks with his father, Verne, and his brothers, Flint and Steve, when the hard times came. The harvests had been thin, then nonexistent, forcing his father to borrow money to make ends meet. The money had come from various sources, but the Bennetts' principal creditor was a neighbor named Hiram Stockton. Stockton owned a successful farm as well as several businesses in the nearby town of Wilbur.

Stockton also had a daughter named Caroline.

Even now, it pained Cord to contemplate her. They had known each other since childhood, and Caroline figured prominently in Cord's youthful desires for love and companionship. Their friendship had deepened into a bantering flirtation that Cord kept hoping would lead to something more. And that very desire, natural though it was, led to his first and greatest heartbreak.

Cord's older brother, Flint, was bigger and stronger than him, and he possessed a swaggering confidence that caused him to treat people and things with casual indifference. Perhaps it was this indifference, and the challenge it presented, that drew Caroline to him. But Cord's gentle dreams of romance with her died the afternoon he heard her and Flint together in the barn, although he hadn't known at the time that it was his own brother with her.

The cries of her enjoyment left no room for doubt what was happening. Cord had fled the sound, fled all hopes of happiness with Caroline, and eventually the Boston Mountains themselves.

It had only been about a year and a half, he realized with a start.

There was no reason to believe that Gordon Anderson and the

other two gunmen had been sent here specifically for him. It seemed more likely they were opportunists seeking to get rid of local law enforcement before taking over the town. But the coincidence of their attacks, along with the Ozark connection Blackstone had ferreted out, unsettled him.

Best to keep calm and keep your wits about you, he chided himself. Nothing would be gained by speculation.

The lawmen met at the office as dusk came down, Blackstone and Cord reviewing the outstanding issues of the day and updating each other about ongoing investigations.

"A ride by Reverend Lomax and his church wouldn't be amiss," Cord said. "We should see if he's had any more trouble with sabotage. And I want to see the progress he's made, anyway."

"That's right!" Blackstone grinned, his teeth pearly white among the black nest of his beard. "You've got a wedding to plan!"

"I do."

"Should I expect an invitation?"

"I'm not sure there's enough beer in town."

Blackstone loosed a howl of braying laughter at this as they exited the office. They mounted up and rode down the street together, surveying the light early evening traffic. Long shadows were appearing as they turned onto the side street that led to the Chinese section. They found Lomax and Li-Sen talking together out in front of the church.

"This place is coming along!" Blackstone enthused, noting that the main portions of the structure were now finished, and work had begun in earnest on the roof. The ceiling joists were all in place, and some of the rafters were up.

"The Lord has been generous," Lomax replied. "So have Li-Sen and his friends. These fellows work like plow horses! You men have been a real blessing."

"The blessing works both ways," Li-Sen said with a friendly shrug. "You pay. We work. Everyone benefits."

"Now, if I can just get you to come to church."

Li-Sen laughed at this, holding up his hands. "We have our own religion where we come from, Reverend Lomax. But we would be happy to come visit someday perhaps."

"You're welcome anytime," Lomax replied seriously. "Given all the work you've done, showing a little hospitality is the least we can do."

Something caught Cord's eye just as Lomax finished speaking—a dark shape looming at the intersection of Main Street and this one. More on instinct than any fully formed thought, Cord wheeled his horse around and headed that way. The dark shape moved out of sight.

"Marshal?" Blackstone's puzzled query faded beneath the sound of Cord's hooves. He reached the corner, turned, and saw a man in black untying a horse from the hitching post outside the Golden Nugget.

"Hey!" Cord cried.

The man in the black duster looked up, surprised to be noticed. With a flick of his wrist, he unfastened his horse, then hurriedly mounted up to wheel toward the edge of town.

Cord drew his gun.

There was no doubt the man was one of the trio that had attacked him. What the hell was he doing in town? *Scouting me out,* Cord thought angrily. He spurred his horse onward, eager to run the man down.

Now he could hear Blackstone's hooves pounding up behind him. The Englishman drew level with Cord as they pursued the man in black. They chased him past the saloon, the hotel, and the land claims office, losing sight of him in the blast of sand and dust his horse raised as he fled Rio Oro into the wilderness beyond.

Chapter 14

"Kat Olmsted? I've got a bone to pick with you!"

Dollie Whittaker's voice cracked across the interior of the Bear Flag Saloon, turning the head of every customer in the room.

Tonight's crowd was a large one, and it was all Kat and her crew could do to fill the drink orders and keep things moving along smoothly. Kat was just about to take a break and retreat to her office when the batwing doors flew wide, and Dollie Whittaker appeared to issue her challenge.

Kat had seen her around town, her eye naturally drawn to the presence of another woman in Rio Oro. She had expected that Dollie would confront her about the situation regarding the Bear Flag sooner or later, when she was good and ready—and it appeared that Dollie had decided now was the time to make her move.

Kat knew this woman to be something of a quick-change artist, having seen her in various getups. By day she affected a sort of schoolmarmish appearance but by night favored low-cut blouses and liberal showings of ankle. But now she stood in the saloon's entrance in a broad-brimmed hat, boots, a silk shirt, a riding skirt—and a riding crop that she whipped through the air to punctuate her words.

"This saloon was financed and founded by my late brother, Patrick Elam," she declared. "And when he passed, you snaked it right out from under his family! This saloon is the rightful property of Patrick Elam's kin. How dare you seize and run it?"

Kat straightened and walked slowly toward the woman, a wary eye on the riding crop in Dolores Whittaker's hands.

Garrison Lomax also happened to be in the Bear Flag just then. Partially concealed by a pillar, he was seated at a private table, speaking quietly to Li-Sen when the commotion erupted. Both had entered earlier, when the saloon was quiet, and had not drawn attention to themselves. A Chinese man was not welcome in a white man's drinking establishment, although it would be the other customers more than Kat herself who were likely to object. Nevertheless, they had decided to conclude their discussion about progress on the church quickly and quietly so as not to force the issue.

Those good intentions were upended when Dollie Whittaker appeared and loosened her angry salvo at Kat. Lomax looked around at the men drinking in the saloon and noted that not one among them was taking the initiative to calm things down.

Kat Olmsted was approaching the furious hellcat herself, narrowing the distance between them until she was in easy reach of more harsh words—or a lick of that riding crop the woman held.

"What is going on?" Li-Sen asked nervously.

"Not sure." Lomax stood. "Li-Sen, perhaps you should slip out the back way."

"Yes. Agreed."

The Chinese man gathered himself and moved toward the

kitchen entrance as Lomax approached the two women by the front door.

"What's all this?" Kat asked, smiling a brave smile despite the fear Dollie inspired in her. "There's no need—"

"Don't lecture me about need, missy!" Dollie Whittaker snapped, brandishing her riding crop. "You've got a lot of damn nerve!"

"I'm not the only one with nerve!" Kat shot back. She wanted to keep things calm, but Dollie seemed intent on pushing her to the brink of losing her temper. "Imagine coming in here and behaving the way you are! It's perfectly scandalous!"

"Scandalous?" Dollie laughed. "More scandalous than stealing a man's property and depriving his family of what's rightfully theirs?"

"Excuse me." Garrison Lomax came to a stop beside them. "Perhaps I can be of some—"

"Mind your own business!" Dollie said. "Who the hell are you?"

Lomax absorbed this calmly, his eyes locked on Dollie, alert for any violent move she might make against Kat.

"I'm a man of the cloth," he said calmly. "The Reverend Garrison Lomax at your service, ma'am. And I'll thank you to keep your voice down and conduct yourself in a civil fashion in this public house."

"Or *what*?" Dollie turned her sneer toward him venomously.

"Or I will be forced to engage the services of the town marshal," Lomax replied. "And assist him in any way he sees fit."

Lomax accented these last few words with a glance at the riding crop. Dollie seemed to catch his meaning: *control yourself or I will control you.* Lomax, for all his politeness, was a big man. Dollie read menace in the hunch of his shoulders. The riding crop dropped to her side. She drew a few large breaths to calm herself before addressing Kat in a still trembling but calmer voice.

"I have business with you, Miss Kat Olmsted," she said. Her

chin lifted in a defiant gesture. "It relates to the proper disposition of this business and building."

"Then I'll be pleased to discuss it with you." Kat gestured toward the back. "In my office. This way, please."

Lomax shadowed them on their way past the tables and bar. Reaching the short hallway in back, Kat held open the door, gesturing for Dollie Whittaker to precede her. Once she was in the room, Kat moved close to Lomax and spoke softly.

"Thank you for your protection, Reverend."

"My pleasure," Lomax replied softly. "Is there anything else I can do for you?"

"I think it would be a good idea to get the marshal. Can you ask him to come and knock on my office door, please?"

"Glad to do so, Miss Kat." Lomax touched the brim of his hat and hurried off to fetch Cord.

Cord was upstairs in his loft, sorting through what food he had and trying to decide what to make for dinner when three sharp taps came from beneath his feet. He had an arrangement with Blackstone: the Englishman could notify Cord when he was needed by thumping the ceiling with a broom. Recognizing the signal, Cord stuffed his feet into boots and grabbed his hat before going downstairs.

"Marshal Bennett." Lomax was standing beside Blackstone in the office when Cord arrived. "We seem to have a peck of trouble over at the Bear Flag."

"What's the matter?" Cord asked, buckling on his gun belt.

"Miss Dollie Whittaker is causing a disturbance. Can you come?"

Dollie Whittaker. Cord groaned.

"Of course, I'll come," he said.

* * *

The crowd had settled down some since Dollie's appearance. Cord pushed through the batwing doors, encountering the flurry of swiveling heads that usually accompanied his sudden appearance. *The lawman is on the scene,* they seemed to say. *Something bad is about to happen.*

Lomax conducted him past the bar.

"What happened?" Cord asked

Lomax led the way back to Kat's office. "Our newcomer, Miss Whittaker, burst in here and began throwing accusations at Miss Kat. Claims she stole the family property. That she was some sort of ne'er-do-well and freebooter. It was *very* upsetting."

Cord's jaw firmed as he reached the door. He had expected Dollie Whittaker to make her move fairly soon. But not like this. This was a direct attack, unsettling folks and threatening the peace, to say nothing of his future sister-in-law's livelihood. Squaring his shoulders, he knocked twice on the door and twisted the knob when a voice bid him come in.

In the small, cozy room sat the two women. Dollie Whittaker, booted feet planted on the floor, simmered in the guest chair before the desk behind which Kat sat, hands folded, back straight, her dignity wounded but steely. She was not prepared to give an inch without a fight.

"What's going on here?" He strove to keep his voice neutral but moved to stand protectively near Kat. "I understand you're causing a disturbance, Miss Whittaker. I thought your preferred haunt was across the street at the Golden Nugget."

"I have business interests there, true," she admitted. "But as it turns out, I have interests here as well. You see, this saloon belongs to me."

"Belongs to you, does it?" A flash of irritation flickered across Cord's face. "That's a bold assertion. I understand you claim to be Patrick Elam's sister. Is that right?"

"Oh, I see." Dollie's eyes narrowed. "So you're aware of my claim? Were you already aware of it when last we spoke at the Golden Nugget?" She didn't wait for him to answer. "Well, of course you were. A careful man, aren't you, Marshal." It wasn't a question. "Play your cards close to the vest. I admire that."

"I don't much care what you admire," Cord shot back. "One thing I don't admire are people who come into town disturbing the peace. And you seem to have done a fair amount of that in your subtle way."

"Are you going to arrest me for being subtle?" The arch tone of her voice was intended to provoke him, he knew. Denied the advantages of strength and forcefulness that come with manhood, Dollie Whittaker made up for this with guile and accusations. She was a skilled infighter, this one. He'd have to watch his temper.

"Miss Whittaker," said Kat, sitting forward. "Regardless of whatever assumptions you've made about me, the marshal, or the circumstances under which I assumed proprietorship of the Bear Flag, you should know that this is no lawless frontier town. We've worked hard to make Rio Oro a decent place—a law-abiding place—in which to live. The marshal, here, may be engaged to my sister, but I don't expect that to buy me any favors where the law is concerned. Nobody in this town would. If you're prepared to lay out your case as to why you should take ownership of this establishment, I'm prepared to listen. And abide by whatever decision the law hands down."

Cord noted how these words unsettled Dollie Whittaker. And it was a telling reaction. Perhaps, he thought, she had come out here counting on this being a lawless frontier town. Maybe that was the environment in which she was accustomed to operating.

"Well . . ." Dollie's eyelids lowered to half-mast and her tone assumed a sarcastic purr. "That's mighty *charitable* of you, Miss Kat. To deign to acknowledge the law's place in all this."

"Let me ask you something." Cord moved in and propped a hip

on the edge of the desk. "Have you brought documentation with you to support your claim?"

"I have everything I need, Marshal," she replied coldly. "All the legal justification I require to claim what is my own."

"And you're prepared to present it?"

"I am. Here and now."

"That won't be necessary." Cord went to the door. Opening it a crack, he was pleased and not unsurprised to find Lomax waiting outside. Seeing him, the preacher hurried over as soon as Cord caught his eye.

"What is it, Marshal?"

"Reverend, would you do me a favor?"

"Of course."

"Would you head over to Judge Davenport's office and inform him of the situation? It's officially closed now, but he bunks in rooms in back. Go roust him out of bed and tell him we're on our way and need his legal expertise."

"Right away, Marshal," the preacher said.

Lomax stepped out onto the quiet night street with a heavy sigh. Squaring his shoulders, he turned his steps in the direction of Judge Davenport's chambers. But try as he might, he could not shake the uneasiness Dollie Whittaker's outburst had provoked in him.

He had served as a minister in many communities and was no stranger to violence. He had stood tall for the Lord under some challenging circumstances, once even taking a bullet defending a parishioner. Garrison Lomax was not a man who was easily frightened. But a chill now gripped his heart.

Evil.

He knew evil when he saw it. Could identify it by smell at twenty paces. The Adversary—the Devil himself—Lomax knew to be a real force in the world. He knew the Devil's ways were subtle and indirect. But those seemingly innocent moves always ended with right overturned, the innocent harmed, and the peace disturbed.

He stopped in the middle of the street, fists clenched, shoulders trembling.

Cord Bennett was a good man. As was his deputy, Blackstone. But Garrison Lomax knew that a new evil had come to town—a subtle evil that tested the foundations of good faith and belief. It was an evil more dangerous than guns or outlaws, for it attacked from within and sent the good scattering for cover.

He would fight it. With words. With prayer. And, if necessary, side by side with Cord Bennett and Deputy Blackstone, gun in hand.

It wouldn't be his first such battle.

CHAPTER 15

Horace Davenport was indeed at home in the residence behind his chambers when Lomax came calling. His heart sank as the clergyman explained what had happened over at the Bear Flag. Certainly Dollie Whittaker deserved her day in court, but the way she had gone about things was troubling. That she would storm into a public establishment yelling accusations spoke to more than just a defect of character—it suggested a willingness to sow public discord to get her own way, consequences be damned. Such a precedent did not bode well for the town's future.

"Thank you for letting me know, Reverend," said Davenport. "Please inform the marshal and Miss Whittaker that I'll be happy to see them at once."

Lomax thanked him and left immediately. In the wake of his departure, Davenport set about lighting the cluster of kerosene lanterns in his chambers that he used when working after nightfall. He set out a few extra chairs, dragooning some from his kitchen table for service. Then he took a seat behind his massive oak desk and waited for the visitors to arrive.

The two women entered first, the lapse between Dollie Whittaker's arrival and Kat's suggesting an effort had been made to keep them apart. Cord Bennett and the preacher followed right behind Kat. It was a conclave representative of the principal authorities in town: business, legal, and spiritual. It occurred to Horace Davenport that such a meeting was the first he'd seen in his chambers. *Rio Oro is growing,* he thought, as he waved them into the chairs in front of the desk.

"Reverend Lomax tells me we have something of a conflict in our midst," he began when everyone was seated. "Miss Olmsted has been acting proprietor of the Bear Flag ever since Patrick Elam's demise. And now you, Miss Whittaker, have something to say about that. If you'd care to elaborate?"

He rolled a hand, inviting her to speak.

"I am Patrick Elam's sister, your honor." Dollie straightened in her chair as she spoke, hand falling to the folder in her lap. "I can prove this with the documents here—birth certificates and a copy of my father's will. I also have newspaper cuttings of major events in our family's lives."

"Did Mr. Elam leave a will?" asked Davenport.

"Not that we know of, your honor," said Cord.

"I don't think so," said Kat. "After he passed, I did a search of his private papers. Found no such thing."

"So you say!" spat Dollie.

"Easy there." Davenport raised a hand. "I am prepared to hear all sides of this matter. But I'll thank you all to keep a civil tongue and tone in my chambers."

Dollie remained silent, neither objecting nor apologizing. Davenport turned to Kat next.

"Miss Olmsted?"

She sat forward. "Your honor, I was Mr. Elam's partner in running the Bear Flag. After he died, I made a good faith effort to find members of his family and any silent partners he may have had in the business. Finding none, I took over the proprietorship and daily management of the saloon—again, in good faith. It was never my intention to defraud anyone of anything. The saloon was there. It needed new management. I stepped in and did what I believed was right."

A muted snort rose from Dollie at this. Davenport flashed her a warning look but said nothing. When Kat was done, he turned to Cord.

"Marshal? Any thoughts?"

"No, your honor," Cord replied with a shake of his head. "Only that public breaches of the peace like the one that's led us here tonight will not be tolerated in future." He looked squarely at Dollie. "I hope that's understood, Miss Whittaker."

Dollie's lips tightened at this, but she gave a curt nod of acknowledgment. Cord let it lie at that.

"Miss Whittaker?" Davenport slipped on his reading glasses. "I'll be pleased to take a look at your documents now."

Dollie leaned forward in her chair and placed the folder on Davenport's desk. The judge drew it toward him and opened it, adjusting the fit of his spectacles and the position of the nearest kerosene lantern to facilitate reading. For several minutes, he examined the papers in the bundle, removing and examining pages individually. When he was done, he tamped the pages back into order and replaced them in the folder.

"Miss Olmsted?" he said as he sat back in his chair. "Do you have any counterclaim you wish to express at this time?"

"Your honor . . ." Kat paused, marshaling her words carefully. "Like I said, everything I did was done in good faith. If I had had any idea that Patrick had surviving family, I would have written them at once. But I had no such knowledge. And over his saloon, I have no claim."

In the ensuing silence, one might have heard the proverbial pin drop.

"Your honor, I abandon all claim to the Bear Flag. If it be your decision that Miss Whittaker is entitled to the property, it's hers." Kat waved a hand. "I'm not a woman who is willing to steal something that rightfully belongs to somebody else."

At this, Horace Davenport grew very still. He remained that way for a long moment before nodding and pushing the folder back across the desk to Dollie.

"Let the record show that Miss Olmsted has abandoned her claim. And that Miss Whittaker has the documentation to press for ownership on the basis of familial relation." He nodded to Dollie. "The Bear Flag is yours, Miss Whittaker."

"Good," snapped Dollie. She turned to Kat. "I want you out of there at once!"

"Hang on." Davenport held up a hand. "Let's be fair."

"Excuse me, your honor?" Kat said as she got to her feet.

Davenport's bushy eyebrows rose in surprise. "Yes, Miss Olmsted? You have something else to say?"

"She can have it. Lock, stock, and barrel." Kat sounded very weary now. "There is nothing personal of mine in the establishment. Nothing I need to retrieve. I don't want any more trouble. Cord, take me home, please? Will you?"

"Of course," Cord muttered, moving to hold the door for her.

"Wait just a minute," Dollie said, causing Cord and Kat to stop where they were. "What about the money she's taken out of the place while she was running it illegally? Shouldn't I be entitled to that, as well?"

Judge Davenport's forehead creased in a frown, and his deep-set eyes sparkled with contained anger. He leaned forward and said, "Miss Olmsted has testified that she acted in good faith, and as far as I can see, she had no way of knowing that you even existed, Miss Whittaker, let alone that you had any claim to the saloon. Therefore, it is the judgment of this court that she is entitled to retain any previous earnings that may have accrued to her from the running of the Bear Flag Saloon, up to but not including today's date."

Dollie didn't look happy about that, but before she could raise any objection, Kat said, "Almost everything the saloon made went right back into improving it. I doubt if I took more than a hundred dollars total out of it."

"In that case, we'll dispense with the legal language and put it simply." Davenport gave Dollie a stern look. "As of right now, you two ladies are square. Do you understand that, Miss Whittaker?"

Dollie nodded.

"I would prefer a verbal acknowledgment," Davenport said coolly.

"I understand," Dollie said. She sounded like the words tasted bad in her mouth.

"These proceedings are concluded." Davenport rose lumberingly to his feet. "Good evening."

Cord put a hand on Kat's arm and escorted her out of the building. Lomax was right behind them.

Dollie left last. Davenport watched her go and then shook his head slowly.

Despite what seemed to be a definitive ruling, he had a hunch he hadn't seen the last of this clash between the two women.

Dollie Whittaker stepped into the street with her head held high.

Victory, sweet and bloody, was hers.

She had been prepared to go further and do much worse in pursuit of her claim than involve a judge. Her experiences in life had schooled her in many languages, including that of violence. Her ever-present straight razor, concealed now in her handbag, was just one weapon in her arsenal. If necessary, she was even willing to use the small, two-shot derringer pistol that she had taught herself to handle with deadly accuracy. The notion of drilling Kat Olmsted between the eyes with a bullet was a seductive one.

But no. It was unnecessary now. Because she had won.

She went back to her hotel room and laid out the clothes she would need for the next stage of tonight's plan. On the bed beside a low-cut blouse, she placed the peasant skirt, a sturdy leather belt, and her straight razor. Then she sat down before the mirror to do up her face, outlining her eyes with kohl and paying special attention to her lip blush.

She stepped from the hotel just as the saloons were conducting their final transactions of the night. The main room of the Golden Nugget was nearly empty when she entered, the eyes that turned to her weary as well as excited for her provocative appearance. She swept past them all to the bar, where Teddy Harville was speaking with the barman.

"Good evening, Mr. Harville," she said demurely.

"Good evening to you, ma'am." Harville gave her a smirk and a slight bow. "Such a pleasure to see you. May I offer you a beverage, courtesy of the house?"

Dollie smiled and leaned across the bar, beckoning him to her. "How about a bottle of that lovely wine we shared the other night?" she whispered. "We could take it together at that little table out on the back porch like we did last time."

"A fine suggestion," he whispered back. "Why don't you go on ahead and I'll join you presently?"

"With pleasure." She caressed the back of his hand surreptitiously with a fingertip before departing.

She made her way through the back-room area to the rear porch. A small table and two chairs had been placed there. Originally built to take deliveries, it had been converted to a place for saloon staff to grab a meal between shifts. Dollie found it reminiscent to the cafes she'd seen in Paris. A happy accident of geography gave the porch a superb view of the moon after dark.

Selecting a chair, she put the finishing touches on her plan and settled down to wait.

Harville emerged a few minutes later, followed by the barman. He took a seat at the table as they were served an open bottle of wine and two glasses. Harville poured as the barman departed, handing a glass to Dollie before raising his own.

"To mutual welfare and benefit," he intoned with a smile. And drank.

Dollie sat watching him as he did. When his eyes returned to her, she had put down her wineglass, its contents untouched. She held Harville with her gaze until his stillness betrayed puzzlement and spoke just as he was on the verge of doing the same.

"Theodore, I think we need to have a talk," she said calmly.

"A pleasure," he responded, affection swimming in his eyes. "I am all ears."

"I think it's time for us to make some modifications to our business arrangement," she said. "You saw fit to advance me with a small cash loan."

"Small?" Harville's eyes warmed, and a chuckle escaped his throat. "It was substantial, and placed in an account for our joint—"

"I have moved the money into my account."

Harville fell silent, puzzled. Into her account? But surely that was a mistake. The money was intended to be administered jointly, given the love between them.

"I think it's time for us to reevaluate and go our separate ways. You see, I've decided to ruin you."

She could not have elicited a more stunned response than if she had struck him with a hammer. Harville sat, immobile, as she prattled on cheerfully.

"It's clear to me that you are heading nowhere fast, Teddy. You have no drive, no ambition—"

"W-Wait a minute!"

"You're content to just sit here on your rump and collect profits from your establishment. But some of us have broader horizons.

More challenging goals. And I won't be able to attain those while anchored down by you."

A trembling seized Harville. The stunned shock was giving way to an emotional response. And at the very base of that response . . .

Rage!

"And so I will buy the Nugget from you."

He laughed angrily. "Buy the Nugget? Why, even with the money of *ours* that you've stolen, you wouldn't be able to afford it. Besides. It's not for sale."

"Not yet." She smiled. "But once I have lured away your customers, undercut your profitability, and shown the local business community what a complete and utter fraud you are, the Nugget will no longer be able to afford to stay in business. And you will accept the offer I will make to take the saloon off your hands."

"This . . . this . . ." Harville was shaking now, his face reddening as his fists clenched and unclenched.

"This is goodbye, Theodore." Dollie stood and made an insolent pirouette, then walked away, leaving him no choice but to sit there and watch her go.

Chapter 16

It began as a few tendrils of smoke.

Against the black night sky, unnoticed, dark and sooty wands of smoke climbed skyward to the stars above Rio Oro. It didn't take long for the pillars to thicken into a sheet that undulated in the gentle breeze, sending scraps of ash into the sky. At first impossible to notice even at a short distance, the smoke's odor thickened into a cloud that could be smelled at ten paces, then twenty, then one hundred.

A flicker of orange appeared at the base of the smoke. Soon, the crackle of flames could be heard. With a snap, wood flexed, popped, and burned. As the moon blazed overhead, the conflagration grew.

"Li-Sen!"

He rushed up from sleep to consciousness at the rough shaking of his wife's hand. "What is it?" Li-Sen asked, rolling onto his side in bed.

"Something is burning!" His wife stood beside the bed, trembling despite the blanket wrapped around her shoulders. "There!" She pointed to the window.

Li-Sen stumbled out of bed. Squinting through the dirty glass at the street outside, he saw nothing for a long moment. Then, suddenly, an orange fireball of flame erupted, and the stench of smoke hit him.

"It's Ponder's lumberyard," he said, voice brimming with wonder. "It's on fire!"

Horace Davenport happened to be awake. Like most men of a certain age, his sleep was fitful. He never managed more than four or five hours in a night. He was ensconced at his desk, a tin cup of coffee within reach, scanning a legal brief, when a sound caught his ear. He stopped reading and set down the brief on the blotter before him.

Voices . . .

A scream.

Davenport rose from his desk, went to the door, and pulled it open. Gathering the robe he wore over his nightshirt close around his shoulders, he stepped out onto the sidewalk.

"My God."

Sheets of flame shot skyward from Ponder's lumberyard.

Bart Blackstone was mounted and patrolling at the far edge of town when the fire began. In fact, he had paused at the sign announcing the town limits and lit himself a cigar, taking a few moments to puff peacefully and stare up at the stars.

It was a far cry from Blackpool, he thought. But it would do.

A voice caught his ear, pitched for screaming but barely above a whisper at this distance. Still, it was enough to cause him to turn in the saddle and look.

Saints preserve us!

A moment later, he was spurring his horse back into town at a hard gallop.

"Marshal! Marshal!"

Cord woke to a beating of fists on the marshal's office door. Rousing himself, he pulled on his boots and stumbled across the floor, hauling open the door to find Hap there, wild-eyed and soot-stained.

"Hap, what is it?"

"There's a f-fire at the l-lumber m-mill! Come quick!"

Cord dashed into the street and was greeted by the sight of flames rising from behind the lumberyard fence. He wheeled on Hap.

"Go to the stable! Get buckets! Meet me at the lumberyard!"

Hap ran off to do as he was told. Cord ducked back into the office long enough to grab the marshal's office fire bucket and then sprinted up the sidewalk toward the mill.

The fire was large but had not yet reached any of the buildings. The closer he came to the blaze, the more Cord grew convinced it was confined to a single stack of lumber near the fence's edge. But it was a sizable fire, growing out of control and very likely to spread if they didn't do something. He saw shapes silhouetted against the flames: the flickering movements of men around a wagon in the rear of which stood a barrel.

"Marshal! Over here!"

Reverend Lomax, clad in a pair of long underwear with his black coat over it, waved frantically from the yard's edge. Cord switched direction and ran over. Reaching the preacher, he noted a line of men stretching from the gate into the yard, most of them mill workers, but a sizable number of Chinese folks had also shown up. He saw Li-Sen directing them into place, shouting orders as buckets were filled from the barrel and passed along hand to hand into the yard.

Cord joined the line and began passing buckets. It was difficult, back-straining work. The buckets were heavy and the rhythm, once a second wagon arrived with two barrels of water, relentless. The men at the far end of the line, nearest the fire, would splash a few bucketsful before retreating from the heat and leaving the duty to the next group of men in line. Sooner than he would have hoped, Cord found himself up near the blaze, splashing buckets of water onto the conflagration until Lomax dragged him away by the elbow.

"Come on, Marshal! You won't be any good to us dead!"

Choking and sputtering, Cord allowed himself to be led back to the wagon, where he allowed himself only a minute's rest before rejoining the line and getting back to work.

Slowly, the flames began to diminish. After a time, the majority of the line was able to come forward and attack the blaze all at once, neutralizing it at its base. Blessedly, no other stacks had caught fire, and the resulting damage had not approached the lumber mill proper.

After a time, the last licks of flame were put out and a cheer went up from the assembled men, with locals and Chinese folks laughing and pounding one another on the backs for a job well done. Cord took time to approach Li-Sen and his wife.

"Thank you," he said simply. Turning to the assembled Chinese group, he spread his hands. "Thanks, all of you. We're in your debt."

"Bloody right we are!" Blackstone shouldered his way through the crowd to stand beside Cord. "I'm buying each of you a drink!"

"That would require a lot of money," noted one man in the crowd.

"You think I'm joking?" thundered the deputy. "I'm an Englishman! And we *never* joke about drink!"

Once this had been translated for those who had not yet learned English, the entire population of Rio Oro's Chinese section doubled over with laughter.

* * *

"Hey, Marshal! Can you wait up?"

Cord turned. Hansen, Ponder's yard foreman, was striding across the lot, waving smoke from before his face with one hand while signaling with the other. Hansen, it seemed, had been working when the fire broke out. He wore boots and jeans, his lumberman's apron tied in place as he jogged up beside Cord.

"What is it, Hansen?"

"Marshal, Mr. Ponder asked me to come get you. He says he's caught the man responsible for setting the fire!"

"Oh, he has?" Cord's lips flattened and his stomach plunged as he followed Hansen back to the mill offices. It was his experience that whenever citizens took the law into their own hands this way, bad things tended to follow. "Who is it?"

"It's that simpleton . . . what's his name?"

"Hap?" Cord was incredulous. "He's got Hap in his office?"

"Why, yes, he does!" Hansen seemed annoyed at the question. "Seems only right if he's the one who started the fire!"

"Did Hap confess to doing that?"

"Well, no."

They went into the building and down a short hallway to Ponder's office. The door was closed, so Hansen knocked twice before opening it and ushering Cord inside.

Cord had no sooner spotted Ponder behind his big desk and the shrunken, trembling form of Hap cowering in a chair nearby, guarded by a big mill worker, than footsteps came pounding down the corridor behind him. An instant later, Lomax burst into the room.

"Jeremiah Ponder, how dare you!" The preacher's rage was palpable. Fire and brimstone danced in his eyes. "Who are you to seize and hold this man?" He went to Hap, warning the guard away with a growl before setting a hand on his shoulder. "You have no right to kidnap and imprison a child of God. *Damn you*!"

Cord suppressed a grin.

But Ponder was not amused. He rose from his desk, rotund figure trembling. "And how dare *you* storm into *my* office, Reverend! This ain't your church! Such an outrage! Marshal? Why are you being so quiet about all this?"

"Because Reverend Lomax said everything I came to say." Cord crossed his arms. "What's this I hear about you accusing Hap of setting the fire? Hap, you don't even like to play with matches, do you?"

"Gadzooks, n-no!" Hap trembled. "Th-They're d-dangerous!"

"Hap is a good man!" Lomax thundered. "He may never get a degree from Harvard, but he's a decent and honest fellow, which is more than I can say for you, Ponder!"

"Hey!"

"Just imagine! The arrogance—"

"Preacher, you're out of line!"

"Quiet, both of you."

At Cord's firm command, the room fell silent. Cord sighed, stepped over to Hap, and drew him up from the chair.

"Hap, you're the one who came and woke me, told me about the fire. Where were you when it started?"

"I w-was w-walking p-past the l-lumberyyard!"

"What were you doing there?"

"T-Talking. T-T-To Yu-Lee."

"The watchman." Cord remembered Lomax hiring a member of the Chinese community to watch the lumber. "You two were visiting together?"

"Y-Yes. He w-was on his w-way to w-w-work. I s-stopped on my w-way h-home. We t-talked a b-bit."

"We'll talk to Yu-Lee," Cord assured Ponder. Turning back to Hap, he asked, "Hap, did you enter Ponder's lumberyard at any time?"

"N-No, sir!"

"Okay, then." Cord turned to the mill owner. "It's your word against his. And the reverend is right. You have no authority to detain Hap or anyone else. Don't let me catch you doing it again. C'mon, Hap."

"Wait a minute!" Ponder was coming around the desk now, moving in an enraged hustle. "You can't just—"

Cord whirled on the mill owner. His voice cracked like a whip. "You don't tell me what I can and can't do in my jurisdiction, Mr. Ponder! Try that again and it'll be the last public comment you make for a good stretch, because you're liable to be behind bars for interfering with an officer of the law."

Ponder shrank back, shocked at the hard edge in Cord's voice. Cord was too tired and had breathed too much smoke tonight to put up with the mill owner carrying on like a pompous windbag.

When Ponder didn't say anything else, Cord gave him a curt nod and left the office. Lomax and Hap weren't far behind him.

Lomax and Cord stood Hap a few beers at the Golden Nugget, which Teddy Harville opened to allow the fire crew to slake their parched throats. To his credit, Hap paused after two glasses and thanked both men once again for their intervention before heading off into the night.

"He's a good soul," said Lomax quietly, watching him go. "How come it's always the good ones, the gentle ones, who get victimized?"

"I suppose to some people the world is a jungle. So, they prey on the weak."

"Who do you suppose started that fire?"

"Well . . ." Cord scratched his chin before taking another swallow of beer. "I figure likely the same fella who torched your wood a while back. Might be somebody who gets a thrill out of setting fires. I hear tell there are people like that."

"I thought the first one was set because he disliked Christianity and the church," mused Lomax.

"Could be he does," Cord replied. "But if it's the same man, then we know his motives aren't necessarily personal. It may have more to do with an illness of the mind."

Lomax mulled over the notion a moment before continuing. "Someone terribly broken. Sick in thought and spirit." His eyes rose to meet Cord's. "Or just plain evil."

"There's always that," Cord allowed.

"Ponder was full of brimstone and rage after you left," Lomax said. "He says that if you don't track down the man responsible, he will."

"Is that right?"

"Cord, he vowed to nail whoever it is to the lumberyard fence. Granted, the man's a bit of a windbag, but if he's angry enough, there's no telling what he might do."

Cord blanched at the thought of a man being nailed to a fence. It was downright medieval.

"Something new has come to town," Lomax said, his voice haunted. "Something powerful. Something evil. I can feel it, moving in its sinister ways in the darkness."

"If that's true, Reverend, it's bound to come out in the light sooner or later."

"And when it does?"

"If I can see a snake," Cord said with a faint smile, "I can stomp it."

Chapter 17

The package that would change Cord's life forever passed through many hands on its journey from the U.S. Marshal's office in Sacramento to his.

The package contained not one letter but two. The first was a neatly folded missive from a deputy U.S. marshal in the Ozark region. The second, thicker document had Cord's name scrawled on the outside in blue ink. The two bundled together and tied with string made for a bulky package. It left the clerk's desk in Sacramento on a Wednesday morning.

The stagecoach carrying the mail brought it in the direction of Rio Oro. It changed wagons at the second stop and ascended into the mountains, spending the first night of its journey nestled snug inside the strongbox as an unseasonal rain fell on the parched land.

The package found its way into Blackstone's hand on the afternoon of its fifth day on the road. The deputy accepted it from the stagecoach driver and took it into the marshal's office. Settling down behind his desk, he cut the string, unfolded the first thinner letter, and went fishing in his vest pocket for reading glasses.

It only took Blackstone a few moments to digest the neatly written words, but another minute to reread the message twice. He wanted to be sure that he understood correctly. Even after a third reading, he could barely believe its contents.

That done, he set aside the sheaf of papers addressed to Cord, glanced at the clock, and settled down to wait.

Cord arrived an hour later to find Blackstone visibly perturbed.

"Hi, Bart." He narrowed his eyes as he hung his hat on the rack. "Everything all right?"

"No, Marshal." The Englishman stood and extended the thick message to him. "This came to you, along with a letter from the marshal's office in the Ozarks. There is no easy way to say this, Cord."

"Ozarks?" Cord examined the handwriting on the envelope. He did not recognize it. "What isn't easy to say?"

"Those gunmen, Cord. It appears they're here looking for you. Been sent, in fact."

Cord's gut plunged.

"Apparently, that letter is from someone you know."

Cord unfolded the pages of looping, heavily flourished handwriting and read:

Dear Cord,

It has been a long time since I last stopped by your farm on my rounds, but since retiring from the postal service, I have had time on my hands to gossip and keep track of people's comings and going here in the Boston Mountains. When a deputy marshal came around looking for information, he found his way to me and I thought to put into writing what I told him.

You will remember Hiram Stockton, though in all likelihood you would prefer not to. Back in the days when I knew your family, your kin were close with him and his. But that changed after you left. I retired right around then but soon heard people talking about it in the streets and managed to put two and two together. It seems Stockton had taken to cursing the Bennett name.

Someone, and who it was, precisely, is not germane to this discussion, told me about what happened to Stockton's daughter Caroline. About two months after you left town, she found herself to be with child. She never publicly said whose baby it was. But Hiram decided it must be you, on account of how sweet on Caroline you had always been. I'm not privy to the truth of the matter, of course, and it's no business of mine. But nature took its course and in this case, the inevitable unfolded in tragic fashion. I'm very sorry to say that neither Miss Caroline nor the infant survived the hardship of childbirth.

The men the marshal is inquiring about—the three killers in the black dusters—I've seen them hereabouts, in Hiram Stockton's company. It seems clear to me, Cord, that Stockton blames you for what happened and desires vengeance upon you. To put it plain, those gunmen are out to get you on account of Miss Caroline and the baby dying. Right or wrong, he wants you dead, too, Cord. That's what's going on, near as I can figure.

Please take care.

Sincerely yours,
Darwin Dixon
U.S. Postal Department, ret'd

Cord absorbed the contents of the letter in stunned silence.

"Are you all right, Marshal?"

Cord folded the sheets, stuffed it into his pocket, and made for the door.

"Keep an eye on things for me, will you? Thanks, Bart."

He let himself out before Blackstone could answer.

Cord swung a leg over his horse and rode fast up Main Street, veering around a stagecoach and blasting out of town at a gallop.

Caroline . . .

He felt mixed anger and sadness about her death. Cord had been in love with Caroline as a youth, only to become disillusioned and enraged when she took up with someone else. That hurt had become even deeper when he discovered that her lover was his older brother, Flint. It was a betrayal not only of his feelings for her but also his idea of who she was, of who she allowed him to believe she could be. But all that collapsed like a house of cards soon before the Bennetts' departure for Rio Oro.

Along the way, he had met and fallen in love with Glory, burying that part of himself that was still infatuated with Caroline Stockton. In his love for Glory, Cord had discovered new parts of himself, become awakened to new feelings and a spirit of optimism about the future. Being reminded of Caroline was like being pushed back into a dark closet and the door slammed, leaving him to suffocate in darkness.

And now Hiram Stockton was blaming him!

The reality of Caroline's death opened a fresh wound for her in his heart. And the unfairness of it all was galling. He would never have touched her without first marrying her, and yet she herself had succumbed to those very sins of the flesh. And with his very own—

He caught hold of himself, reining his horse to a stop and taking a deep breath. He had ridden out the burst of raging emotions that had filled him, and now it was time to think calmly and rationally again.

He would have to tell Glory and her family that tragedy and danger had followed him from the Ozarks. There was no way out of it. They deserved to know, and besides, it was absolutely necessary that they be kept safe. That meant honestly sharing information, no matter how painful it might be for him. Their safety was more important than anything.

Even his marriage to Glory?

The realization it might come down to that was one he pushed out of his mind at once.

He took his time gathering his thoughts, measuring the words he would use to explain things. He rode back into and through town, head down, asking himself if there was anything he was missing or had left out of the story. He wanted to make sure Glory understood everything. He would leave nothing out that could pop up down the road and cause her pain.

No, the pain came now with him admitting the past. That pain was his, he thought. All the pain should be his, not hers.

He rode past the city limits and upriver into the area where the claims were staked out in this part of the canyon. Even though he took his time, Cord arrived at the Bennett Claim and Abraham's cabin faster than he would have liked. Although he expected to linger chatting with the old man before going up to the cabin to see Glory, it was her and not her father he found out front. Sleeves rolled up, the front of her skirt stained with mud, she was shoveling a bucket full of runoff into the sluice.

"Cord!" She stopped shoveling and waved, blowing away an errant strand of red hair from her eyes. "Aren't you a sight for sore eyes!"

"Hello, Glory." He slid from the saddle with a grin brighter than what he was actually feeling and wrapped his arms around her waist, drawing her up onto her toes in a fierce hug.

"Well, what brings you up here this time of day?" She pushed her shovel point first into the ground and wiped the sweat from her face with a kerchief.

"I came up to talk to you," he said. "What are you doing working the sluice?"

"Pa has an errand he needs to run and asked me to finish these last few buckets for him. Come on up to the house and have some lemonade."

"Sounds fine."

They made their way to the cabin, Cord pausing on the porch as Glory went inside to get the drinks. She emerged with two glasses that had been cooling in the shaded dark. The lemonade went down smooth on this warm day. After they had settled in their chairs, Cord began.

"I got some news today," he began, a tad ruefully. "It has to do with those men Blackstone and I encountered on the street—the trio of gunmen who came after us."

"Have you caught them?"

"No, although we almost caught one the other day." Cord swilled the lemonade around hesitantly in his glass. "He got away. Near as we can figure, they're camped out in the wilderness somewhere around town. But a while back, we sent out some letters asking about them, and we got a response this morning. Glory, there's no easy way to put this."

"What is it, Cord?" Her face was serious now, her gaze direct.

"They're hired killers. And they've been sent here from the Ozarks to kill somebody."

"Who?"

"Me."

Glory accepted this news in stunned silence. For a long moment, she sat staring at him, disbelief clouding her eyes. At length, she shook her head as if unable to accept what she had just heard.

"Why?" she asked simply.

"Before we left to join the gold rush, my family and I farmed in the Boston Mountains in the Ozarks, near the town of Wilbur. I've told you about that. Our neighbors were Hiram Stockton and his family. He had a daughter named Caroline." He smiled again, but it was a haunted expression. "When I was younger, I was sweet on Caroline."

Glory was watching him now, unspeaking, eyes focused like a deer scanning the forest for danger.

"Anyway, she didn't return those feelings. Or, if she did, she only pretended to." He shrugged. "It was my older brother who ended up, ah, having . . . I mean, he . . ."

"He won her heart and disappointed you?"

"Well, he certainly *won* her, but I'm not sure her heart was what he had in mind, exactly." He sighed heavily. "I found out what was going on by . . . Well, I discovered them together in the barn, only I didn't know it was Flint until later. All I knew was that she was with somebody." Cord shook his head. "That was enough to tell me I had everything all wrong."

Glory stayed silent.

"Anyway, Caroline got, ah, with child. Didn't discover it until after we left."

"Would you have gone back if you'd known?"

"No." He shrugged again. "I'd have no cause to. Like I said, she'd been with somebody else."

He noticed she had stopped looking at him.

"Caroline died in childbirth. The baby didn't survive, either." The silence during his next pause felt bottomless, so he did not linger there. "She's laid in her grave, God rest her, along with her child. But Hiram Stockton isn't content to let it end there. He's convinced I'm responsible. He never had any idea Caroline was involved with Flint. And so, he's hired this trio of gunfighters to come after me and settle the score."

Glory sat for a long time, staring out at the river. The silence stretched out until only the whisper of the current could be heard.

"And are you?" she asked, her voice firm.

"Am I what?"

"Responsible?"

"No!" Despite his resolve to stay calm, he grew annoyed. "I told you, it was Flint."

"I see," she said. But it was clear to him she did not.

Cord felt frustration build within him. Glory's reaction didn't make any sense. It was almost as if she considered him, Cord, to be responsible for Caroline's pregnancy and death, not Flint. But he wasn't. He had explained that. So why did she imagine he was lying?

"Glory—"

"I need some time, Cord." She stood, brushing the front of her dress. "This was completely unexpected and . . ."

"And what?"

"I suppose it's part of being a marshal's wife that I never considered. The notion that I would have to wait up nights wondering if you were going to come home alive. Or—"

She stopped and turned away from him. He could tell by the hunch of her shoulders that she was fighting tears.

"I just need some time, Cord. Please just give me some time."

She went inside and shut the door.

Chapter 18

Cord sought out Lomax late the next afternoon. He discovered the preacher down at the building site, supervising the roofing crew atop his church. Cord came upon him calling instructions up to the two Chinese men nailing shingles into place on the sloping surface. Cord, who had never been partial to heights, marveled at their balance.

"Afternoon, Marshal," said Lomax with a grin. "Come to help?"

"Actually, I've come seeking help." Cord dismounted and tied the reins to the rail of the porch steps. "I find myself in need of some spiritual counsel."

"Then you've come to the right place," Lomax said quietly. Turning to the men on the roof, he called out, "Li-Sen! Why don't you and your brother go ahead and have your lunch now? I need to go inside and talk with the marshal, here."

"All right," replied Li-Sen. He spoke briefly to the other man in Chinese before waving to Cord. "Hello, Marshal!" he called. A moment later, he and his companion were shinnying down the ladder and then moving up the street toward home for a meal.

"Come on in." Lomax guided Cord through the main doors and into the sanctuary. Cord looked around, impressed by the interior. It wasn't finished, but it was certainly shaping up nicely.

The pulpit and the altar, both freshly completed, dominated the room. A few pews had been built and put in place, but the rest had yet to be constructed. They existed now as a row of wooden planks propped against the back wall beside a box of tools. The stained-glass windows, brought out from San Francisco, spilled light and color over everything.

Lomax guided Cord to a door in the back of the room which opened into a small office.

"There's not much here yet," said the preacher. "Just some tables and chairs. But I can offer you a mug of coffee if you like."

"That sounds really good," Cord said.

"Coming right up."

A small stove provided warmth and a cooking surface. Lomax had a pot of coffee brewed and poured two cups before drawing out the chair behind his desk to sit by Cord's. It was more companionable that way, like two friends talking. Lomax handed over one of the cups, then took a seat.

"Got no milk or sugar," Lomax said. "Sorry."

"I prefer to take it black, anyway. Thanks." Cord took a sip of the good, strong brew and waited for it to settle in his stomach. Lomax, he noticed, had fallen into a waiting silence. A stillness moved into the room. After a few moments, there was only the sound of the wind outside.

Might as well get down to it, Cord thought. Putting things off seldom made them better.

"It turns out the three gunmen who came after me and Deputy Blackstone are hired killers. Professionals sent from the Ozarks and paid to kill me."

"Why?"

"They were hired by the father of a neighbor we had back in the

Boston Mountains. Man named Stockton. His daughter died in childbirth. He's decided I'm responsible."

"Were you?"

"No. But my brother was. I didn't know that then, but Flint told me after we got out here." Cord sipped his coffee. "Flint's gone, now. Buried up out beside my other brother, Steve, near the claim. But Stockton figures I was the man who got his Caroline with child and caused her death. And he wants his revenge."

"That is a tough cross to bear," Lomax admitted.

"It is." Cord sighed. "But the worst damage has been to my marriage plans. See, I spoke about this to Glory. Tried to explain to her. But she's decided to pull back. Withdraw from me because of this news."

"Right when you need her support the most."

"Yeah. Although I can't say I blame her for being hesitant. I mean, I understand it. It's not just the business about Caroline, although that's bad enough. She's realizing that being married to a lawman is always going to have its share of worries. More than its share."

Lomax nodded, agreeing but saying nothing.

"What is it about women, Preacher? Why do they think with their feelings instead of their heads?"

"One might just as well ask what it is about men that they lead with their brains and not their hearts," Lomax answered. "I've been preaching and counseling a good while now, and troubles between men and women usually boil down to this one central difference between us. It's often a point of contention. But it can also be a point of connection. Joy, even."

"How do you figure?"

"Ever seen a bunch of women attend a wedding?" Lomax grinned. "The love and joy they give to someone celebrating that occasion, the excitement they generate, that's a woman thing, Marshal.

Something *they* do, and part of the magic they give to our world. If we didn't have it, we'd sure miss it."

Cord chewed on this. It made sense.

"She loves you, Cord." Lomax's voice was firm as he said it. "I know a woman in love when I see one, and she definitely fits the bill. She's upset right now because she's scared. She may not recognize that herself yet, but I think that's what's behind this. Fear."

"That's understandable."

"It is." Lomax set down his cup and crossed his arms. "Remember that she is willingly taking on a vast burden—one most women wouldn't dare assume. And that is the burden of being a lawman's wife. The women able to do that are rare, Cord. Rare as diamonds. Because each time such a woman kisses her husband goodbye at the start of the workday, she doesn't know if he'll return to her alive."

Cord nodded, clouds clearing from his mind as Lomax helped him to see.

"She needs room right now, I reckon," Cord said.

"The most loving thing you can do is give that to her."

"It's hard."

"Trust usually is."

"So, what you're saying is that I should let this go and allow God to work?"

"I am, Marshal," Lomax said. "Sometimes in life, we have to just wait and see how things work out."

Cord chuckled. "And here we came out West, figuring we'd be masters of our destinies."

"God lets us do that," Lomax said. "To a certain extent, anyway."

Cord nodded. It was difficult to accept. But he had no choice.

Another person who had no choice was Dollie Whittaker, now ensconced as proprietress of the Bear Flag Saloon.

No choice but to enjoy herself, she thought languidly.

Wearing a blue dress and a red scarf tied at the throat, her hair pinned back and her cosmetics freshly applied, she held court at what she thought of as the "high table" in her establishment—a small round table with two chairs on a slightly elevated platform near the bar.

Once it had served as a stage for traveling entertainers, but changes to the dimensions of the room and the extension of the bar made it impractical as a stage. The piano had been moved to the other side of the room, where a more suitable stage had been added. Now the small platform was the perfect perch for the modest table, allowing Dollie a place to work as well as a lookout from which to survey her kingdom.

Right now, her eyes were set on the Golden Nugget's entrance, partially visible through a window by the batwing doors. She had taken to studying its patrons in detail as they went in and out, noting the faces and names of the ones she recognized.

She had already made a thorough study of Teddy Harville's business, knew its strengths and weaknesses, and understood its finances better than Harville himself. The question now was how to leverage those weaknesses to her advantage.

It didn't take Dollie long to puzzle out *how.* Her success would depend now on the *who.*

And she had an intuition about that.

She waved over one of the serving girls, a shy farmer's daughter named Angie. Dollie liked Angie because she was pretty and stupid—too stupid to ask questions. As Angie approached, Dollie finished inking a short message onto a note card, which she blotted, then folded into an envelope. Before sealing the envelope, she deposited one of her business cards inside.

"Angie, dear." She handed over the envelope. "I would like you to run up to the lumber mill. Ask to speak to Mr. Ponder. Give him that *personally.* Don't leave it with anybody. Put it into his hands yourself and wait there until he has read it. Then return. Understand?"

Angie nodded, accepted the envelope, and scurried off.

The late-afternoon crowd began to drift in for drinks. The bar grew busy. Dollie watched the men enter and order their beers, noting with satisfaction that her observation about the differences between her clientele and that of the Golden Nugget had been accurate. She was reflecting on this when Jeremiah Ponder entered.

Many of the men recognized him. A number of his employees nodded deferentially as he walked by. Dollie Whittaker stood and waved as he approached the bar.

"Over here, Mr. Ponder." She smiled and gestured toward the empty chair beside her. "Won't you come up and be my guest here at the high table?"

"Don't mind if I do." The rotund, sweaty little man climbed onto the platform and dragged the chair toward himself, dumping his body into it with an exhale. He requested a cold beer, which the bartender brought immediately. Dollie toasted him with her teacup.

"So good of you to come and visit, Mr. Ponder," she said breezily.

"Good of you to invite me." He sipped the foam from his beer. "Ah, that's good!" He set down the glass. "And of course your note made accepting the more attractive option. Any invitation to consider making a deal with another business owner is always worth examining."

"I do agree." Dollie gazed around the main room. "Extensive remodeling of this room ended a few months ago. I understand your mill was significantly involved in the process."

"We supplied the lumber." Ponder nodded. "A few of my workers came and earned extra pennies doing some carpentry on their days off. All in all, it worked well for everyone involved."

"It did." Her eyes twinkled. "I was thinking about extending and continuing that cooperative partnership."

"You planning more renovations?"

"Not at the moment, no." She leaned forward and placed her hand on his. "I am thinking more in strategic terms, you understand. A partnership with an eye on the future, so to speak."

Ponder smiled. "What did you have in mind?"

As he finished the question, the piano player appeared and began thumping the keys of the upright in the corner. A bouncy dance hall tune jangled into the room.

"Let's repair to the back to discuss the details, shall we?"

They took their drinks into the office once used by Kat Olmsted. Dollie had taken special delight in seizing and converting this room to her own use. Once Ponder had taken a seat, she closed the door and turned to him.

"Mr. Ponder, I am not insensitive to the problems your mill has been having of late," she began. "You and your workers are being harassed by an organized group of malcontents among the mining community. These provocations have been ongoing and may have contributed to the fire that broke out in your yard the other night."

"Interesting," he muttered. "Yes, you're right. Go on."

"Malcontents. Among the mining community," she repeated. "Many of whom drink at the Golden Nugget."

She had his attention now. Ponder put down his glass and folded his hands, paying close attention to Dollie as she continued.

"Being able to marshal and organize one's forces . . . having a base at which to gather and from which to launch action . . . having a sympathetic backer who can provide support . . ."

A slow grin began to spread across the mill owner's face.

"What say you we make a deal?" she asked. "Your lumbermen can drink here at a discount. Announce that to them. Let's make the Bear Flag the saloon of choice for Ponder's mill. It's a win for them because they get cheap beer. It's a win for you because you will always know where to find them after hours. And it's a win for me."

Ponder sat back for a few moments and mulled over what she had proposed. Then he said, "My men already drink here because of the decree handed down by Marshal Bennett to try to keep the peace here in town. But such a discount would increase their loyalty to you."

Dollie smiled. "Loyalty is beyond price in business."

"Indeed. Because that would give you a ready-made army in house for your vendetta against Teddy Harville." Ponder laughed, then added, "Don't look so surprised. There are few secrets in this town."

"So true," Dollie said with an elegant shrug that made her breasts move enticingly under the tight dress. Ponder took note of that, as she had known he would.

He wasn't completely distracted, however. He said, "Since those men are my employees, I'd like to think that they're loyal to me. Loyalty is a quality that's difficult to share."

"But if we have the same goals, then we both profit from that loyalty, don't we?"

"I suppose," Ponder allowed.

Dollie reached over and rested the fingertips of one hand on his forearm. That nearly always worked. "Then shall we discuss the future?"

"Yes," he said. "Let's do that."

CHAPTER 19

The next morning, Glory came into town early to buy some things at the general store. Main Street was quiet as she tied her wagon to a hitching post near the city limits and began hiking the wooden sidewalk to the store. She was just passing the Bear Flag when Dollie Whittaker appeared wearing her schoolmarm getup. She smiled and nodded to Glory as they passed.

"Good morning," she said kindly. "We have hot coffee at the Bear Flag if you're interested."

Glory's jaw clenched. She was furious with Dollie Whittaker for what she had done to Kat. But the matter had been decided legally, fair and square, by Judge Davenport. She considered ignoring the woman and passing on by, but that would suggest she was upset. She refused to give Dollie Whittaker the satisfaction.

"No, thank you," she said tightly. "I am very definitely not interested."

"That's a shame." Dollie Whittaker's lips spread in a slow smile. "You know, we have made great strides in improvement under new management."

"I'm sure you have," said Glory, trying to maneuver her way around Dollie.

"Your sister made a show of running the place, but she made poor decisions. It was no secret why the business was in such difficulty."

A hot rage began to kindle in Glory's belly. *No secret why the business was in such difficulty?* The insinuation was there on the table, right in front of everybody. Glory could not let it pass.

"What are you suggesting?" she asked icily.

"Why, I'm not suggesting anything." Dollie batted her eyelashes. "It's just that the saloon does excellent business. Always has. Lots of drinks get poured. Lots of coins change hands. As for where those coins end up?" Dollie shrugged.

"And where is that?" Glory's voice held an edge of real danger.

"Why, in your sister's pockets, of course! She was known to cheat her employees—"

It was as far as Dollie got. Glory dropped her shopping basket and flew at Dollie, hands clawed, a growl escaping her throat. How *dare* anyone accuse her sister of theft!

Dollie Whittaker was taken completely by surprise. She had always taken Kat's quiet sister for an easy target. Maybe that red hair should have been a warning. The hellcat that launched herself spitting fire and rage was a fury. They collided, arms entangling. Grappling, their skirts flew as they reeled across the boardwalk.

Glory threw a punch that slammed into Dollie's stomach and knocked the wind out of her. Dollie reared back, trying to escape, but Glory had hold of her and refused to let go. For a moment, they teetered at the edge of the sidewalk, paralyzed by the strain of their opposing strengths.

Then they tumbled into the dusty street. Glory landed on top, pushing far enough away from Dollie to line up a punch. But Dollie used this opportunity to flip Glory to the side and roll on top herself, balancing on her knees. Holding Glory's wrists pinned to the ground, she pushed her face toward Glory's with a wicked leer.

"What a pretty face," she hissed. "Be an awful shame if anything happened to it!"

She released one wrist, curled her hand into a fist, and punched down hard. Glory shrieked under the impact of the blow, her nose bloody. Dollie laughed at her pain and raised her arm, fingers clawed now, ready to go after Glory's eyes.

When suddenly Bart Blackstone grasped the back of Dollie's collar and yanked her into a standing position.

"That's not very nice," he said quietly. He held her so that her legs dangled and only the tips of her toes touched the ground.

Dollie twisted against Blackstone's grip in an attempt to get free, but it was too tight. She realigned her body and swung a punch at his face. Her fist landed with a soft, harmless tap and Blackstone responded by holding her out at arm's length, lifting her even higher so that she flailed helplessly.

"Miss Glory?" he asked without looking around. "Are you all right?"

"I am, thank you, Mr. Blackstone." Glory rolled to all fours and pushed herself to her feet, brushing the dust from her dress and wiping the blood from her face as the marshal's office door banged open and Cord came running.

"What the hell did you do to her?"

The words were out of his mouth before he could control himself. He saw the blood discoloring Glory's mouth and cheeks, saw the dust on her rumpled clothes and the ineffectual squirming of Dollie Whittaker at the end of Blackstone's arm. Figuring out what had happened here was no great challenge.

"It's under control, Marshal," said Blackstone. "I have Miss Whittaker in custody. Perhaps you'd care to see to Miss Glory?"

"Come on," Cord said, grasping Glory's wrist and whisking her across the street into his office.

He tended to her carefully, wiping the blood from her face with a clean handkerchief. Then he brought out a basin of water for her to wash with. After a few minutes, now reasonably presentable, she dropped the soiled towel by the washbasin and went to the window. Across the street, Blackstone was still looming over Dollie Whittaker.

"Are you all right, Glory?" Cord fought to control the worry in his voice.

"I am, Cord. Thank you." Her voice was soft as she stood watching Blackstone and Dollie. She turned to him. "Tell Deputy Blackstone to let Dollie Whittaker go, Cord. I don't plan on pressing any charges."

"Why not?" Cord's voice filled with wonder.

"Because I attacked her first." Glory drew a shuddery breath.

"You did?" Cord frowned. It seemed so out of character for her.

"Yes. She insulted Kat. I couldn't help myself."

Cord smiled. Defending her sister was very definitely in character for Glory.

Loyal to her bones, he thought. He had chosen well.

He paused for a moment, then added: *Assuming the wedding happens at all.*

A few minutes later, the big Englishman stepped into the marshal's office long enough to report that Dollie wanted to press charges but that he had told her firmly that was impossible.

"What reason did you give?" Cord asked, amused.

"Rio Oro city bylaw five-thirteen," Blackstone replied.

"What's bylaw five-thirteen?" asked Glory.

Blackstone shrugged. "Beats me," he said. "I just made it up on the spot. Filthy bloody woman!"

He handed Glory her shopping basket, which he'd retrieved from the boardwalk, where she had dropped it when the fracas began.

Cord and Glory laughed as the deputy left the office. The situation wasn't really funny, but they couldn't help but admire Blackstone's way of handling things.

"I have a surprise for you," Cord said, growing serious again.

"You do?"

"Sure thing." He rose from his chair. "Do you feel like taking a walk?"

"Why, of course!"

They left the office, stepping onto Main Street as the morning traffic of horses, carriages, and pedestrians filled the town. Rio Oro was growing, and Cord was surprised by how happy this made him. Each day brought new, prospective gold hunters to Casterline's office to stake a claim, and those claims seemed to be paying out more often than not. A gold town rich in strikes was more likely to survive and thrive, making the leap from prospecting camp to a full-fledged municipality. Cord's job as marshal was likely to remain secure for the foreseeable future—something that gladdened his heart enormously. He felt as if he were making a difference here and found that very gratifying.

They walked to the intersection of Main and the unnamed cross street. Turning, they started in the direction of the Chinese area. Cord paused once they reached the church.

"Here it is, Glory," he said. "It's almost done."

She took in the new façade. Lomax and Li-Sen had hung the doors yesterday, so the sanctuary was now enclosed. The shingles had been laid on the roof and a workman at the far end toiled to erect a tiny bell tower. Cord conducted Glory to the door and knocked twice. Garrison Lomax answered promptly.

"Ah, Marshal. And you brought your lovely fiancée! I don't believe we've met. Garrison Lomax." He extended a hand.

"Gloriana Olmsted." She shook. Then added: "Soon to be Glory Bennett."

Cord's heart surged with hope at these words. Bringing her here had been the right idea.

"Cord is a lucky man." Lomax grinned. "Are you two busy right now? Care for a tour?"

"We'd love one," said Cord. He was pleased to feel Glory's arm loop into his. Perhaps the passage of some days and this morning's donnybrook with Dollie Whittaker had inspired her to overcome the doubts caused by their conversation about the Ozarks. Perhaps she realized now how much she needed him—how much they needed each other.

Cord was delighted.

"We don't have much for pews yet," Lomax admitted, conducting them down the aisle between rows of rough wooden benches. "These should do for now. But I aim to order some proper pews and get them freighted out here. Once the, ah, collection baskets start coming in . . ."

"You'll need collection revenue," Cord noted. "But also some more substantial donations. Maybe some of the more well-to-do citizens could be induced to pony up."

"They usually can. Particularly as they age and become more concerned about the state of their souls." Lomax waggled his eyebrows comically. "A canny preacher knows to get close to the elderly."

"Reverend Lomax!" Glory laughed. "You're awful!"

"Oh, I don't know if I'd go that far," Lomax joked. "Call me . . . strategic."

This prompted a healthy laugh from both of them. Lomax continued the tour, showing off the finished pulpit. It was a fine, simple speaker's box a short three steps above the floor. The altar was a rough wooden table, but large. A big wooden crucifix stood in the corner beside a coil of rope.

"Li-Sen is going to come and help me hang that later," Lomax said.

"We're here," said Glory. "Why don't we do it? We'll help you. Won't we, Cord?"

"Sure!" Cord grinned, pleased with her initiative. "C'mon, Reverend. Let's hang that thing!"

Lomax, sensing that no argument could dissuade them, shrugged, shouldered the coil of rope, and pointed out the hook that had been set in place in a cross beam behind the altar from which to hang the cross. Cord threw both ends of the rope over the beam and Glory caught them, drawing the ends together so a loop remained on Cord's side of the beam. Lomax and Cord wrestled over the cross, pushed both arms through the loop, and then steadied it. At Cord's suggestion, Glory came to hold the cross steady while he and Lomax manned the rope. She held the cross straight as they raised it, guiding it until it clicked into place on the hook.

"There!" she cried.

The men slackened and slowly released the rope. The cross hung straight and true, adding the finishing touch to the house of God.

"It's beautiful," Glory marveled, her eyes shining.

"Looks very fine," Cord agreed.

Lomax stood there gazing up at the cross for a long time. Cord noted the trace of a tear in the man's eye.

"Always wanted a church of my own," he said quietly. "I've preached in mining camps, cavalry forts, other men's parishes . . . but never in a place of my own. This . . ." He paused briefly, overcome with emotion. "This is very special to me."

Cord and Glory, arms around each other, studied Lomax with fond respect.

"Rio Oro is lucky to have you, Preacher," said Glory.

"We are," agreed Cord.

Lomax seemed on the point of weeping. But then he coughed

into his hand, squared his shoulders, and sniffed, regaining control of himself.

"This is a fine town. And a fine church," he announced, conducting them back down the aisle to the door. "It will be a pleasure to have your wedding be the first of many in this place. Have you set a date?"

Cord and Glory looked at each other.

"I'm thinking the sooner the better," he said.

Glory seemed to hesitate for a moment. Cord relaxed when she smiled and nodded.

"Why don't you figure it out and let me know?" Lomax opened the door and led them onto the small porch. "We can—"

The sound of gunfire cut him off.

Then Lomax was dragging Glory back inside as Cord crouched and drew his Colt.

CHAPTER 20

Gunfire thundered through the town, sending the citizens scurrying for cover. A bullet whined off of a rock near Cord and ricocheted down the street to smash a window. Two more shots thudded into the doors of the church.

It was them, Cord thought. Had to be!

The gunfire was concentrated up at the intersection, perhaps a hundred yards away. Cord squinted against the smoke rising from the guns.

There!

The man with the rifle—the one who had been on the balcony of the rooming house—was firing on the church from a kneeling position. He had fashioned himself a secure little blind between a horse trough and the edge of the general store. Cord withdrew behind the church steps and searched for the other two.

More shots from the rifle cracked, followed by the thinner reports of pistols. Cord looked for them. It seemed one was out of sight across the street from the rifleman, long range for a handgun but not impossible. And the other . . . ?

Cord caught sight of the man as he burst into view, sprinting down a narrow alley beside the warehouse across from the church. He was moving fast and coming right this way!

Cord stood, aimed the Dragoon, and fired two well-placed shots that sent the man sprawling. The wind-rip of a rifle slug passing much too close to his ear made him break into a run.

He had to lead the gunmen away from the church, otherwise Glory or Lomax risked catching a stray bullet. So, he did the unexpected. Crouching as low as he comfortably could, he ran straight for the rifleman, firing as he went.

Startled, the rifleman managed to get off one more round, which went wide, before getting spooked. He retreated into his narrow little hiding place, ducking behind the trough.

The third gunman was drawing a bead on Cord, who flung himself full length on the ground just as the man squeezed off his shot. The bullet narrowly missed him. Rolling, he came up on his knees and fired two bullets back in the direction of the gunman. Neither one hit, but the second came close enough to ricochet off the wall beside the man. Cord felt a swell of satisfaction as the would-be killer's eyes widened in alarm. A second later, he dove for cover.

Cord figured to do the same. The Dragoon was empty, and he had to reload.

A wagon was parked just a short distance up the road, a few yards from the intersection. He made for it at a dead run.

By now the rifleman had recovered his wits after being startled by the lead flying around him and was ready to get back in the fight. A blast from the rifle sent another bullet whining past Cord's ear. He clenched his teeth, poured speed into his legs, and gained the rear of the wagon before a second shot came.

"Hee-yah!"

The full-throated bellow cut through the echoing gunfire. With a thunder of hooves, Blackstone appeared astride a huge black horse. The big man and even bigger horse barreled down

Main Street with a strangely balletlike grace. Blackstone rose in the stirrups, reins in his left hand and a cocked pistol in his right. He bore down on the first gunman as that varmint rose from cover.

Despite the speed of his approach, Blackstone was confident enough in his marksmanship to hazard a try. His Colt roared, and the gunman's hat flew off. The man's eyes widened as he dove for cover. A few inches lower and Blackstone would have ventilated his skull for him.

Cord took advantage of the respite to reload the Colt, then began sidling his way around the wagon, maneuvering for the edge of the street. Gaining the corner of the box, he peered around, seeking a look at the rifleman.

Who was gone.

The man had moved, Cord thought, as gunfire rose again, much of it aimed at Blackstone. The Englishman thundered past on his horse, laughing and blazing away at the killers with merry abandon.

Blackstone was out of his mind, thought Cord, and was grateful for it.

Blackstone snapped his head around, gathered the reins, and, performing a tight turn, galloped straight back at the hatless man, firing gunshots like there was no tomorrow. The gunman went belly-first on the ground. Blackstone's horse vaulted over his prone form like a steeplechaser. Then Cord heard the rifleman's weapon boom again. The shot went wide, smashing one of the windows in a nearby rooming house.

Cord broke into a dead run, the rifleman in his sights now. He somehow knew this man was the leader of the group—the one calling the shots, so to speak. Cord remembered how he had positioned himself on the balcony during the last gunfight, elevating his view as if to survey and direct what happened below. This was the most dangerous of the bunch. *Anderson.* Cord was determined to stop him.

He aimed and fired at the man, who was still trying to bring down Blackstone.

The shot caught the rifleman off-guard. His head whipped around. Then he was twisting his body to bring the rifle to bear. Cord let him have more lead. His second round whined off the wall near the rifleman's face, causing him to grimace and retreat down another alley.

The pounding hoofbeats from Blackstone's horse filled the air. He had circled around for another attack. The loud boom of his coach gun echoed through the town like the crack of doom.

Their strategy a failure, their ambush in shambles, one of them wounded, the gunmen were eager to just get the hell out of town with their hides intact. As Cord hurried back across the street, he spotted all three of them regrouping at the corner and aiming their weapons at Blackstone, hoping to take him down with one combined volley. Cord wasn't about to let that happen.

He fired the Dragoon at the nearest of the three—a man down on one knee, aiming along the barrel of his pistol. With that weird marksman's intuition that can only be developed with time and practice, Cord knew the moment he squeezed the trigger that he would hit his target.

The bullet struck the gunman in the shoulder, shredding the fabric of his shirt and the skin and bone underneath as well. He went down with a cry of agony. The rifleman swung toward Cord.

And then Blackstone galloped through them. Cord couldn't be sure at this distance, but it appeared the Englishman managed to bump one man with his horse on the way by, for the second man with a pistol stumbled in his efforts to drag his wounded comrade to his feet. The rifleman abandoned his effort to target Cord and started yelling and gesturing toward the livery stable.

They were giving up the fight and trying to escape. But Cord vowed this time they wouldn't succeed.

The three men scrambled through the door of the livery barn, the wounded man being helped along by one of the others. Cord sprinted up to Blackstone as the deputy reloaded the scattergun.

"You get on up the road and block them!" Cord said. "This ends here!"

Blackstone shoved the second cartridge into the coach gun, nodded, and spurred off down the street.

Cord approached the open door of the stable, flattening himself against the wall and edging toward the open doorway. He heard the sound of voices and the jangle of horse tackle inside. They would be mounted soon. Throwing caution to the winds, he leaped for the door but was almost run over by a trio of stampeding horses as they burst out into the street.

The men charged toward Blackstone, galloping like hell for the edge of town. Cord and Blackstone both opened fire again, taking advantage of the distance between them to put the gunmen into a crossfire. Cord could see the rifleman bent forward in the saddle, flattening himself against the horse's neck to reduce his size as a target. The first pistol fighter was right behind him and the second, wounded and barely hanging on, lagged behind.

Cord was aiming his final round when a spray of sparks erupted in the road ahead.

What happened next happened too quickly to absorb all at once. It was only later that Cord would piece together the actual sequence of events.

Blackstone was a shadow looming in the dust kicked up by the horses. And he held something in his fist—a round object attached to a sputtering fuse.

Oh, my God, thought Cord, Blackstone had lit the fuse on a keg of blasting powder!

Boom Boom Blackstone had fallen back on his weapon of choice.

The Englishman waited until the trio sped past him to lob the small keg. It sailed through the air before landing between the hooves of the wounded gunman's horse.

Cord threw himself to the ground as an explosion rocked the town. The blast kicked up dust into the air and shook every window on the street.

Two hours later, Cord sat mounted on a hilltop, surveying Rio Oro in the valley below.

There had been nothing left of the gunman and his horse—just a smoking crater in the center of Main Street. Around it were remnants of clothing and bits of charred horseflesh. Fortunately, no townspeople were injured in the explosion. But effective as the blasting powder had been in reducing one gunman to ash, the other two apparently had escaped.

But he and Blackstone had taken a bite out of them, Cord thought. There was that to consider.

So why did he feel so shaken?

His nerves had taken a pounding since accepting this job. Protecting the good citizens meant facing all manner of dangers, and this was not the first time he had come close to catching a bullet.

But it *was* the first time Glory had been so close to danger. Had Lomax not acted quickly and pulled her inside the church, anything could have happened. She might even have been—

He drew a deep, shuddery breath and fought to control his trembling.

This was his fault.

There was no other way to figure it. He had come out here from the Ozarks with his brothers beside him and Caroline Stockton in his past. And he had dragged that past right up to the door of the church where he was planning to marry Glory.

But now he was having second thoughts.

Did he love Glory? More than his own life, he knew with an

ironclad certainty. But could he live with himself if anything happened to her?

There were risks to marrying a lawman, he realized. He had always known this, and so did Glory. But now the risks had multiplied to the point where they could no longer be ignored.

Maybe he should pack up and head back to the Ozarks, he thought. Confront Hiram Stockton in person and tell him the truth.

But that would take the better part of a year, and there was no guarantee the man would even listen to him. Plus, the town would be left without a marshal. And he could not allow that to happen.

No, this business with Stockton's hired killers would have to play itself out. Cord would have to hunt down the last two and finish them if he and Glory were to have any chance at a life together.

A burning resolve filled him.

He would find these men and rid the Earth of them. He knew there was no other way. It was not the way he wanted things to be. But it was the way things were.

It was kill or be killed.

BOOK II

Chapter 21

In the hilly wilderness east of Rio Oro, two men in black dusters crouched by a cooking fire.

To any casual observer, they appeared to be nothing more than two pilgrims on their way to or returning home from somewhere. With their frying pan and stacked saddlebags, home-rolled cigarettes, and unsaddled horses grazing contentedly at the edge of the firelight, they looked for all the world like simple travelers on the open range.

Only closer examination of their weapons—the gleaming, freshly oiled sidearms and rifles and the wear on their holsters—hinted at the true nature of their vocation. Anyone observing from a distance who cared to linger long enough would note their unnatural stillness and silence. These were men accustomed to moving unobtrusively, making little noise, and leaving no trace of their passage.

At length, one spoke as the dark night pressed in around them like fog.

"Shame about Bill," he said quietly.

"He knew the risks," came the reply from the second, older man.

"Still," said the first man. "Hell of a way to go. Blown to smithereens. Wonder what that feels like."

"Not too good, I reckon." The older man, name of Anderson, had set down his coffee and taken up his rifle, passing a rag along its oiled barrel. He did this meditatively, the weapon being an extension of himself. Anderson, like his dead friend Bill and his present companion, Leamas, had served in the Mexican-American War. Killing suited them well enough to make a career of it.

"Ain't never seen no lawman use blasting powder before," Leamas admitted. "They allowed to do that?"

"Well, who's going to tell them they can't?"

"Reckon you're right." Leamas sipped at his coffee. "Still. A damn shame about Bill."

Silence returned for a while. A few minutes passed like that. Then Leamas spoke again.

"He have any kin?"

"Who?"

"Why, Bill of course!"

"No idea." Anderson shrugged. "Doubt it."

"Why?"

"You got any?"

"No!"

"Me neither." Anderson shrugged. "Our line of work don't lend itself to family life, if you catch my meaning."

"Reckon so." Leamas sighed, pitched out the dregs of his coffee, and rinsed his tin mug with water from a canteen. "But that marshal is going to be a tough nut to crack. Hell, we already tried for him twice and missed. Second time, we lost a man!"

"That'll be the last man we lose."

"You figure?" Leamas was sounding testy. "You don't seem too bothered about it."

"I ain't." Anderson spat. "Bill knew the risks. Same as you or me. He came and he died. Damn shame, but there's an upside. Reward money gets split two ways, now. Not three. So, there's that."

"You're a cold son of a gun, Gordon."

"Reckon you're right."

The silence returned. The fire crackled. The wind moaned thinly in the deepening night.

"So how are we gonna do it?"

"We can't take 'em in a stand-up fight," Anderson admitted. "We've tried ambushing him twice, and both times he beat us back. Second time, he killed one of us, or his deputy did, anyway. No, this marshal's a dangerous one. We're gonna have to get sneaky. Creative."

"I reckon sneaky is about the size of it."

"He sleeps in a loft above the marshal's office," Anderson said. "We could wait until late one night when his partner is off somewhere and just set fire to the building. Lay for him outside in case he escapes."

"Just shoot him down as he runs from the fire?"

"Reckon so."

"That's a low-down, dirty plot if ever I heard one, Gordon."

"Sometimes low-down and dirty is what gets the job done."

"Reckon you're right."

"I know I am."

Gordon Anderson was no stranger to low-down and dirty tactics. He had used plenty of them in the war against the Mexicans. To Anderson, killing was just killing. Blasting a rattlesnake to bits was no different than killing a man. He viewed the world in very simple terms. Some things were living. Others were dead. Anderson and his gang made their money moving people from one state to the next. Easy as moving numbers in a ledger from one column to the other.

But this job was proving difficult. They had been told that Cord Bennett was a mere farmer—a simple hayseed who could be easily dispatched. As such, the price Stockton had offered to pay for proof of Cord's death had seemed outlandish.

Not so now. The simple hayseed had been transformed into the town marshal. His skills with a gun suggested he had managed to gain a great deal of experience during his tenure in office, too.

And that other one—the man with the blasting powder. Anderson was nursing a special hatred for him.

He would kill them both.

Leamas, sitting quietly with his coffee, suddenly grew still. Anderson stopped breathing, narrowing his eyes and squinting in the direction his partner was looking.

"What?" he whispered

"We ain't alone, Gordon." Leamas breathed these words as he raised his pistol. He jerked his chin out into the blackness.

Anderson closed his eyes. There it was—that sense that they were being watched. It was a feeling Anderson had come to know well during his time on the blood trail. Now the feeling was backed up by a sound—the scuff of boots on rocks. A fall of pebbles. Then the shifting of a body somewhere out there in the night.

Leamas stood suddenly, gun arm outstretched, as his nerve cracked. Anderson knew he might as well stand up too. No point anymore in pretending they hadn't heard anything.

"Who's there?" demanded Anderson with as much authority as he could muster as he tracked his revolver from side to side. "Show yourself or you're a dead man!"

Again, the shifting of footsteps on stone. The silhouette of a man appeared out of the darkness, approaching the fire.

Jeremiah Ponder stepped carefully along the rocky ground, his hands held out from his sides, palms visible. He owned a pistol but never carried it because he had no desire to be shot in "self-defense" while armed. So, he moved, unarmed and cautious. As he edged toward the gunmen's cookfire, Ponder began to seriously consider the possibility that he had lost his mind.

Cutting a deal with a woman like Dollie Whittaker was dangerous—like trying to shake hands with a rattlesnake. Ponder was under no illusions about his new ally. He was running a huge risk associating with her, sensing that she could turn on him at any time.

But along with the imperative to protect himself was another more urgent one: to demonstrate that Dollie Whittaker's trust in him was not misplaced. Their partnership required him to bring something to the table. It was for this reason that he had taken the risk of following the outlaws out of town.

He fully emerged now into the light of their fire, hands raised, round glasses reflecting the flames, a sheepish look on his sweaty face.

"Hold it right there," snarled the man who looked to be the older of the two. "Who the hell are you and what do you want?"

"N-Name's J-Jeremiah Ponder," he stuttered, annoyed that he sounded like Hap. But he was terrified. He cleared his throat and did his best not to show it. "I own the lumber mill in Rio Oro. I've come with a business proposal."

At this, both men exploded in laughter.

"A *business* proposal? Y'hear that, Joe?" the older one asked. "This fella wants to proposition us."

"Sounds kinda dirty," sneered the other man.

"I'll say. Go on over there and give our new friend Mr. Ponder an inspection."

The one called Joe sprang up and scuttled over to Ponder. The lumberman lifted his arms, and Joe ran his hands over the man's jacket and waist. For good measure, he dug into Ponder's pockets and removed his wallet and pocket watch. He began riffling through the money in the wallet.

"So, you have a business proposition, eh?" The older man

crossed his arms. "I should tell you right now, Mr. Ponder, that I have no interest whatsoever in the lumber business."

"Well, that's a good thing," exclaimed Ponder. "Because I don't need the competition." He managed a thin chuckle. "No, fellas, I'm not interested in taking you on as partners in the mill. But I do have a problem that could be solved with the help of, ah, professional gunmen."

"And what problem is that?" Joe emptied Ponder's wallet and tossed it back at his feet. He handed the pocket watch to his companion, who opened and studied its face disinterestedly as Ponder continued.

"My mill employs a number of men in the town. We do good work. And we've done good business so far! But there's a movement of sorts among the miners. They're pushing me to compromise my product and lower my prices."

"How are they doing this?" the older man asked. He dropped Ponder's watch into a vest pocket.

"They show up at the mill. Big groups of them. Stand at the gate. Fuss and complain. Block my men from coming to work some days! There have been confrontations in town. Fistfights. It's bad enough now that the miners and the lumbermen drink in separate saloons!"

Both gunmen listened with grave attention.

"This sort of thing can't be allowed to continue," Ponder said, winding up his pitch. "It's bad for business, to say nothing of our civic life in town."

"Why don't you ask the town marshal to do something about it?"

"The marshal?" Ponder spat. "Well, he's useless. Him and his great, big British deputy, Blackstone. Worthless as rotted apple cores, the both of them! I have no use for the law as it currently stands in Rio Oro. In fact, I'd like nothing more than to see them replaced."

"We might be able to help you with that."

"Well, that would just be gravy to an already welcome partnership." Ponder spread his hands, his smile now genuine. Now more relaxed, he continued, "I'm thinking the miners need to be warned off from interfering with the mill and its operations."

"You mean you need some enforcing done. You need someone who can protect your interests."

"Exactly!"

"It just so happens we need somebody who can help us achieve our aims." The man smiled, but it wasn't a friendly expression. "And you, Mr. Ponder, may be just the man."

"Is that right? Why, I'd be happy to help!"

"Happy to help. Hmm." The man shot a sidelong glance at his companion. "Well, there's nothing we like more than a helpful partner. Isn't that right, Joe?"

"A man can use all the help he can get," Joe affirmed. With a big grin, he let out the ugliest laugh Ponder had ever heard.

An hour later, Ponder guided his horse to the main road and began picking his way back to town in the darkness.

He was trembling.

He had not expected Anderson—that was the older killer's name, Gordon Anderson—to make the request that he had. It was far beyond anything shady that Jeremiah Ponder had ever done before. In the past, he had cheated the occasional employee, billed the odd client too much, bilked a business partner here and there. But the level of deception and skullduggery that would be needed to give the gunmen what they wanted was of an entirely different order.

He was no con man, Ponder thought. And he was certainly no

gunfighter. No, sir! But he might have to be both to ensure that this plan worked.

He drew his horse to a halt and sat breathing heavily on the dark, deserted road.

He knew that success required sacrifice. He knew it also involved cutting corners here and there. A man who could do something with the right hand while ignoring the actions of his left had an advantage over the competition. This meant sometimes turning a blind eye to one's own wrongdoings. Could he do so now?

He had no choice, Ponder realized. Because if he didn't, he was fairly sure Anderson would kill *him*.

He swallowed hard and urged his horse toward the lights of town.

CHAPTER 22

Although their hands were full riding herd on the town, Cord and Blackstone had arranged their schedules so that they could each take the odd day off now and then. Clyde Casterline had provided backup for Cord before Blackstone's arrival, and he could occasionally be induced to close his claims office and help out whoever was left holding the duty.

On the morning of his next free day, Cord waved goodbye to Casterline and Blackstone as they sat drinking coffee outside the marshal's office door and turned his horse toward Ghost Canyon. He intended to get some work done on the cabin today.

He passed out of the sleeping town and started up the river with his head full of thoughts. Since the shoot-out at the church, he had seen Glory just once, and then only in passing. Everything had seemed normal when they spoke, but Cord could not shake a sense of guilt for endangering her. It was a notion that had been tormenting him since that day.

They would have to talk. Puzzle this out together. Because married folks were supposed to trust each other and work as a team.

He passed through the newest claims and turned into Ghost Canyon, following the river tributary into the lee of the sheltered valley. It was with a sense of relief that he drew on the reins and dismounted, removing his hat and jacket and addressing himself to the pile of lumber and rack of tools he had left there. After a review of the tasks to be completed, he took a swallow from his canteen and set to work.

He had always enjoyed building and repairing things. Back on the farm, his brothers had always grumbled when the time came to patch the barn or mend a fence, but Cord never complained. He felt at home with a hammer in hand. He focused on completing the rear wall of the place before taking a break and helping himself to some of the food he'd packed in a saddlebag. Sitting by the river, he enjoyed some bread and cold meat washed down by water from a freshly filled canteen.

He was up on the roof when the wagon came up the path, pulled by two horses. Abraham Olmsted managed the reins, his two daughters beside him on the seat. Glory grinned and waved as they drew to a halt in the front yard. Cord wiped sweat from his face with a rag and clambered down to greet them.

"Hello, Cord!" Glory climbed down from the wagon and hurried to him, wrapping her arms around his waist in a fierce hug.

"Hello, sweetheart." Pressing himself against her, he noted the look on Abraham's face. There was something bothering the old man, and Cord had a good sense of what it might be.

"We came to lend a hand," Abraham said quietly. "And have a talk."

"I'm grateful for the help," Cord replied. "And the talk. What's on your mind?"

Abraham hesitated and turned to Kat, who was unloading a hamper and a cookpot from the wagon.

"We brought dinner fixings," she said, her tone a tad cold to

Cord's liking. "Why don't you and Pa finish up your day's work on the cabin and we'll talk about it over a meal?"

Cord nodded. "Sure thing," he said, keeping his voice neutral. After a quick huddle with Abraham, the two men set to work finishing up the doorframe.

"It's the shoot-out," Glory whispered to him when they caught a moment together alone. "They've been at sixes and sevens over it."

"I've been at sixes and sevens over it myself," Cord admitted.

"Cord." She grasped his sleeve as he turned to go. With a fierceness he had never seen before, she said in a fiery whisper, "It makes no difference. I'm still marrying you, mister!"

"Glad to hear it." Efforts to keep his answering smile casual could not hide the relief he felt at these words.

Work on the frame went smoothly. To Cord's surprise, they were able to hang the door at sundown. Despite the tense atmosphere of their gathering, all were enthusiastic when Cord suggested they eat their meal indoors.

"Might as well christen the place," he said. "Seems fitting for us to do it all together as a family."

He noted how Kat and Abraham exchanged a look at that. A sense of foreboding filled him.

They improvised a table with a couple of sawhorses and some boards. Kat and Glory served up a fine mess of beans and fresh-baked biscuits. They gathered around, seated on whatever they could rustle up: a bale of straw, two stumps from the firepit, and the one chair for Abraham. Cord and Abraham took off their hats as they all bent their heads for grace.

"Lord, we give thanks for this meal and this fellowship," Abraham intoned. "And we give thanks for the refuge of family and friends in this dangerous time. Amen."

An uncomfortable silence settled. Cord flashed a smile at Glory as he reached for a biscuit.

He was going to let Abraham start this talk. If there were uncomfortable things that needed airing, he was of a mind to let someone else go first.

"How are you, Cord?" asked the old man.

"Good, thanks." Cord broke a biscuit in half and studied its rich, soft interior, still steaming from the pan. "Things are going well in town. Blackstone and I have it all in hand."

"Do you, Cord?" Kat's question was pointed and came out sounding shriller than she likely intended. "After what happened the other day?"

Cord bit back his initial reaction to this, which was one of annoyance. Kat couldn't possibly understand the pressures under which men like he and Blackstone operated. If a miner made a mistake on the job, he might lose time or money. If a marshal made a mistake, people could lose their lives. That knowledge, combined with the impossibility of predicting who might show up in town, made for a difficult job. He and Blackstone did their best, but people only seemed to take notice of them when things went wrong.

"You have every right to be concerned," he replied evenly. "Glory and Reverend Lomax were placed in danger. They could have been killed."

"Because of you," Kat said. "Because of the vendetta that man Stockton has against you."

"Yes, I could have been killed," Glory admitted. She seized Cord's hand. "But I wasn't."

"Glory," Abraham said gently. "You've got to understand, honey. It likely won't be the last time something like this happens."

"How many enemies do you think you make in a month, Cord?" Kat softened her tone, but her words were still cutting. "It's not you. We know you're a good man. But this job of yours . . . You put yourself in harm's way, dealing with dangerous men—men who hold a grudge. What happens the next time Glory is in their way, too, and you're not there to protect her?"

"I won't allow that to happen," Cord affirmed.

"Cord." Abraham cleared his throat. "You ever think of maybe taking off your marshal's badge and just working your claim? It's paying out well! You and Glory would make a comfortable living and you'd be, well, safe."

"You have to think about your family, Cord," said Kat. "You have to think about the future."

Cord sighed. He heard them loud and clear. What was more, he could feel the deep concern underlying their words. He had to admit—they had a point. He had once viewed the world in much the same way they did. But being the marshal had changed him.

"I never expected to become town marshal," he admitted. "When this job came up, I wasn't sure I had what it took to do it. Heck, I wasn't sure Rio Oro even *needed* a marshal. But I don't see it that way now. Not by a long shot."

"Well, then, how do you see it?" Abraham's question floated in the air like an accusation. Cord took his time answering.

"I used to take things like law and order for granted," he said. "Never gave much thought to what it takes to keep the streets safe, or people's property protected. Just took it on faith that those things would always be there. Never considered what it took to provide it."

Abraham and Kat had fallen silent. They were all watching him now.

"Safety is like freedom," he continued. "It's not free. A few generations back, our ancestors had to fight the British. That's what it took to make us free. Lots of good men died in that effort. Hopefully, we won't ever see a war like that again."

"Hopefully," whispered Glory, a shine of pride in her eyes as she listened to him talk. That pride urged him on.

"Amen," Cord agreed. "Thing is, most people don't realize that there is a kind of war happening every day, all around us."

"What war?" Kat asked.

"Not sure how to put this, but . . ." Cord frowned. He chose his words carefully, not wanting to be misunderstood. "People labor for their daily bread. Work for wages, cultivate their crops, ply their trade, whatever it takes. And it's hard. Getting up every day and doing the right thing just to survive takes gumption. So, I suppose that's one side in this war."

"And the other?" Kat's question contained a note of impatience.

"Well, people like the ones who attacked us at the church," Cord answered. "People like the ones who'd rob you in the street or who break into our homes and businesses to steal our property. They're the other side."

"But surely they're rare," Kat objected. "I mean, most folks—"

"Most folks have no idea," Cord said flatly. "They have no idea what it takes to keep criminals in check. What do you imagine would happen to this town if there was no marshal? Wouldn't take long for lawlessness to rule over everyone. That's a tyranny no different from old King George. Because without someone to control criminal behavior, criminals quickly get out of hand. And all that hard work you put into earning your daily bread counts for nothing because they can just take it on a whim."

Everyone at the table was surprised. None had ever heard Cord speak this way before.

"You challenged me to think about the future, Kat. And I am." Cord put his hand on Glory's. "This town deserves a future. And our children deserve a future. That won't be possible without law and order. And securing that takes sacrifice."

"Not many people are willing to make that sacrifice, Cord," Abraham said quietly.

"I know." Cord nodded. "But I am."

An hour later, Cord and Glory stood together outside the cabin door as Abraham and Kat waited in the wagon.

"Your kin don't seem too happy with me being marshal," he said quietly. He stared hard at the ground before raising his eyes to meet hers. "I would understand if you—"

"Cord. Shh." She placed a finger on his lips. "I've never been prouder of you than I am tonight."

A deep joy surged within him at these words.

"You're right," she said simply. "Without the work you do, this town—our family—have no future. You're ready to make the sacrifice, Cord, and so am I. No matter what it takes."

He stood speechless, moved by her courage.

"I'm going to marry you and have children with you. We'll make a life as a family and you'll do your work. And I'll support you every step of the way."

CHAPTER 23

The miners assembled before the lumberyard gates at dawn. Ponder worked his employees in shifts. During busy months, he added late and early rotations to the schedule. The completion of the church, renovations to the Bear Flag, and a new construction project in the Chinese section ensured plenty of contracts, so lumbermen were working late into the evening, departing the yard just as the saloons declared last call.

So, too, were lumbermen seen arriving in the early morning, straggling in from boarding rooms and shared housing, yawning and wiping sleep from their eyes as they made their way up the street. A passel of them came now, foot-dragging their way past the land claims office, shoulders hunched against the predawn chill. One looked up and noticed the miners blocking the gate.

"What's that all about?" he asked.

"No idea," replied one of his companions.

Both men had seen miners attempt to disrupt mill operations in the past and so agreed that discretion was the better part of valor. They would wait until more of their fellows arrived before daring the gate. They withdrew into the shadow of the livery stable and waited.

Slowly, in twos and threes, other lumbermen approached. Seeing their fellows sheltering in the lee of the stable, they joined them, swelling their numbers. As the hostler appeared and opened the main door, the crowd of lumbermen grew until it was almost as many as the number of miners. At length, Hansen, the yard foreman, approached the miners.

"What's going on here?" he demanded. "What are you men doing blocking the gate? I've got people who need to get to work."

"You've got a lot more than that!" snarled an angry man in a bowler hat who Hansen recognized as Bowles. "You got a heap of trouble coming your way!"

Hansen stood tall, his chin jutting out defiantly, and answered Bowles, "Is that right? Well! We'll see about that!"

He spun on his heel and stalked across the street to the stable.

"What are you men doing?" he demanded as he confronted the mill workers. Jabbing a finger at the yard across the street, he added, "There are boards to be cut over there."

Muttering and much shuffling of feet came from the lumbermen. They were angry at the miners for causing trouble, but it was mighty early in the morning for a ruckus. Nobody moved despite the scowl on Hansen's face.

The tension just grew worse as the sky lightened overhead. The sun rose on the two groups glaring at each other from across the street. Muttering, contemptuous spitting, and obscene gestures escalated to taunts and, eventually, shouts. Two men, one from each side, broke from their respective groups and took a few hesitant steps toward each other. They paused about twenty yards apart, yelling and shaking their fists. One of the lumbermen, upset at being denied entry to work, bent and picked up a stone.

"Don't you dare!" yelled Bowles, who was one of the men who'd ventured out from the crowd of miners.

The lumberman hauled back his arm and threw. The rock missed, sailing harmlessly past Bowles to bounce on the ground, but that didn't matter because the mere fact that it was thrown was enough of a spark to ignite both mobs.

They lunged toward each other with shouts of rage, fists and cudgels swinging, to collide in the middle of the street. The driver of an early morning delivery wagon drew to a swift halt and leaped down from the driver's box, grasping the reins of his horse and guiding it away, barely reaching the stable before violence swamped the street.

The chaos broke into individual melees of miners versus lumbermen. Fists and curses flew as blows were struck and punches landed. The angry, bloody pandemonium surged one way and then the other. Hats were knocked off and noses bloodied. Bowles and Hansen, locked in a clinch, twisted around in a circle, throwing clumsy punches at short range. Hansen had just gained the upper hand when gunfire erupted.

Watching all this from his refuge behind a post, Hap quaked in fear. Accustomed to the ridicule of other men, he tended to avoid the townspeople for the most part, but the scene he was witnessing impelled him into action. When a clearing appeared in the melee, he dashed between clots of paired fighters and up the stairs of the marshal's office. Blackstone was already knocking on Cord's door when he arrived.

"Hap!" Blackstone turned. "What—?"

That's when they heard the gunfire.

Cord pulled open the door, his boots already on, his hat in hand. "What's all the commotion out here?" he demanded.

"There's a bloody riot at the mill! And now—" Blackstone paused as more gunfire sounded. "There's shooting!"

"Hap, you stay clear!" snapped Cord. He and Blackstone pounded down the stairs.

They arrived at street level to see the mobs dispersing in a panic, fleeing to the edges of the street. Cord absorbed it all in a blur of impressions: the thunder of gunshots, the surge of rioters in the haste to gain cover, three—no, four—bodies lying in the street.

Then the guns fell silent, the dust settled, and calm returned to Rio Oro—an eerie calm, as if nothing had happened. Still, Cord and Blackstone drew their weapons and stood back-to-back, scanning the surrounding buildings for any sign of a continued threat.

"Shooting's stopped," Cord said.

"What a damned bloody mess," Blackstone said.

Cautiously, Hansen limped out of the stable doorway. He had a black eye and a split lip and was holding a bloodied bandanna to his forehead as he approached.

"Those damn miners!" he shouted. "They were waiting for my men at the mill yard gates! Ambushed them as they were coming into work!"

"Any of them bring guns?" Cord frowned as he knelt beside the body of a miner. The man was dead, no doubt about it.

"I didn't see any guns," Hansen admitted.

"This one's a miner too," said Blackstone, kneeling alongside the body closest to Cord's. Cord looked over, nodded, scanning the other two.

He caught his breath, his jaw tightening at what he saw.

The next body sprawled beside a bowler hat that lay partially crushed in the dirt.

"Bowles," Cord said. He sat back on his haunches and, just to be sure, gazed at the fourth body for a moment. "All miners. All shot."

"Precision shooting." Blackstone breathed the words where he knelt beside one of the dead, examining the bullet hole at the center of the man's forehead. "See here? And there." He pointed. "Only miners. And all shot in the head. This is the work of a professional."

"Or *professionals,* plural." Cord's lips thinned in frustration.

"You're thinking of the men in the black dusters?"

"They may be nearby somewhere." Cord stood up and cast around, turning in a complete circle to study every doorway and window in the vicinity. Seeing no trace of the killers, he turned back to Blackstone.

"Let's split up and search. See what we can find."

Blackstone checked the row of buildings along the same side of the street as the marshal's office while Cord took the other side. The search they carried out over the next half hour failed to yield any results.

Cord figured whoever had done the shooting was long gone by now, so he went back to the site of the riot, where Blackstone was waiting to report his own lack of success. Cord saw Hap helping Forbes, the town undertaker, wrap the dead in canvas.

The gate to the lumberyard stood open and the day's work was underway. As Cord noticed this, he saw Hansen step out and approach them.

"I wonder what he wants," Blackstone grunted.

"Likely won't be anything good," Cord said.

Hansen pulled up in front of Cord, sweaty and out of breath. He said, "Mr. Ponder thinks he has some idea of who might have done this."

"The shooting, you mean?"

"Of course."

"And who might that be?"

Cord tried to sound interested, but he still had a foul taste in his mouth from when Ponder had detained Hap based on nothing more than a hunch.

"Honestly, I don't know," Hansen said. "He wants to talk to you about it. Only you."

"I see." Cord's tone was skeptical.

Hansen seemed to read his meaning. "Listen, Marshal, I understand that him accusing Hap that last time was just plumb stupid.

But Mr. Ponder seems right agitated about this idea he's got. He genuinely believes he's got some valuable information for you."

Cord held up a hand. "All right. I'll go listen."

"Much obliged."

Leaving Blackstone to mop up, Cord followed Hanson through the office door and down the hall to the room where Ponder kept his huge desk. He sat up straighter when Cord came in.

"What's this Hansen is saying that you may have a lead on the gunman from this morning?"

"I may, actually." Ponder flicked a nervous gaze at Hansen. "That'll be all, thank you, Charlie. The marshal and I are going to have a word in private now."

"Sure thing, Mr. Ponder."

Hansen stepped from the room, pulling the door closed behind him. Cord waited until he heard footsteps fade down the hall before turning to Ponder.

"Well? What do you have for me, Mr. Ponder? I've got killers to catch."

"I understand, Marshal. It's complicated."

"I have time."

"All right." Ponder exhaled. "It's like this. Last December, at a gathering over in Wakefield, I bumped into William Argyle. He has a ranch, you know, a spread he bought from one of those old Californio families who got it originally in a land grant from the king of Spain."

Cord shook his head, tamping down the impatience he felt welling up inside him. "Don't reckon I know the man."

"He almost never leaves his ranch," Ponder went on. "The thing about Argyle is how he keeps his eye on the frontier. He's from Texas, came out here after the war with Mexico, and is interested in raising cattle, not mining. So he ranges over quite a bit of territory and knows when any strangers pass through his ranch."

"What does that have to do with what happened this morning?"

"I'm coming to that." Ponder's facial expression was briefly irritated. He didn't like being interrupted, even though he was taking forever to explain what he knew. "Like I said, it's complicated. Anyway, he told me he'd run across some men last winter passing near his ranch. Argyle confronted them, of course, but there was no trouble because he had several of his vaqueros with him. The strangers admitted that their profession was that of professional gunmen."

Now Ponder had Cord's attention. "Go on," he said.

"Argyle said these men wore black dusters. Three of them. Black hats, black dusters. Said they were returning from a mining town that needed some simmering down. They went in, laid down the law of the gun, and now were on their way back East."

That didn't quite jibe with what Cord knew about Gordon Anderson and his two companions, but the description sure as blazes matched.

"Well, Argyle told me that story over a whiskey in the saloon where we ran into each other, and I filed it away in my memory and forgot about it completely. Until the other day, when Moses Avery came through town."

"I saw him myself but didn't talk to him," Cord said. Avery was a traveling attorney-at-law, a hard-bitten but scrupulously fair man who drove a special box wagon fitted out with all manner of official papers and seals and legal reference books crammed into a small office on wheels. Avery went from place to place, offering basic legal services for a reasonable fee. His main stock in trade was land deeds, of which there were many to be documented in the growing state of California.

"Avery usually makes a point of stopping by," Ponder said. "I always have a contract or two I need drawn up, and I'd just as soon he'd do it. I've been using Avery's services for quite a while now. He's more of a friend than a lawyer. Had dinner with me. Mentioned he did some business at a stagecoach station east of here.

One of the passengers on a westbound coach that was stopped wanted a will drawn up, so Avery handled that while he was there. He said he saw three men in black hats and black dusters getting into that stagecoach when it departed."

Cord nodded slowly. This part of the story fit in better with what he knew about the situation regarding Anderson and the other two gun wolves.

"Those men are somewhere in this region, and I think I may have an idea where they're holed up too," Ponder said. "It's near here. How much do you want to bet they had something to do with the deaths of those miners?" Ponder huffed in outrage. "It was ruthless, efficient butchery so far as I could tell. Looked like the work of professional gunmen. I'd lay money it was them."

Cord couldn't disagree with the conclusion Ponder had drawn, even though it had taken a long time to get there.

"So where is it you think they're holed up?" he asked bluntly.

"Moses Avery said the men in black were in the company of Paul Errins."

Cord recognized the name. Errins, like many another man, had come to California intending to find a fortune in gold, only to fail in that. But he was an excellent hunter and had carved out a place for himself as a supplier of fresh meat to the butchers in the mining camps scattered through the hills. Cord knew the man by sight but had never had any dealings with him.

"I know where his cabin is," Ponder said. "They must be hiding out with him. I mean, why else would they be seen in Errins's company?"

"And you say you know how to get there?"

"I do. Are you going after them, Marshal?"

"If the two who were left alive after that last trouble were responsible for what happened here this morning, they have to be brought to justice," Cord said.

"I'm very happy to hear that, Marshal," Ponder said with a smile. "Very happy indeed."

Cord wondered briefly why it mattered so much to Ponder. After all, it had been miners who were gunned down, not lumber mill workers.

Maybe the man just didn't like seeing murder being carried out on the streets of Rio Oro.

Cord didn't care, because apprehending—or killing—Gordon Anderson and the other gunman would take care of the threat to Cord's life, as well, and ease the minds of Glory and Kat and old Abraham Olmsted.

He leaned forward, rested his hands on the front edge of Ponder's desk, and said, "Tell me where I can find them."

CHAPTER 24

Dollie Whittaker stared through the main window of the Bear Flag Saloon at the Golden Nugget across the street.

Harville had served his purpose. Having afforded her a foothold from which to step up to greater and better things, he was now a liability—someone with whom she had been intimate. For this reason, he had to be destroyed. But destroyed in such a way that his business and assets were kept intact so she could claim them for her own.

She had plans.

"You've spoken to your men?" she asked, without turning from the window.

"I have," said Hansen.

"And they're on board?"

"They're willing to do it," Hansen replied. "You ready to hold up your end?"

"Of course."

"All right." Hansen jammed his hat on his head. "We'll get right to it, then."

He left through the batwing doors of the Bear Flag and headed up the street to the lumber mill.

The quitting bell sounded and the mill gates opened. The afternoon shift of lumbermen poured through the opening, a gaggle of movement and voices and lazy jostling as they left work for the day in search of diversion.

Hansen and Fillmore, one of the senior lumbermen, broke from the crowd and began leading them surreptitiously in the direction of town. The main body of lumbermen followed, straggling in staggered groups so as not to be too obvious. But as Hansen and Fillmore reached the Golden Nugget and turned to go inside, the majority of lumbermen followed.

It was a solid chunk of men that swelled in through the entrance to occupy the place. Within moments, the majority of tables were occupied and a line of timbermen had occupied the bar rail. It was early enough that only a handful of miners were in the place. Seeing they were outnumbered and weren't even supposed to be there in the first place, they withdrew toward the rear tables, keeping a cautious eye on the mill workers as they sat, careful to be within easy reach of the door.

The piano player came in and sat down, pushing back the cover and taking an experimental stab at the keys. Notes tinkled as the bar girls moved between tables, setting down pitchers of beer, bottles of whiskey, and glasses. They just got the first round served when all hell broke loose.

It started with a whoop. Then someone grabbed one of the girls and dragged her down onto his lap. A cackle of laughter rose as a man stepped over to the piano player, snatched his hat from his head, and poured it full of beer before slapping it back on, soaking him in a cascade of warm suds.

A thrown bottle smashed against the back wall and a riot started.

* * *

When Harville arrived later, summoned from his home by a frantic barman who ran all the way there with a dishtowel still crammed in his belt, the sight inside his own business appalled him.

The main room looked like a hurricane had blown through it. The front window, smashed entirely in places, was a network of cracks and punctures. The walls were a spiderweb of fractures. The dance floor was awash with spilled beer and broken glass. Smoke still hung in the air, a pall of it dwindling out through the open rear door that had been propped open by one of the bar girls. Harville stepped over to the origin of the smoke, the charred wreckage of the piano that someone had doused in kerosene and touched a match to.

The paintings above the bar were blotched with splashes where hurled drinks had exploded.

The bottles on the back shelf were mostly gone or smashed.

The whole thing was a dead loss.

"Boss?"

Harville looked up and recognized Jim, one of his bartenders. Jim's left arm was in a sling, and he sported a black eye the size of a ripe apple.

"What the hell happened here?" demanded Harville. "And why didn't you stop it, Jim?"

"We tried, Mr. Harville. But there were just too damn many of them."

"Just too damn many of *who*?"

Jim told him.

Harville's next steps were taken carefully and with much attention to detail.

First, he had the smashed section of the front window boarded up. Then he directed the bar girls and his men to clear out the main barroom. The glass was swept up and the floor mopped to remove every trace of spilled liquor. Then the furniture was inventoried.

Less than half was usable. The rest was taken out back for repair or final disposal. Harville visited the town rooming houses, restaurants, and public buildings, hat in hand, and managed to scrape together a decent number of chairs on loan until his furniture could be replaced. He sent out his men with a wagon to collect and transport the borrowed chairs to the Nugget.

The smashed bottles were a dead loss, but there remained enough liquor for the saloon to limp through another night or two of commerce. Fortunately, there were plenty of barrels of beer in storage. Harville had these rolled out and tapped, ready for the evening rush.

By the time the miners began straggling in for their nightly revelry, the place resembled something like the establishment it had once been. A few tapped barrels had been left on the bar top as a distraction, hiding the damage and lost bottles and providing a space to hang a hand-lettered sign:

WANT TO MAKE SOME EXTRA CASH?

The sign occasioned some notice, as well as lively discussion, among the cash-strapped miners. As the beer was poured, men began questioning how that extra money might be made. Speculation abounded. Perhaps Harville was looking to hire bartenders? Enforcers? The talk was spirited but inconclusive.

Kat Olmsted arrived in the midst of this ferment, slipping into the Nugget unobtrusively and lingering by the wall near the batwing doors to observe. She had been meaning to call on Harville for some time, both to catch up with her former business rival and get a sense of how things lay between him and the Bear Flag just now. She noticed the absence of furniture and bottles behind the bar, the hastily rearranged feel of the place, and the charred space on the wall where the piano had stood. To her mind, it seemed obvious what had transpired here.

She would bet money Dollie Whittaker was behind the destruction. Her anger at the newcomer over the tussle with her sister grew even stronger at this latest realization. Hurting Glory, and now attacking the Golden Nugget . . .

Dollie Whittaker was a lawless woman who respected no authority but her own. Now she had the financial and political clout of the Bear Flag at her disposal. The amount of havoc she could wreak in town from such a perch was massive.

Teddy Harville appeared, entering the saloon through one of the rear doors. His normally flashy attire was more subdued this evening. His arrival brought cries of welcome. He waved to the assembled miners before drawing off a schooner of beer for himself and climbing atop the bar.

Well, thought Kat. *This should be interesting.*

"Friends! Patrons! Fellow citizens!" Harville hoisted his glass of beer on high. "As you can see, we've been through some changes recently here at the Golden Nugget! But what hasn't changed is my gratitude to *you*—the hardworking miners and prospectors who've come out to the frontier in search of your fortune! You are the heart and soul—the *lifeblood*—of this saloon! And for that, I lift my glass to you in gratitude!"

Cheers arose in the glow of a newfound camaraderie as the men drank. Here was Harville, welcoming them as if into his own home, knitting them together as a group. For men who had forsaken their families to come out to the frontier, his words had a uniquely warming quality to them.

"Friends, I won't lie to you." Harville's change in tone riveted the assembled customers to silence. He drew out the moment as long as he could before continuing. "I've been here in Rio Oro since the earliest days. I've seen a great deal of change. Many folks have come and gone, and the town remains—for the most part—

better for their contributions. But the shape and future of this town rely on us. If we don't protect it, what will become of our home?"

An undercurrent of troubled muttering filled the room.

"We suffered a blow today," he told them. "A blow from a sinister new element in our midst. I don't have to tell you that the trouble between you miners and Ponder's lumber mill has been unsettling. But now that conflict has extended to engulf other businesses. Today, men from the Bear Flag Saloon came over here and deliberately destroyed the sanctuary I have tried to provide for you."

Kat turned and left, moving fast.

She stumbled onto the wooden walkway, almost losing her footing before crossing to the edge and leaping down into the street. She could no longer hear Harville's rant, but a cheer rose among the assembled miners. To her mind, it boded no good for the Bear Flag—or anyone. He was trying to incite a riot!

She bent her steps toward the marshal's office, where a single light burned in the window. She moved as fast as she could, willing herself to run faster, willing the office door closer until she reached it. Skidding to a stop, she pounded on it several times before twisting the knob and crossing the threshold.

"Deputy Blackstone! You'd best come quickly!"

Blackstone looked up from where he sat at the desk, poring over paperwork, blinking at her over the top of the quaint hexagonal bifocals he used for close work. He drew a ponderous sigh before fetching them off his face.

"Miss Kat!" he exclaimed. "What on Earth—?"

Teddy Harville was pleased with himself. He had whipped his patrons, most of whom had downed several drinks, into a frenzy of anger and resentment. All that was left was to unleash them on the enemy.

He bought them all one last round on the house, made a few more incendiary remarks, and then casually suggested they pay a visit to the saloon across the street. This suggestion was greeted by whoops of agreement. Clenched fists shot into the air, the final swallows of beer were downed, and mugs thumped decisively on tabletops.

The miners made for the door. Much to their surprise and delight, they discovered a pile of rocks and short wooden planks just outside. Without bothering to ask how they had ended up there, the miners helped themselves to the makeshift weapons before turning their attention toward the Bear Flag and surging into the street.

Where they stopped short.

Seated on his horse between the two saloons, Blackstone glared at the mob. Something in the big Englishman's face was frightening enough to drain momentum from the crowd. The fight left them and they lingered, shuffling their feet and muttering.

"I declare this an unlawful assembly!" Blackstone bellowed. He drew his pistol. "The Golden Nugget is closed for the night by city ordinance! Any man still in the street one minute from now will be hanged in the name of public order!"

Shocked by that draconian decree, the crowd stared at Blackstone. But despite the wide eyes and trembling hands of most, a few angry mutters rose. They were armed, after a fashion, and they far outnumbered the deputy.

Blackstone raised his gun and fired a shot into the air.

"Disperse now! Or face the consequences!"

One by one, the men thought better of it, dropped their rocks and wooden planks, and slunk off down the street.

Blackstone watched them go. It had been touch and go there

for a moment, and he knew that if they had decided to attack him, they would have overwhelmed him without much trouble.

But not before he sent several of them into eternity before him, and none of the mob had wanted to risk being among that number.

He waited until the street was empty before turning his horse and riding back toward the marshal's office.

Chapter 25

Cord and Ponder rode through the morning and into early afternoon, Ponder leading while Cord followed at a discreet distance.

Ordinarily, men taking such a long journey on horseback would ride closer together so they could talk, but Cord was not overly inclined to converse with Ponder. The mill owner was a persnickety sort—the kind of man whose main conversational gambit was to pull apart and question everything said to him. Even the simplest declarative statements would be turned back on the person with whom he was conversing. Cord found it tiresome and so avoided speaking to Ponder except when absolutely necessary.

As they rounded the base of some hills, it was Ponder who broke the silence. Cord urged his horse ahead a few quick steps to hear what the man was saying.

"—just past the valley here." Ponder pointed. "That notch between those two boulders is the start of the footpath. Errins's cabin isn't far beyond that."

"How far?" Cord produced a bandanna and wiped sweat from his neck.

"Not more than an hour's ride. That's at a slow pace. You want me to go ahead?"

"Hold on." Cord raised a hand. "Let me take a moment and think about this."

There were no tracks in the soil between them and the start of the trail. Of course, that meant nothing. Any gang being hunted by the law and holing up in a secluded cabin would take care to erase their tracks. Cord drew his horse to a standstill and closed his eyes, opening his nose and ears and drawing a deep breath. And waiting.

No sounds. No smells. No tracks.

No trace of men.

"All right," Cord said. "This path. It'll take us straight to where we're going? No detours, branches, nothing like that?"

"It's straight from here to the cabin," Ponder affirmed. "I've been there. Errins took me hunting last year. It's a nice place."

"Describe it to me."

Ponder climbed down from his horse and found a stick. Kneeling, he sketched an outline of a small cabin in the sand. "It's just a single story. Three rooms. The door's here." He tapped the diagram. "Two windows, one to either side. And there's a porch out front. Got a roof over it."

"Anything else?"

"A nice stone chimney." Ponder sat back on his haunches and studied the shape in the dirt. "The cabin is set back in the trees a bit. Right where the path dies out. It's hard to miss."

"And it's deserted except when Errins is using it?"

"That's what he told me," Ponder said. "It's just a hunting cabin. A good-enough place to eat, sleep, and warm up in overnight. Not a permanent home at all. Or valuable enough to post a guard on or keep anyone there year-round."

"All right." Cord sighed. "I'm going to go scout it. You might as well wait here. It's a long way back to town and you wouldn't want to go alone. So just make yourself comfortable. Brew a pot of coffee and I should be back in an hour or so."

"Right you are, Marshal."

Ponder guided his horse over to a boulder where he seated himself as Cord rode through the notch and onto the footpath. He waited until Cord disappeared into the trees, counted slowly to one hundred, and then mounted up and headed back in the direction of town.

Cord's plan was to scout out the cabin in advance of a full-scale raid by himself, Blackstone, Clyde Casterline, and whoever else he could rustle up as a posse. It would take some time and work to arm and equip such a party. But all that effort would be worthless without a good sense of what they were up against.

He kept his senses alert as he advanced up the rise into the trees. This area was heavily wooded, with plenty of places from which to launch an ambush. Cord moved cautiously, pausing often to look and listen. Once or twice, he dismounted and led the horse quietly through the undergrowth. But after an hour or more of furtive advances, he encountered no sign of the gunmen.

Maybe they were off elsewhere at the moment, he thought, and hoped he was right.

The cabin suddenly appeared as a bulky shadow in the forest. The moment Cord saw it, he dismounted, led the horse to shelter behind a stand of trees, and settled down to watch. He was so careful to conceal his presence that he didn't even risk a swig of water from his canteen. He relaxed into the stillness, breathing through an open mouth to hide the sound of breath, listening as the wind rustled the tree branches. For a full quarter of an hour, he saw no sign of anyone. Leaving his horse behind the stand of trees, he approached the cabin.

If he had any doubt it was uninhabited, the open door laid those worries to rest. The place was about as obviously deserted as it could be. Cord did a careful circuit of the area around the structure, scanning for blinds from which to launch an ambush but found nothing. Nobody.

He drew his Dragoon and advanced on the doorway. A faint odor of mouse droppings greeted him as he stepped onto the porch. Two chairs stood there, joined by a thick spider's web. The atmosphere of the place was musty and claustrophobic.

Nobody had been here for a good long while, he thought.

He considered searching the place from top to bottom but satisfied himself with a quick scan from the front room. To search further would belabor the obvious.

There wasn't a soul here and hadn't been for a long time.

He felt annoyance flare inside him. Damn that Ponder for wasting his time! But, drawing a deep breath, Cord calmed himself. Ponder had *not* wasted his time, he told himself. Ponder was a concerned citizen with information he thought might be of use to Cord and so had shared it. It wasn't the lumber boss's fault that the lead hadn't panned out.

Cord took one last look around, walked out to the porch, and stretched. It would be a long ride back to town. Cord reoriented himself to the stand of trees behind which he had left the horse.

The animal was as he had left her, head down, noisily munching on wild grass. Cord ran a hand along her neck, took the reins, and gently began guiding her back down the path. When he came to a clear area, he raised his left boot to put it in the stirrup—and paused.

Something wasn't right. Hard to put his finger on, but something was very definitely amiss.

Cord could tell, even if he wasn't familiar with this part of the country, that something was out of place. He turned in a full circle, scanning the trees, taking stock of his senses. Smell? Hearing? What *was* it?

There!

A shadow shifted in the forest shadows, then broke loose, a hidden observer relocating to another vantage. He managed two steps before Cord whipped out his Dragoon and fired, aiming high since he didn't know who the lurker was.

The bullet caused the shadow to stop, pivot, and return to cover. Cord heard a voice raised in alarm, followed by another gunshot. The bullet missed by a mile. If this was meant to be an ambush, they hadn't thought it through.

More likely he had spooked them while they were coming home, he thought.

He jumped into the saddle and galloped back toward Ponder. Once he had put a little distance between himself and the attempted ambush, if that was what it was, he ducked off the trail and guided the horse behind a cleft in the rocks. Dismounting, he drew his rifle from its saddle scabbard and waited, listening.

The sound of hooves increased from a thin rattle to a thundering. Cord sighted on the nearest bend in the trail. Soon the sights filled with the shape of a horse and the black of the rider's duster. That distinctive garment was enough evidence for him. Cord held his breath and squeezed the trigger.

The shot came close enough to spook the man's horse. The mount shied away from the bullet. The rider fought to get the horse under control, jerking the reins as it whinnied and stamped and danced around. Cord lifted his revolver as he saw the shadow of another rider appear behind the first. He fired a second shot, but by then both men had turned tail and fled.

Cord followed suit and lit a shuck out of there, heading in the opposite direction. The bushwhackers were spooked right now, but they still outnumbered him two to one and knew this ground better.

He rode hard until he figured he was well clear of them, then slowed his horse to a walk. Forty minutes later, he came to the spot where the trail began. He wasn't surprised to find Ponder long gone.

The gunfire had spooked him, Cord thought. It was understandable. The mill boss had come unarmed and anyway, Cord hadn't brought him along to take part in a gunfight and didn't expect that from him.

He returned to Rio Oro in the late afternoon. The streets were quiet, just the occasional horse or wagon raising dust as it passed through town. Blackstone met him at the door to the marshal's office, coach gun and saddlebags already in hand, ready to light out.

"You all right?" the big Englishman asked, obviously relieved to see Cord. "Ponder was just here. Looked like he'd seen a ghost! Said you were in trouble."

Cord reined in and tied the horse to the hitching post. "I was. I took care of it," he said as he swung down from the saddle. "Not that it amounted to a lot. Turns out our gunslingers had holed up in Paul Errins's hunting cabin. I surprised them as they were returning home."

That wasn't strictly the truth. Cord was convinced the duster-clad killers hadn't been holed up in the cabin. It wouldn't have looked so dusty and deserted if they had.

He was going to have to mull that over for a while yet, though, and he wasn't ready to share his suspicions with anyone else yet, not even his deputy.

"Well, let's go get them!" Blackstone grinned, relishing the prospect of another battle with the gunmen.

"Whoa there, partner." Cord put a hand on the man's arm. "They'll have their wind up by now. More than likely, they'll be long gone. I was hoping to plan an ambush, but that's not going to work out now."

Blackstone sighed. "Fair enough," he grumbled. "But those two have a reckoning coming their way. A good, old-fashioned English trouncing!"

"You mean Yankee trouncing." Cord chuckled. "Don't forget—you're in America now, Bart."

As Cord and Blackstone conferred, Ponder and Dollie Whittaker were ensconced in a back room of the Bear Flag—and Dollie was not pleased.

"What, exactly, were you hoping to achieve, Jeremiah?" she asked in a voice tightly controlled against the anger she felt.

"Well, I figured that—"

"You figured that if you got the marshal killed that would make our lives, what? *Easier*?"

"Well, it was the price I had to pay to—"

"To do *what*?" Dollie's voice climbed a tone, eyes flashing as she clenched a fist.

"To get those gunfighters on our side." Ponder's voice crumpled to a raspy whisper. "See, they demanded Bennett as tribute for helping us and . . ."

"You idiot."

Ponder's temper rose, but he bit back an angry reply. He reminded himself that he needed Dollie Whittaker to help him deal with the miners' vendetta against him and his business. But now she was on her feet, pacing back and forth behind her worktable, her fury as palpable as a live tiger in the small room.

"Jeremiah, it is important that we be seen as law-abiding business owners," she lectured him. "We need to have Cord Bennett and his lummox of a deputy on *our* side for when we make our moves. Mine against Harville and the Nugget. You against the miners."

Ponder swallowed, nodding. Even as he realized the extent to which he was relying on Dollie, he was also suddenly aware that she could put him in prison for his role in the shooting outside the mill.

He had best tread carefully with her, he thought—for now.

Until the time came when he didn't need her anymore.

Of course, she might very well be thinking the same thing about him . . .

Chapter 26

It didn't take much to ignite the next incident between the miners and lumbermen.

Bitter feelings persisted between the two groups after the street brawl that led to the shooting. Miners and mill workers gave one another a wide berth in the street, glaring as they passed. Wherever lumbermen and prospectors found themselves in close proximity, raised voices, insults, and the odd scuffle were sure to follow. These minor collisions simmered for a long time, gaining steam, occurring with increasing frequency.

After a few days of it, the first vandalism occurred. Someone got hold of red paint and daubed a rude word on the wall of the Bear Flag. It became the object of heated conversation among the lumbermen, who noticed it on the way to work the next morning. In the street, a group of twenty or thirty muttered angrily to one another before going as a group to the door of the Golden Nugget to relieve themselves.

Most had already drunk their morning coffee, so it was no hardship to join with others in leaving behind a large puddle on the wooden walkway in front of the saloon. As the day's heat came on, its unmistakable stench rose, forcing one of the bar girls to come out with a bucket, lye soap, and a scrub brush. Even after she was done, traces of the sharp, unpleasant smell lingered.

Absorbed as they were in hunting the black-clad gunfighters, Cord and Blackstone registered the growing tension as a series of unrelated but minor incidents. Cord intended to follow up on the provocations, but it was Clyde Casterline at the land claims office who was first to realize how out of hand the disputes were getting.

His office was a frequent destination for prospectors. The front room where he kept his assaying counter was a normal stop for miners in town to pick up supplies—an unofficial social club where men could make a pretense of trading tips and sharing news as an excuse to swap gossip and size up potential rivals for promising claims. Anyone searching for a given prospector could usually count on him stopping by Casterline's at least once a week. Everyone knew this, including Ponder's men.

Clyde Casterline was behind the counter, listening to two prospectors argue. Pan-head Peterson and Linus Butler were old-timers with prior experience in Mexico who had been among the first men to stake claims in the region. Both functioned as mentors to newcomers and so shared a half-hearted rivalry that manifested itself in joking japes and side-of-the-mouth comments that were never quite insults. On this day, they happened to be arguing about mules.

"Best one I ever owned spoke French," Pan-head declaimed.

"Get out!" snapped Linus. "Ain't never been no mule that ever spoke no French!"

Working his ledgers behind the counter, Clyde Casterline suppressed a grin. *Here we go again,* he thought.

"Damn right there are mules who speak French!" Pan-head seemed downright incensed about the topic. It was obviously a point of honor with him. "They're descendants of the Army mules trained by the French and left behind after Napoleon tried to invade Mexico! They only understand commands in French!"

"Why?" demanded Linus. "Because Napoleon taught 'em? That's the dadblamed craziest thing I ever heard. Ain't it true, Clyde? Ain't that the craziest damned thing—"

He had not finished when Hap stumbled through the door, wide-eyed and trembling.

"M-Mister Casterline? W-We g-got trouble outside here!"

Clyde Casterline peered over his bifocals at Hap. He personally found the man's behavior annoying but knew from experience that Hap had his ear to the ground around town. Whenever news broke, he was sure to hear and share it first.

"What's up, Hap?" It came out a little sharper than Casterline intended, but that didn't faze Hap.

"Th-there's a g-group of lumber mill men! J-Just ou-outside here!"

"What the devil do they want?"

"I d-don't know, M-Mister Casterline . . . b-but they sure d-do look *angry!"*

"Oh, good grief!" Casterline pulled off and tossed his glasses onto the open ledger and stalked out from behind the counter. He took two steps toward the door and, seeing the shapes of the men outside, retreated just long enough to pick up a club that he kept on a shelf beside the cash box. Then he stepped out into the street.

The men gathered there had been among the muttering mob he had seen the morning of the shooting, and they bore the same look of desperate, directionless anger.

"Can I help you, boys?" he demanded in a wintry tone, hands behind his back.

The muttering and shifting stopped, the lumbermen stiffening as one. It was one of Hansen's men, a tall, bearded drink of water named Sven, who stepped up and puffed out his chest.

"We have business with those two river rats in there!" he boomed. "Now you send them out to us or else!"

"Or else *what*?"

Sven was a full five inches taller than Casterline, fifty or sixty pounds heavier than the slender land claims agent, and twenty years younger. He had the well-muscled look of a man accustomed to expending an entire day immersed in physical labor. To most men, he would be intimidating as hell.

But Clyde Casterline was a canny judge of men. Sven did not frighten him. And violence was a language Casterline had come to speak fluently. He didn't look imposing, but his lean frame was corded with muscles like steel cables.

"Or else"—Sven jabbed a finger at the older man—"we will come in and—"

That was as far as he got. Casterline's right arm came out from behind his back with the club, swinging hard. Its weight connected solidly with Sven's left temple and the giant crashed into a heap on the ground. The other lumbermen drew back in alarm, eyes widening, the fight draining from them immediately.

Casterline pointed the club at the lumbermen and jabbed the air with it to emphasize his words. "Next man who comes to my office threatening anybody gets their head busted wide open! Now *git*!"

He took one angry step toward the group and they fled.

Casterline watched them go, hitched up his trousers, and turned to go back into the office with a look of satisfaction on his face.

This was one potential riot that he had nipped in the bud!

"Marshal?"

"What is it, Bart?"

"We've got trouble."

Cord turned to see the Englishman peering out through the window in the direction of Casterline's office. One man lay in a heap at Clyde Casterline's feet. Then as one, the men grouped watching turned and fled down the street and into the Bear Flag.

"What in tarnation is going on?" Cord moved to the door, Blackstone right behind him. They went out into the street just as Pan-head and Linus stepped out of Casterline's office.

"Hot damn!" said Pan-head as he stared down at the motionless form. "Lookee there! That's big Sven!"

"He's takin' a nap," observed Linus.

"He ain't takin' no damn *nap!"* retorted Pan-head. "He's laid out good and proper, like a stunned fish in the bottom of a canoe!"

"Canoe?" Linus howled. "How do you come up with this nonsense? Mules that speak French and fish in canoes. Ain't no damn *canoes* anywhere near this cotton-pickin' town!"

While Linus was talking, a group of perhaps half a dozen prospectors gathered around to listen. They were all gazing in awe at Sven's body when Cord and Blackstone arrived.

"He dead?" Cord glanced down at the prone giant.

Casterline had followed Pan-head and Linus out of the office. "No," he said, still looking pleased with himself. "But I reckon he'll have one hell of a headache when he wakes up."

"What happened?" asked one of the miners.

"Sven come up here all liver and lightning!" cried Pan-head. "Set hisself right outside Mr. Casterline's office, all rough and tough-like! Made a threat and *boom*! Clyde laid him out like a fish in the bottom of a canoe!"

Linus scoffed and rolled his eyes at the word *canoe.*

There was a sudden commotion in the doorway of the Bear Flag. Sven's companions were returning in the company of a half dozen more fellows from the mill. Their appearance caused a sudden flurry of angry muttering from the prospectors.

"Them damn timberjacks!"

"What the hell do they think they're doin'?"

"Why they comin' thisaway?"

Cord moved out to intercept the group in the street before the men could reach Casterline's office.

"Wait just a minute." He held up a hand. "You—whoa!"

One of the men attempted to ignore Cord and step around him, so Cord grabbed him by the collar and swung him around 180 degrees until he faced the group again. He whirled when Cord released him.

"Don't you touch me!" the man cried, shaking a finger at Cord. "Don't you dare—"

That was as far as he got. Cord drew his Dragoon, cocked it, and jammed the pistol up under the man's jawline.

"Don't I dare *what*?" he asked icily. "You do understand I'm the marshal in this town, right? Which means I'm the law. Right?"

The terrified lumber mill worker sputtered, eyes wide, a dribble of spit rolling down his chin.

Cord let the hammer down on the Dragoon and pouched the iron. "It's plain and simple, mister. When the marshal tells you to stop, you stop and listen good."

He addressed the remainder of the group.

"You fellas need to just drop your grievance. Those miners had nothing to do with Sven getting coldcocked. That was Mr. Casterline's doing, and he was well within his rights to do it. Touch him and I'll have no choice but to shoot you. Understand?"

The fight appeared to drain from the timbermen, but after a moment, one stepped forward and pointed.

"Ain't that Pan-head Peterson over there? Ain't it? That pot-lickin' son of a gun! Step out here, Pan-head, you rat! I got me a grievance with you!"

Before Cord could intervene, old Pan-head had shoved his way through his fellows and stepped out to face the timberman. His bearded chin jutted out angrily.

"Well, what is it?" he demanded.

"That mule you sold me!" The timberman hooked a thumb back

over his shoulder at the stable building. "You said he was *trained*! By the *army*!"

"Well, he is!"

"He don't respond to no commands! He don't even know how to giddyap!"

"Well, that's 'cause you got to say it in *French*! I told you that when I sold him to you!"

"I don't believe you! I think he's just deaf! What kind of low-down varmint sells a deaf mule to a working man, I ask you?"

These remarks were a match to the tinder of the situation. The group behind him grew bold again, as if suddenly realizing that they outnumbered the two lawmen, weapons be damned. Men could be disarmed easily enough if swarmed. And Cord was having the uneasy feeling that might be in the cards.

A muttering arose from behind. Blackstone had his hands full, as well, holding back the miners who had gathered in front of the land claims office.

That was when the man who had tried to brush past Cord earlier decided to try again. Cord was ready for him, but he wasn't ready for the other two who charged past on his other side. He turned on his heel and called after them, "Stop! In the name of the law!"

He reached for his Dragoon. And that was when several things happened very quickly.

The first was that someone grabbed Cord's gun hand by the wrist from behind. He wheeled around and saw his assailant—a bearded man wearing a set of ragged and stained overalls. The man gritted his teeth as he dug in his heels, hanging on for dear life and preventing Cord from pulling his weapon.

At the exact same time this was happening, one of the prospectors in front of Casterline's office broke from the crowd and smacked one of the two men who had brushed by Cord. The second man leaped on the prospector's back. And then, suddenly, they were raising massive clouds of dust in their struggle.

Blackstone made his move, starting to push his way through the crowd of prospectors, when suddenly big Sven woke up and bounded to his feet, pushing his chest into Blackstone's and snarling, "You back down now, big man! Or else!"

"Or else *what*?" Blackstone snapped back. "Do your worst!"

At that point, it was inevitable.

All hell broke loose in Rio Oro.

CHAPTER 27

Blackstone hauled back his right arm and swung, fist connecting with Sven's jaw and dumping him to the ground for the second time in less than half an hour. One of Sven's pals seemed of a mind to retaliate. He lunged forward, reaching for the big Englishman with clawed fingers, only to crumple into a dazed heap beneath Casterline's club.

Cord, meanwhile, had the one prospector holding on to his wrist and refusing to let go. Rather than resist, he pushed into the man and stomped hard on his feet, causing the man to leap back with a yelp.

Cord shoved him away, drew his Dragoon, raised it into the air, and triggered a shot that boomed and echoed as it reverberated against the storefronts along Main Street.

As one, the groups of prospectors and timbermen froze. They all raised their arms simultaneously, as if some puppet master had decided to pull everyone's strings at once.

"Go on!" Blackstone shoved two of the prospectors from behind. "Line up! Over there!"

"Next to them timbermen?" whined Linus. "I won't—"

"Yes, you bloody well will!"

It took some manhandling, but Cord, Casterline, and Blackstone managed to get everyone arranged in a ragged column. To a man, every one of them wore a hangdog look as Cord holstered his Dragoon and addressed them.

"I've had just about enough of this!" he said. "Every time I turn around, you miners are getting into it with these lumber workers! It's a disruption of the peace and a threat to public safety. And it's going to stop. Now!"

The column of men watched him intently. He had their attention.

"You men are going to go back to work at the yard or at your claims. And you're going to pass the word. No more riots! No more brawls! No more nonsense between these two groups. Or we're going to start having some *hangings*!"

The last word, barked loud and clear, made several of the men wince.

Good, thought Cord. He wanted them spooked.

"Now git!"

With a wave of his hand, the group broke up, the men bolting off in separate directions.

"Let's just hope they listened," grumbled Casterline.

Dollie Whittaker watched all this unfold, unobserved by Cord and Blackstone as she stood at a second-floor window of the Bear Flag Saloon.

Her campaign against Harville was proceeding according to plan. These continued clashes between the miners and the lumbermen only served to strengthen her. It wasn't enough to drain business from Harville's saloon. No, she wanted him on his knees, ruined, cashed out, and closed down. She wanted to ruin him. And this latest disturbance provided her with just the excuse she needed to push her plan forward a bit.

She descended quickly to her office, sat down at the desk, and wrote something on a card, which she sealed in an envelope and passed to one of her bar girls for delivery to Judge Davenport. Then she returned upstairs to choose appropriate attire for the next act in the drama she was directing.

The first to receive a summons was Clyde Casterline. He was just finishing up his morning's work and getting ready to close down for his midday meal when Hap appeared in the doorway with a fistful of envelopes.

"M-Mister C-Casterline? H-here." Hap thrust out an envelope with Clyde Casterline's name written on the front in copperplate script.

"What's this, Hap?" Casterline accepted the envelope, slit it open, and withdrew a sheet of formal stationery.

"It's from J-Judge D-Davenport. I'm t-to d-deliver this p-posthaste."

"I see." Casterline cast his eyes on the contents of the letter and frowned.

Hap's next stop was the Golden Nugget. The barroom was nearly empty at this hour. Teddy Harville stood talking to one of his men when Hap arrived. He scuttled in through the batwing doors and approached Harville nervously.

"Well, hello, Hap." Harville looked up from his conversation. "You're in awful early today. You want a beer?"

"N-No, sir." Hap cleared his throat. "I g-got s-something for you f-from Judge D-Davenport."

Hap handed over an envelope. Harville accepted it with a hum of surprise, opened the flap, and withdrew the paper inside. He read the words there once. Paused. Then read them again. Then he folded the paper and put it in his pants pocket.

"Thank you, Hap," he said tonelessly.

Hap found Blackstone at the stable, talking with one of the hostlers. The big Englishman was surprised when an envelope was thrust into his hand.

"What's this?" he asked.

"From J-Judge D-Davenport," Hap said. "I'm t-to d-deliver th-them."

"I see." Blackstone frowned, opening his envelope. When he read the contents, he hoisted his eyebrows in surprise.

Davenport delivered Cord Bennett's envelope personally. The marshal was surprised when a knock came on the office door, and he opened it to find the justice standing on the threshold like a messenger boy.

"Your honor!" Cord grinned and held wide the door. "What can I do for you?"

"Wanted to come and give this to you by hand." Davenport extended the hand holding the envelope. "It's a summons. I've had Hap delivering them around town."

"What's this about?"

"This morning's street altercation outside of Clyde Casterline's office." Davenport sighed. "That Dollie Whittaker doesn't miss a trick. She's leapt at the opportunity to pin the blame for the disturbance on Teddy Harville and made a formal request for a hearing on the matter."

"Is that right?" Cord glanced at the verbiage on the summons before refolding and pocketing it. "Well, I'll be happy to help set her straight. Harville had nothing to do with things. At least, so far as I could see."

"Every bit of information helps," said Davenport. "I've convened the hearing for my chambers, this evening at sundown. I figure we should be able to wrap things up fairly quickly."

"All right."

"Having you and Blackstone there to help keep order should expedite the process." Davenport shrugged. "I look forward to seeing you there."

Oddly enough, Cord found himself looking forward to it, as well. This might be a good chance to clear the air and maybe even head off future ruckuses.

At sundown, Cord locked the marshal's office and headed across the street to Judge Davenport's chambers. Blackstone was already waiting outside when he arrived.

"Anyone else here yet?" he asked.

"Casterline and Teddy Harville just left," said Blackstone. "Apparently, Davenport wanted a word with them. Harville didn't seem too pleased when he departed."

"The judge probably grilled him about this morning's brawl." Cord shook his head. "Lord knows that man has been through enough without getting blamed for every disturbance of the peace that occurs around here."

Cord knocked on the door and let himself in. Davenport was standing by the window, reviewing some documents. He peered over the top of his bifocals at Cord.

"Good of you to come, Marshal. Mr. Blackstone." He took a seat behind his desk. "I expect Miss Whittaker will be along shortly. I wanted to have a word with her privately first before bringing Mr. Harville back into the picture. I had a discussion with him and Clyde Casterline earlier, and I'm convinced Harville had nothing to do with this morning's altercation."

"I agree, your honor," said Cord. "Based on everything we saw, the whole thing was a spontaneous affair. It just up and happened."

Davenport was still nodding over this when the door opened and Dollie Whittaker made her entrance, followed by Jeremiah Ponder.

"Miss Whittaker." Davenport smiled at her. "I see you've brought company."

"I have, your honor." Dollie planted herself defiantly in the center of the room. "I am coming with a concern—and a complaint. But I also have a solution for the problem in mind. I've been discussing the matter with Mr. Ponder and he seems to agree with me."

"I do, your honor," Ponder affirmed. "With your permission, I'd like to stay. And it's good to see you, Marshal," he said to Cord. "I alerted Mr. Blackstone as soon as the shooting started up at that cabin."

"Mr. Ponder." Cord nodded to him. "Yes, I'm all right, thank you."

"Well, let's get started." Davenport consulted his pocket watch. "We have some time before Mr. Harville joins us. What is it you wished to bring to the court's attention, Miss Whittaker?"

Dollie Whittaker marched over and took the seat directly in front of Judge Davenport's desk. Rummaging briefly in her purse, she extracted a sheaf of papers.

"This morning's attack on mill workers by the local ne'er-do-wells is just the latest in a series of provocations Rio Oro has been forced to endure," she began. "The frequency and persistence of these attacks—as well as their preferred target, the mill—can leave no doubt that they are part of a coordinated effort to undermine public order."

"Is that right?" Davenport put his hand to his chin, his thumb worrying the stubble along his jawline. "I think there is considerable room for debate on that point. But please do proceed."

"No doubt they are part of a coordinated effort," she repeated. "And I believe I—*we*—know who is behind it." She brandished the sheaf of papers. "I have statements here from a number of witnesses who claim that conspiracies are regularly hatched by the prospectors against the mill workers."

"It's true, your honor," said Ponder. "We've had numerous attacks on the mill and on mill workers."

"I am aware of those," Davenport allowed, glancing at Cord and Blackstone.

"The object of these conspiracies is Mr. Ponder's mill. And my establishment."

"The Bear Flag?" Davenport leaned forward and extended a hand. "Let me see those."

Dollie Whittaker handed over the sheaf of papers. Davenport unfolded and read them quickly. Cord noted his stillness as he absorbed the contents of the pages. Harville knocked and entered just as Davenport was finishing.

"These actions have been discussed and planned in the Golden Nugget saloon," Dollie announced with a cold glance at Harville. "It's obvious there is a conspiracy afoot to shake up the town, and Mr. Harville is an active participant."

"Wait just a damn minute!" cried Harville as he swept off the top hat he wore and clutched it angrily. "I have nothing to do with—"

"It's all right, Mr. Harville." Davenport held up a hand. "You will have a chance to speak your piece. And as for your claims of a conspiracy, Miss Whittaker?" Davenport folded and handed the papers back to Dollie. "I don't see that these statements prove anything."

"On the contrary, your honor," she objected. "They prove that the Golden Nugget Saloon is a cesspool of corruption and violence! And we have a proposal to limit further incidents in town."

"And that is?"

"We ask that the court order Mr. Harville to accept an offer to purchase his business so—"

That was as far as she got. Harville exploded in laughter, throwing back his head and hooting loud enough to shake the rafters. He was so overcome with mirth that he was forced to grab the back of a chair to remain upright. He got himself under control upon finding himself in the icy stare of the judge.

"I'm sorry, Judge," he said, chuckling. "But the Golden Nugget isn't for sale. And I don't reckon there's a law anywhere that can compel a man to accept an offer on his business that he doesn't want to."

"You're correct on that point, Mr. Harville." Davenport's glare settled on Dollie Whittaker. "This is what you're bringing me? An attempt at a takeover of the Golden Nugget? On the basis of this flimsy accusation? For shame, Miss Whittaker. There's no legal basis for such a thing. This is an absolute waste of my time."

She cast her eyes on the floor. "I am sorry your honor sees it that way."

"I do." Davenport sighed. "Believe me, if there was the slightest chance this would mitigate the violence in town, I might consider it. But no, it won't. Besides, it's illegal, and even suggesting it is an abuse of the law. We have lawmen who can handle the violence without violating anyone's legal rights. Isn't that right, Marshal?"

"It is, your honor," Cord said. He suppressed a grin at Dollie Whittaker's furious glare at the judge.

Then she turned that look on him, and he didn't feel like grinning anymore. He remembered what Reverend Lomax had said about evil coming to Rio Oro.

The good reverend might be on to something there.

CHAPTER 28

Cord awoke, memories of last night's meeting in the judge's chambers fading away in a sudden wave of excitement.

This was the day, he thought.

He rose and dressed quickly, donning a clean shirt and combing his hair before pulling on his hat and boots and heading downstairs. The main street was quiet. Blackstone was just pulling the kettle from the stove when he let himself into the office.

"Good morning, Marshal," the big Englishman said. "Coffee is ready."

"Mighty helpful of you," Cord said. He held out a tin mug as Blackstone poured a healthy serving of coffee. The Englishman's tea, Cord noted, was already filled and steaming on a window ledge.

"So! Today is the big day, if I am not mistaken." Blackstone took up his tea and sipped. "Nervous?"

"Shoot, no." Cord grinned. "Glory and I have been anxious to sit down and firm things up with the preacher. We've got a date set. Next up is the planning. She wants to keep things simple."

"Marriage is a wonderful institution," Blackstone affirmed. "I should know. I've tried it several times myself."

"You were married?"

"Oh, once or twice. Maybe three times. I can't keep them all straight."

"What happened?"

"Ah. Well." Blackstone shrugged. "When one wife finds out about the others, things can get very complicated . . ."

At least that was one thing he didn't have to worry about, Cord told himself.

Glory, for her part, was equally anxious as she prepared to leave the cabin she shared with her father and sister. She had cleaned and pressed her best dress, put out her best sunbonnet, and run a damp cloth over her boots. She wanted to look her best when she and Cord sat down with the minister.

"Well, look at you!" enthused Abraham when he saw her. "You're the right prettiest Glory in Rio Oro."

"Oh, Pa!" She laughed. "You know good and well I'm the only woman named Glory in this whole town!"

"So, I'm not wrong!" Abraham grinned as he sat down at the kitchen table. "Shoot, for all I know, you're the prettiest Glory in the entire territory!"

"Now you're just being silly."

Kat emerged from her room. Seeing her sister, she broke into a wide smile.

"You're looking very stylish this morning, Miss Glory," she said. "If I didn't know better, I'd think you're off to meet your beau."

"It's the big day," Glory said. "Cord and I are sitting down with Reverend Lomax to finalize plans for the wedding."

"Wedding!" Abraham looked bewildered. "Why, it was only yesterday I was teaching you two how to ride a horse! Now one of you is up and getting married! Where does the time go?"

"You ask that question an awful lot, Pa," said Kat.

"She's got a point," Glory added. "You're forever complaining about how time slips away."

"Just wait until you're my age," Abraham warned. "Then you'll understand how fast it all goes."

Garrison Lomax sat in the front pew of the darkened church and gazed around with a sense of satisfaction and well-being.

The building was complete.

All those years spent riding the trails as a saddlebag preacher had culminated in this, his very own church. Lomax chided himself that it was, in fact, God's church. But he was its builder and first custodian. He felt a justifiable sense of accomplishment and protectiveness.

Events involving Cord Bennett troubled him. He had grown fond of the lawman and his comely bride-to-be. Lomax considered himself a good judge of character and Cord Bennett met every criterion Lomax held for a good man. And that, to his way of thinking, was part of the problem.

Good people, in Lomax's experience, were like lanterns that blasted light into the world. That light benefitted their community and those around them.

But it also attracted evil souls who despised the light and sought to extinguish it. For this reason, men like Cord were often in danger. By extension, so was Glory, given events the last time they visited the church.

What would become of them and their family? Lomax nursed a nugget of worry on that score. A man like Cord was a natural target in a lawless world. But with a wife? Children? The danger multiplied.

Lomax was a preacher, true. But he was also a hard man, and fiercely loyal to those under his protection as given him by the

Lord. While he waited for them to arrive, he bent his head in prayer to be loyal to that trust.

Lomax opened the church doors and stood waiting when Cord and Glory arrived. Arm in arm, huge smiles on both their faces, they looked for all the world like the happiest couple in history.

"Good morning!" he said with a chuckle. "Well, if I had any doubts about this wedding, I'd say they're well and truly laid to rest. Don't think I've ever seen two folks more pleased to be caught in one another's company!"

Cord laughed and extended a hand. They shook. Glory surprised both men by grasping the preacher in a one-armed hug and squeezing him.

"Reverend," she said, "you have no idea how happy we are to be putting this to rest!"

"No surprise there," he replied. "Leastways, not as surprising as your strength. You nearly broke me with that hug!"

"She's a strong woman," Cord said. "That's part of what I love about her."

"A man with a tough job like yours needs a strong wife," Lomax said. "Come on inside and let's start making some plans."

The preacher conducted them to the front pews of the church where he had a piece of paper and a pencil laid out, along with a Bible and several prayer books. They all sat. Glory gazed around the interior of the church in silent wonder.

"What a lovely place," she said.

"It is." Lomax smiled. "Why don't we start with a short prayer?"

Cord and Glory bowed their heads as Lomax spoke a simple and heartfelt benediction, asking the Lord to bless the upcoming union and shower grace upon the ceremony. The blessing complete, they set to work on practicalities related to the wedding itself.

"So, when is the big day?" Lomax took up his paper and pencil as he spoke.

Cord and Glory looked at each other.

"One week from today, Reverend, if that suits you," Cord said.

"That's a fine day," Lomax replied. "How many can we expect in attendance?"

"Only a dozen or so," Glory said. "We aim to keep the circle small. We'll hold a reception at the hotel. And of course you're invited."

"I accept!" Lomax beamed. "Glory, your family will be attending. Cord? I understand your family has passed . . ."

"Clyde Casterline is coming at my invitation," Cord said. "And Deputy Blackstone has agreed to be best man."

"I see." Lomax jotted this down. "And, Cord, forgive me, but you haven't been married before, correct? You have no in-laws or children?"

"No."

At the mention of children, Cord felt a shift in the room. When he looked over, Glory's eyes were on the floor.

She was still thinking about that business of Caroline Stockton's death in childbirth, he realized, suppressing his frustration. Her suspicions cast a persistent shadow over their plans.

Lomax noticed, too, but pushed on with the discussion of wedding plans.

Once arrangements had been finalized, Cord excused himself to get to work for the day. He closed the door behind him, leaving Glory alone in the chapel with the preacher.

"You're troubled." Lomax spoke the words softly.

Glory sat very still. Lomax could sense her discomfort, even at a distance. She was a circumspect woman—one accustomed to behaving with restraint and dignity whenever in public. But Lomax had been a minister too long not to recognize true emotional anguish when he saw it.

"Caroline Stockton," she whispered.

"Who is that, Glory?"

"She was a neighbor of Cord's in the Ozarks. A young woman he was sweet on when he was younger. She . . ." Glory drew in a deep breath as if gathering her strength and courage. "She died in childbirth."

Lomax listened intently, saying nothing, nodding just slightly so Glory would know to go on.

"Cord found out about this only recently." She stared out the window, lips tightening as she struggled to maintain her composure. "Reverend Lomax, I can't help harboring suspicions. My God, it sounds terrible to say it aloud! But I can't hide what's in my heart."

"And what is that, Glory?"

"I can't help wondering." She raised her face, eyes glistening with tears. "Was the child Cord's? Did he have relations with her? Before he left to come out here?"

"Your suspicions are understandable. Justified, even. Have you spoken to Cord about this?"

"I have. He denies the baby was his. Says it was his brother's."

Lomax nodded. "And you don't believe him?"

"I—" She stopped short, digesting his words. "Well, now that you put it that way, I . . ."

Lomax waited.

"How *can* I feel that way?" Glory seemed genuinely puzzled by her own doubt. "I mean, here we are, talking to you about a wedding. And here *I* am . . ."

"Doubting."

The word fell in the silent church like a dropped rock.

Glory was silent too.

"Glory, if you have any doubts about the wedding . . . Well, you should speak freely on the matter." Lomax spoke these words calmly, neutrally. "And if you want me to mediate on this matter between you and Cord, well . . ." He sighed and looked up at the roof. "I feel a great fondness for you both. You're wonderful people. I want happiness for you both."

"Thank you, Reverend." Glory relaxed visibly. "I haven't felt able to talk about this freely with anyone."

"So the feelings have backed up inside you like something blocking a drain?" Lomax asked. "That's why we're here. And by *we,* I mean other people. Remember that the Cross has a vertical dimension that represents our relationship with God. And a horizontal dimension that signifies our relationship with God through each other. And as God's bound servant, I am here to do whatever I can to help you two through this. No matter the cost. It's my sworn duty as a minister of the Word."

Glory was listening intently. Lomax was pleased to see her brightening. When she spoke, her words surprised him.

"Just talking about it helps," she admitted.

"Do you want to marry Cord?"

"Yes." She spoke the word firmly, conviction audible in her tone. "Yes, Reverend. I want that more than anything."

"Do you trust him?"

"I do." She was nodding now. "How silly of me to think I can not trust a man, but then go ahead and marry him. He says it's not true that Caroline's child was his. And I should take his word on faith."

"Faith is what this God business is all about." Lomax laughed. "It isn't always easy."

Now Glory was laughing. It began as a low chuckle but steadily built into a great, thunderous, rolling laugh that Lomax could not resist joining.

"Yes. I have faith in God. And in Cord." She smiled. "Thank you, Reverend. Thank you."

Back at the marshal's office, Blackstone paused on his way out the door and turned to Cord.

"You're troubled," he said. It was not a question.

"Just worrying about Glory," Cord admitted. "By marrying me, she becomes a target."

Blackstone drew himself to his full, impressive height.

"Marshal," he said, addressing Cord with unaccustomed formality. "As your deputy—and friend—I'm here to tell you that your enemies are mine. Same goes for your family. Anyone who tries to harm either of you will face more hell from me than any man can imagine. Anyone who *actually* harms either of you can count on me making war on him. Total war. No surrender and no quarter."

Cord had no doubt that the big Englishman meant every word of what he said. It made Cord feel a little better, too.

But only a little, he realized, as he thought about those elusive black-clad gunmen.

CHAPTER 29

Later that night at the Golden Nugget, Teddy Harville started to get nervous.

So far it had been a quiet night, the controversies and disturbances of the past days and weeks casting no shadow over the barroom. Trade was slow but steady. Things picked up a bit when a group of prospectors stopped in to celebrate their luck at a recent strike but quieted down again after they left. The poker game in the corner began shortly afterward, along with Harville's misgivings.

A hard-looking stranger was ensconced at a table with two prospectors, the local tailor, and a traveling salesman who was staying at the hotel. Poker was the game. So far as Harville could tell, the game was for dollar stakes.

At first, everything seemed fine. But as the night wore on, things began getting tense.

The drummer was trying to cash out. It became obvious to Harville at sometime around nine p.m., because he kept trying to rise from the table, but the stranger would pull his sleeve to delay him, call for another round of drinks, and deal another hand.

The salesman returned to his seat willingly enough after two such episodes. But as ten o'clock approached, his moves became more urgent. Voices began to rise. Polly, one of the barmaids, pushed close to Harville as she came to the bar to pick up refills.

"Mr. Teddy, sir," she said, glancing nervously over her shoulder at the table. "I think something is about to happen. Something bad."

"Why's that, Polly?" Harville asked, keeping his voice low and moving a little closer so they could speak privately.

"That man at the poker table." Polly could not conceal her nervousness at even mentioning the man. "He sat down at the table a while ago and, next thing you know, he's taken over the game and raised the stakes. He's been winning for most of the night. But the salesman arrived and began to cut into his winnings."

"I notice that sales fella keeps trying to leave," Harville whispered.

Now Polly was nodding. "You got that right, Mr. Teddy. He says he needs to catch the morning stage. But the other man won't let him go. Insists he stay and keep playing hand after hand."

Harville swallowed. This wasn't good at all.

When the drummer began making moves to rise again, Harville decided to risk a visit to the table in person. Maybe he could ease the situation. He grabbed a half-full bottle of whiskey from the back counter, hung a towel over his right forearm like a waiter in a fancy restaurant back East, and approached the poker table.

"Well, hello, gentlemen!" With a smile, he leaned in and set the half full bottle of whiskey on the table's edge. "You fellas have been playing quite a long while and giving us good trade. I don't mind saying the kitty's larger tonight because of you. By way of thanks, here's a half bottle of our finest. On the house."

Smiles all around. Except for the stranger and the salesman. The stranger kept his head down on his cards, face obscured by the brim of his hat. But the salesman greeted Harville's interruption as just the break he needed to make another bid for freedom.

"That's mighty kind of you, sir," he said to Harville. "And in fact . . ." He pushed back his chair and rose, digging in his pockets for change. "I owe you for that last schooner of beer. I have to get going, so let me pay you now."

"Sit down."

The stranger's voice was soft but menacing. The salesman froze.

"Now, there's no need for *that*!" Harville chuckled as he said it. "Allow me to offer—"

But the stranger raised his face, stopping Teddy Harville in mid-sentence. Within the cold, silent gaze that greeted him, the bar owner felt the man's rage at the interruption of whatever spell he kept casting over the drummer.

"We don't want it, whatever you're offering," the stranger rasped. "Now go away. And you." He turned to the salesman. "I told you to sit down."

With a sigh, the salesman dragged his chair from the table and sat back down again. Harville chose that moment to beat a hasty retreat. Once back behind the bar, he pretended to fiddle with his accounts ledger as he tried to figure out his next move before violence erupted and blood was spilled on the sawdust-littered floor.

At that exact moment, Deputy Blackstone happened to be passing by on the sidewalk outside. As he glanced through the front window, Blackstone caught sight of the stranger sitting at the poker table and got a good luck at the man's face. He froze for an instant as the shock of recognition went through him.

The man wasn't wearing his black duster tonight, but he was unmistakably one of the pair of gunmen who had tried more than once to kill Cord.

What on earth was the man doing in town? It flummoxed Blackstone. He must have known that he ran the risk of being recognized. And yet for some reason, he had floated into town unnoticed after dark and taken a seat at a poker game in the Golden Nugget. It was every bit as much an embarrassment that he could have gotten away with that as it was a clear and present danger to the town and Cord Bennett.

What to do?

Blackstone weighed the benefits of charging in there alone against rousing Cord for backup. If he did, he risked missing the gunman should he slip out during the minutes Blackstone was gone.

No. He would take the risk and do this alone.

Blackstone dropped a hand to the butt of his holstered revolver.

It was better to risk a bullet than forsake this opportunity to put a stop to one of the gunmen. The duster-clad killers had wreaked havoc upon Rio Oro. Blackstone had a chance to end this here and now, and he owed it to Cord and the town to try.

He was just making ready to slip out from behind the pillar when a roar of gunfire exploded inside the saloon.

Harville would recall the events of the next few seconds for the rest of his life.

He was still at the bar when he saw the stranger's hand sweep toward his holster beneath the table. By the time the man stood up, the gun was out and in his hand and pointed directly at the salesman's heart.

"I know you been cheating," the stranger said. "And you know I know. Which is why you keep trying to leave."

The drummer was armed too. No man traveled the frontier without some sort of protection in case of trouble. He jerked up out of his chair and his hand darted under his coat.

The stranger fired his gun just as the salesman drew and fired his. The resulting roar was like a peal of thunder breaking in the middle of the room.

* * *

Blackstone hurled himself through the batwing doors and into the saloon as customers scattered and bartenders dove behind the bar for cover. Muzzle flame lanced through clouds of powder-smoke and rounds sang in the air like bees as the two men exchanged fire. Harville crouched at the end of the bar as the stranger and the drummer retreated behind upturned tables and continued blasting away at each other.

Blackstone began firing from the doorway at the hired killer he had recognized through the window. His first bullet blew a hole in the table's edge. His second shattered the side window behind the man.

The killer swung to meet this new threat and fired back at Blackstone. The big Englishman was forced to duck back outside the doorway.

The salesman chose that moment to stand to his full height and fire over the top of the table he'd been using for cover. Unfortunately for him, his bullets missed, whining past the gunman's head.

The killer dropped behind his table again, leaned to the side to fire around it, and triggered twice. The salesman reeled backward, clapped his free hand to the hole in his chest that had suddenly started welling blood, and collapsed.

Silence fell as gun smoke billowed through the saloon.

Blackstone barreled through the doorway again, a gun in each hand now, firing wildly as he approached the killer's table. He was just a dozen feet away when the gunman leaped through the shattered window, busting out the frame, and tumbled into the alley next to the Golden Nugget.

Blackstone turned and dashed out onto the boardwalk. He lunged toward the corner, but by the time he got there, the man had disappeared into the darkness.

The deputy was debating whether to reload and go after him when he heard a swift rataplan of hoofbeats behind the saloon.

They dwindled rapidly. Blackstone grimaced. The rapscallion had had his horse hidden back there and was making his getaway—again.

Blackstone heaved a sigh and went back indoors. Harville was down on his knees beside the prone salesman.

"He's dead," Harville announced.

"Pity, that." Blackstone threw both his empty guns on the bar. "But at least it means you're not too busy to get me a tall whiskey. The good Lord knows, I need one."

CHAPTER 30

Cord was about to hurry out of the marshal's office when Blackstone returned.

"What the hell happened?" he asked. "It sounded like a war broke out."

"It was one of those black duster killers," Blackstone said. "In town and playing cards at the Golden Nugget. Ended up starting a gunfight with a salesman from back East who came into town a couple of days ago."

"How many killed?"

"Just one." Blackstone paused. "Although two of the bar girls caught stray bullets. Doc is looking at them now."

"And our gunfighter?"

"Galloped out of town about ten minutes ago. Heading that-away." Blackstone pointed north.

"All right." Cord went to the gun cabinet and put up the shotgun he had grabbed as soon as he pulled on his boots following the outbreak of gunfire. "The sun will be up in a few hours. We should have a fresh set of tracks to follow. If we light out now, bring lanterns, and keep at it, we should be well along his trail by sunup."

It's time to end this, Cord thought.

There was no way around it anymore. The gunmen were here to kill him and they would not let up. Removing one member of their group had failed to dissuade them. So long as the two survivors persisted, no one in town was safe.

Cord and Blackstone lit out before dawn, both carrying lanterns, Cord in the lead. The gunman had been in too big a hurry to cover his tracks, and so the first third of their journey was easy. They blew out their lanterns as dawn softened the eastern sky and paused to take a drink of water from their canteens.

"He's headed toward that hunting cabin," Cord noted. "They used it as bait for their trap before, but now I'll bet they're actually holed up in it."

"They'll be lying in wait for us," Blackstone said. "So, what do we do?"

What indeed? These were canny men they tracked, treacherous and experienced. Cord considered the matter at length for several minutes before an idea occurred to him. He turned and inspected the horses.

"What do we have for supplies?" he asked.

"The usual." Blackstone shrugged. "Stuff we keep packed for emergencies. Enough to stay on the trail for a week. We're light on water, but there are streams around here."

"There's a creek up ahead," Cord confirmed, remembering his last ride through these parts.

"What are you thinking?" Blackstone's eyes narrowed as he asked the question.

Cord told him.

* * *

They split up. Blackstone kept to the column of tracks left behind by their quarry while Cord cut trail into the wilderness.

Errins's cabin lay farther up in the hills. Blackstone was making a beeline toward it. So somewhere up ahead, the gunmen would be lying in wait for him. Which was why Cord had left the Englishman instructions to call a halt to his pursuit well before nightfall and build a fire.

Cord, meanwhile, was following a route that circled around the base of the hills. With the gunmen's attention drawn by Blackstone's campfire, it was his intention to approach the cabin from behind and take them unawares. He was counting on boredom to make them careless. Blackstone would help enormously in this regard.

The Englishman did exactly as instructed. Cord reined to a stop when he saw the plume of smoke from the Englishman's fire rise from the trail below and smiled thinly, imagining the puzzlement of the gunmen.

They were tricky varmints, but they were about to have a trick pulled on them for a change.

Blackstone kept his fire burning through the afternoon.

Cord, for his part, pushed on. His path was a wide circle around the base of the hills where Errins's cabin was located. A ridge rose parallel with one side of the hills, and as he cantered between its thickset trees, he caught sight of the track upon which Blackstone had paused and caught sight of one of the gunmen riding in the Englishman's direction, too puzzled by what was going on to just sit back and wait.

Perfect.

Once he reached the backside of the hills, Cord dismounted and watered the horse. Although he was loath to spend the time, he also fed the animal and forced himself to take a few generous bites of hardtack. The next few hours would involve a great deal of work for both of them. He wanted to be ready. When he reckoned they were, he grasped the reins and began guiding the horse up the side of the hill.

The afternoon wore on. Cord and the horse fought their way up the steadily steepening hillside, pausing to rest in the occasional sloping meadow. After a while, the ground leveled out again. Sunset was coming soon.

He mounted and rode on, allowing the horse to pick its way through the underbrush. Cord kept one eye on the west as the sun lowered. Just as the light flattened into an orange bar on the horizon, the plume of smoke resumed from Blackstone's cookfire. Cord could almost hear the frustrated groans of the two gunmen lying in wait up the trail. Blackstone had timed things so that it would be full dark within minutes, and risky to anyone trying to approach his camp from a distance with lanterns. Cord had to conclude that their plan was working almost too well. They didn't want the gunmen to give up and return to their hideout.

Cord used the fading daylight to press on across the level hilltop. After another fifteen minutes, the back of Errins's cabin appeared in the distance ahead. Cord dismounted, left the horse with its reins dangling, and crept forward through the underbrush to view it more closely.

He remembered the cabin's features from his last visit and could tell, even from here, that it was deserted. The gunmen were down the trail, hunting Blackstone. Which was exactly where he wanted them.

Turning, he crept back through the forest to where he had left the horse. Then he settled down to wait.

Blackstone had made good use of his enforced halt. He now had a healthy fire going, a good stock of wood to fuel it, and his horse was gnawing contentedly on a nearby patch of grass. The

Englishman had unfastened one of his saddlebags and laid out his cooking gear, looking for all the world like a weary traveler who had simply paused along the trail to whip up dinner. Which he most definitely was. With one small caveat.

He had chosen his campsite with some thought, taking care to situate it at the bottom of a low rise with only a single approach. To get at him from up top required struggling through a thicket of trees and brush and then crossing a rock-strewn section of open ground. It would be impossible to do that without making a considerable amount of noise. Blackstone had built his camp so that these obstacles faced anyone approaching from behind.

The back side of his fire ring was built up a little higher than the other three sides. Tucked in among the stones was Blackstone's shaving mirror, positioned so that he could watch the tree line while his back was turned.

At first, he had not been sure, but now he was satisfied the stirring he spied amongst the trees was not caused by wind but human movement. One or more of the gunmen were over there, watching, but he was making no effort to advance on Blackstone's position.

He was probably on his own, the Englishman thought. He watched until the movement ceased.

Then he threw sand on the fire, mounted his horse, and went after the man.

Cord's vigil ended with him catching sight of a figure approaching the cabin through the trees.

It was one of the two gunmen. Cord could not tell which at this distance, but the black duster and the furtive movements were enough to tip him off. The man was moving quickly, making for the door of the ruined cabin before disappearing inside.

Now was the time to move, thought Cord.

He finally had one of them alone, and that was likely about as even as the odds were going to get. Killing one of the surviving pair would leave the last gunman on his own. Cord felt confident he would abandon the mission at that point.

He began creeping toward the cabin from the back side, which had no windows. Placing his boots cautiously, he walked a tightrope of clear ground along a narrow track, careful not to rustle the grass or snap any dry twigs. A breeze rose as he moved, drowning out smaller noises, so he picked up the pace and came to within ten feet of the cabin, where he crouched behind a stand of rocks he found there and closed his eyes to listen.

The breeze died. Birds chittered. And the sound of cookpots rattling around came from within the cabin.

Cord grinned.

He had him now.

The gunman Blackstone was following had almost reached the cabin. Blackstone saw the second horse tied to the porch rail and knew the other hired killer must be inside, so he decided to make his move sooner rather than later. He drew his coach gun, brought the weapon to his shoulder, and cocked both hammers as he nudged his horse forward out of the trees. The ominous, unmistakable sound caused the gunman to stop short.

"Don't move," Blackstone said. "Put your hands up over your head."

The horseman's stiffness betrayed his fear. Blackstone noted the slow, cautious way he raised his hands. This wasn't the slowness of a man seeking to be uncooperative. It was the slowness of a man taken by surprise, worried and anxious as hell he was about to get plugged by whoever had him covered.

"Draw your gun out backward with your left hand and toss it aside," said Blackstone.

The man was complying, reaching across his own body with a cross draw, when gunfire sounded from the cabin.

* * *

Cord wasn't sure how the gunman spotted him—perhaps he had carved a knothole in the back wall and checked it from time to time—but spot Cord he had. He leaped off the end of the porch, a gun in each hand, and began firing into the underbrush. Cord barely managed to avoid being hit.

Hooves came thundering up to the cabin. It was the other killer, in full flight, with Blackstone right behind him. The first one spun to see what was going on, and Cord stood upright from the brush and opened fire on him. The bullet narrowly missed the man on the ground, but it sailed past him, and fate guided it home. The slug smashed into the chest of the mounted gunman and drove him backward out of the saddle.

In the second afterward, the remaining gunman managed to snap off a shot at Blackstone. The Englishman tumbled off his horse to land beside the man Cord had shot.

Instead of staying to continue the fight, the black-clad gunman dashed to the corner of the cabin and disappeared around it just as Cord reached the front of the structure. Cord crouched and lifted his gun, expecting the man to use the cabin for cover and throw more lead at him.

Nothing happened. His revolver up and ready, Cord eased around the cabin and spotted the gunman disappearing into the trees. Cord's head turned one way and then the other as his gaze moved back and forth between the killer and the motionless shape of his friend and deputy lying on the ground.

With a grimace of frustration, Cord turned and hurried to Blackstone's side.

"Is the dastardly scum dead?"

"He is."

Cord knelt beside Blackstone, where he sat with his back propped against the porch steps. Cord kept pressure on the wound to Blackstone's left arm with a thick bandanna he'd fished from a saddlebag. The blood flow was slowing, but it would still be some time before the big Englishman was fit to ride. They would have to spend the night here and light out in the morning.

"Did you see which way the last one went?" Blackstone asked.

"Out into the trees. That way." Cord indicated the direction with a lean of his head. "Moving quicker than a snake."

"Do you happen to have a bottle of painkiller handy?"

"I do." Cord grinned and drew a flask of whiskey from his saddlebag. He had fetched his horse from the trees behind the cabin once he'd made sure the fallen gunman was dead and helped Blackstone to the porch. "A few sips of this should set you right."

"Ahh. Mother's milk. Thank you, Cord." Blackstone accepted the flask and took a healthy pull. As he lowered it, he said, "My guess is we've likely seen the last of that scoundrel. Three of them came out here. Now there's only one left. If I was that lad, I'd cut my losses and head back East."

"Agreed." Cord accepted the flask when Blackstone held it out and took a deep drink himself. "He can try to finish the contract from Stockton and die. Or abandon it, lose the money, and keep his life. Which do you think he'll choose?"

"His life," said Blackstone. "Any other choice would be madness."

CHAPTER 31

Cord's return to town with Blackstone the following morning generated considerable attention. A small crowd gathered outside the marshal's office as Cord dismounted and helped the wounded Englishman down from the saddle.

"What happened?" cried one of the saloon girls from the Golden Nugget.

"Deputy Blackstone was wounded in the line of duty," Cord announced. "It's regrettable. But the gunmen who were terrorizing our town have been dealt with. They're gone."

A cheer went up from the assembled townsfolk, with men stepping in to pound Cord on the back and congratulate him as a flock of saloon girls descended on Blackstone with much petting and clucking over him in concern. The big, hearty Englishman was well-liked in the community.

"We'd better get you to the doc," said Cord.

"Don't worry, Marshal!" cried the saloon girl who had spoken earlier. "We'll take care of this big, strong, handsome man! Won't we, girls?"

Cord watched with a smile as the group conveyed him down the street toward the town physician's office. Blackstone looked back over his shoulder with a helpless but happy grin. Much as Cord wanted to be there when Blackstone arrived at the doc's, he realized that his partner was in excellent hands.

Slowly, the crowd dispersed. Cord went into his office and closed the door, leaving a solitary figure remaining behind.

Jeremiah Ponder studied the closed door of the marshal's office. Then he watched Blackstone and his caretakers disappear inside the doctor's office. He was shaken to the core in a manner he found deeply troubling.

He never thought things would go this far.

Ponder had no great fondness for the law. And he didn't particularly like the burly Englishman who helped Cord Bennett keep order in town. But his arrangement with Dollie Whittaker, intended to free him from the attacks of the miners and help her undermine Teddy Harville, had moved way beyond a mere alliance of convenience into a constellation of violence that was threatening to consume the town.

Put simply? He didn't trust her anymore.

Not that he ever had, to any great extent. They could cooperate to achieve common goals. But now Ponder was having second thoughts. Dollie Whittaker's mission of vengeance—against Kat Olmsted, against Teddy Harville, against the Golden Nugget, against the peace of the town itself—had gone off the rails and was threatening to take Ponder and his business along with it.

This has to stop, he thought.

He would have to do something. Confronting Dollie in a straightforward fashion made sense but came with substantial risks. He didn't wish to be added to her list of enemies. She had already demonstrated how ruthless she could be.

But neither could he continue to function as her unquestioning ally. It would be wise to put some distance between the two of them. But how?

He would have to speak with her. It wasn't something he looked forward to doing, but he had no choice. He would put his affairs in order and make sure that his interests were covered. Then he would sit down and renegotiate his deal with the devil.

Ponder put in a full morning's work at the office, conferring frequently with Hansen regarding pending and upcoming projects and scheduling men and shifts accordingly. Then he sat down with his accountant and examined his ledgers. His accountant, a balding, bespectacled man named Bartley, sat by, ready to explain discrepancies in the accounts.

"So, we cleared one thousand in profits last month?" he asked.

"On paper," Bartley clarified. "About one third of that is in bills coming due. Some are actually overdue. But that's where we sit right now."

"Comfortably in the black?"

Bartley tugged his glasses from his face and polished them furiously. "In the black, yes. Comfortably? Well, that's a matter of interpretation, I suppose."

"I'm going to be withdrawing some cash from the safe this afternoon, Bartley." Ponder stretched and sat back. "I have some business that's going to require cash."

"Of course, Mr. Ponder." Bartley took back the main ledger. "I'll reflect the withdrawal here, of course. May I ask? How much are you talking about?"

"A thousand dollars."

Bartley's surprised disapproval manifested in a sudden rush of inhaled breath and a sucking of teeth. "A thousand *dollars*? Oh my. Oh my."

Ponder waited.

"All right, Mr. Ponder," Bartley said at last. "I've made the adjustment. We do have some bills pending, but if we hold off a few days, we should be able to make our payroll and operating budget projections. We should be fine."

"That's good. Thanks, Bartley."

Ponder waited until the office staff had gone home before entering the back room, where the huge brass safe was kept. Kneeling, he twirled the lock until the tumblers clanked and hauled open the door.

Inside, amidst sheaves of legal documents and bags of gold, were piles of legal tender. Ponder reached in and withdrew several stacks of bills. Kneeling before the safe, he counted out one thousand dollars and placed it in his pants pocket before returning to his office.

Putting on his coat and hat, he locked the office door and headed out. The yard was empty except for one late team cutting planks for a construction project. Their foreman would lock up the yard when they finished for the day.

On his way down the street, he saw Cord Bennett lounging in the doorway of the marshal's office with a faraway look in his eyes as he leaned a shoulder against the jamb. Ponder stopped and spoke to him.

"How is Mr. Blackstone doing?" he asked.

"Well enough, I suppose." Cord sighed. "Doc says it's too soon to tell, but he thinks my deputy will keep the use of his arm. And that's good news."

"It is." Ponder paused for a moment, considering. "You know, Marshal, I don't reckon enough people thank you properly for the risks you take doing the job you do. I appreciate it. I really appreciate both of you for all the work you do."

"You're welcome, Mr. Ponder." Cord smiled tiredly. "We're glad to do it."

Ponder tipped his hat and continued down the street. Coming to the Bear Flag, he paused, seeming to consider his options, before finally turning to push through the batwings and go inside.

The saloon was doing a brisk business at this time of day. Dollie Whittaker sat at her customary table on the raised dais, occasionally looking up from her papers and ledgers to appraise the room. Her acknowledgment of Jeremiah Ponder's arrival was a glance and a pause—a form of genteel startlement. The mill owner steered in her direction through the wilderness of tables, returning the greetings of the mill workers who recognized him and said hello.

"Oh, evening, Boss." Hansen looked up from a poker game he was playing with a group of lumbermen. "Care to sit in? Penny stakes."

"Thanks, no." Ponder patted Hansen's shoulder on the way by. Dollie Whittaker was closing her ledger now, watching him with puzzlement. They had agreed never to meet openly, so this sudden breach in etiquette was unusual.

"Good evening, Mr. Ponder," she said coolly as he approached. "To what do I owe this *unexpected* pleasure?"

"Miss Whittaker." Ponder doffed his hat. "I would like to request an audience. Something has come up."

"Very well." She smiled and drew a slip of paper toward her, upon which she scrawled a note. Folding the paper, she handed it to him. Ponder pocketed the note without reading it, ordered a beer at the bar, drank half, and left.

He unfolded the slip of paper in the street outside. The curtly worded instructions were to present himself at the back door in fifteen minutes. He did so at the appointed time and was admitted by one of the saloon girls, who conducted him to Dollie's rear office. He arrived to find her waiting behind the desk.

"Please close the door," she said imperiously. "It would not do for people to see us associating, don't you agree?"

"Why, yes, I do."

"Then *why* did you risk coming here so openly?" There was no raising of the voice, no violent gesture needed. All she had to do was widen her eyes slightly to convey menace. "That was never part of our arrangement, so I can't see why you would do this now."

"I had a visit from the marshal," he said.

These words had the desired effect. Dollie Whittaker was suddenly caught up short, skidding to a stop and considering her next words carefully. Ponder noted the hesitation in her eyes, even as she rolled a hand and affected nonchalance.

"Go ahead," she urged.

He waited a beat. Ponder had given his lie lengthy consideration, convinced all the bases and loopholes were covered. Nevertheless, he proceeded slowly.

"I was surprised when he showed up at the mill the other night. I was working late when Bennett came sniffing around, asking questions about those gunmen. I gather he's been able to run one or more of them down—"

"How did he tie them to you?" Ponder noted how she refrained from using the word *us*.

"I'm not sure. And I'm not convinced he has. Not conclusively, anyway. But it's enough to give me pause." He drew a deep breath and studied the ceiling. "Look, I'm having some second thoughts about the direction things are going. I think that we should maybe pull in the reins and slow down a bit. Hold off on further action against the Nugget and the miners. I understand this cuts into your plans and your bottom line, so . . ."

He fished in his pockets and produced the money he had taken from the safe.

"I'd like to propose an adjustment to our arrangement. We hold off on any further provocations. And in acknowledgment of the difficulty this may cause you . . ." He stacked the bills on the desk. "Here is a little something to see you through."

Dollie Whittaker's eyes fell on the stacks of bills. As Ponder had anticipated, the sight of so much money was enough to get her attention. She appeared to be counting in her head, squaring up Ponder's request with the amount on the desk before her. Then she looked up and spoke in a cold voice.

"Coward."

The word fell in the small room like an axe.

"Coward!" She leaned forward and brought her fist down on the desk, raging now and filled with contempt. "You expect you can just come in here and buy me off? What kind of a despicable creature are you, Ponder? The kind to shrink from a fight? The kind to flinch back and retreat the moment you encounter some kind of resistance? What kind of a worm behaves that way?"

Ponder jerked back, as if struck in the face.

"We have an agreement, Mr. Ponder." Dollie Whittaker rose, fists on the desk in front of her, chin raised imperiously as she glared down her nose at the lumber baron. "This is not the sort of arrangement you can just back out of when you get scared, or because it suits you! I can see that I am going to have to assume a position of guidance and leadership where this situation is concerned. And the first step I am going to take is to remind you of the trouble you would be in if I brought your relationship with those gunmen to the marshal's attention!"

"W-Wait." Ponder held up his hands. "*Relationship*?"

"You admitted to me right here in this room that you engaged their services to fire on the miners outside the lumberyard! It surely would not take much, even for a man of Cord Bennett's limited intellectual gifts, to tie you to them! Especially after what happened when you led him out to that ambush. No, Mr. Ponder."

Ponder stared at her. "I . . . I had nothing to do with that ambush."

"Please," Dollie said, rolling her eyes. "It's patently obvious that you led Bennett into that trap. I'm sure even he's figured that out by now. Whatever possessed you to do that, anyway?"

Ponder looked stubborn and defiant, but only for a moment. Then his shoulders slumped and he sighed. There was no denying what Dollie had worked out.

"They approached me," he admitted. "Or rather, their leader did. He showed up at my office at the mill one night when I was working there alone. He frightened me considerably at first. I thought he was there to rob me! But then he explained that he'd been watching for an opportunity to make a business proposition to me. He and his partners had come to Rio Oro to kill Cord Bennett, he said, but he didn't see why they shouldn't make some extra money on the side by helping me break the power of the miners."

"You want to break the miners so that you can move in and grab their claims," Dollie guessed. "Probably working behind the scenes with some proxy owners."

Ponder shrugged in acceptance of her theory. "Something like that," he said. "In the long run, the more miners abandon their claims, the more wealth I would get my hands on, sooner or later. And then . . ." He made a face. "And then those hired killers had me over a barrel. They threatened to expose what I was doing unless I helped them in their primary objective, which was to get rid of that damned Cord Bennett. I never liked the way the man was sniffing around my business, so I went along with the idea." He shook his head dolefully. "But that didn't work, either."

"That seems to be a common thread running through your efforts, Jeremiah," Dollie said. She smiled thinly. "Thinking for yourself just doesn't seem to work out for you. Which is why I think our arrangement will remain exactly as is, with one exception. Going forward, you will do what you are told when you are told to do it. By me. I hope that's clear." She sat, not waiting for his response, and didn't even deign to look at him as she added,

"I think that will be enough for today, Mr. Ponder. You can show yourself out."

Ponder heard rather than saw the burly barman appear in the doorway. He had no idea how Dollie had summoned the man, but the aura of menace radiating from him was unmistakable.

Ponder was out the back door and in the alley before he realized that Dollie Whittaker still had his thousand dollars.

Chapter 32

The tip, when it came, was unexpected and most definitely a long shot. But Cord and Blackstone agreed they had to check it out.

As before, it was one of the Griffith brothers who shared the news. Members of their family had a habit of wandering far and wide for various reasons, so they often returned with news from the wider world. A few hours' ride west of town lay a mining camp where three score miners in the employ of some company back East sought to wrest precious metals from the Earth. Blackstone reported what he had heard to Cord—that a man in a black duster had recently ridden into the miners' camp offering his services as an enforcer.

"Sounds like our man," Cord admitted.

Although satisfied the danger to Rio Oro was past, they agreed that a trip to the mining camp was in order—if for no other reason than to clap irons on the leader of the trio that had wrought so much havoc in their town. Although the wound on Blackstone's arm continued to nag at him, they made arrangements to set out that very morning.

"He'd be a fool to stay around there too long," Blackstone said. "Anything more than a day or two would be a surefire ticket to the gallows."

"The gallows is where I aim to put him," Cord said. "After a fair trial in front of Judge Davenport, at any rate."

"Fair or not so fair, I'll be happy just to see the scoundrel swing."

"We both will. I'm convinced they're the ones who gunned down those miners in cold blood."

It was a long, hot ride. After two hours, they were only too pleased to stop in some trees by a still pond. They made a quick pot of coffee, ate some rations, and were preparing to mount up again when Blackstone noted a plume of dust rising in the distance.

"That'd be the mining camp," he said. "You can tell they've just dumped a big pile of tailings. Probably from the back of a wagon."

"Is that right?"

"Plenty of mines back in England," said the deputy. "It's a sight I recognize and know well."

"I'll take your word for it."

They rode on. Narrow trails appeared, widening to become wagon roads the nearer they approached the mine. It was by one of these that they spotted the sign.

TAYLOR MINE
ANDREW TAYLOR, ESQ., PROPRIETOR
EMPLOYEES AND OFFICIAL BUSINESS ONLY BEYOND THIS POINT
TRESPASSERS WILL BE SHOT

"Friendly bunch," quipped Blackstone.

"Given the way things are here, can't say I blame them." Cord touched the badge on his vest, glad of the authority it provided. Technically, of course, his jurisdiction only included Rio Oro and the surrounding area, but most folks would think twice before shooting at somebody wearing a lawman's badge.

Up ahead, around a bend in the trail, they met the first employee of the Taylor mine. Astride a mule and cradling a sawed-off shotgun, the grubby, grizzled old-timer wore a flat hat and a flea-bitten black overcoat. He recognized the badge on Cord's chest and nodded respectfully.

"Afternoon, Marshal," he said. "Mine office is right at the end of this trail. It's the first building in camp."

"Boss likes to keep an eye on comings and goings?"

"You could say that." The old-timer's cheeks spread in a grim smile. "George Taylor's the foreman's name. He'll see to whatever you need."

"Much obliged." Cord touched his hat brim.

"You fellas hire any new talent lately?" Blackstone asked, wincing briefly as his arm pained him. "Anyone, say, wearing a black duster?"

Cord saw a flicker of recognition in the man's eyes, but he answered with a shrug and repeated, "Mr. Taylor will see to whatever you need."

Cord thanked him again and they moved on, slowly walking their horses down the last quarter mile of trail. The unpainted wooden building that was the mine office appeared up ahead, right where the sentry had said it would be. The access to the mine entrance, shunting and grading yard, and outbuildings lay beyond a narrow cleft in the rock that formed a natural wall and gate around the Taylor holdings. As they approached, Cord could see two figures at work near the mine entrance.

"I wonder if George is Andrew Taylor's son?" Blackstone asked as they dismounted and led their horses through the cleft toward the office.

He turned out to be Taylor's grandson. A bookish man with prematurely graying hair and a pair of thick spectacles, George Taylor immediately ceased working with his papers to give the two lawmen a serious hearing.

"We're following up on some information we received regarding a fella we'd like to locate," Cord began. "We'd heard tell he might have signed on with you here. Wanted to ask about it."

"Sure thing. Glad to help." Taylor stepped over to a work counter and took up a leather-bound ledger. "Do you have the man's name? We get men in and out of here quite frequently. Mine work isn't for everyone."

"This man wouldn't be working in the mine. We heard he was looking for a job as an enforcer. Man in a black duster. Fellow about fifty or so. Graying hair. Craggy features. He might be going by the name Anderson."

Taylor immediately started and looked up. "Gordon Anderson," he said. "That's the man's name. And yes, he was working here. Until this morning. Gave his notice and left about an hour ago."

Cord's heart began to pound. "Any idea which direction he was headed?" he asked.

"He said he was going back East." Taylor shrugged. "I didn't press him. To tell you the truth, he was the sort of man who gave me a bad feeling. We have a number of guards, and they're tough men, make no mistake about that. But there was something different about this one. I was glad he decided not to stay. Saved me the trouble of telling him I'd changed my mind and he would have to move on."

Cord and Blackstone exchanged a look.

"Reckon we got what we came for." Cord touched his hat brim. "Much obliged to you, Mr. Taylor."

"This fellow Anderson, was I right about him? Is he bad news?"

"The worst," Cord said.

They rode hard and found trail sign within a few hours. Anderson had stopped to rest himself and his mount, built a fire, and watered his horse at a stream before continuing on. His path led in the general direction of Rio Oro.

"He's making tracks, and fast," Blackstone noted as they mounted up to resume pursuit. "Where do you think he's headed?"

"My guess is he'll keep heading East, probably all the way back to Missouri. He's run into one wall after another since he and his partners came out here. But the way he's going, he might be planning on making one last stop in Rio Oro. His failure to kill me and carry out the job Stockton sent him on could be eating at him. That might be why he gave up the job at the mine as fast as he did." Cord squinted at the ground where the tracks were. "I reckon we'll know soon enough. He's not that far ahead of us."

The sun was high in the sky when the buildings of Rio Oro appeared in the distance. They were gaining on their quarry now, the tracks fresher with each passing hour. Cord's throat was dry, his heart hammering in expectation.

"What do you think he's going to do when he gets there?" asked Blackstone.

"Hard to say," Cord muttered, squinting. "He'll look for me first, and when he doesn't find me—"

Right then, gunshots popped faintly in the distance.

They were still a ways from Rio Oro, and the trouble had already started. Could they get there in time to keep the crazed gun-wolf Anderson from killing anybody else?

Cord didn't know, but they had to try.

His stomach plunged as he thought about Glory. There was a good chance she and Kat and their pa weren't even in town right now. They were probably safe up at the claim.

But he didn't know that for sure, and even if they were, there were other people in Rio Oro he cared about, innocent people who didn't deserve to be gunned down by a lobo like Anderson. He gritted his teeth and rode as hard as he could, but after a few minutes, he sensed that something was wrong. Slowing, he turned.

Blackstone was doubled over in the saddle, right hand up to his left arm. Cord rode back to him hurriedly. As he approached, he could see the Englishman's face had gone a stark shade of white.

"Bart, what—"

"No, no." The deputy whispered fiercely, shaking his head. "I'll be fine. Bloody arm just started bleeding again." The realization of what he'd just said jerked a harsh laugh out of him. "Cord, you go ahead. You go get that killer."

"You sure?"

"Go!"

Cord swallowed, nodded, and galloped off toward Rio Oro as fast as he possibly could.

The gunfire had ended well before Cord reached the settlement, and knowing that plunged his spirits to the bottom of his guts.

Quite a few people were in the street as he rode in, including a small crowd in front of the assayer's office. Cord headed for there first, conscious of the attention he was drawing from the townspeople. When the knot of men in front of Clyde Casterline's office heard his horse coming, they turned to look and parted enough for Cord to spot the slender figure lying on the ground.

He recognized Casterline, and that was like another punch in his belly. He swung down from the saddle before his horse completely stopped moving and ran to the assayer and land agent's side.

Casterline was alive, Cord saw to his great relief. The man even sat up as Cord dropped to a knee beside him. The left leg of Casterline's trousers was bloody, and he had a streak of crimson on the side of his forehead too.

Cord gripped his shoulder and asked, "Clyde, how bad is it?"

Casterline was a little wild-eyed. "I saw him, Cord!" he blurted out. "That varmint in the black duster. I saw him ride in and go charging into the marshal's office with a gun in each hand. He was looking for you!"

Cord wasn't surprised to hear that. Anderson was making one last-ditch, near-suicidal effort to fulfill the task Hiram Stockton had paid him to do.

"I grabbed my rifle and headed for your office," Casterline went on. "I was going to try to trap him in there. But he came out shooting and winged me right off, the blasted skunk! Knocked a leg out from under me, and then a bullet grazed me on the head. Knocked me silly, it did. I reckon I must've blacked out for a minute. When I woke up, he was gone."

"That's the truth of it, Marshal," one of the bystanders put in. "Plenty of us saw Clyde go after that varmint."

"What happened to the gunman?" Cord asked tightly.

"He got back on his horse and lit a shuck out of town, headin' East."

Cord turned back to Casterline and asked again, "How bad are you hurt?"

"I don't think it's too serious. That first bullet knocked a chunk of meat out of my leg. I suppose I lost enough blood that it made me a little lightheaded. I keep—"

Casterline's eyes rolled up in their sockets, and he would have fallen backward from his sitting position if Cord hadn't grabbed him.

"That's the second time he's gone out like that, Marshal," a man said.

"Here comes the doc!" added another bystander.

Carefully, Cord lowered Casterline and then turned him over to the doctor when the medico bustled up. He stood and looked around at the crowd.

"Was anybody else hurt?"

Several men shook their heads.

"No, that fella in the black duster got out of here in a hurry after he ventilated ol' Clyde," one said.

"He must've been lookin' for you, and when he didn't find you he just wanted to get out of town," added another.

"He was headed East, you said?"

More nods all around.

Cord's face was grim as he drew in a deep breath. Casterline was in good hands, and he had to see to it that Blackstone was as well.

But once that was done, he would get back on Gordon Anderson's trail. That man had to answer for all the damage he had caused since he'd come to California.

CHAPTER 33

Blackstone rode slowly into town on his own before Cord could go and fetch him. He leaned over in the saddle, favoring his injury. The wound in his arm had broken open again from all the bouncing around he'd done in the saddle during the past twenty-four hours, but the doctor cleaned and redressed it and pronounced that it ought to be all right, adding a stern warning to Blackstone that he should take it easy for at least a week.

Cord knew how unlikely it was that would happen, especially with Anderson still on the loose. So he threw his saddle on a fresh horse, grabbed a few supplies, and set out on the killer's trail while Blackstone was still groggy from the painkillers the doctor had given him.

As Cord rode out of Rio Oro, Teddy Harville was relaxing in more civilized surroundings, thanking his lucky stars for the way things had turned out.

He realized he was fortunate. To be sure, a crisis still gripped the town, what with the conflicts between the prospectors and the lumber mill, the intrusion of the gunfighters hunting the marshal, his own problems with the Bear Flag and its proprietor. But all things considered, he had made out better than most, his establishment existing now like an island of relative calm in a windswept ocean.

The Golden Nugget was doing a brisk business following the shoot-out in the street a while earlier. People were excited and wanted to talk about what had happened, and they wanted to wet their whistles while they were talking. Men crowded the bar in the Nugget.

Even over the buzz of that excited discussion, Harville heard the rattletrap clanking of wagon wheels. He looked up and spotted the vehicle through the window as it slowed, recognizing the specialized conveyance of Moses Avery, the traveling attorney-at-law whose business often brought him through town.

Jeremiah Ponder had recommended the man's services. Harville had filed that information away in case he ever needed it. But as it happened Avery was the one who approached him today.

The special box wagon fitted out with all manner of official papers and seals and legal reference books crammed into a small office on wheels pulled to a stop before the saloon doors. Avery himself descended from the driver's box before entering the wagon briefly to grab something. He emerged holding a sheaf of papers. Pausing to examine the state of his hair and suit in the mirror inset behind the door, he adjusted his glasses, flicked dust from his collar, and turned to business.

He came through the batwing doors and approached Harville with a broad smile on his face and a hand extended.

"Teddy, how are you?" They shook. "Hope I'm not interrupting anything."

"No." Harville was a bit startled but not alarmed. Avery was a fine, if sometimes hard-bitten fellow. He had a reputation for scrupulous fairness. "How long have you been in town?"

"Just rode in, actually. May I?" The lawyer placed his hand on a chairback. At Harville's nod, he took a seat. "Been making the usual circuit of the mining camps and towns in this area. Stopped in on a few ranches. I spent my off-hours drafting a contract here and there. Teddy, I wanted to broach the topic of a sale with you. I mean the sale of your property here in Rio Oro. You've been in business a while and have built up a steady business. No doubt you could push a hard bargain if someone was offering to buy."

"Offering to buy?" Harville's eyebrows shot up toward his hairline. "You looking to get out of the lawyering business, Avery?"

"What if I was?" The man shrugged. "Don't you think I could run a saloon?"

"Why, sure." Harville was startled. "But why would you want to? Lawyering pays much better, I'd imagine."

"But just *say* I was interested. Just for pretend." Avery signaled the barman to come over. He ordered a half bottle of whiskey and two glasses. "What kind of terms do you think I could get for a place like this? This is the kind of information that could help me down the road, say, with a sales contract."

Harville considered all this carefully. The bartender arrived and, as he set down the two glasses, Harville reckoned it seemed he was having a drink whether he wanted one or not. He considered Avery's question carefully.

"Well, I'd say for a down payment nothing less than three thousand dollars. I know it's a lot, but I do good business here. Cheers." He clinked glasses with the lawyer before resuming. "I might be willing to negotiate some, but not too much."

"What's the lowest you'd consider for a cash price?"

"Nothing under five thousand." Harville shook his head. "Considering that I'd walk away with the money and the buyer would be stuck with all the headaches. A lot more goes into this place than people imagine."

"No doubt that's true." Avery drank off his glass and poured himself another. "And I'm guessing things like inventory on hand, glasses, cutlery, all that sort of stuff would be included?"

"Why, I—" Harville paused abruptly. Something about this conversation struck him as peculiar. "Moses, let me ask you something. Is all this talk just hypothetical? Or are you actually . . . ?"

"Actually what?"

"Negotiating." Harville said the word firmly, his tone leaving no doubt to his resolve. "Because this has all been very vague so far, but when you start asking me to factor in the price of crockery and movables, you get me wondering."

"All right, look." Avery held up his hands. "I'm not going to dissemble with you, Teddy. I've heard a fair amount of talk about this place. And not just here in Rio Oro. It's seen as a desirable property—a business on the rise in a fortunate town. Others are taking notice."

"Are you here representing a prospective buyer?"

"Truthfully?" Avery paused. "Truthfully, I have been approached by multiple parties about making an offer on the Golden Nugget. You can imagine, Teddy, given my line of work how that sudden flush of good luck struck me. It makes *me* curious to learn more about the value of whatever so many consider desirable. So, my questions are sincere. And I suppose I have to ask, too, *would* you consider selling it? Ever?"

"For the right price, sure."

"And if someone were to meet your right price? And then some?"

"You mean more than five thousand?"

"More than *seven.*"

Now Avery had his attention. Teddy Harville leaned his elbows on the table, clasping his hands and resting his chin atop the knuckles as he examined the itinerant lawyer with real interest. Someone prepared to offer more than *seven thousand dollars* for his humble establishment was a person of real significance. That kind of money could see Harville set for life, provided he played his hand well in negotiations. He drew a breath and opened his mouth, prepared to ask a probing question when Avery surprised him by unfolding the sheaf of papers he held.

"I have a draft offer here for eight thousand. It's a contract. Go on and examine it if you like." Moses Avery refolded the sheaf and pushed it across the table.

"Well, I'll be." Harville shook his head, eyeing the papers admiringly. "You mean to tell me you've had multiple discussions with multiple parties interested in my business and one was serious enough to have you draft a contract?"

"For *eight thousand dollars,* Teddy. I'd think this offer over carefully, because it may not come again."

"Don't I know it." Harville took up the contract and flipped to the first page. "Everything looks to be in order."

"I think you'll find it quite satisfactory." Avery's smile suggested that he had been promised a handsome commission on the sale.

Harville got to the third page and stopped.

"This is from—"

"Dollie Whittaker. Yes."

Harville closed his eyes. "Are you *serious*?"

"Quite. Why, I—"

Harville hurled the papers back with a will. Rising from his seat, he pounded the table, enraged. "You've come in here to offer me a sales contract from that damned *Dollie Whittaker*?"

"Well, yes." Moses Avery was aghast. "I don't understand why you're upset about that."

"Because she's tried to ruin my life multiple times now!"

Harville began pacing back and forth furiously. "She . . . she . . . she came in here and became my partner. My lover! Then she turned around and stabbed me in the back! She went and took over the Bear Flag. She's been trying to run me out of business. Stealing my customers! Bad-mouthing me to anyone who will listen! Getting her patrons to come over here and trash my place."

"I can see I've made a mistake." Avery hurriedly began to gather up the pages. "Teddy, I'm *so* sorry. I had no idea—"

"Then she tried getting me in trouble with the law. The *law*, Moses! and my business declared a menace to public safety. Tried to force me to sell out to her right then and there!"

"Teddy, I assure you." Avery rose from his seat and backed away, one hand up in front of him. "I won't ever say a word about this to you again. As God is my witness—"

Harville stood trembling, his eyes locked on the ceiling, fists clenched. It was clear to Avery that the man was cracking up before his eyes.

"Dragging me into a judge's chambers with the town marshal in attendance! People see these things! They gossip about 'em! If it ain't one thing, it's another!"

"Tell you what, Teddy." Fingers trembling, Avery fished a few dollars from his vest pocket and extended them to Harville. "Here's a donation. To the cause. To your saloon. To help with medical costs. *Whatever.* Just please, for God's sake, don't hurt me."

"Get out!"

"Okay." Avery paused. "You sure you don't want—"

"Out!"

After Avery scuttled back outside, Harville stood leaning on a chair and breathing heavily for several minutes. The bartender noticed Harville's distress and exchanged a glance with one of the saloon girls. They had never seen Teddy Harville behave this way before, and it was unsettling to say the least.

"What do you think is the matter?" whispered the saloon girl.

"Moses Avery was just in here," replied the bartender softly.

"The lawyer? What did he want?"

"Can't say. But I—"

The bartender broke off as Teddy Harville straightened, turned, and marched straight toward the bar, a look of baleful determination lighting his face. The saloon girl scampered out of the way as he rounded the far end and bustled along the row of shelves containing liquor bottles.

"Is there something I can help you with, Mr. Harville?"

"Shut up!" Harville barked. Reaching up, he grabbed two full bottles of whiskey and dragged them down to the bartop, where he unscrewed the caps and cast them aside.

The bartender watched in horror as Harville soaked two handkerchiefs in whiskey before pushing them into the open mouths of the bottles.

Dollie Whittaker was working late when Hap hurtled through the batwing doors and into the half-full saloon.

"Mr. Harville's g-gone crazy and he's coming this way!" he cried. "I'd clear out if I w-was you!"

Dollie Whittaker half rose from her table on the dais, ready to speak some calming words to Hap and her patrons. But Harville appeared in the street outside before she could do so.

"Dollie?" he cried. "Dollie Whittaker, you in there?"

"I'm here, Harville!" she called back as she started toward the batwings. "What do you want, sir?"

The men at the tables exchanged looks, rose, and left the saloon hurriedly, their drinks unfinished.

"I came to buy you a drink, you witch!"

Harville produced a book of matches and set the whiskey-soaked rags hanging from the mouths of the bottles alight.

Dollie took a step back, her hand rising to her mouth as Harville hurled the first of the improvised explosives at the Bear Flag. It missed by a wide margin, crashing in the street and flaming out.

The second one hit the batwing doors and shattered, and blazing whiskey splashed flames over them and the boardwalk.

CHAPTER 34

Every sense, every instinct in Cord's body was honed to a high level of alertness as he trailed the black-clad killer through the rugged hills east of Rio Oro.

He knew there was every possibility in the world that Gordon Anderson was lying in wait for him somewhere up ahead. Foiled at every turn, Anderson might give up on his murderous quest and rattle his hocks out of these parts, but there was just as good a chance that he'd try one more ambush.

The varmint was nothing if not stubborn. Cord had to give him credit for that.

Unfortunately, this rough country provided plenty of hiding places where a man intent on killing could take good cover. Cord knew that, and knew he would have to draw Anderson out, even if it meant increasing the risk to himself.

Because of that, he rode in the open, practically inviting a shot. His muscles and nerves were pulled tight, and his skin crawled as he anticipated the smashing impact of a bullet at any moment.

All he asked for was even a second of warning, anything that might give him even a sliver of a chance to escape death.

He got it in the wink of a stray beam of sunlight glinting off something metal in a thicket of brush atop a hill to his right.

Cord dived out of the saddle to the left as he heard a rifle shot crack. The bullet whined off a rock about ten yards from where Cord landed, telling him that it had passed through the space he'd occupied an instant earlier. He was drawing his Colt as he rolled toward another rock. He yelled, hoping the noise would spook his horse into moving on, out of the line of fire.

The horse spooked all right, dancing around wildly for a moment before galloping on down the trail as Cord reached the slab of rock. It was a couple of feet tall, tall enough to give him some cover if he stayed low. He pressed his face to the dirt as another shot blasted and a second slug ricocheted off harmlessly.

Knowing that Anderson would have to reload—there was no doubt at all in his mind that the bushwhacker was the man in the black duster—Cord pushed himself up on his left hand and used his right to thrust the Colt over the rock. He triggered two shots at the brush under the spot where a haze of powdersmoke floated in the air.

The range was a little long for a handgun, but Cord had elevated the Colt's barrel a little and believed the shots would carry that far. A sudden thrashing in the brush seemed to indicate that he was right. He hoped he had hit Anderson.

Hell, he hoped he'd blown the varmint's brains out.

The crack of another rifle shot a moment later told him that wasn't the case. He ducked. The bullet kicked up dirt behind his legs, which he had drawn up as much as he could. Anderson had shot high, but if this kept up, he might find the range.

Cord fired another round toward the bushwhacker and dropped down again. What Anderson did next surprised him.

"Bennett! You hear me, Bennett?"

The killer wanted to talk to him. Cord didn't have any idea what Anderson might have to say at this point. The time for talking had passed, if indeed it had ever existed.

Even so, curiosity prompted him to return the shout. "I hear you, Anderson! What do you want?"

"So you know my name." Anderson sounded a little surprised by that. "I reckon you probably know why I'm here too."

"I'd have to be a damned fool not to! Hiram Stockton sent you to kill me."

"You shouldn't have run out on his little girl and left her like that!"

"I didn't run out on Caroline, and I wasn't responsible for what happened to her. That was my brother Flint."

A harsh laugh came from Anderson. "I heard tell that he's dead! Mighty convenient to blame everything on him, ain't it?"

"It's the truth," Cord insisted. "You go back and tell that to Stockton."

"I'm not gonna tell him anything except that the man he paid me to kill is dead. You might as well step out in the open and get it over with, Bennett!"

Cord risked another look. He spotted a darker patch in the brush and thought that might be Anderson's duster. If he'd had his rifle and time to aim, he could drill the man from here, but under the circumstances, all he could do was snap another couple of shots in the right direction and hope.

That glance was enough to draw another shot from Anderson. It struck the slab so close to Cord's face that rock dust got in his eyes. He dropped down again, blinking furiously for a few seconds until his vision cleared. He knew Anderson would be reloading during that interval, but he risked pushing up and taking the shots anyway.

The Colt roared and bucked in his hand as he fired twice. At the same time, he heard Anderson's shot and felt the wind-rip of the slug as it passed close beside his left ear.

The brush thrashed again, even more wildly this time. Cord saw Anderson lurch upright and start to turn away. With one round left in his gun, Cord fired.

The black hat flew from Anderson's head, but the man kept moving, ducking back out of sight. Cord bit back a curse and dropped behind the rock slab again. As he started to reload as quickly as he could, he heard hoofbeats. The swift pounding of them came clearly to his ears, and then they began to diminish. Anderson was abandoning the ambush and making his getaway. Cord knew at least one of his shots must have found the killer. He had no way of knowing how badly Anderson was hit, but it must have been serious enough to make the man give up—for now.

But Cord had heard the deranged determination in Anderson's voice. If Anderson survived the wound, he would be back. The knowledge that he wasn't finished with the hired killer after all was a bitter, sour taste under Cord's tongue as he retrieved his horse. He would have to go after Anderson.

He had barely swung up into the saddle, though, when he realized the horse was favoring its right front leg. It had gone lame, probably from its violent reaction when the shooting started. With the bitterness inside him growing, Cord dismounted, checked the leg, and then began leading the horse back toward Rio Oro.

His pursuit of Gordon Anderson was over, and there wasn't a damned thing he could do about it except wait for the gunman to make his next move.

"Teddy?"

Harville opened one eye and immediately shut it. His head was pounding like a steam engine. He shifted his position, suddenly aware of his surroundings. He was very definitely *not* in his own comfortable bed at home but rather on the narrow wooden frame of a bunk.

That was when he remembered being banged over the head

and dragged into a cell by that big English deputy. Blackstone had had his wounded left arm in a sling by then, but there was nothing wrong with his right arm, which he had used when he slammed a gun butt into Harville's head.

With a heavy sigh, Teddy Harville opened both eyes and gingerly came to a seated position.

Cord Bennett was standing outside the cell with a bemused smile on his face. Harville mostly liked the marshal; considered him an asset to the community and a good man. But the smile on Bennett's face made him hate the marshal a little bit this morning.

"You remember what you did last night?"

Harville blinked. Shook his head. And remembered.

"They managed to put the fire out quickly enough, I'm told, although there was damage to the Bear Flag's doors and a set of chairs. The boardwalk will need to be repaired too. You'll be expected to pay for all that, Teddy."

Harville waved a hand dismissively. The costs would be incidental. Of course he would pay.

"I don't like coming back into town and finding that a man I've considered a friend tried to burn it down," Cord went on.

"I wasn't trying to burn down the town!" protested Harville. He winced as the reaction made his head hurt even worse. "Just one particular building."

"You know how fast fire can spread. That's one of the biggest dangers any settlement out here faces." Cord shook his head. "You really must not have been thinking straight. We're going to arrange for you and Dollie Whittaker to sit down with Judge Davenport again. Time to put this feud between the two of you to rest."

"But we've already *tried* that!" Harville's voice was a fierce croak.

"This time *I'm* the one requesting the meeting," Cord said. "And we're not leaving until things are settled."

Harville's mouth firmed, and he glared down at the floor, obviously frustrated. Cord could tell he wanted to say something but was restraining himself out of fear of making things worse.

"We have to come to some sort of solution about this, Teddy." Cord withdrew the key from where it was looped to his belt. "This town can't have you and Dollie Whittaker continually going at each other, using the prospectors and lumbermen as your soldiers. No, you're going to find a way to get along, or both your businesses will be shut down as hazards to public safety. You understand?"

Harville nodded miserably.

"Good." Cord opened the cell door and stood aside. "You're free to go. We'll see you and Dollie at Judge Davenport's later. Until then, I need you to stay out of trouble."

"I understand, Marshal."

"Good." Cord patted him on the shoulder. "Go home and get some rest."

Harville collected the contents of his pockets, which had been emptied into a box on Cord's desk upon his arrest. Then he slunk from the office, head down, shoulders slumped. A more defeated-looking man Cord had yet to see. He let Harville out, closing the door behind him and settling down to finish his report on the trouble he had found when he trudged back into Rio Oro the night before. He worked quickly, eager to finish. He had an important errand to run.

"My word, Glory! How much stuff do you intend to take with you?"

"Oh, Kat!" Glory heaved the box up onto her hip, blew a strand of hair from her forehead, and grinned at her sister. "I'm only taking what we'll need to get started!"

"Do you really need that extra kettle?" Kat, herself sweaty and disheveled from helping Glory load the wagon, squinted at the crate in her sister's hands critically. "And that bedspread was made by our mother!"

"So? She'd want me to have it!"

"You sound awfully confident." Kat lightened these words with a playful grin. "Well, go on ahead, then. I suppose I'll give my permission for you to take it."

"Ha! Like I need your permission!"

Kat swatted at Glory playfully and then stood in the doorway, watching her sister head out to add her crate to the load on the wagon parked out front.

She sighed, knowing this would be one of the last chances she and Glory would have to banter together as sisters living together. In just a few days, Garrison Lomax would be tying the knot for them, and she would leave Abraham's house forever to begin life as Cord Bennett's wife. A better life for her sister Kat could not imagine.

Cord appeared just as Glory was loading the crate onto the wagon. She set down the box with a thump, turned, and went to Cord, steadying his horse as he dismounted and took her into his arms.

"Well, hello there, good sir," she whispered, crushing him to her.

"Hey." He hugged her back, delighting in her softness and fresh scent. "Looks like you're piling up the whole house on the back of that wagon!"

"Well, I want us to be prepared!" She grinned teasingly.

"Sure, but are you fixing on leaving anything for your dad and sister?"

Kat laughed out loud at this. She leaned against the side of the wagon, arms crossed, an approving smile on her face.

"I told her she can take as much as she wants," Kat said. "The more she takes, the more excuses I'll have to come visit."

"You'll be welcome any time," Cord said. "You and your pa both will."

"I know." Kat's smile softened. "But you won't see too much of us at first. We want to be sure to give the happy couple their privacy."

Cord and Glory laughed at this. They were surely looking forward to those private moments.

"Shall I accompany you up to our place?" Cord asked.

"That would be nice, Cord. But I think Pa could use a hand with the sluice." Glory gestured at the damaged machine, where it sat partially disassembled. "It's been a caution for him this past week. Another strong pair of arms would do wonders."

"All right," Cord said as he stepped back from her. "You go on ahead. But be careful, you hear? I want you in one piece for our wedding."

"So do I, Cord. So do I."

Cord and Abraham were laboring together over the sluice as Glory pulled out of the yard, reins in one hand as she waved goodbye with the other. She rode onto the wagon trail, guiding the horses with a twitch of the reins and setting out for Ghost Canyon. She made good time, moving past the newest claims into territory that had not yet been registered and apportioned at the assayer's office. Sooner or later, she knew, prospective gold hunters would appear, and Clyde Casterline would divvy up these pristine plots. But for now, they were open space. Glory enjoyed the sensation of being out beyond the hustle and bustle of the townsfolk.

She was a mile or two into her excursion when a curious prickling rippled the back of her neck.

She was not a woman given to mistrustful thoughts. And she had given consideration to what marrying a lawman would mean regarding her personal safety. She had yet to accept Cord's invitation to shooting lessons but knew that she eventually would be forced to learn. Yes, his was a hazardous profession. But now that the gunmen had been killed or driven off, she had no reason to imagine she was in any danger.

So why couldn't she shake the weird sense that someone was watching her?

She reined the horses to a stop, twisted in her seat, and examined the trail behind her. There was no sign of anyone. Not a soul.

She was just nervous because the wedding was approaching, she told herself.

She resumed the journey, turning off the trail and into the cut of Ghost Canyon. As ever when she undertook this trip, she marveled at the scenic beauty of the place Cord had chosen as their home. High rock walls clawed the sky to either side of the canyon, the sloping hills at their base forested and the little lowland enriched by the tributary from the main stream that ran through it. She found the nearly finished cabin as they had left it the other night, spotting the makeshift table and chairs still in place through the open door.

They needed to put a lock on that thing to keep wild animals from wandering in, she chided herself as she climbed down from the box. The wind blew, perfuming the air with the scent of pine. She closed her eyes and stood there, enjoying the hushing of the branches as they danced in the breeze. Opening her eyes, she felt a wave of happiness and—

That same weird feeling that she was being watched.

She looked around.

And saw no one.

Shaking off the suspicion, she began unloading items from the wagon. This was the main load of household items—the last big delivery of goods prior to the Big Day. She had been careful, making a list of things she and Cord needed to ensure they would not be forced to leave the cabin for several days. She wanted that private time. They both did.

For forty minutes, she shuttled back and forth between the wagon and the interior of the cabin, pausing only to take sips of water from her canteen. Once the majority of the bric-a-brac was inside, she yawned and stretched, ambling down to the river. Glancing left and right to ensure she was unobserved, she sat down and pulled off her boots and stockings. Setting them aside, she scooted down the bank to the water's edge and plunged her feet into the river.

The cold water hit her like a train—hard and frigid and wonderful. It made her head swim as she sat enjoying the breeze, planning and dreaming. As she leaned back, supporting herself on her elbows, a twig snapped behind her.

She whirled.

A baby deer stood twenty feet away, alert and quizzical. Glory grinned at the little creature, scanning around for signs of its mother and seeing no trace of her. At length, the young deer bent and chomped a mouthful of grass before turning and sauntering away through the brush, plainly unconcerned.

I'm starting to act like a real fraidy-cat, Glory told herself.

She enjoyed the cool water on her feet for twenty minutes before deciding enough was enough. She pulled them out, letting her skin dry in the breeze before pulling her stockings and boots back on and returning to the wagon. She reached for a stack of linens and paused, again troubled by the sense that she was being watched.

She dismissed the notion and got back to work.

In point of fact, Glory *was* being watched.

The pair of eyes locked on her every movement from a vantage point high in the trees were gray and cold and remorseless.

Gordon Anderson's trail of blood and vengeance had crossed many state and territorial lines over the years. Men, women, and even children had died under his gun. He had heard bullets singing their deadly song around him, he had seen partners gunned down, but he had remained unscathed and triumphant in his grim work. He had reached a point where he felt, in unguarded moments, that he was somehow untouchable.

But he had never encountered a situation like the one he now experienced, one in which he had felt the hot sting of lead, and all the cunning and force of his efforts had been foiled by . . .

What?

Was it luck? Strength? Superior tactical planning? He could not for the life of him figure out what it was about Cord Bennett that made disposing of him so troublesome. He and his men had almost had Bennett at the church. Hell, Anderson had dropped his own sights on the lawman!

But instead of the marshal's death, here he was, wounded and alone following the loss of his two associates.

But no matter, he told himself as he shifted in the brush to ease the pain of his wounded arm and the bullet graze on his left side, just above his hip.

He would have his revenge. And soon.

Chapter 35

"It's a damned shame," sighed Horace Davenport, looking down at the burnt section of doorway and boardwalk in front of the Bear Flag Saloon.

"Luckily, no one was hurt." Cord stretched, relaxing and repositioning himself where he stood nearby. He had just returned to town after two hours of repairing the sluice on his claim with Abraham Olmsted.

"Mmm." Davenport sorted through a heap of shattered glass with the toe of his boot. The half-soaked, half-burned label of a whiskey bottle clung to one shard. "A damned unfortunate waste of good liquor too."

"Agreed." Cord squinted at the frayed label beneath Davenport's boot. "Not to mention a hazard to public safety."

Davenport nodded, cutting his eyes across the street in the direction of the Golden Nugget. "Come on, Marshal," he said. "Let's go pay Teddy Harville a visit."

"Right you are, Judge."

They crossed the street, pausing to let a wagon trundle by before gaining the boardwalk and passing through the batwing doors of the Golden Nugget. A half dozen customers filled the tables and a few places at the bar.

Teddy Harville, collar loosened and shirtsleeves rolled up, was poring over his ledger book behind the counter beside a bartender, who stood serving beers and making change. He looked up with a grimace, straightening self-consciously as Davenport and Cord approached.

"Mr. Harville." Davenport smiled. "I understand you and the marshal had a chat this morning about your actions of last night across the street."

Harville swallowed. "Yes, your honor," he said. "We sure did."

"All right, then." Davenport reached into an inside pocket of his jacket and produced a folded document. "You're being summoned, along with Dollie Whittaker, to my chambers. This is a civil mediation with the intention of resolving the conflict between you in the interest of public order. Your attendance is mandatory, Teddy. If you're not there, Cord, here, will be coming along to arrest you for contempt of court. You understand?"

"Y-Yes, your honor." Harville accepted the paper meekly.

"All right, then." Davenport favored him with a faint smile. "Nobody likes being pushed or intimidated. But it's no cause to engage in public violence. Let's solve this and we can all get on with our private business."

"Yes, sir." Harville nodded obediently.

Davenport and Cord declined the offer of a free drink and left the Nugget, angling for a return to the Bear Flag. They entered the saloon to find it mostly empty. Dollie Whittaker's clientele tended to congregate later in the day. Nevertheless, the lady herself was present, seated at her usual table on the raised dais beside the bar counter. She nodded and rose as the two men entered.

"Why, Marshal Bennett! Judge Davenport. I have been expecting you." She indicated the empty chairs at her table with a wave of her hand. "Won't you please be seated as my guests?"

Cord kept his facial expression neutral. He didn't much like Dollie Whittaker, so he was pleased to take his cues from Davenport on this one.

"Thank you, no." Davenport softened the refusal with a pleasant smile. "This is not a social call."

"I see." Dollie Whittaker's voice dropped a little on the last word. She folded her hands contritely before herself and raised her chin slightly. "Of course I am at your service, Judge. You have my complete attention."

Davenport, Cord noted, ignored all these social nudges, denying Dollie the role of reasonable citizen she was portraying. He suppressed a grin. The judge definitely had this woman's number.

"Miss Whittaker, you're being summoned to my chambers along with Teddy Harville. This is in response to last night's incident."

"Oh, I am *so* pleased to hear that the law is taking an interest in last night's assault on my establishment." She turned and reached for some pages on the table. "I have drafted—"

"That's fine." Davenport held up a hand. "I am sure you have everything in order as regards documentation of your position. But this is not a criminal matter. This is in the nature of a civil mediation."

"I'm sorry." She frowned. "Did you say . . . *not* a criminal matter?"

"It's a mediation. The—"

"How can it *not* be a criminal matter?" Her voice rose slightly. "Teddy Harville came over here last night and started a fire in the doorway of my—"

"Enough."

Davenport's tone was soft, but it had the paradoxical effect of stopping Dollie in her tracks with the force of a hammerblow. She opened her mouth to speak, but then immediately clamped it shut.

"Miss Whittaker, let me make myself perfectly plain." Davenport planted his hands on his hips. "Both you and Mr. Harville are becoming clear hazards to the public safety of Rio Oro. Mr. Harville's actions of last night speak for themselves. But your continued harassment of the man—to say nothing of your attempt to involve the legal system in your vendetta—also speak for themselves. This nonsense is going to stop before one or both of you cause serious harm to the citizens of this community. You are therefore instructed to appear in my chambers for a mediation at the date and time indicated in the summons. Failure to do so will lead to your immediate arrest and seizure of your business by the state."

"Seizure?" Her face was white. "Why, you can't—"

"Excuse me?"

Davenport's angry bellow thundered through the barroom and spilled into the street. It was so loud that numerous passersby stopped. Even a wagon passing in the street outside came to a halt as the driver squinted in through the door to see what was the matter.

"Do not tell me what I can and cannot do as a justice of the peace in this territory!" Davenport's expression was as dark and threatening as a storm cloud. "The law stands, Miss Whittaker, in this territory so long as I am on the bench. No exceptions, no preferential treatment." He smiled, but his eyes remained cold and glittering. "You have a good day, now."

With that, he and Cord left the saloon.

"They're fools, naturally." Davenport lounged back behind his desk, a glass of bourbon in hand. Cord sipped at his own glass as he stood by the window, studying the street outside. "Both engaging in unbelievable idiocy and wasting my time. Wasting the *court's* time."

"That is unmistakably true, your honor."

Davenport swirled the bourbon in his glass and squinted. "Truth be told, though, it's that damned woman more than Harville who sticks in my craw. A man pushed to his limit and striking back is one thing. I can understand that! But someone who connives and consistently undermines her neighbors, her community, the legal system . . ."

"She beat up Glory too."

Davenport's eyes shifted, piercing Cord. "You don't say? Why haven't you charged her?"

"Glory declined to pursue the matter." Cord shook his head. "She's a good woman. A better woman than Dollie Whittaker will ever be. Damned if I didn't want to go over to the Bear Flag and do something myself to settle the score for what she did. A dozen times I've wanted to, but I've refrained. It's just about driven me mad sometimes."

"If she can make a man like you feel that way, Teddy Harville's outburst is understandable." Davenport sighed. "All right, then. We'll take it one stage at a time. Get them both in here and hash it out."

"Sounds good to me. I hope we can get everything settled before the wedding."

"That's right!" Davenport grinned. "The big day is coming up! I was pleased to receive your invitation, by the by, and I'm planning to attend. When is it again?"

"The day after the mediation. In the late afternoon."

"I'm looking forward to it." The judge chuckled. "Although, I daresay, not as much as you are, my boy." Davenport paused and frowned. "You didn't invite either Harville or Dollie, did you?"

Cord laughed. "No. I felt kind of bad about not inviting Teddy, too, since he's been here in Rio Oro since before Glory and I ever got here. But we're trying to keep the ceremony fairly small."

Davenport lifted his glass. "Then we are guaranteed a most pleasant afternoon!"

* * *

Cord, still chuckling, headed across the empty street toward his office. The sounds of revelry seeped out of both saloons. In the quiet evening, Cord heard a girl squeal and the tinkling of piano keys. Somebody was playing "Consider the Lilies." The tune stuck in Cord's head, and he hummed a snatch as he stepped onto the sidewalk and let himself into the marshal's office. Blackstone was putting a pot of coffee for the night's duty on the stove when Cord came in.

"We're going to have another mediation with Judge Davenport," Cord began.

"Not Harville and Dollie again, I hope."

"That's right. We should probably both be there in case of trouble."

Blackstone groaned. "God restrain me from burning both of those saloons to the ground—with their owners inside!"

Cord laughed. "Judge Davenport wanted to know if I'd invited them to the wedding."

At this, Blackstone threw back his head and joined in the laughter.

"Are you ready?" Blackstone asked after a moment. Cord could tell from the way the deputy posed the question that he was serious.

"About the wedding? You bet." He smiled. "I've been waiting for this for a long time, Bart. Glory and I are ready to take this step. It's something we both need and are ready for in our lives. And we're right for each other."

"I couldn't agree more," Blackstone replied. "It's splendid when people find out where they're supposed to fit in."

Cord thanked his lucky stars that the labyrinth of his wayward and troubled path had crossed Glory's. How would life have been if they had never met? Cord could barely imagine the possibility. Finding out where he belonged had been the most precious and healing experience of his young life.

"I'm looking forward to the church service. I'm eager to give thanks for all of this."

"Praise be," said Blackstone, nodding.

In the darkness of the stable down the street, a shadow shifted.

There was no one in the darkened stable after-hours. One of the men who rousted beer barrels and the occasional rowdy customer from the Golden Nugget was paid a nickel each week to stop in on his way home from work and check on the horses in stalls. But that was still many hours away.

The shadow moved, briefly silhouetted in a diagonal shaft of light from the moon before disappearing back into shadow. Softly, the figure reached out and opened a stall door before slipping inside, a tangle of reins dangling from his left fist. In all this, he made barely the slightest noise in his passage. The horse, a brown gelding, whinnied and shifted as he entered the space. But it took the dark figure barely a minute to get the horse calmed and the reins slipped in place over face and head. Ten seconds later, he was walking the gelding out, shutting the stall door behind them, and heading for the rear door of the stable.

Outside was his own horse. Working quickly, he transferred his saddle and saddlebags to the new mount before tying it to the door. Again moving in near total silence, he led his tired horse into the stall and removed the reins before exiting, leaving her there in exchange for the horse he had taken.

Then, returning outside, he left town, keeping to the shadows before emerging onto the trail to Ghost Canyon, the tails of his duster flapping lightly in the breeze behind him.

CHAPTER 36

Well, this is it, Cord thought. *Last day as a free man.*

The truth, of course, was that he could not wait to get married to Glory. But as his horse picked its way along the trail beside the river, Cord was mindful enough to take stock of the moment's gravitas, and of the significance of the change his life was about to undergo. This would be among the last times he would ride this trail as an unmarried man, among the last times in his life he would be responsible for himself alone. He reckoned he might miss that one day, and so he gave it some thought.

The individual claims floated by to his right as he rode. A number of them had either yielded nothing or been played out because many were very definitely abandoned. This didn't worry him too much. There remained many claims, his own included, that were paying out handsomely. The gold rush would endure in Rio Oro for many seasons yet. But it seemed the major claims were claimed and consolidated. Going forward, there would be more moguls and fewer gentlemen of fortune.

Change. It was inevitable.

He guided his horse along the trail until arriving at the turnoff to the Olmsted cabin. Abraham was outside, operating the sluice they had repaired together. The old man was spry and strong despite his years. Cord felt a rush of warmth and gratitude for the man as he drew near. One could not choose one's own father, true enough. But Cord was glad old Abraham would be his father-in-law. He could hope for none better.

"Hello, Cord!" The old man set down the bucket in his hands as Cord dismounted and came over. "Seems you've got an extra saddlebag or two on that horse!"

"I do," Cord admitted with a chuckle. "This is the last of my belongings from the room above the marshal's office. I'll sleep tonight in our cabin in preparation for tomorrow."

"Tomorrow. Lord . . ." Abraham's voice took on a dreamy tone as he cast his gaze skyward. "Seems just yesterday Glory and Kat were little kids who came up just to my knee. Oh, go ahead and laugh now. But you'll see how it is! Children come, time goes by . . . and next thing you know, you're busting your back, slaving over your son-in-law's claim!"

He gave a hearty chuckle at the end of this, and Cord joined in.

"Family's a good thing. And you'll never have to worry, Abraham. As you get on, we'll take care of you. That's a promise."

Abraham raised his hands and took a step back. "I don't care to be no burden on you! No, sir! You and Glory got a life to make for yourselves!"

"It's no burden, Abraham," Cord said. "It's a privilege."

Glory was stacking piles of clothing into crates on the kitchen table when Cord knocked. Her answering grin when he walked into the room and swept her into his arms was bright as two suns.

"Cord," she breathed. "Only one more night apart."

"One more night," he whispered.

They stepped apart, eyes locked together. They were so lost in each other that Kat's entrance almost went unnoticed.

"Good morning, you two," she said in a jocular tone. "I'd imagine you're both pretty hot and bothered right about now."

"Why, *Kat Olmsted*!" Glory whirled and chased after her sister, who dodged playfully behind the kitchen table, her hands on the back of a chair as Glory swayed left and right, teasing moves in either direction.

"How many more times am I going to get to bedevil my beloved sister before breakfast?" Kat said. At this, both women fell into a hearty laugh and embraced, tickling and shoving each other playfully. Cord laughed at this girlish expression of sisterly love.

"Oh, you'll be a welcome guest in our house," Cord assured Kat. "You're welcome to come up anytime for a night or a weekend, if it suits you. I want a nice, close family for our children. Lots of time with Aunt Kat."

"Aunt Kat." She smiled. "I like the sound of that."

"You heading up to our place?" Glory asked, spying the extra saddlebags on Cord's horse, where it grazed in the front yard.

"I am." He gestured upriver. "Moving the last of my stuff from the office up there. I'll stay the night. Are you heading up now?"

"No. I have more boxes to pack. I have to do my dresses and—I almost forgot. Forks and dishes! Can't neglect them."

Cord chuckled as she turned away to begin pawing through the cupboards.

"You should have made a list," Kat taunted.

"Well, why don't you sit down and make one for me, Kat Olmsted, if you're so all-fired smart."

"I will, by damn!" Kat yawned and wandered to the stove. "As soon as I have my coffee. Cord, you want some?"

"I dearly would, thanks."

She set them up at the table with a pair of tin cups. Both sat as

Glory found and stacked dishes, then disappeared into the bedroom to empty some drawers.

"You planning to help Glory take the stuff up to our place?"

"No." Kat took a tentative sip of coffee. "I'm heading into town to do a few hours down at the Nugget."

"How's that been working out for you?"

"You mean working for my former competition, the one and only Teddy Harville?" She laughed. "It's actually fine. We get along better than I expected. But it won't be a good fit for the long run. We're both too bossy."

"You just have to find a good man of your own and get married." He winked. "Like your sister."

"Wouldn't I like to!" Kat shook her head. "I suppose, now that my sister is getting married and I'm not, I'll be expected to dance barefoot at the wedding. Isn't that the tradition?"

"I've heard it said," Cord admitted. "But you're good people, Kat. You shouldn't have any trouble finding a good man." Cord added nothing to this aloud but privately resolved to see that she danced with Bart Blackstone at the wedding.

"Do I hear you out here playing matchmaker with my sister?" Glory had reentered the room clutching a mess of socks to her chest. She lost a few on her way to the kitchen table, where she set down the rest with a sigh.

"I suppose I am," Cord admitted, reaching out and picking up the socks she'd dropped. Handing them to her, he asked, "Don't you want to see your lovely sister hitched up with a good man?"

"You know I do." Glory paused to beam at Kat. "Of course I feel bad for her since I've already snagged the best man in Rio Oro. But I'm sure we could find someone who runs a close second. How about that deputy of yours, Cord?"

Cord suppressed a chuckle and didn't mention that the same thought had crossed his mind only a few moments earlier.

"Bart Blackstone?" Kat sniffed. "He's that Englishman, isn't he? A mite hairy for my taste, but . . . Is he a good man, Cord?"

"The best," Cord affirmed.

"My daughter asks about good men and here's Cord saying, *He's the best*." Abraham stepped into the kitchen and stretched. "While I'm standing right here!"

Cord smiled as Kat and Glory burst into laughter, joined by their father. A better family he could not possibly have chosen to marry into.

"Pa, Kat's headed into town to work for a few hours down at the Nugget," said Glory. "And I'm taking the wagon. Can she have Jasper for the day?" Glory gestured toward the mule tied to a tree outside.

"Jasper needs a rest," Abraham said. "But I have to go into town too. Kat, I'll walk with you."

"Thank you, Pa."

"And once you're done working, if you ask Bart Blackstone real nice, he might give you a ride back home," Cord said with a straight face. But he nudged Glory with his elbow and she winked at him.

They visited over another pot of coffee before finally deciding to get the day started in earnest and head their separate ways. Abraham shouldered the canvas bag he used to haul supplies up from the store as Kat pulled on a sunbonnet and walking boots. Cord and Glory walked out to the porch with them to say their goodbyes.

"Tomorrow's the big day!" said Abraham. "You two say your goodbyes now, because you're not allowed to see each other until the wedding."

"That's true." Kat's tone was severe. "Glory, I expect you back here early this evening so we can do your hair for tomorrow."

"Don't worry," Glory said. "I don't intend to let that detail slip. And Cord, just wait until you see my wedding dress!"

"I'm sure it's beautiful," Cord said.

"It sure is," Kat said. "Just wait and see!"

They stood watching Abraham and Kat descend down the trail until they vanished among the trees. Then they put their arms around each other, delighting in the feel of each other and enjoying the sound of the rushing river.

"This is our last day apart, Cord," Glory whispered.

"I know." Cord's voice was filled with a species of wonder. "By this time the day after tomorrow, we will be husband and wife."

"Husband." She turned to examine him, top to toe, with her arm still around his waist. "Wife. Those words have a new meaning now, don't they?"

"They do now," he agreed. "And probably even a newer meaning tomorrow."

"You never know how something is until you're in the thick of it," she agreed.

"I reckon this will be the last time I see you before the wedding," Cord said.

"Reckon so."

They released each other and stepped back.

"I choose you, Cord," she said simply. "Out of all the men in this town—in this *world*—I choose you."

"And out of all the women in this town and this world, I choose you, Gloriana Olmsted." He reached out and seized her hand. "My life, my fortune, my everything—I dedicate it all to you."

"Same," she whispered, squeezing his hands back.

They stood staring into each other's eyes a while longer.

"Well . . ." He released her hand. "I reckon this is it."

"Reckon so." She grinned at him. "See you at the altar."

Cord rode the trail into Ghost Canyon. He found himself enjoying the trip, moving at a leisurely pace as the last claim vanished behind him and he turned into unclaimed land.

The cabin was in good shape. Cord's initial goal had been merely to make it ready for habitation, but between his own efforts and the help he had received from Abraham and Blackstone, he had made far better progress—better than he had thought possible. The house was not only ready but also cozy. Secure. The kind of place to call a home.

Cord reined in by the front door, tied his horse to the porch railing, and took his saddlebags off the animal. He piled them on the kitchen table and began to sort through their contents, putting away his shaving gear and other personal effects. He didn't have much in the way of clothes, but he unpacked and stowed what he had in the dresser Abraham had procured for their use and installed in the bedroom. His suit was carefully rolled and stowed in a separate canvas bag. He withdrew and unrolled the clothes, examining the jacket and pants with a critical eye before brushing and hanging them in preparation for tomorrow's big day.

The big day.

Cord walked out to the porch.

By this time tomorrow, he would be walking down the aisle, changing his life forever. He couldn't wait.

Checking his pocket watch, he noted the time for the mediation with Judge Davenport was fast approaching. Cord mounted his horse and headed back to town, his progress watched by a single pair of dead gray eyes.

CHAPTER 37

"Well," sighed Glory, "I think that's just about everything." She and Kat stood gazing at the boxes, piles of clothing and kitchen items stacked around them. Glory was bringing a great many things from the house into her new life. There was a sense of finality now that she had finished packing. All that remained was to load all of this into the wagon for the trip to Ghost Canyon. Once that was done, the inevitability of her departure would be a tangible thing.

"I can't believe it's happening," Kat said. She laughed suddenly, and Glory was surprised to see a tear roll down her cheek. "Silly me! Here I am, getting all emotional."

She burst into tears and embraced Glory, crushing her sister's body to hers with a kind of desperation, equal parts sadness and joy.

"Oh, Kat . . ." Glory hugged Kat back and stroked her hair. "I'm only just moving up the canyon a ways."

"I know."

She grasped Kat's shoulders and held her at arm's length. "It's not like I'm moving to France or something!"

This broke the tension between them and they began to laugh. It gained momentum until they were giggling uncontrollably, having to grasp at chairbacks to remain upright as their mirth threatened to overwhelm them.

"France!" hooted Glory, shaking her head. "The very thought of it!"

"I don't know," said Kat, picking up a box and stepping toward the front door. "I hear tell those French fellas are awful romantic!"

"What's this about French fellas?" Abraham asked, stomping up onto the porch. "Are there Frenchies hereabouts somewhere?"

The sisters' laughter redoubled, and Abraham stood there puzzled for a few seconds before finally shrugging and grabbing a crate to take to the wagon.

"Did you leave us anything in the house, Glory?" he asked during his sixth trip back into the house. "Or am I going to have to eat my dinners straight out of the pan from now on?"

"Oh, Pa." Kat shook her head. "Don't you worry. I didn't let Glory clean out everything."

"Thank goodness!" he said. "Because some of those dishes were picked out by your mother, God rest her. They're about all I have left to remember her by."

"What about us?" asked Glory.

Abraham paused in the doorway. "Of course," he said quietly. Then, turning, he added, "Kat and yourself. And whatever grandchildren you have with Cord!"

"What kind of grandchild do you want, Pa?" she asked. "A boy or a girl?"

"How about a few of each?" Abraham joked, ducking inside to grab another box.

It took them the better part of a half hour to finish loading the wagon. As Glory stacked the last pile of clothes in the back, she marveled at the amount of stuff she was taking.

"Lord, there really is an awful lot there!" she exclaimed. "Maybe we should unpack some of it."

Kat and Abraham shook their heads vehemently. "We just loaded all this," Kat objected. "We're not doing it again!"

"Fair enough," said Glory.

"I promised Cord he could have that old saddle blanket we brought on the trail out here," Abraham said. "It's in the shed out back. Let me go get it."

"All right, Pa." Glory nodded and watched her father head around the back of the house.

Gordon Anderson watched from the tree line, his gray, unblinking gaze following every movement as the old man and the two girls loaded up the wagon. He was savvy enough to understand that the redheaded girl was leaving. His guess was that she was about to marry the marshal, the man he had been hired to kill.

And now here they were, alone and vulnerable—the girl, her sister, and the old man. Cord Bennett was miles away in town. A plan was forming in Anderson's mind—a good one. He would not find an opportunity like this again.

Quietly as a wolf, he slipped along the tree line until he was on the blind side of the house. Then he followed the old man out to the shed.

"I spoke to Pastor Lomax," Kat was saying. "Looks like we'll have about twenty people for the wedding. But he says lots more have been asking him about it."

"Is that right?" Glory laughed.

A sudden shout came from around the back of the cabin, cutting her off.

* * *

Abraham found the shelf where he kept the horse blankets and began rooting around among them. It was too dark to tell the individual blankets apart, so he lit a lantern, set it on the shelf, and searched until he found it. Pulling the fading gray blanket loose, he lifted the lantern, turned, and came face-to-face with a stranger.

"Who—?" Abraham's words stumbled on the shock of the man's sudden appearance. "How did you get in here?"

The man said nothing. He merely stepped forward, seized the lantern, and knocked the blanket from Abraham's hands.

"Hey! That—!"

An instant later, the man had drawn his gun, cocked the hammer, and rammed the end of the barrel up under Abraham's chin.

"You stay real quiet now, mister," he said softly. "We're going to go out and have a friendly chat with those pretty daughters of yours."

Abraham complied nervously, sidling ahead of the man in response to a flick of the pistol. He stepped outside, conscious of the loaded weapon at the small of his back. What was happening here? Where was Cord? He had no answers for this. But he knew his daughters were in danger.

They had proceeded maybe a dozen steps from the shed and were close to rounding the side of the house when Abraham cried out, and the man hit the back of his head with his gun.

Kat and Glory rushed around the corner to find Abraham on all fours, blood pouring down his neck to stain his shirtfront. Above him stood one of the men in black dusters that Glory recognized from the shoot-out at the church. Anderson, that was his name, Glory recalled Cord telling her.

The barrel of his pistol was smeared red with Abraham's blood, and he snapped his eyes up at the girls when they appeared.

"Get away from him!" shrieked Kat. Hands raised and fingers clawed, she lunged for Anderson.

Anderson raised his gun and fired, putting a bullet in the ground six inches in front of her left shoe, stopping her short.

"Pa?" said Glory. "Pa, are you—?"

"I'm all right!" Abraham managed, his voice shaky. He held up one hand. "I'm bleedin', but I'm all right! You stay where you are!"

"Smart words, old man," said Anderson. He turned to the women. "I reckon neither of you ladies is armed. But you never know these days. Some ladies like to carry a little gun in their handbag."

"We're not carrying handbags, you vicious monster!" said Kat. "Get away from our father!"

Anderson's eyes swiveled toward her. Glory thought they resembled cannons in their depth and menace.

"Now, ain't that something?" Anderson replied. "Here I am, gun in hand, your father at my feet, and you both unarmed. And yet you take it into your head to tell me what to do. Stupid woman."

Kat, seething with rage, made to take a step forward, but Glory stopped her.

"That's right," said Anderson. "You mind your sister now, you stupid damned woman. Take another step and I'll put a bullet in you, I don't care that you're a girl. You wouldn't be the first one I've shot."

"So, you shoot women," said Glory. "Do you kill children too?"

"Shot a pregnant woman in the belly in Arkansas one time," Anderson said, his eyes taking on a faraway look. "It took her a long time to die."

"I wouldn't be proud of that if I were you!" snapped Kat.

"I ain't." Anderson shrugged. "It's just business. And business is business. You." He nudged Abraham with a boot. "You able to get up?"

"Don't reckon I can," muttered Abraham.

"Well, that's a shame." Anderson turned to the women. "Why don't you two come on over here and help your daddy get up? We'll bring him inside and have a talk, all nice and civilized."

Glory and Kat rushed forward and pulled Abraham upright. Standing on either side, they wrapped their arms around him and made their way indoors, shadowed by Anderson, who stood in the doorway and smirked as they lowered the old man into a kitchen chair.

"You." Anderson jerked his chin at Kat. "Feisty one. My pony's tied up in the trees by that cut over yonder." He pointed. "You go on up, untie him, and bring him down. I know you won't run."

"How do you know that?" she spat.

"Because if you aren't back as fast as I think you ought to be, I'll kill the old man and skin your sister alive. Now get moving."

Kat and Glory exchanged a look before Kat moved toward the door. Anderson stood aside to let her pass and followed her with his eyes as she made for the trees.

"So, that cabin up the trail apiece," he said. "The one in the cut by the river . . ."

"I don't know what you're talking about," said Glory stiffly.

"The one you were at the other day." Anderson smiled. "Saw you pull up in your wagon and stow a bunch of your belongings inside. That where you and the marshal are planning to move once you're hitched?"

Glory's rage poured out through her eyes and posture although her mouth remained shut.

"Yes, I figured it was something like that." Anderson chuckled. "That day I saw you in town together at the church, I figured a wedding must be in the offing. And soon, too, I reckon, if you're already moving in your stuff."

Glory swallowed. Said nothing.

"We're going to take a trip up there together." Anderson beamed. "Head on up and get ready to give the marshal a good old-fashioned homecoming! Yes, sir."

"He will kill you," Glory said. "He's a good man. Better than you'll ever be."

"Good, huh?" Anderson turned to glance at Kat as she approached the house with his pony in tow. "Oh, you don't know Cord Bennett, sweetheart. Not one bit. He got a girl back in the Ozarks pregnant, then ran away when he found out."

"That's a lie!" snapped Glory. "He told me all about it. It was his brother who got that poor girl with child. And his brother's dead! Your little mission of vengeance is over. Why don't you go back to where you came from?"

"Because I'm a professional," said Anderson. "And a professional always keeps his word." He turned and barked at Kat, "You! Firecracker! You tie my pony to the back of that wagon and get in here now!"

Kat tied Anderson's horse as instructed before joining them in the kitchen. Abraham was more alert now, his blood loss stemmed by a rag Glory held to the back of his head. Although bleary-eyed, he was following the conversation.

"All right, then." Anderson moved in, grasped Glory by the elbow, and hauled her toward the door. "You." He pointed his gun at Kat. "I want you to get your pretty little behind into town and find the marshal. You tell him if he ever wants to see his bride-to-be alive again, he'll drop what he's doing and head on up to his new place. We'll be waiting."

"He'll kill you," Kat seethed. "And if he doesn't, I will. That's a stone-cold promise, mister."

"Promises, promises." Anderson sighed. Then he laughed and dragged Glory out to the wagon.

Chapter 38

Cord was doing a good job of holding his tongue, but it wasn't easy.

They were convened in Judge Davenport's chambers: himself, Blackstone, Dollie Whittaker, and Teddy Harville. Davenport had the meeting under control, despite Dollie's near-continuous attempts to derail proceedings with a litany of complaints that she was only too pleased to enumerate. Harville, for his part, sat quietly with his top hat perched on his knee—the reasonable party in this dispute. Blackstone stood, arms crossed by the door, hiding his disgust as best he could and mostly succeeding.

What a happy group, thought Cord.

" . . . so I think Mr. Harville's culpability in this matter is clear," Dollie was saying. "He's very obviously at fault in trying to burn down my establishment."

Davenport waited until she was done, then sat very still for a long moment, absorbing her tirade. It washed up against him and evaporated like waves on a rocky shoreline. He turned to Teddy Harville.

"Do you have anything to add, Mr. Harville?"

"Your honor, I take responsibility for my stupid, *stupid* actions. And I'm sorry. I genuinely am!" He looked around the room as if seeking validation from the listeners. "But your honor is right. This nonsense can't continue between us. I love this town and don't want to cause any trouble."

"So, you should accept my offer and sell your saloon to me, Teddy," Dollie began.

"Enough."

The word from the judge, softly spoken, silenced Dollie Whittaker as effectively as a gunshot.

"Mr. Harville, I appreciate your statement of contrition. I do believe it is sincere." Davenport turned to Dollie. "I am actually inclined, in this instance, to also take into account Miss Whittaker's part in all this."

"But your honor, I—"

Davenport silenced her with a sharp glare.

"This can't continue." The judge spoke firmly, addressing the entire group. "Public order must be maintained, and this simmering rivalry between the two of you is a threat to that—one I am no longer prepared to tolerate. So, we can do this one of two ways. You two can come to a reasonable accommodation or I am prepared to shut down both establishments."

Cord was surprised when Dollie began laughing. Davenport broke off until she calmed herself.

"Judge," she said finally, giggling and wiping tears from her cheeks. "You *can't* shut down the only two saloons in town. Why, you'll have a riot!"

Now it was Davenport's turn to laugh. It was a low chuckle, almost sinister in tone. Dollie sat in silence until it ended.

"There you go again, Miss Whittaker, telling the law what it can and can't do in my jurisdiction. I believe I already warned you about this one time before. And yet." He rolled a hand. "You don't seem inclined to take my warnings seriously."

Dollie's eyes widened and she held up her hands, as if in surrender.

"You have something you want to add?" Davenport's glare was back.

"N-No, your honor." She licked her lips. "I, um, misspoke."

"I'll say you did." Davenport's jaw firmed. "Watch what you say in my chambers, young lady, or I will find you in contempt. And you *will* spend a few nights in Marshal Bennett's jail. Marshal, you *are* prepared to accommodate female prisoners?"

"We sure are, Judge."

"All right, then." Davenport spread his hands. "Here is what I propose. You, Mr. Harville, will refrain from further violent acts against the Bear Flag."

"Will do, your honor! You have my word!"

"And you, Miss Whittaker, will cease your attempts to take over the Golden Nugget. And both of you will avoid speaking to each other. You will also take steps to ensure the clientele of both your establishments avoid mob violence directed against each other. Agreed?"

Harville was nodding enthusiastically, pleased to be let off so lightly.

Dollie measured those words carefully before looking up. "Yes, your honor. I will do as you say."

"Very well. There remains now the question of—"

A knock came at the door, breaking into what the judge was saying. At a nod from Davenport, Blackstone hauled it open to reveal Kat standing outside, distraught and shivering.

"Your honor, I'm sorry to interrupt."

"Miss Olmsted." Davenport looked concerned. "Please come in. Is everything all right? You seem quite disturbed."

"Your honor . . . Cord . . ." She grasped Cord's arm. "She's been taken. Glory. And Pa's been attacked."

"By whom?" Cord's face seemed to have turned to stone at Kat's words.

"A man wearing a black duster. Cord, he's taken her up to your cabin in Ghost Canyon. Told you to meet him there or he'll kill Glory."

A low rage began simmering in Cord Bennett's belly. Throughout all the violence he had encountered in his role as marshal, he had never succumbed to anger or felt hate toward wrongdoers. But this was different. This was *Glory*! A monstrous wave of anger ripped through him and he felt, for the first time in his life, what it was like to truly hate and wish harm upon another person.

"All right."

Cord spoke with an icy calm that was unsettling. "Your honor," he said, gesturing at the door. "With your permission . . . ?"

"Go." Davenport waved a hand. "I'll finish up here. You go and be safe. And God be with you."

With a glance at Blackstone, Cord made for the street, his deputy and Kat right behind him.

They stopped in the marshal's office long enough to collect every gun and scrap of ammunition they could lay their hands on.

"Kat, I want you to stay here in this office. Lock the door when we leave and don't open it for anybody. Understand?"

"Yes, Cord."

Blackstone grabbed up the coach gun. With its sawed-off barrels, he could fire it one-handed.

"Ready, Marshal," he said coolly. "What's the plan?"

"We're going to check on Abraham, then ride up to Ghost Canyon and fetch Glory."

"And then?"

"And then?" Cord buckled on his gun belt. "And then I'm going to shoot that man graveyard dead."

They mounted up and rode out of town, unobserved by any except Lomax, who paused in sweeping the church stairs to lean on his broom and watch them go, a worried expression on his face.

CHAPTER 39

"Stop *pushing* me!"

Glory whirled on Anderson, who stood by the wagon. He had been silent and aloof throughout the ride, ignoring her questions and grasping her roughly by the forearm when she tried to jump out. Upon arrival, he had shoved her roughly toward the cabin the moment they climbed down from the driver's box.

"Well, ain't you the little firecracker?" Anderson muttered. "If you know what's good for you, you'll do as I say."

"Or what? Are you planning to knock me out like you did my father?"

"Maybe."

She spat in his face, lunging at him with her fingers clawed and grasping for his eyes. Anderson blocked her effortlessly, his facial expression blank, his eyes unfocused, as if recalling a memory. Having deflected her attack, he sighed before backhanding her across the jaw. The slap was hard enough to cause Glory to spin around before collapsing to the ground in a heap.

"Stupid," said Anderson. He bent and pulled her upright by her hair. She came to her feet, screaming, and Anderson pushed her toward the cabin door.

"Abraham!"

Cord leaped from his horse and rushed to where Abraham Olmsted sat on the front step of his cabin, holding a bloody rag to the back of his head. Cord was worried the old man might be seriously injured, but the fire in his eyes when he looked up was blazing.

"Cord, he took her. He took my little girl! I tried to fight him. I did! But he . . ."

"Abraham, it's all right. You did what you could. He's taken her up to—"

"I know where he's taken her. Ghost Canyon. Your place. You going to get her?"

"Damn straight we are."

"I'm going with you. No, don't you argue, Cord!" Abraham surged to his feet. The wound on his head had stopped bleeding and he appeared steady enough. "I'm coming with you so I can shoot that blasted snake myself!"

Cord couldn't help grinning at the old man's fire. "Abraham, we're on horseback and armed. I'm not sure . . ."

"I've got a mule and a shotgun and I'm coming with you and that's all there is to it!"

"All right, then." Cord stood. "Let's go get Glory."

They rode through the trees, alert for ambush. Anderson, knowing they would come, might be lying in wait for them. But as they turned into Ghost Canyon, they remained mounted and unharmed. So far, it seemed as if Anderson was keeping to his word.

Cord struggled to manage his emotions. Anderson was clever, he thought. Grabbing Glory and threatening her life exploited Cord's one major vulnerability, and effectively at that. He knew the marshal would arrive scared, frustrated, off-balance. Cord could not allow this to happen. He forced his outrage deep inside him, set his jaw, and focused on the trail ahead.

"He'll be expecting you, Cord," said Blackstone quietly as they approached the outskirts of the cut where Cord had built his cabin.

"Yeah."

"He might even expect Abraham . . ."

"What are you getting at, Bart?"

The Englishman reined his horse to a stop. The others followed suit. A sly smile appeared within the forest of Blackstone's beard.

"I think we should set up an ambush of our own," he said, pointing to a narrow trail that cut into the forest. "That trail right there leads around to a place where a man can climb down into the canyon behind the cabin. I roamed around up here quite a bit when I first came to these parts, while I was still trying my hand at prospecting."

Cord's eyes narrowed. "So, you're thinking . . ."

"I'm thinking that you two should come in by the front door while I'm coming in the back."

"Sounds like a good idea, Cord," said Abraham. "The sight of you and me riding in there together would flummox him, maybe enough that he'd forget about old Bart, here."

"It's not a bad plan," Cord allowed. "Can a man your size be sneaky, Bart?"

"An Englishman? Be sneaky?" Blackstone chuckled. "One day, Cord, I'll tell you about the Battle of the Plains of Abraham." He grinned at the old-timer next to him. "No relation."

Still chuckling, he nudged his horse onto the path and disappeared into the trees.

Anderson made Glory pick up one of the chairs she had brought to the cabin and carry it outside. Glory thought of swinging it at his head, but Anderson was canny enough to remain just out of range. And the memory of his brutal slap made her hesitate.

"Set it down right there," Anderson told her, pointing to a spot in the front yard. Glory did as he said and set down the chair. "Now sit."

She sat. The moment her rump hit the seat, Anderson grasped and pulled her wrists together, binding her arms behind her. Then he lashed her to the back of the chair. As a final precaution, he bent and tied a rope around her ankles, hobbling her.

"I'm sorry," said Glory. "I had no idea I frightened you so much."

"You're funny for a stupid little girl," he said, and spat on her shoe. "You might want to keep that trap of yours shut."

"Or else what?"

"Or else I might carvé your tongue out of your mouth with my knife. Now hush."

Glory hushed. She watched Anderson pull his pistol and begin checking it over.

When Cord and Abraham rode into the canyon, they could see Glory roped to the chair. But no sign of Anderson.

"Glory!" Abraham cried. The name echoed back from the walls of the canyon "Glory, sweetheart! Are you all right?"

"I'm all right, Pa!" she called. "I'm not hurt! Are you?"

"I'm fine!" Abraham turned to Cord. "What do we do now, Cord?"

"Just follow my lead," Cord said, and nudged his horse closer to the cabin. He stopped about two hundred yards away.

Stillness settled over the yard.

"Anderson! I'm here!" Cord shouted. "Show yourself, you coward!"

Anderson did show himself. He appeared from around the side of the cabin.

And he was shoving Bart Blackstone ahead of him.

The big Englishman had taken a beating—a bad one. Cord had

no idea how Anderson had managed to overcome the deputy in the first place, let alone deliver such a terrible thrashing. But he had managed somehow. Blackstone's left eye was blackened and swollen, his beard covered with blood, his breathing ragged and irregular. He limped slightly, moaning, as the gunman pushed him out to the center of the yard.

"Nice try, Marshal." Anderson's smile and voice were both soft, and all the more sinister for it.

"You let my daughter go!" yelled Abraham.

"Shut up, old man." Anderson delivered this in a chillingly offhanded fashion. "Me and the marshal here have some business, don't we? Some very *old* business having to do with Caroline Stockton. You remember her, Bennett? The girl whose belly you put a baby in and then abandoned before leaving the Ozarks?" He leered at Glory. "Does your little bride-to-be, here, know about her? Did you tell her?" He seized a handful of Glory's hair and jerked her head back. "Did he tell you, sweetheart? Do you know about this man's past?" He finished up by kissing Glory's cheek.

Instinctively, Cord's hand flashed for his gun. But Anderson's revolver twitched in his hand, making Cord freeze.

"I wouldn't if I was you, Marshal. It'd be a damn shame to have to kill this little lady. Don't you think?"

Cord eased his hand away from the gun.

"Cord didn't get Caroline Stockton pregnant!" cried Glory. "And yes, he *did* tell me! I already told you all this! It was his brother—"

Anderson's backhanded blow struck Glory on the mouth, cutting off her words and bloodying her lips. Cord fumed in rage. He could hear Abraham moan softly beside him.

"You got her fooled, Cord." Anderson chuckled. "Did you fool Caroline the same way? By telling her you loved her?"

"Caroline's baby belonged to my brother Flint," Cord said. "And he's dead. Your vendetta is done. You can go back and tell Hiram

Stockton that you found and killed the father of Caroline's child and he'll never be any the wiser."

"Well, I suppose so." Anderson shrugged. "But he *did* specify you by name, Cord Bennett. And I'm a professional. A professional *earns* his pay."

Cord said nothing.

"Now, I want you to unbuckle your gun belt, Marshal. Use your left hand. Nice and slowlike."

Cord's hands dropped to his belt and unbuckled it.

"Now throw it over yonder. And the old man can toss that shotgun too. Go on, now."

Cord did as he was told. Abraham did too.

"Now, I want you to take ten steps toward me, Bennett." Anderson was exultant. "Nice and slow. Hands out at your sides where I can see them. Go on, now."

Gritting his teeth, Cord advanced one slow bootstep at a time into the yard. He counted silently to himself. It seemed to take forever to reach ten, but he finally did. He stopped where he was.

"Kneel," Anderson said. "And put your hands on your head."

Cord raised his hands and did as he was told. For a moment, the wind and birdsong ceased and a great stillness fell over the yard, broken only by the sound of the river rushing in the distance.

This is it, thought Cord. *This is where I die.*

Anderson addressed Abraham next.

"You can get out of here now, you old fool," he said. "You and the Englishman. He can take the marshal's horse. I want you two to git. Right now."

"Not without my daughter!" cried Abraham.

"She stays here with me, just to be sure you don't try any more tricks." Anderson grinned. "Once I'm done with Bennett, I'll cut her loose. But until then? She stays and you go. Vamoose."

Abraham said nothing, merely helped Blackstone up onto the saddle of Cord's horse after the deputy had stumbled forward. Cord heard the sound of the hooves diminish as the two riders receded into the distance. Only silence remained.

Anderson studied Cord with lively interest.

"You've been a tough nut to crack, Bennett. I'll give you that." He produced a cigar from his vest pocket. Fishing a lucifer from his pants, he snapped it to life with a thumbnail and held the flame to the point of the cheroot. "I've killed well nigh a hundred men in my time, but nobody's ever given me as much trouble as you. Now here we are. Just you and this gal, here. And me. Ain't nobody coming to help you now. The hunt ends here."

Cord ignored him. "Glory," he said. "I want you to shut your eyes. I don't want you to see this."

Anderson threw back his head and laughed.

"Ain't that sweet?" he crooned. "Protecting your little sweetheart's tender sensibilities. I suppose it does no harm. A condemned man is allowed his last words. Anything you want to say, Cord? Any last thoughts you care to share with the world before you leave it?"

"Glory." Cord spoke firmly. "Glory, honey, I love you."

"I . . ." Her voice was a rasp. "I love you too, Cord."

"I now pronounce you man and wife," Anderson said, then brayed with laughter. "Ain't that a hoot? I ain't much for preaching. But I do know they abandoned Jesus on the cross. Just like all your friends abandoned you. Time to say goodbye, Marshal."

Anderson cocked and raised his pistol.

A deafening blast of gunfire sounded, and Anderson stiffened, as if alarmed. Then his arm fell as his body grew slack and he tumbled to the ground.

A figure stepped out from behind the cabin. Cord's shock mingled with the memory. . . .

The memory of how, when he had first met the man and demanded his gun, he had reached around and plucked out a revolver from the belt at the small of his back.

A modified Colt Walker with a short barrel.

The Reverend Garrison Lomax.

The preacher moved quickly to the fallen man's side and hooked a boot toe under Anderson's shoulder. Keeping the gun trained on the killer, hammer poised to fall again if need be, Lomax rolled the duster-clad gunman onto his back. Anderson's arms flopped limply, and his shock-widened eyes stared sightlessly into the blue sky above Ghost Canyon.

Cord surged to his feet, ran to the chair, and began untying Glory.

"Preacher," he said in a voice choked by emotion. "We sure are glad to see you!"

Lomax lowered the hammer on the Walker and replaced it at the small of his back. Then he grinned at Cord and said, "Couldn't have anything ruining the first wedding I'm going to perform in Rio Oro, now could I? The first of many, I hope!"

CHAPTER 40

Dollie Whittaker sat alone at the high table in the Bear Flag Saloon. The bar had closed a half hour before, and all the lights were extinguished except for the kerosene lantern by the light of which she now worked. The accounts were coming along beautifully. Profits had been rising steadily for the past two weeks, and she now had enough money to follow through with her plans for both the Bear Flag—and beyond.

She set down her pen, stretched, and looked into the darkness beyond the front window.

Rio Oro.

She would make the town hers. Of this she was supremely confident. She already had Teddy Harville over a barrel. Jeremiah Ponder was a cowed wreck of the man he had once been. Those Olmsted sisters were wise enough to keep away. And she was fairly sure that busybody Judge Davenport wouldn't be bothering her anytime soon. She had his number and knew exactly how to step carefully around him and those two clowns they called lawmen.

No, she wouldn't be facing any serious obstacles.

She would use her charm. Her money. Her body again, if necessary, to push her conquest. She already had her eyes on a few influential citizens. She planned to sidle up close to a few of those men and work her magic. She was confident she could win them over. There was only one man in town she feared.

Lomax.

The preacher frightened her, although she wasn't sure why. Perhaps it was his immunity to her physical charms. Men of the cloth could be seduced, to be sure. But Lomax was not one to stray from the straight and narrow path. He was a hard-core, certified do-gooder who sent shivers up her spine anytime his stare found her on the street. Religion was nonsense, of course. But there was something unsettling about that man . . .

But it didn't matter now.

Dollie could have her way with the local worthies, expand her influence through money and manipulation, and achieve a position of real prominence in this pathetic, one-horse town—a position that would make her unassailable. Then she would deal with Lomax. It was just a matter of time.

She rose and went behind the bar. Reaching beneath the counter, she withdrew a bottle of her favorite Spanish wine and poured a glass. She had just resumed her seat at the high table when she heard a noise.

At this late hour, the town should be silent. But no, there it was again—the sound of footsteps coming down the wooden boardwalk. A shadow moved outside the window. The steps halted and the batwing doors squeaked in the darkness and silence.

"Hello?"

A figure was approaching from across the darkened barroom. Instinctively, her hand slipped to the straight razor in her belt.

She was just about to draw it free when she recognized who had entered.

Ponder.

"Well, Jeremiah." She smiled coldly. "I must say, you did startle me a bit. But it doesn't matter. We're closed. I'd offer you a drink, but the bartenders have all gone home for the night."

Ponder said nothing. He merely crossed the last few steps to the raised dais and stood behind the other chair at the table. Putting his hands on the chairback, he leaned into the light of her lantern.

He's drunk, she thought. She knew the signs.

And Ponder *was* drunk. He had been sure to down a few stiff drinks before this meeting. So, he was slightly intoxicated. But not enough to prevent him from doing what he had come to do. He remained bent over the chair, facing in her direction. After a few seconds of silence, he opened his mouth and spoke in a low voice, his lips dry from the alcohol he had consumed.

"Well, here we are, Dollie," he said. "Just you and me here in the Bear Flag Saloon. In the dark and quiet. After-hours. The perfect time to have a conversation."

"What would you like to discuss?"

Without asking, Ponder dragged the chair from the table and sat heavily, sighing as he relaxed into the seat. To Dollie's eye, he seemed remarkably calm.

Unnervingly so.

"You've really been busy around town, haven't you," Ponder said. It wasn't a question. "Making your little inroads. Forming your little alliances before abandoning and betraying them. You've left quite a trail in your wake, lady."

"Trail of what?" She was growing impatient with his clowning.

"Of broken hearts and bodies," he replied. "And promises."

"I don't break promises," she said, smiling. "Because I never make any."

"You don't, do you?" He laughed. "It's actually pretty remarkable how you operate."

"Jeremiah, it's late, and I'm working."

"Take Teddy Harville, for instance," Ponder said, as if he hadn't heard her. "You just seem bound and determined to ruin that man. After everything he's done for you! Why, he was the first to welcome you to Rio Oro. Brought you in as a partner. Helped set you up. Gave you some money, too, or so he said."

"I don't know what you're—"

"Sure. Sure." He waved a hand. "I understand. Actually, saying these things out loud is probably difficult for you. You prefer things to remain unsaid. Unspoken. Silence is like shadows. You can slip through it unobserved. Concealed. In the darkness . . ."

He smiled as he finished his thought.

"Like a *rat*."

She stood. "I'm going to have to ask you to—"

"Sit down."

The sharp command froze her in place, but Dollie was determined to show no fear. Not to *this* man. Not to *Ponder.*

Nevertheless, she graciously complied, smiling and pulling out her chair to sit again, fingers brushing the handle of her straight razor as she did so. Determined to make him pay for his defiance, she leaned forward, fingers under her chin, and gave him courteous attention.

She opted for the cautious approach.

"Jeremiah, you do seem a bit agitated. Perhaps you can tell me what the problem is."

"I know you set the fire at my mill."

An uncomfortable silence prevailed. Then: "That's ridiculous."

"Is it?" Ponder's eyes, shining with drink and false courage, fixed on her with unsettling focus. "It's the only explanation that makes any sense. And it fits with your methods. Doesn't it? Sure." He scratched his cheek and belched before continuing. "You blow into town. Size up the situation. Sense the tension between my men and the prospectors. You knew a fire would rile everyone up."

"I heard a rumor you accused Hap of doing it. I heard you held him in your office and the marshal had to come rescue him."

"That's true." Ponder shrugged. "Thought for sure it was him. But after a while, I thought better of it. Made a *list*." He slapped the table with a flat hand. "Went through it one name at a time, crossing off everyone until only one name was left. Yours."

She said nothing.

"And then there's the money." He held up his hands. "You took Harville's. And mine. You just never stop, do you? Take, take, take . . ."

"Jeremiah, please . . ."

"Take!" He slapped the table again. *"Take!"* Slap! *"Take!"*

"Calm down—"

"How much is enough, Dollie? How much of these people, how much of this *town* do you intend to . . . to *take*? How many people here do you plan to ruin to get your way?"

"As many as it takes, Jeremiah."

The frankness of her answer caught him up short.

"As many as it *takes*!" She laughed and toasted him with her fancy Spanish wine. "All right, Jeremiah. It's true. I *did* try to burn down your lumberyard. I heard about the lumber fire that happened at the church and thought that was a perfect excuse to start one elsewhere. Get the good citizens riled up and afraid, so I could do whatever I wanted to in the midst of their confusion! How much of this town do I plan to take? Well, I'll tell you, Jeremiah. *All* of it. Every last building and business. I'll take them over one at a time until I'm the only one left standing. Because there can only be one queen. And that's *me*."

She drained her glass and set it down triumphantly. Ponder sat for a long moment after she was done.

"But I know something you don't," he said at last.

"And what's that?"

"You'll never be queen."

She opened her mouth to object, but his hand flashed before she could speak, emerging from his pocket clutching a small, polished revolver.

The shot echoed through the empty room. The bullet split Dollie Whittaker's forehead, driving her backward from her chair to land on the floor with a crash.

Ponder stared blearily at his handiwork. *Dead.* She sure as hell was.

Unsteadily, he rose and carried the lantern to her office, where he rifled her desk until discovering a quantity of cash, which he pocketed. He figured he was due some reimbursement. Then he extinguished the lantern and picked his way through the darkened saloon to slip through the front doors, unobserved.

Or so he thought.

CHAPTER 41

Dollie Whittaker's body was discovered the morning of Cord and Glory's wedding. Cord, already wearing his best suit, was talking with Blackstone in his office when one of the Bear Flag's employees came over in a panic to report the killing. Cord and Blackstone, still bruised from his thrashing by Anderson but functional, hurried over together to find a trio of saloon girls gazing down at the prone form of their dead boss.

"She's dead," moaned one of the saloon girls.

"What a shame," said another.

"Good riddance," muttered a third.

Cord knelt by the body. Dollie Whittaker had been shot in the head at close range—close enough for powder burns to ring the edge of the bullet hole. He stood and examined the area. No indications of violence, no scuffed footprints on the saloon floor, no traces of a visitor.

"No surprise she's met a sticky end," said Blackstone.

They searched the rest of the place, finding no trace of the intruder. Blackstone questioned the staff, all of whom said they had left Dollie in place at her usual perch, working on her account books, when the place closed for the night.

"Well, we have a killer in town," Cord said after Blackstone reported back.

"Can't say I disapprove of his or her choice of victim."

Cord frowned. "Every citizen deserves protection under the law. Even . . . Well, even her."

They stepped outside. The town was just beginning to stir. A few of the townsfolk paused to wish Cord all the best in his nuptials. He was touched by their show of support.

"You're a well-liked man, Marshal," said Blackstone. "As you well deserve."

"Thank you, Bart." Cord looked up as a wagon passed, the tarp in its rear covering a figure. "That'd be Anderson's body, on its way to Mr. Forbes's place. That's a loose end I need to tie up."

"Right you are, Marshal." Blackstone nodded vigorously. "You leave this matter of Dollie Whittaker with me and go enjoy your honeymoon with your missus. The town will be in good hands while you're away."

"I have no doubt." Cord grinned, clapped Blackstone's shoulder, and followed the wagon down to the undertaker's place.

As Blackstone stepped down from the sidewalk and into the street, Hap hurried over to him.

"D-Deputy B-Blackstone?" Hap asked tentatively. "May I h-have a w-word with you, p-please?"

Kat arrived in town, dressed for the wedding. She saw the commotion around the Bear Flag. Li-Sen and his wife were at the edge of the assembled crowd, watching as the town doctor and an assistant draped the body in a sheet and prepared to transport it away.

"What's going on?" she asked.

"It is Miss Whittaker," Li-Sen informed her. "Someone murdered her last night."

"Oh." Kat blinked. "That's a shame."

That was the right thing to say, whether she actually meant it or not.

The batwing doors on the saloon swung wide. The assistant walked out backward, looking over his shoulder as he eased his end of the stretcher through the door. The doctor held the far end, his black bag closed up and being carried on his behalf by one of the saloon girls. Kat watched them transport Dollie's remains to the doctor's office—the necessary first stop for any homicide victim before arrival at Mr. Forbes's undertaking parlor.

"Violence is never good," Li-Sen observed. "But, ah, I somehow feel as if very few people will truly mourn that lady's death."

Kat nodded and said nothing.

Li-Sen and his wife made their way back home. Kat watched them go before turning and spotting Judge Davenport, who stood outside his office in shirtsleeves, sipping a cup of coffee as he watched Dollie disappear into the doctor's office.

"Good morning, Judge," said Kat.

"Good morning, Miss Olmsted."

"May I have a word with you?"

"Of course." Davenport smiled. "I've been expecting you. Do come in."

A small burying ground had been established on the outskirts of town, a short distance from the main road. Cord followed the wagon containing the remains of Gordon Anderson, now sewed inside the covering sheet. He would be buried in his shroud. Forbes saw no point in wasting wood on an outlaw's coffin. Cord didn't object.

Lomax was waiting for them at the freshly dug grave, Bible in hand. He, Cord, and the burial party were the only ones in attendance as Gordon Anderson was lowered unceremoniously into the ground. Lomax opened his Bible and read aloud as Forbes and his assistant began shoveling dirt into the grave.

"'I am the resurrection and the life, saith the Lord.'"

Cord watched the dirt shower down upon the remains of the man who had tried to kill him and Glory. He felt nothing other than a mild relief.

It didn't take them long to cover Anderson up. Lomax finished his prayers as the assistant jammed a simple wooden cross into the ground at the head of the grave.

"'Ashes to ashes, dust to dust,'" said Lomax. "'From dust we came. And to dust we shall return.'"

He shut his Bible. Forbes and his assistant loaded their tools into the wagon and pulled away.

"Rest in peace," muttered Lomax. Then he turned and walked slowly back to town. Cord followed, thoughts preoccupied with the wedding. He was still thinking about it when Blackstone caught up with him.

Jeremiah Ponder sat in his office at the lumber mill, counting the money he had taken from Dollie Whittaker's desk—compensation for what she had stolen from him. He felt a welling of satisfaction as each bill passed through his fingers. At length, he had a fine, neat stack of currency before him. He had just tucked it into a cashbox and sealed it in a drawer when Hansen appeared at the door.

"Mr. Ponder? Marshal Bennett and Deputy Blackstone are here to see you."

Before he could respond, the two lawmen entered, followed by Hap.

"Good morning, Mr. Ponder," said Cord.

"Good morning, Marshal." Ponder scowled at Hap. "What can I do for you?"

"Nothing. You're under arrest."

Ponder's jaw dropped.

"What?" He half rose from his chair before Blackstone stepped over and pushed him back down.

"For the murder of Dollie Whittaker." Cord smiled. "You shot her where she sat at her table in the Bear Flag Saloon last night around midnight. We have a witness."

"Who? *Him*?" Ponder jabbed a finger at Hap and laughed. "He's a fool! Doesn't even know how to tell time! And you believe him?"

"I'm n-not a fool!" Hap thundered, startling even Blackstone with the volume. "Y-You went in th-there when sh-she was alone. Argued w-with her and c-called her names! Then y-you sh-shot her!"

"Ridiculous!"

"N-No, it ain't!" Hap turned to Cord. "I'll s-swear t-to it right now, M-Marshal! In f-front of Judge Davenport and all! On m-my *honor*!"

Cord nodded and turned to Ponder.

"We have a witness willing to swear testimony to what he saw. And Hap may not be perfect, but he's honest." Cord clapped the boy's shoulder. "Never told a lie in his life. Everyone in town knows that about him. So, I'd say you're in a peck of trouble, Ponder. Deputy?"

"Yes, Marshal?"

"Place Mr. Ponder in irons and conduct him to a cell."

Ponder, stunned, allowed himself to be pulled from the chair and handcuffed. With surprising gentleness, Blackstone led him out through the door and down the hall to the exit. A minute or two later, Cord and Hap followed.

Kat was just leaving Davenport's office when they arrived. She stood chatting with the judge as Cord and Hap stepped up.

"Hello, Kat. Your honor." Cord gestured to Hap. "Hap wants to come in and make a sworn statement."

"Sure thing." Davenport checked his pocket watch. "We should have just time enough before the wedding."

"We have an hour until Cord and Glory tie the knot," Kat said. "Enough time for me to get things set up in the Bear Flag for the reception. Forget the hotel, Cord. We're celebrating at the Flag."

"If you say so." Cord laughed. "Are you back in business there?"

"Ownership of the Bear Flag Saloon has now devolved back to Kat by virtue of her prior claim," Davenport affirmed. He stood aside and held the door wide for Hap. "Come on in, young man," he urged. "Whatever you have to say, we'd best get cracking if we're going to get to the church on time!"

CHAPTER 42

Well, Cord thought. *This is it.*

He stood at the altar, Blackstone and Lomax at his side. Familiar faces filled the first two rows of pews—Kat, Casterline, Judge Davenport. At Kat's insistence, Teddy Harville was permitted to attend. Although not a close friend to either the bride or groom, he was a lonely man who had been through a lot. Once Kat confided the details of his run-in with Dollie, Glory had assented. So, he and a half dozen other familiar faces sat in rapt anticipation. Any moment now, things would get underway.

There was movement in the doorway, and suddenly Glory stood there on the arm of her father. Her white dress was breathtaking, and she concealed her face behind a traditional lace veil. When they stepped across the threshold, Lomax nodded to Linus Butler, who stood by the door holding an accordion. With some hesitance, the old prospector began to pick out the wedding march.

Glory and Abraham began advancing toward the altar.

"Any second thoughts, this is the time to bow out," muttered Blackstone.

"Shut up, Bart," Cord muttered back.

Lomax rolled his eyes.

Blackstone chuckled.

Glory and Abraham arrived at the altar and Cord stood forward. Abraham handed Glory off to him, and they stood together before Lomax, their backs to the congregation.

"Dearly beloved," the preacher began. "We are gathered here today in the sight of Almighty God to join this man and this woman in the bonds of holy wedlock. Marriage is a sacred estate, ordained by God and affirmed by the presence of Jesus at the Wedding feast in Cana."

Cord half listened to Lomax, his eyes fixed wonderingly on those of his bride. She was so . . . so . . .

Good Lord, he loved her so!

"Cord Bennett, do you take this woman to be your lawfully wedded wife? To have and to hold, in sickness and in health, from now and for the remainder of your life?"

"I do." He spoke with firm confidence.

"And you, Gloriana? Do you take this man to be your lawfully wedded husband? To have and to hold, in sickness and in health, from now and for the remainder of your life?"

"I do."

"All right, then." Lomax closed his Bible. "By the power vested in me by the Union Theological Seminary and the Lord God Almighty, I now pronounce you man and wife. You may kiss your bride."

Cord reached out and lifted her veil. She was crying tears of joy.

"We made it," she whispered.

"We sure did."

They kissed, and the entire church erupted in cheers.

* * *

There was quite a crowd outside when they emerged. A number of townsfolk had come down to offer their best wishes. Li-Sen and a dozen or so members of the Chinese community were there, too, crying out their well-wishes in their native tongue. Cord looked out over everyone and was deeply touched.

Home, he thought. *I'm finally home.*

They swept down the sidewalk and into the Bear Flag Saloon. The wedding party, along with Lomax and Blackstone, joined them. Linus Butler tagged along with his accordion and immediately set about playing some sort of polka music. It wasn't Cord's first choice for a tune, but he did lead Glory out to the dance floor and held her at arm's length.

"Hello, Mrs. Cord Bennett," he said quietly.

"Hello, Cord. My dear, dear husband."

They kissed. And the crowd roared.

Slowly, they began to dance. Butler hadn't much of a melodic sense, but at least he could keep time. They twirled and pirouetted together through a clumsy waltz, until slowly they were joined by other couples. Drinks were ordered and the merriment began in earnest.

Teddy Harville wandered through the door and headed over to the bar. Kat was there, pulling a beer from the tap when he arrived. She turned to him with a grin.

"Well, here we are!" she cried. "Just like old times. You over there in your place, me here in mine. Competing fair and square for the customer's honest dollar."

She placed a beer in front of him. Harville grasped it up in a toast. "Here's to that!"

He drank.

"You know," he said. "It might be an interesting idea to have joint events. Like poker nights. Or dart tournaments. Between our two establishments."

"We could charge money for tickets."

Teddy Harville's eyes narrowed. "Now you're talking."

Linus Butler paused for a breather and looked up to see Panhead Peterson seated at a nearby table, watching the performance.

"Don't you know any *good* music? Like 'Rock of Ages'?" demanded Peterson.

"Ain't nothing wrong with the music I'm playing!" retorted Butler. "It's Ukrainian."

"What the hell are you doing playing Ukrainian music? You're not even Ukrainian!"

"No, but my uncle Mischa was, and he taught me to play, so there!" Butler spat.

"Fine!" Peterson poured himself another whiskey from the bottle he'd bought. "But try to play 'Rock of Ages' for me, would you? It's a good song."

At a far table, Antiglione sat with Li-Sen and another Chinese man named Wong. They had consumed a decent amount of alcohol fairly quickly, but it had not yet occurred to any of them that they might be drunk.

"America is very strange place," said Antiglione. "Nice people. But strange."

"They are a young nation," said Li-Sen.

"This is true," grunted Antiglione. "Long before America, was Rome. World empire!"

"And long before Rome was the Xia Dynasty." Li-Sen shrugged.

"Empires come and go." Antiglione raised his glass. "Friends are forever."

Li-Sen smiled. "I'll drink to that," he said. And did.

Horace Davenport, for his part, sat at the bar in his shirtsleeves, bent over a chessboard. Sitting next to him, turned so she could reach the board, was Angie, the youngest of the Bear Flag's bar girls. He watched as she reached out, seized her queen, and took his last bishop.

"How old are you?" Davenport demanded.

She raised her chin. "I'm seventeen!"

"Nonsense. *Nobody* is this good at chess at seventeen!" He moved his rook to block her next advance. "Anyway, why aren't you in school?"

"Don't need no school. I'm gonna find me a nice rich man and marry him. Schooling don't help that none. Just like it ain't helping your chess, old man."

"Hey, I'm a *judge*, blast it! You call me *your honor* from now on, you hear?"

"All right." She sat forward, moved her rook, and smirked at him. "Checkmate . . . *your honor*."

"See this?" Blackstone stripped his right sleeve and thrust forward his pale white forearm. A livid pink scar extended from elbow to wrist. "Got that when I was eleven. In a street fight in Blackpool."

"See this?" Lomax tapped his nose. "My dad broke it for me when I was ten."

"No offense, Reverend, but it must surely have improved your looks."

"Curse you, you infernal Englishman." Lomax grabbed up the bottle on the table before them and filled both their glasses to the brim. "You dare insult a man of the cloth?"

"No! I was merely complimenting your handsome features." He raised his left arm and winced. "Still feeling that bullet wound I got from one of those bloody gun-wolves."

Lomax pulled down his shirt collar to reveal another scar. "Apache did that to me."

"That's nasty, that is." Blackstone shook his head. "You've got me there, Reverend. I've never been a guest of them."

"It's not like I *planned* to visit them."

"Of course not."

"But some invitations?" Lomax shrugged. "Some invitations you just dare not refuse."

The revelry continued, with dancing and drinking and general merriment, until an hour before sunset. Glory sidled up to Cord.

"I think it's time we're on our way, Cord," she said. "If we're to make Ghost Canyon by nightfall."

"I agree, Mrs. Bennett." He smiled and patted her forearm. "Let's leave on a toast. You get everyone's attention, and I'll bring us a glass of champagne."

Cord went off to the bar. Glory climbed atop a chair and banged a spoon against a beer mug until she had everyone's attention. Cord appeared shortly and handed her a glass of champagne.

"Hello, everybody!" Glory cried. "And thank you so, *so* much for coming! Thank you for helping to make this a fabulous wedding day and for making me the happiest bride west of the Mississippi! I'm truly, truly grateful, Cord and I both. Truly grateful for *everything.* Thank you all so much!"

The wedding party guests all applauded, crying out their best wishes as Cord lifted Glory down from the chair and carried her across the saloon and out through the batwing doors to the wagon. Blackstone and Lomax stood there, both beaming.

"Congratulations, you two," said Blackstone.

"God bless you both," added Lomax.

Cord grinned, nodded, and lifted Glory into the wagon. Out to the east, the sky was beginning to darken. An amazing dusk glow of bright orange and gold shot across the rugged landscape, igniting the clouds and casting the sky to the west in streaks of purple and silver.

"What an amazing night," whispered Glory.

"I'll remember it forever," agreed Cord.

A gaggle of people drifted out from the saloon to see them off. They were just making ready to depart when Li-Sen and two of his friends rushed out into the main street and stabbed what appeared to be stakes into the ground.

"Before you go!" he cried. "Congratulations! Best fortune to you both."

He struck a lucifer. His friends did likewise and lit the tails of something attached to the stakes. Moments later, sounds like gunfire reverberated and streaks of light shot into the sky.

"Oh!"

Glory's cry coincided with the blossoming of the first firework, a constellation of bright red stars against the sky. It was followed by explosions in blue and purple from the other rockets. The amazing show went on and on, explosion blossoming from explosion. Cord marveled at it, shaking his head in wonder.

What a day!

With a final wave to the crowd, he whipped the horse and drove the wagon fast down Main Street, eager to get home before dark.

The crowd drifted back inside. With a discordant clang, Linus's accordion wheezed back to life and the oompah music returned. The only folks left on the sidewalk were Blackstone, Lomax, and Clyde Casterline, who had arrived late but now stood with a whiskey glass in hand, watching the wagon disappear into the distance.

"Well, that's that," said Lomax.

"It is. Well done, Reverend," said Blackstone. "Thanks for making it a great day."

"Glory to God, my son."

Pan-head Peterson pushed through the batwing doors, shaking his head.

"I'm not sticking around for more of that rotten noise," he complained. "Who the hell ever told Linus Butler he was a damn *musician*?"

Pan-head crossed the sidewalk, unhitched and mounted a donkey at the rail.

"Alors, ma petite," he crooned to it. *"Allons-y."*

The donkey wandered off down the street, Pan-head wobbling on its back.

"I'll be damned," said Clyde Casterline, taking a sip of his whiskey. "The *damn* thing *does* speak French after all. . . ."

The road spiraled ahead as the town fell away behind them. Cord and Glory were together in the driver's box, snuggled close together as he guided them toward their home in Ghost Canyon and a future together. It was a future they had come very close to losing.

But we kept it, he thought. *Thanks to our friends.*

Kat . . . Abraham . . . Blackstone . . . Lomax . . . Casterline . . . Davenport . . . Hap . . .

I am truly a blessed man.

"What are you thinking, Cord?" Glory squeezed his arm as she grinned into the oncoming breeze.

"Just thinking about how lucky I am," he replied. "What are you thinking about?"

"I'm thinking about babies." She squeezed his arm again. "You *do* know how babies are made, don't you, Cord Bennett? Think carefully before you answer."

"Why sure. My older brother had the talk with me about the birds and the bees. I understand the overall principle."

"Silly." She swatted him. "I'm just teasing. Anyone who's ever worked a farm knows how babies are made!"

"Well, like I said." He grinned. "I understand the overall principle. The second part is more important. It's the part I can't wait to learn about with you."

"And what's that?"

"How to love well."

She pecked his cheek. "You're already doing very well that way," she assured him.

Cord's grin widened. He had come to California to find his fortune, and right now he figured he had discovered treasure beyond his wildest dreams.

He flicked the reins and drove the team forward into the fading light, eager to get them home before nightfall.

TURN THE PAGE FOR AN EXCITING PREVIEW!

JOHNSTONE COUNTRY.
WHERE TEXANS FIGHT FOR FREEDOM, HONOR—AND WHISKEY.

Welcome to the Whiskey Capital of Texas, where a proud family of distillers faces off with a ruthless rival who's trading shots of liquor with hot lead. . . .

The small but lively town of Glen Rose, Texas, is famous for its home-brewed whiskey—thanks to the Stark family's secret recipe. Over the years, Civil War veteran Jed Stark and his tough-as-nails mom, Minnie, have managed to turn their small family distillery into a highly successful business. But whiskey's not the only thing that's brewing in Glen Rose. There's plenty of trouble, too—namely Merlin Sheldrake, a rival distiller who's got the money, power, and connections to swallow the Starks' operation in a single gulp. Sure, his rancid brand of rotgut whiskey is no match for their smooth Texas blend. But this is more than friendly competition. This is nasty, all-out war. . . .

First, Sheldrake sends a couple of goons to the Stark ranch to steal their family recipe—but they get a load of buckshot from Minnie instead. Then, he sets fire to the Stark distillery, burning everything to the ground. Thankfully, Jed has a stash of stills hidden in a cave and no intention of backing down.

But then the whiskey wars take an even darker turn—when Minnie is kidnapped by Sheldrake's hired guns. Now Jed has no choice but to fight this fight to the bitter end. Even if the blood flows faster than whiskey, Jed is prepared to teach these lowlifes a lesson: Don't mess with Texas. Especially when there's family, honor, and whiskey involved . . .

CHAPTER 1

Jedediah Stark, a lean, whip-hard man in a faded blue, sweat-stained shirt beneath worn leather braces leaned back from raking a steel poker over a bed of hardwood coals.

He watched them for a moment as they pulsed and glowed beneath a wide steel pan. This, as very few folks knew, was one of the tricks the Stark family had used for generations of making whiskey, first back in Tennessee, then there at Whiskey Woods, the longtime family ranch outside of Glen Rose, Texas.

Stark stood up straight, stretching his back and letting out a long, pent-up sigh, sounding like steam from a worn valve. He rubbed the small of his back and squinted at the drops of sweat sliding down his forehead.

Jed, the third-generation Stark to live most of his days and nights on this land, was a tall, broad-shouldered fellow with a gaze difficult to look away from if you were a lady, and daring to meet eye to eye if you were a man.

He tugged free a rumpled red kerchief from a trouser pocket, mopped at his sweat-stippled brow, and thought about how fine a nice, long, cool drink of water would taste then. Movement to his right, below the long eave of the open entrance to his still, caught his eye.

He shifted his gaze and squinted out into the hot, midafternoon sun cooking the dooryard. There lay his old, droop-eared, long-boned red hound named Redeye. The dog was a solid if lazy beast, but performed admirably the only real task asked of him—to lend a cold eye and a gruff bark of warning to strangers.

So far as Jed knew, Redeye was past the ten-year-old mark, but it didn't really matter. The beast had been born old, as if he had had no youth nor prime middle years. For a whole long time, for as long as Jed had known him, which was most of the beast's life, Redeye had acted as if each movement cost him an incredible amount of effort. It seemed only by the grace of good fortune was he able to perform the task of rising, walking slowly to his water bowl or his grub. Once sated and filled, it was all the hound could do to drop, as if clubbed on the head with a sledge, into another of his lengthy, snore-filled, snooze sessions.

That it had turned out to be another hot day, especially for April, was not a surprise to Jed, but this hot this early in the season only meant more of the same, in his experience, born of roving this spot all his days thus far.

All that was save for three years during the cursed war, when he was called away and was nearly killed every moment of it, or so it had felt. And at the end of it, or at least of his time in it, never had a man been more relieved to return to his place of birth.

From then on, he vowed to never roam farther than thirty or so miles from it again. Glen Rose was as good a town to live near as any other, in his experience, and Whiskey Woods an ideal home place.

The thousand-acre ranch had been established by his grandpappy,

Hawcliffe Stark, long years before, on reaching the region and deciding to sink roots after he arrived from Tennessee.

Jed cast his gaze once more on ol' Redeye, who had roused himself enough from his usual slumberous pose to raise his head from the dirt, droopy hound-dog eyes taking in whatever it was he had first heard.

Normally, on a steaming day such as this, the old dog would slump, slow-walking, from shady spot to shady spot, only to collapse once more as if shot. It never failed to elicit a chuckle from Jed.

As the whiskey maker wiped sweat from his trim beard, he saw the dog not drop his head back to the earth but do the opposite and force himself to sit up. Must indeed be something out of the ordinary, thought Jed. He looked again, visoring his eyes against the day as he walked closer toward the sunlight from where he had been toiling before the fire at his still.

Jed looked up the long, winding lane that led from the plateau above the ranch toward the road that led to the town of Glen Rose. He had learned as a boy to always trust a beast's attention, no matter a dog, a cat, a cow, or a horse. They sensed disturbances, differences, far sooner than humans could.

He continued to squint up the road, glancing back once at Redeye, whose flopping ears now showed slight boldness, as if they had sprouted a little dignity. He saw the first possibilities of telltale puffs of someone, or something, approaching the ranch along the dusty roadway. He adjusted the angle of his big, visoring hand against his forehead.

"It's likely Loud," said Jed, not looking over again at his silent conversation pard, ol' Redeye.

Loudon Paley was his newspaperman friend, a chubby Easterner who had made his way West some years before, seeking the woolly and the raw grist for his story mill, revenge tales resulting in foolish gunplay and unnecessary mayhem.

What the man had found instead was a town, one Glen Rose, Texas, pretty enough, and sizable enough with 216 residents and another couple of hundred in the immediate surrounding area.

What he also found was that Glen Rose had need of a newspaper. In fact, it had never had one, and as the self-proclaimed "Whiskey-making Capital of Texas . . . and maybe the world," Glen Rose seemed ripe and ready, at least to the residents and to the puffed-up mayor, Fendall Hawkins, to welcome the services of a back-East-educated journalist.

Much to Loudon Paley's lasting regret, he had, in a fit of whiskey-fueled pique, agreed to be that man, and to fulfill that role for Glen Rose. Regret because nothing much ever happened in Glen Rose.

And as Paley was a chatty type and not prone to sitting in the shadows and listening for news, he found himself knowing lots of people but not having all that many friends.

Somehow, Jed wasn't quite certain how it came to be, he and Paley had become friends. For Jed's part, being with Loud was simple enough. Jed was inclined toward quietness, and as Loud was, well, *loud,* they struck a perfect balance.

Many afternoons, practically year-round, Loud could be counted on to visit Whiskey Woods, on foot or more often riding his old flop-eared mule, Alice, out to the ranch for conversation and a sip of whiskey from the shop bottle.

But as Jed continued to watch the clouds of dust puff up and grow, closer and larger, he noticed that whoever it was, for it surely wasn't Loud, was neither a single man afoot nor a rider on horseback—or muleback.

As Jed continued to watch and sip tepid water from a canning jar, he saw steady plumes of dust rise up, closer, ever closer on this hot day. It was someone in a buggy. A small, two-wheel buggy. And this was no person intent on doing anything but getting to the end of the long, winding lane quick.

It wouldn't be his sweetheart, Lilly, because she would be busy at the diner. Besides, he'd seen her the night before and hoped to do so again this night.

Of course, Jed received visits from folks every few days, and sometimes with more frequency than that, but he knew well the schedules of all the saloon owners and others who made regular trips to Whiskey Woods to buy whiskey.

This was not one of those days and, from the approaching look of this buggy, it was not one of his regular visitors. But within another half a minute, Jed Stark knew who this visitor was. And despite his predilection for calmness, level thinking, and even acting in his life, Jed felt his guts tighten a smidgin. For he realized that this visitor was one Merlin Sheldrake.

And Sheldrake, while he had only been to the ranch two previous times, had been there for the same reason each time. Jed didn't think this time would be any different. The man would once again make him an offer that most other folks in the region, or perhaps the state, would be hard-pressed to refuse. Sheldrake wanted to buy Stark's distillery, his whiskey, the recipe—everything about it.

For certain the land would never belong to anyone but a Stark, at least not while Jed lived. And with even more certainty, he knew that they would never sell the distillery and certainly not their family recipe for Whiskey Woods whiskey. Never ever ever, even if he was killed defending it. He would take it to his grave.

And if Jed was that certain about that point, then his mother, Minerva Florabelle Stark, known as Minnie, or by Jed as Mama, or to folks who knew the family well enough, Mother Stark, was doubly certain. For they were the only surviving Starks of their line in the world, and that coveted recipe was not written down anywhere. Never had been, no sir. It resided in his head and in his mother's head, and that was it, that was all.

It would die with them. And then where would his so-called rivals be—the folks such as Sheldrake and other whiskey makers who thought they could make a golden liquid half as good as Whiskey Woods brew?

Jed sighed and rubbed a hand over his weary face. This was not something he had suspected was going to happen yet again, and it was certainly not an encounter he was looking forward to. For he would have two knobheaded folks to deal with. Sheldrake and Mama. The thought that they were similar in so many ways made Jed chuckle. And doubly so when Jed mused on Mama's reaction should such a proclamation ever crawl out of Jed's mouth.

Life in Glen Rose had been fine before Sheldrake came to town four years earlier. He recognized that this area of the country was growing as more folks moved in and settled.

With that fact in mind, he reasoned rightly that Glen Rose, famous for its whiskey-making traditions and culture, would be an ideal place to set up operations for the whiskey production and distribution arm of his business holdings, of which booze was the fastest growing and most lucrative.

Jed knew that the man had made much money as an industrialist and railroad man in the upper Midwest and had been slowly broadening his empire. The rangy whiskey maker sighed in silence and walked into the sunlight from the darkened, albeit hotter interior of the whiskey shed. It was a largely open-sided affair with long, low overhangs of roof, which in the infrequent wet times kept the rain from soaking him while he worked.

The cooler months were such that Jed was plenty warm even without the protection of much in the way of walls, as he spent much of his time tending the fire and receiving plenty of heat.

In fact, the winter months were about the only time when Jed felt about right, not too hot and not too cold. The ever-present urge to make another successful, consistently Stark-tasting whiskey kept the man from caring all that much about his own comforts.

"What are you thinking, eh, dog?" said Jed, barely glancing at Redeye, who sat erect now and was working up a growl deep in his old chest. That didn't bother Jed much. Redeye looked to be more of a menace than he was.

Despite Sheldrake having met the dog on two previous occasions, the rangy hound remained unimpressed with the rich fat man, something of which Jed approved. It was an attitude, to Jed's relief, that his dear, surly Mama shared with the dog.

As if his very thoughts cued her, Mother Stark strode on down from beneath the shade porch of the house. She looked, as Jed knew she would, tight and hard and working up a case of mean. And she was toting Ol' Shredder, a single-barrel shotgun that had been in the Stark family, according to Mama, "since Methuselah was in knee pants."

The gun, so named because it had been known to make a rib-boned mess out of whatever it was that it was aimed at and trigger squeezed at, was now aimed and ready.

This was due in part to the fact that the shells Mama used were nasty things brimming with lead nuggets the size of a child's fingertips. And when she gave that trigger a tug, Ol' Shredder spoke like a dragon that had been kept shut up in a dark place for far too long.

It would roar and growl and cough and belch flame and smoke, and it would spit those maiming nuggets as if for the pure enjoyment of it.

Jed also noted, with mild relief, that she had not yet cocked the vicious, barking thing, which, with Mama as the wielder, didn't mean all that much.

The woman was adept at ratcheting back that hammer and sending a dose of "Mother Stark's spicy mix!" at anything or anyone she deemed in need of her attention.

"Mama," said Jed in a low, even voice. "You don't even know what he wants yet."

She swung her gaze from the fast-approaching, dust-clouded buggy and fixed her big son with a hard eye. "I know and you know what that thieving brute wants. And you know and I know he ain't about to get it. But I do know what he's going to get. Held my trigger finger at bay for far too long where that fat rascal's concerned. No more, I say!"

Jed sighed. "Mama, don't kill him. Stark or no, the local law, as you well know, is no friend of ours. Marshal Chiswick will lock you up on murder charges quick as a wink."

"I'd like to see him try!" she said, cackling and squaring off.

Sheldrake's buggy, driven by the man himself, slowed and turned so that all he had to do was stay seated and address them from there, as he had done on his two previous forays out to Whiskey Woods. But then Jed noted that Sheldrake set the brake and looped the lines. It looked as if the fat man in the fine but dusty suit was about to step down.

Yep, he was, and it was not a pretty sight.

"What in tarnation do you think you are doing, Sheldrake?" said Mother.

The man did not reply until he grunted himself down half backward, out of the buggy.

In a none-too-quiet voice, Mama said to Jed, "That backside of his looks like two pigs fighting under a blanket!"

Red-faced, out of breath, and now facing them, Merlin Sheldrake once more stood on the firm earth of the Starks' dooryard. "Well, now, it is nice to see you both again, I'm sure."

Redeye hadn't yet moved, but Jed noticed the dog was tense all over, every muscle tight and set to hurtle his lean form into a lunge. The growling sound he'd made earlier had only increased in volume.

The hound's floppy ears were angled back, as if he were already darting forward at tremendous speed—something that Jed had never considered would be possible for the beast. All it would take was one step from where Sheldrake stood and that dog would be on him like stink on dung, thought Jed.

And if it happened, he didn't think he would work too hard to stop the beast. He would come to Sheldrake's aid, but Jed didn't think he would hurry himself at it. Time might tell, he thought, getting small pleasure from watching everybody work through their various stances.

He regarded the smile on the rich man's fleshy face, pink and clean-shaven save for a thin, fancy-man mustache that always looked to Jed to require more effort than it was worth, given its meager showing.

Sheldrake turned to Mama with what Jed had to assume was intended to be a winning, ingratiating smile. "Mother Stark, I must say it is lovely to see you. Why, you look younger with each week that passes, I do declare!"

As Jed watched, doing his best but not succeeding in suppressing a wincing smile, he was about to say something to help suppress the ruckus that he knew was on its way. He was too late.

"First off," growled Mama from somewhere down deep in her throat, the sound she was making matching that steady, menacing gurgle that Redeye had maintained all the while Sheldrake had been there, "you didn't answer my question, curse you!"

Sheldrake's smile began to slip, but he yanked it back up again and began to splutter, but the old woman cut him off because she kept right on talking.

"You great, greasy-jowled, slop-bellied fool! What makes you think you can set foot on Stark land?" Even as she said this, she raised Ol' Shredder from the near-waist height she lugged the heavy thing at, taking her time and seeming to enjoy the fact that Sheldrake's beady eyes were locked on the thing, the brows rising with the gun.

"Why, my dear lady," he said, offering a slight bow, his derby shucked and clutched tight to his chest. His gleaming bald head was pink, and Jed saw the sweat stippling the thing.

On anyone else he might think the man was sweating extra out of nervousness, but with Sheldrake, Jed didn't think so, not given the bold, swaggering way Sheldrake normally carried himself in life.

The fat man held up his free hand, palm out, and wagged it as if he were waving bye-bye to them, which Jed wished he would do, and soon.

"My dear, dear Mother Stark!"

Jed winced again.

"And that's another thing, you pathetic mess! What in the name of all that is kind and decent in the world gives you the right to address me as anything other than Mrs. Stark? Huh? I ain't *dear* or *sweet* to you, and I certainly ain't your mama, and for that I count myself among the luckiest of folks."

Mama certainly was on a roll today, thought the whiskey maker. Speaking of, he had things to do, and this unexpected and annoying visit had best get to its inevitable end. Jed cleared his throat and Sheldrake looked over at him, with what Jed thought was a begging look, as if Jed might rescue him from the hole he'd dug for himself.

Nothing doing, Jed thought. "See here, Sheldrake. I have things to do, and standing here listening to you jaw and seeing you sweat and stammer and not get to the point is nothing but annoying. Hop to the game, man, or get gone."

"Right, yes, sir, Jed, eh, Mr. Stark." Here Sheldrake glanced quickly at the old woman toting the shotgun before looking back to Jed. "The reason I am here." He straightened and stiffened his back, seeming to remember that he was not a mewling, pathetic man but a wealthy, confrontational businessman who always gets what he wants. "I came here today with nothing but the best of intentions."

The old woman snorted and spat at the dusty earth before her boots.

"Mama," said Jed. "Let the man speak his piece."

She mumbled something but didn't commit to a yes or no.

"Yes, yes," said Sheldrake. "You see, I know my previous offers to purchase your fine whiskey recipe fell short of the mark you have in mind, and I respect that. I really do! That is why, on reflection and consideration of the fact that you have been an established presence here in the Glen Rose region for a good many years—"

"None longer!" howled Mama.

"Yes, well, I drove all the way out here on this stifling day to make you a third and final offer." Here he had to once again hold up his hands because he saw on Mrs. Stark's face what was coming. "No, no, please, ma'am, please let me finish."

He glanced at Jed, who nodded.

"Thank you, sir. Now, my final offer effectively doubles." Here Sheldrake's voice faltered as if the words were causing him no small amount of grief to utter. "I . . . I offer you double the amount of my last offer. I daresay you recall that figure, Mr. Stark?"

Jed eyed the man through squinted eyes, his arms folded over his chest. He didn't really recall the specifics of that offer, aside from recalling that the amount was substantial even then, and double that was nothing but a foolish figure, to be sure. But it was no use, never would be. But how to convince the man of it? Sheldrake was a hard learner.

"Look here, Mr. Sheldrake, we both appreciate—"

"Ha! Curse your hide, Sheldrake!"

Jed sighed and glared at Mama, then back to the visitor. "We both appreciate your coming out here on this fine day, prettier than a picture if you ask me," said Jed, digging a little at the fat man's complaint about the day being sweltering.

"But as we told you last time, and the time before that, the Stark whiskey recipe is not for sale. We like it here fine, and we like what we do, making whiskey. That's it, that's all, man. I'm sorry you wasted your time."

Jed wasn't really sorry. The man was a grown fellow—overgrown, more like. Sheldrake made his choice and so did Jed, a whole lot of them on this day alone.

"But I don't think you understand me, Mr. Stark!"

Sheldrake's tone, Jed sensed, had shifted, changing from soft and placating to something with a harder edge. Not much, but it was there. "What I am offering you is twice the amount of cash. And for that all I want is a piece of paper with the recipe written on it. Naturally, too, for that amount of money I have to ask that you both not share that recipe with anyone else for a period of, say, a dozen years. But!" Here Sheldrake held up a thick, pink index finger, as if prodding the underbelly of the air itself. "Since we are, shall we say, friends, and since we are both men of the world and seem to know each other's mind, I am prepared to make certain, albeit limited, concessions."

Sheldrake tapped his chin and pooched his lips a moment as if deciding between pie or cake at a diner. Finally, a smile broadened on his face and he nodded. "Yes, here is what I am prepared to do: I will allow you both to retain ownership of this pretty homestead the Starks have carved for themselves here.

"You will not, of course, be allowed to make whiskey yourselves for another dozen years, it's true, but with money such as that, only a fool would wish to continue working like a galley slave, eh?"

He chuckled and regarded them.

Jed wanted to ask the man if he was funning them, but he knew the answer. He was surprised that his mother hadn't jumped down the fat man's throat almost at once. He glanced at the old woman and saw a rare sight indeed.

Mama Stark was staring at the fat stranger, her shotgun halfway poised to deliver, the hammer uncocked. But it was her mouth that surprised Jed. It was sagged open and her eyebrows were raised high. He knew about what she was feeling. He himself could hardly believe what he'd heard.

Jed cleared his throat. "Sheldrake, you have to be joshing me."

He advanced a half step on the man, Redeye tight to his right knee, advancing with him with steady dog half steps.

"As long as Starks are on this land, we will make whiskey. With our recipe. And we will sell our whiskey. That will never change, and we aren't going anywhere," said Jed, advancing. He paused when he was within a foot and a half of the red-faced, sweating man.

He'd only come this close because he was not a little worried that after all that insulting blather, Mama was about to twitch on that trigger and turn the richest man in these parts into a slopped, oozing, bloodied heap of dying fat man.

A sheen of oil, likely grease oozing from Sheldrake's pores, slicked the fellow's features, a look that made even the normally placid Jed want to punch the man. It smacked of laziness and overindulgence and craven cowardice in the face of life's everyday challenges. None of these were something Jedediah Stark tolerated in himself, and barely so in others.

He made exceptions, of course, for folks who were good at heart, such as his chubby pal, the newsman Loudon Paley. Loud liked his pie, perhaps a pinch too much, but he was intelligent, challenging, and worried about the plight of the less fortunate in life. And Loud woke up each day, Jed was convinced, with an earnest desire to help other folks. A good man.

On the other hand, given what Jed knew of Merlin Sheldrake, he had to say that there was very little kindness or good-hearted intention to the man. He was a loudmouthed, brazen braggart with one urge and one urge only—to own everything he desired.

The closer he drew to Sheldrake the more Jed realized the fat man also had an awful stink wafting off him, like a ditch critter gone bloated in the sun. Time to get him gone.

"Look here, Sheldrake, I'm not your friend, I don't know your mind—a freakish thought at best—so I will tell you now for the last time, we don't want to sell our whiskey recipe. The only thing we sell is the whiskey itself, to folks we know and folks we like.

Now, we didn't ask you to come here once, let alone three times, each time with the same unwanted offer. Stop it and go. Now."

As Jed spoke, he straightened and knew his face was growing redder with the heat of the moment. His right arm assumed a long, straight point to it that whiskered by the fat man's head and aimed at one thing—the fool's silly little buggy.

For one, two, three gulps, all Sheldrake could do was work his thick, wet lips like a banked fish, his eyes round and wide.

He was about to speak when Jed, in a lowered tone, said, "If you don't do as I say, and do it right now, Mr. Sheldrake, I will have no choice but to turn Mother Stark loose on you."

As if to slam the point in place, like a well-smacked nail, from slightly behind and off to Jed's right rose up the deadly, oiled, throaty cold clicking of a shotgun hammer knocking back all the way to the deadliest position of all.

"And I ain't never, not once, failed to hit my target, mister. Keep that in mind, you great sloppy oaf. Now do as my son says and get gone!"

Standing less than an arm's length from Jed—a head taller and a good deal fitter, leaner, and more muscled than Sheldrake—the rich man looked up at him, then over at Mother Stark, his newly narrowed eyes locked on her sneering face. And he did something that once more surprised the two Starks.

Sheldrake spoke, this time in a low, cold, grating voice that rivaled the steely ratcheting of the shotgun's hammer in menace. "And I have never, not once, failed to get what I want in life, woman." The words curled from his mouth like smoke on the slightest of breezes. "I will have your recipe. Or I will see you both barking in the netherworld, begging for my forgiveness. Keep that in mind."

He turned and walked to his buggy and climbed up into it with a smoothness and speed that Jed thought impossible by the fat fellow, considering his bumbling entrance and descent from the same buggy not long before.

Sheldrake gathered up the reins and looked over at them. "Keep it in mind, but not too long. Merlin Sheldrake won't be kept waiting." With that, he smacked the lines hard on the horse's rump, and the buggy lurched forward.

Mama walked over and stood beside Jed, and they both watched him maneuver the buggy in no hurry out toward the end of their wide yard.

For one of the very few times in his life, Jed found himself wondering if what he was doing was worth risking the lives of those he cared for, namely his mother. And sure, the Stark recipe and name and home, too. Not to mention his own life.

More to the point, he wondered why it was that, when backed right up to the wall, he and Mama didn't do anything more than stand there like turtles sunning on a log and listen to the great, blustering fellow.

He looked down at Mama, and to his surprise he saw a smirk on her face as she watched the slow, low cloud of dust that was Sheldrake's buggy roll away from them.

The old woman raised the shotgun the last few inches to her shoulder, snugged her cheek down, and touched off the trigger.

The shot whipped forward, parting the air like a clot of kill-crazy bees.

Jed saw that she had aimed a pinch high, no doubt in hopes of having the pellets arc down on the retreating buggy. Nothing sounded as if it met with its half-hearted intended target.

Neither one spoke for a time. Then Jed said, "I will hand it to Sheldrake, he isn't one to give up on a thing."

"It's because what we do we do better than anybody in these parts. Heck, in the entire country. Maybe even the world!"

Jed smiled. "I think the Scots might have something to say about that."

"Bah," she said. "They're always whining and yowling about how great their whiskey is. I don't see it, myself."

"You don't drink the stuff, Mama," said Jed, smirking as he tidied up for the night.

"That doesn't matter a whit. I know what I know."

Jed did not respond, knowing after a lifetime of such traded comments, there was no arguing with Minnie Stark and coming out on top. She would not, could not, be bested.